Chris saw.

"No!" The sight knocked the breath out of her: His head was gone, sliced off with surgical precision. His hand was still warm, his grip on her fingers tightening in death. As she pulled away, his body toppled onto the redwood floor with a soft thud.

Then Margot saw.

"What have they done with the head?" she screamed. *"What have they done with the head?"*

PAUL BOORSTIN

BERKLEY BOOKS, NEW YORK

SAVAGE

A Berkley Book / published by arrangement with
Richard Marek Publishers

PRINTING HISTORY
Richard Marek edition / July 1980
Berkley edition / December 1981

ISBN: 0-425-04938-8

A BERKLEY BOOK ® TM 757,375
Berkley Books are published by Berkley Publishing Corporation,
200 Madison Avenue, New York, New York 10016.
PRINTED IN THE UNITED STATES OF AMERICA

For Sharon

Savage

Prologue

June 12, 1970

DAWSON FELT THE TWO GRENADES ON HIS CHEST
bobbing like breasts. Now that they were approaching the target, the miraculous transformation had begun: he became both
man and woman, a terrifying beast that was complete only
now, only when blood was about to flow. He felt the tingle
of an erection, and the nipples of his steel teats seemed ready
to spurt milk. He would be the bearer of extravagant gifts.
"We three Kings," Dawson's mind chattered, "three wise
men." But instead of a crown, Dawson wore a baseball cap, the
name of the ball club obscured by mildew, perverted into an
insignia for another, more ominous team. His jaw was a thicket
of stubble, his eyes bloodshot. "The Star of Bethlehem," his
mind rambled. "The Goddamn Sahara." In spite of the lush
growth, it *was* like the desert here, for all paths looked alike,
and all led nowhere, like the roads that had drawn and quartered
the Texas badlands where he grew up. He spoke no Spanish,
the two hunters with him little English. Their mission would
not require words.

Old Andrés watched Dawson's lips moving silently, shaping
private obsessions. He knew Dawson was mad. He had seen
him drive a pike through the flesh at the front of his neck and
hang a full bucket of water from it to prove his ability to
withstand pain. And standing there, bloodied like some twisted
santo, Dawson had grinned. Mad, yes, but here, madness could
mean strength. He would be a fool in so unreasonable a place
as this to count on reasonable men.

The hunters' fatigues seemed to congeal out of the tedious
green of the jungle, sweat staining crescents under their arms.
They had passed the sacred volcanoes Yalí and Kolon, the
black mountains where the Indians believed the world was
spawned in hate. They had passed the gorge of the dead ser-
pents. And when they had reached the fork in the Jacará River,
where jutting rocks stabbed the water white, Andrés led them
west toward the sun, which burned like a deadly flower in the
fronds of a royal palm. Taking the lead, he swung his machete
skillfully, so that the weight of the steel blade rather than his

own muscle gave it cutting force, splitting the vines with swift strokes. His bearing was deceptive—a potbelly, a stoop—for like his old guns (a World War II Garand 30.06 and a Smith and Wesson .38 in his belt), he had been honed by the years to achieve a killing grace. His row of gold teeth was his bank account, proof of his prosperity. And as if protecting his life savings, he seldom opened his mouth to speak.

Only *he* knew where the trail would lead, for unlike Dawson, the American, or Felipe, the pale young one, dark-skinned Andrés had Indian blood. They were following what was, for Andrés, a familiar path through the northwest corner of the vast rain forest that stretched from the Andes's western slope to the Pacific. The trails had changed in the forty-odd years since he had learned them as a boy, but not the sixth sense that enabled him to thread the labyrinth. He sniffed the air. He could smell a salt breeze. It would have been quicker to travel by motor launch to the remote beach that was their destination. But approaching by sea would have cost them the advantage of surprise. And that would have cost them everything.

Andrés stopped, his machete blade poised in midair, sticky with sap from the branches. He ran a hand along the scar that slashed from the base of his neck across his cheek. Carefully he pulled aside a veil of leaves to reveal the first hint of the village: a thin vine had been stretched across the trail and knotted to the trigger of an ancient percussion-cap shotgun. When a creature—a capybara, a jaguar, even a man—snagged the vine trip wire, the gun would fire. The weapon had already discharged, and a trail of blood along the ground indicated the victim had crashed off into the forest to die.

Their feet squished through the muck. Dawson's combat boots had been carelessly tied, for he lacked the patience to lace them all the way up. But he was meticulous about his M-14. He had served in Vietnam three years as a sniper and would have reupped for another tour of duty if they had let him. By night, his rifle equipped with noise suppressor and starlight scope, he had launched murderous initiatives, obeying the cruel voices in his mind. Soon he took such delight in his work his commanding officers feared for their own lives. They discharged one who had learned his trade too well, lest the fever spread. For Dawson was a carrier.

Not so Andrés, a sober, practical man. Superstitious, but as only the practical can be, he obeyed even the most morbid of rituals if they stood a chance of prolonging his life. He had robbed his shoes off a corpse, believing a dead man's shoes would protect their next owner from harm. As he slogged through the forest, the oxfords had become so caked with muck it looked as though he had stepped from the grave.

Young Felipe planted his boots in Andrés's footprints, following the older man, learning from him step by step. In contrast with Andrés's frayed straw panama, Felipe's khaki forage cap was new. Traces of naphthalene packing grease still clung to his AR-15 assault rifle, and his shiny boots blistered his feet raw. An aristocrat by birth, he had a handsome, even pretty, face, his fair skin delicate as a girl's, his eyes blue with long lashes. His father was a colonel in the Guardia Nacional. Felipe had enlisted in the Guardia, too, but when he discovered he would be a Sunday soldier with a plywood gun, he had looked for work better suited to his restless temperament. After plying him with brandy, Andrés had recruited the youth for this, his first hunt. In the *veterano*, Felipe felt he had finally found a father worthy of his devotion.

The three men were so close to the village now Felipe could smell the smoke from the cooking fires. Andrés raised a finger to his lips. Overhead a dozen red howler monkeys clung to the latticework of liana and branches. If they were alarmed, their screeches would be heard three miles away. The men looked up, as if seeking a blessing from heaven, hoping that the monkeys would not betray them.

Dawson's mouth stretched into a grin: *Bethlehem*. Beyond plaintain and banana trees and a garden of manioc and sweet potatoes, a longhouse straddled a hillock overlooking the ocean fifty yards away. The thirty-foot structure was built without windows, the walls buttressed with a double thickness of chonta palm staves for defense. The barricades were impregnable, even against Dawson's 7.62 mm bullets, protecting the men of the tribe, who were inside taking their customary siesta. Squatting at the entrance to the hut, a fat Indian woman, naked except for a swatch of cloth around her hips, nursed a four-month-old baby at one breast, a puppy at the other. *"Madonna and child,"* Dawson murmured, wild-eyed, and fingered his M-14 expectantly.

The light of the clearing was unsparing, a far cry from the jungle's chairoscuro which hid killer from victim until the act of murder had been discreetly consummated. Felipe turned from the woman to the only other human being on the red clay of the clearing: a naked child of seven. His belly swollen with intestinal worms, the little boy was collecting moth larvae, squeezing them between thumb and forefinger like a delicacy. Felipe had steeled himself to face a hostile enemy, but how could he have prepared himself for this? Doubt gnawed at him, like the flies buzzing over nearby heaps of excrement. A heat rash crawled up his neck so that the chain of his gold crucifix chafed and cut him. "Why are we going to *this* village?" he remembered asking Andrés, and the answer had been: "Because they are killers and must be exterminated." Had Andrés lied? Felipe looked to his companions, seeking the answer. They had raised their guns to firing position. He mimicked their action, hoping to mirror their calm, but in his haste, his rifle's trigger guard clicked against the hilt of his hunting knife.

Had he given them away with the sound? In the clearing the child tensed and gazed intently into the shadowy vegetation. He was looking straight at them. How much could he see through the leaves? Felipe held his breath. Suddenly the boy dropped the moth larvae and ran over to a hollow log, the signal drum. Felipe framed his target in his sights, but his trigger finger froze. He could not bring himself to kill a child, even when the boy snatched a club to pound out the alarm. Seemingly Felipe's fleeting death wish alone was enough, for the boy toppled in the dust, hitting the ground hard as if hurled from a great height. Andrés's shot had been muffled by a silencer. The woman on the front steps stood up, her teats popping from the mouths of baby and whelp alike. Before she could duck into the lodge, Andrés killed her, too.

"Gift of the Magi..." Dawson murmured, and heaved a grenade toward the hut. Bright as the Star of Bethlehem, it exploded. The blast sent a shower of splintered palm staves into the air, flame igniting the thatch of the roof. Billowing smoke drove the warriors out, a blur of barrel-chested men running into the clearing. And the moment he laid eyes on them, Felipe felt afraid. It was as if their bodies had been created solely for combat, as if all the frills devised by "civilized" men since had only dulled the primal urge to kill. Faces painted with red bands of achiote, black shoulder-length hair flying, they were hungry to fight. Felipe opened fire at last, aiming for their torsos, grunting as the gunstock rammed into his shoulder with each recoil. He realized the Indians' crude muzzle-loaders shooting the hard seeds of the etsa tree were no match for his assault rifle. He felt giddy with power to watch them fall, their bodies jerking like marionettes with tangled strings.

A girl, lighter-skinned than the others, darted into Felipe's line of fire, and his finger faltered on the trigger. The teenager's lips and nipples were pink instead of brown, her hair almost blond. The child of a trader and an Indian girl, he guessed. Killing Indians was one thing, but she was almost white. It was not until she lunged for an antiquated Winchester .44 carbine at the doorpost of the hut that he summoned some as-yet-untapped anger. Squeezing the trigger, he sent her toppling to the ground. There was no time to look back at her corpse. He was grateful for that.

The survivors had barricaded themselves in a small hut built on high ground, a seemingly impregnable position. Etsa seeds hissed from it toward the attackers. When Felipe started to crawl toward the hut, Andrés grabbed his arm and pointed at Dawson. *"¡Déjale hacerlo!"* Let him do it. This was why Andrés tolerated the American's madness. Dawson had already snaked on his belly up to the hut's blind side, grinning like a child playing hide-and-seek. Flattening himself against the wall, he yanked the pin to a hand grenade, counted to three, and flipped it inside through a chink in the palm-stave logs. The explosion sent four men or, rather, shreds of them flying. A haze of smoke drifted across the clearing, and in the silence, Felipe could hear the roar of the nearby waves.

Andrés wiped his brow with a sweaty wrist and trudged into the open. He peered inside the burning hut, and finished the body count— eighteen men, eight women, six children. Then, his expression easing from a soldier's vigilance to a bargain hunter's curiosity, he fingered a jaguar skin stretched on a rack of palm staves to dry. In the firefight, slugs had slashed an ugly wound across it. Worthless.

As Felipe walked into the clearing, he felt the pain of his blistered feet once again, the heat rash burning his neck. The stillness was unnerving. The corpse of a fallen warrior stared at him, and he took a wide detour, as if death were contagious. Had Dawson already become infected? The American was loading the one weapon both Felipe and Andrés refused to touch: a 35 mm camera. To pull a trigger was a spontaneous reflex, but to take pictures of the aftermath, that was more difficult, demanding a sober scrutiny of the dead. *El Jefe*, back in the capital, insisted on the photographic "documentation." It was the only way to assure an accurate head count. *El Jefe* knew he could rely on Dawson. His coverage was always thorough, his pictures sharp, for he snapped them the way he fired his M-14, with a terrible precision.

Dawson triggered bursts with the Nikon, careful not to disturb the corpses where they lay. To Felipe the warriors seemed hopelessly obsolete. Yet Andrés had told him "they are the deadliest tribe of all." How had they earned their fearsome reputation? According to Andrés they had been forced out of their ancestral lands at the foot of the Andes years before by prospectors seeking gold and oil. Driven toward the coast, they had waged a last-ditch war until finally, at the ocean's edge, they had nowhere left to run. They weren't just the last of a tribe. They were the last of an entire race. Extinct.

His official photography complete, Dawson loaded a fresh roll of film into the camera and broke into a crooked grin. He slipped the dead baby back into its mother's arms and snapped a picture. Madonna and Child. *Venite adoremus*. He bent over two warriors lying side by side, their bodies contorted in agony, and wrapped their arms around each other. "They're just good friends," he cackled. "Just good friends." Dawson dragged two young women into the open—a dark one and the light-skinned half-breed. The *veterano* knew from past experience what was coming next. *"Está loco,"* Andrés told Felipe, and shook his head. Felipe did not want to see what Dawson would do to the light-skinned girl. He was glad to follow Andrés behind the longhouse, searching for something to eat. The *veterano* found the carcass of an agouti stored under palm fronds, but the ten-pound rodent had turned green with rot. A bowl of cocoons holding butterfly grubs was no more appetizing. Then Andrés discovered a gourdful of manioc beer. "The women chew the manioc and spit it into this bowl to ferment," he explained. "The younger and more beautiful the woman who chews the manioc, the sweeter the taste." He sipped some with a calabash. "Good," he nodded. "It must have been chewed by a virgin." The stench of the brew disgusted Felipe. He took a taste and spit the mouthful out.

When Andrés and Felipe returned to the other side of the longhouse, the wild gleam in Dawson's eyes had yielded to satiety. "This is your rifle, and this is your gun," the American hummed. "One is for killing, the other's for fun." Andrés's gaze met Felipe's. Both men loathed Dawson's excesses as much as they despised the vultures which had scuttled down to peck at the corpses.

In the windless air, the fire had dwindled, and Dawson and Andrés walked around the longhouse with copal torches, igniting the corners that were still standing. Inside, through the flames, Felipe glimpsed a blackened pot and strange cutting, scraping, and stirring implements. Somehow they didn't look like cooking utensils. Were they tools of magic? Could a tribe's sorcery continue after its annihilation? He sensed an ominous question left unanswered and felt compelled to ask Andrés. But the old man had already turned his back on the blazing huts, trudging up the trail. Dawson followed, with a jaunty bounce in his step. Felipe looked at the American, and at himself, and wondered if there was any difference between them after today. A veil of flies had settled on the face of the pale-skinned girl. Felipe turned his back on her but it was no use—she lay in an open grave in his mind. For a moment he longed to run toward the ocean, to cleanse himself in the waves. But he didn't dare. He had to hurry or be left behind to rot with the corpses. He jogged to catch up with Andrés.

"We were wrong to do this." The youth spoke in a whisper when he reached his friend, as if even here, in the middle of nowhere, they might be overheard.

The *veterano* struck a match and lit a cigarette. "It gets easier." He exhaled the smoke through his gold teeth. "After a while, it all gets easier."

As the mercenaries dissolved into the surrounding green, eyes followed them—ageless eyes that were wise and utterly without pity. Eyes of a supreme hunter, they could read the hieroglyphics of light and shade, track down trails too devious for humankind. The eyes had watched the devastation with sadness, but they shed no tears. Unblinking as the moon, they burned with a cold hunger for vengeance, a rage that could reach across space and time and into the deepest jungles of the mind. Instead of compassion for the victims, this supreme intelligence felt only hatred for the guilty. And in its visionary strength, it plotted a deadly course.

There was a hidden meaning here, beyond the massacre, beyond the savagery of "civilized" men. The incident would be etched in time, with a grave significance only the unseen hunter knew. The cutting edge of its revenge would not be dulled by time, nor would the coming torrential rains wash away the stench of blood. For the crime was not merely against the tribe. The crime was against the jungle itself.

1

4 A.M. AS USUAL, IN PITCH BLACKNESS, SULEIMAN, the houseboy, left a tray of tea and cold chapati on the porch of the guesthouse, and as usual, crows flapped down from the roof, knocking the china over with a crash. No matter. Christine Latham couldn't stare breakfast in the face. Her mouth had the rotten-egg aftertaste of Daraprim, the malaria pills she took to escape the fever, and she was nauseated from the Ampicillin that helped her fight a chronic case of dysentery. Unable to muster the energy to climb out of bed, she lay on her cot, listening to the crows fighting over the scraps, their cacophony echoing her own troubled thoughts. The Gir Forest, in the northwest corner of India, was bleak under the best of circumstances, but to make matters worse, Chris had arrived during the worst drought in twenty years. So what else was new? *View* magazine had sent her to Siberia in the dead of winter and to Timbuktu in July. Par for the course, she thought.

That night, as usual, Chris had been tormented by what she called the mosquito net dilemma. If she slept under the cheesecloth shroud, it suffocated her. But if she didn't use it, the mosquitoes attacked in force. Chris had chosen to go without, dozing naked, and she regretted it. The mosquitoes had eaten her alive.

She stood up and bent down to touch her toes with a groan. Then she attempted a few *pliés*, the last vestige of ballet lessons she had taken when she was ten. She had a firm, supple body for a woman of thirty, for her work kept her limber. Her work also kept her exhausted and, too often, alone.

Chris walked over to the sink to rinse her mouth out with sour-tasting boiled water. In her ten years of roughing it, she brooded, this had to be the low point. The Gir Forest "guesthouse" consisted of a dozen cinder-block cubicles with cots filled with moldy straw and squeaking ceiling fans that seemed designed solely to keep her awake. Chris might have been more comfortable camping in a tent if it weren't for the cobras. She was the sole guest and had been forced to endure alone the cook's infamous curried goat five times that week. She would have sold her soul for a pizza. But even worse than eating goat was watching Suleiman dry the dishes afterward with the soiled bed linen. In the fetid 110-degree heat, she couldn't even drown her sorrows. Gujarat, Gandhi's birthplace, had been declared a dry state in his honor.

Chris stared at herself in the mirror as if facing a firing squad. Under a dying bulb, her russet hair was a dingy brown. But even at this hour, her eyes were bright. They transformed a face of striking conventional beauty into something else, less soft perhaps, less delicate, but more intelligent and open. She licked her chapped lips. Lipstick might help, but why bother? The men here didn't care how she looked. In their eyes a woman doing "man's work" was hardly a woman at all. Well, she sighed, maybe they were right. She sniffed under her arm and made a face; she stank like a Harijan, one of the untouchables whose job was to scrub the guesthouse toilets. The sun had brought out the freckles on her fair skin, and she ran a wistful hand along her cheek as if wiping away tears. It had been a long time since a man had touched her face. Chris reined herself in on the brink of self-pity. She had chosen this life, God damn it. If her relationships with men were as fleeting as the images in her Nikon viewfinder, she had no one to blame but herself.

Chris slipped on her rumpled uniform: khaki shorts and a faded L.A. Dodgers' T-shirt that had shrunk a size too small, revealing firm breasts beneath it. Stifling a yawn, she snapped onto her belt the pouch that held her smelling salts, malaria pills, insect repellent, Valium, and Lomotil and laced up her boots. Then she lovingly removed her cameras from the Haliburton case under her cot, squirted the dust off the lenses with a blower brush, and selected fresh rolls of film for the day's shoot.

"Essential to have mating coverage," the telegram from Graner, her managing editor in New York, had read, and then, even more absurd: "Please photograph *tastefully*." Though the rest of her story on the Asiatic lion was complete, getting the mating sequence had already delayed her departure two weeks. From the looks of it, she'd go on eating goat stew until doomsday or at least until two oversized alley cats felt the urge to copulate. But then, she wondered, was waiting for a pair of lions to get it on any more absurd than traveling hundreds of miles to cover a murderer's execution when there could be no outcome but one?

Chris wasn't a wildlife photographer. She lacked the patience—and the iron bladder—to crouch for hours in a leafy blind to record quirks of animal behavior. But when *View*'s regular nature man had taken a spill out of a baobab tree in Kenya and wound up in a cast from the waist down, she had been assigned his photo essay on the endangered Asiatic lion. Once this subspecies, the biblical Lion of Judah, had ranged from North Africa through India, but now it was reduced to the 200 in this remote bramble forest. Compared to Chris's recent assignments in Teheran, Northern Ireland, and South Africa, a sojourn with the cats of the Gir had seemed a welcome change of pace. After spending years watching the ugly spectacle of people acting like animals, she had, perhaps, hoped to find animals acting human. Which, of course, they didn't. But once she reached the Gir, Chris had been impressed by the predators' instinctive code: to hunt only for food; to kill with merciful swiftness. A far cry from the terror of a pipe bomb exploding in an Ulster schoolyard or a machine gun spraying a mob of blacks in Soweto.

Inevitably, however, the human element had intruded in the Gir, for the Indian government was less than delighted to have Chris Latham publicizing the sorry state of its big cats. The local authorities had assigned her Mr. Singh, a "guide" to distance her from the incriminating truth, a spy to harass her while supposedly assuring her safety. She hoped that the danger of this morning's task might discourage him from joining her, and spare her the pleasure of his company.

Chris nestled her cameras back into their case and snapped it shut. She stepped out onto the porch and sniffed the predawn air. It reeked of a dead water buffalo that had been rotting for days. Was this really her worst assignment? she wondered. The most rancid place of all the pleasure spots *View* magazine had sent her? Well, she had had it up to here. Get the shots, she told herself. Catch the lions fucking so you can get the hell out.

A motor grumbled outside. Just as he had for the past five weeks, Pamarbai had driven up to her door at 4:15 A.M.. That jeep. Chris shook her head. It had taught her the most useful word in the Gujarati language: *kalas*. Broken. A story that should have taken ten days had dragged on for weeks, thanks in part to the vehicle's intestinal afflictions, even more troublesome than her own.

Pamarbai sat behind the wheel in his khaki uniform and

puttees. Tugging at his black handlebar mustache, the turbaned driver seemed to have stepped from the pages of Kipling. Unfortunately the Gunga Din devotion was lacking. He felt that working for a woman was unworthy of him. Today Pamarbai seemed even sterner than usual, and when Chris heard a sniff from the back seat, she knew why. Mr. Singh had shown up after all, wearing his starched green forestry uniform and a frosty look. "Good morning," she said. He didn't reply. A suspicious man with a bulbous head and no neck, he had stood in her way from the beginning. "Good morning," she repeated, her smile more forced. He nodded stiffly. They would be facing danger today, thanks to her. He resented it. Before she could even slam her door, the jeep lurched off down the dirt road.

Under their headlamps, the bramble thicket seemed dead from the drought. This hour before dawn was the coolest time of day, and Chris relished a shiver, knowing that scorching hours of heat lay ahead. The headlights' glare turned the eyes of a nilgai to glass as the antelope darted past. Then, as they jolted through the darkness, they were surrounded by crows, dozens of them, black sentinels perched among the brambles.

"I am telling you just now," Mr. Singh's stilted English rose over the jeep's rumble, "this journey today is most perilous, and you will please take no unnecessary risks."

"I'll do my best"—she nodded with strained cordiality—"but if I get what I want today, I can leave. You'd like that, wouldn't you?"

He pursed constipated lips. "Yes, I hope you will go home soon, please."

The road dead-ended in a ravine, and the jeep rattled across a rock escarpment that wore a crown of thorns. A figure loomed ahead of them, hunched beside a teak tree, as stiff as one of the crows. Sidibai, another shikari, was stouter than Pamarbai. His khaki jacket was too tight for him, and he carried a rusty double-barreled shotgun. His left thumb was missing, thanks to a bad habit of sticking his finger into its muzzle, a habit that had ended the day the gun went off. It was Sidibai's responsibility to track the lions through the wildlife sanctuary, for so few remained that a single disaster—a forest fire, an epidemic—could spell the breed's extinction.

"Find them?" Chris asked Sidibai.

"Yes, memsahib."

Pamarbai switched off the motor, and Chris could hear the moan of a predawn wind.

After climbing from the jeep, she followed Sidibai and the driver into the thicket, the brambles scratching her bare arms. Singh took up the rear. Ahead of her in the shadows Sidibai tapped the ground with a stick like a blind man, in the belief that the vibration would warn any cobras of their approach in time for the reptiles to slither away. Even so, Chris placed her feet with more than usual caution. She glanced at the sky. The twilight would provide barely enough illumination for photography, forcing her to load in High Speed Ektachrome and push it one stop to ASA 400. She hoped the light would increase soon enough for her to use Kodachrome 64 for a less grainy effect. As she took a reading with her light meter, Chris lost the two shikaris in the web of thorn branches. When she caught sight of them a moment later, they were standing perfectly still. She saw why.

The predators lolled side by side in a clearing fifty feet beyond, the big cats, the brambles, the earth seemingly carved from a block of ebony. She judged that the male and female each weighed about 400 pounds. As Chris edged up to the shikaris, the light grew, warming the feline bodies from coal black to the batik of fur. The Asiatic lions were the image of their African cousins: proud, sensual, powerful—part kitten, part killer.

Her hunting instincts stirred, and she clutched her Nikon by the lens as if steadying the barrel of a gun. Her longest telephoto, the 300 mm, had been cracked a week before during a scramble over boulders, so she had to rely on her 105, which was barely powerful enough to do the job. It meant the risk of working at close range, and as she edged toward the lions, Mr. Singh scowled. The shikaris held their guns at the ready. During mating, the predators were unpredictable. To interrupt an assignation could prove fatal.

Click. Chris felt immune to danger, swept up in a trance. She had entered a world the width of her viewfinder, to frame, focus, set exposure, then snap the shutter—*Click.* She bracketed her f-stops, holding the camera rock-steady to keep the image from blurring at the perilously slow shutter speed of ⅟₃₀ second. *Click—click.* All in a single continuous movement, as natural as her next breath. *Click.*

The rim of the sun glinted over the barren hills, tinting the lions and the earth shades of palomino. After loading in a fresh canister of ammunition, Chris crept forward, less than thirty feet from her prey. The male stirred. He licked his chops and stretched luxuriously. Then he mounted the female from behind. Chris triggered her camera's automatic-drive and cranked off a burst. *Click-click*. The male's haunches quivered, and he sank his teeth into the lioness's neck. His mate twisted her head in a snarl. *Click*. It was over in one fierce second, and then they were lazy felines once again. Chris and her camera had been created for this moment. As long as it lasted, she felt a rare blend of serenity and exhilaration. This was why she put up with the goat curry, the obstinate bureaucrats, the threat of disease—this moment beyond orgasm. No, in spite of her hunter's stance, her sniper's eye, she wasn't firing the Nikon like a gun. She was using her camera to make love to the world.

And now that the mating ritual was over, Chris edged closer to catch the lioness raking her claws across a rotting log. Singh cringed behind the shikaris, his eyes bulging in terror. "Yes, you cannot do that!" he gasped. The lioness stiffened at the sound of his voice, and the male bared his fangs, a growl escaping his jaws. Lost in her viewfinder world, Chris was the last to know her presence had been betrayed. In the next thirtieth of a second, the instant it took the shutter to guillotine one frame, the lion sprang toward Chris. She never saw her attacker, for with a deafening explosion, both barrels of Sidibai's shotgun belched flame. Crows shot skyward, like a disintegrating fragment of the night, and the startled lions scattered, vanishing into the forest.

"You lady will pay for this!" Singh shrieked. He had stumbled backward into a dry riverbed and was soaked with muck. "You cannot do that!" he sputtered.

"But I did." Chris grinned and removed the roll of film from her camera, to tuck it safely into her pocket. She had her ticket home.

It was ten in the morning when the jeep rolled up to the guesthouse. In the 105-degree heat, the putrefying buffalo stank worse than ever, but Chris didn't flinch. In half an hour she would be able to pack up, and make good her escape. Her body had other ideas. Now that the job was done, the weeks of exhaustion seemed to pounce on her. Unable to muster the energy to open her suitcase, she collapsed on her cot, and sank into a deep sleep. It was late afternoon when she awoke, the blades of the ceiling fan slicing shadows across her body.

"Memsahib!" Suleiman, the houseboy, was rapping on her door, his voice quavering with excitement. "Telephone!" She had placed a call to the United States a week before and had forgotten all about it. Now a faint ringing told her it had come through at last. She dashed to the park superintendent's office, a bare cubicle with a chair, a desk, a chart of poisonous snakes on the wall, and dived for the receiver. Even after she snatched it up, the phone kept on ringing, like a miscue in a high school play. Finally, the ringing stopped. It sounded as if her boss in New York were shouting down a sewer pipe.

"Hello?"

"Hello!"

"Chris? Graner. I can hardly hear you."

"Can you hear me now?"

They were shouting so loudly she wondered if they could have done as well without the telephone. "I got the shots!" she said.

"The lions fucking?"

"Yes!"

"Fantastic!" His exclamation came through faint as a whisper.

"I'm leaving Miami Beach tomorrow," she said.

"What did you think of my letter?"

"What letter?" Chris shouted.

"Did you get my *letter?*" Graner's voice was fading in and out.

"*What* letter?"

"You know. The letter. The one that tells..." But before he could utter another syllable, he drowned in a maelstrom of static.

Chris jiggled the hook in exasperation. The line was dead. "Damn!" She slammed the phone down and turned to Suleiman, who leaned sheepishly in the doorway.

"Suleiman, what happened to my letter?"

"Letter? Memsahib, I—"

"Come on, Suleiman."

He reached into his slipper and pulled out a folded envelope, unopened, but with the postage stamps steamed off. "As you can see, Memsahib, I have placed it here for safekeeping."

She shot him a dirty look. How many weeks ago had it arrived? Before she could find out, he made his getaway, mumbling something about helping with the goat curry. Chris hesitated before opening the envelope. What if Graner assigned her to the Black Hole of Calcutta, as long as she was in the general vicinity? A famine, a civil war, an outbreak of the plague—she knew he would come up with something delightful. When a glossy brochure dropped out of the envelope, she couldn't believe it. Graner had attached a note, in the scrawl it had taken her years to decipher. "I thought you might find your next assignment a pleasant change of pace. Just don't make a habit of it." The brochure showed a high-rise hotel on the edge of a perfect beach. In another rendering, the artist had depicted a candlelit dining room. Chefs at a smorgasbord sliced roast beef, flanked by carved ice swans.

Chris walked back to her room and flopped down on the filthy cot in her filthy clothes, gazing at the brochure as if it were a message from heaven. *"The Hotel El Dorado . . . The ultimate resort. . . ."* She tugged off a boot and kicked it in a dusty arc across the room. How long had it been since she had worn high heels instead of those damn clodhoppers? *"The most beautiful beach on earth. . . ."* How long since she had sprawled in the sun with a tall drink and a tall man? Maybe Graner realized what a bloody good reporter she was after all. Maybe they really *were* afraid she would go over to the competition, the newsmagazine they jokingly called Brand X. She wondered if there was a catch. Nonsense. Her boss had sent her into the lion's den, and now that she had survived, even Graner recognized she had her R & R coming. "The Grand Opening of the El Dorado Hotel. Cover it," he had written, "and enjoy."

A raucous cry disrupted her reverie. Through the window, shimmering in the heat like a mirage, an emerald-blue peacock perched in a distant tree. Its tail feathers were spread in a fan, as improbable a sight amid the desolation as the brochure she held in her hand. The peacock's plumage looked so extravagant against the scorched brambles, that she wanted to reach out and touch it. After Graner's good news, Chris told herself, she was through with crows. Through with crows for good.

2

WHEN CHRIS DISEMBARKED FROM HER VARIG JET
at Tierra del Mar, capital of Panaguas, a Pan Am representative
in a blue blazer was standing beside the runway to meet her.
The American introduced himself as Arthur Ashby and beckoned her to be seated in a wheelchair. "They said you would
be tired," he said. "I brought this."

"*They?*" Chris asked. But she could guess who "they" were.
She strode ahead of him toward the terminal. In spite of her
irritation, she had no intention of taking it out on Ashby. He
was the one who looked like a basket case. His eyes were
puffy, his face ashen. It seemed to take all his strength to push
the empty wheelchair ahead of him, as if it were holding the
tonnage of his problems.

"So where's the phone?" she asked.

He seemed flustered. "How did you know there was a call
for you?" Chris didn't answer. She'd been through this enough
times to know plenty.

Ashby left the wheelchair just inside the terminal building,
and his pace quickened. He took the lead as their feet clicked
across the marble floor of the main concourse. Chris was surprised to see it was deserted. Only two flights, both of them
international, were posted on the arrival board. "We used to
be the third largest air traffic hub in South America," Ashby
said. "That was *before*...." He turned away from the idle
baggage carousels, as if they were a slap in the face. Blue-
uniformed police with machine pistols were stationed along the
walls as motionless as caryatids. "It's funny," he continued.
"A week ago, when all the Americans were killing each other
to get out, I was working around the clock. But now that they're
gone and there's nothing to do, it's worse. It's death." He led
her down a corridor and stopped at a door marked "*Se Prohibe
Entrar.*" He unlocked it and switched on the overhead fluorescents. The room was a shambles, computer terminals gutted,
tape reels mangled. "This used to be our reservations center,"

he said. "Until the guerrillas remodeled it."

Ashby seemed so grieved by the sight Chris felt compelled to comfort him. "I'm sorry."

He shrugged. "Not that it matters. About the computers, I mean. You know how many passengers we booked on our wide-body flight from New York yesterday? Eight. It's you journalists." He said it in a tone that showed he held nothing against Chris personally. "You're murdering us. Talk about bad press."

He beckoned her to a corner of the room that had escaped destruction. On a desk, sat a phone with buttons for ten incoming lines. All of them were open except for a single flashing light.

"For me," Chris said.

"For you."

Calculating the time difference in her mind, she conjured up the party on the other end as clearly as if the receiver in her hand were a picturephone. Graner's shirt was rumpled, his tie askew. The searchlights on the Chrysler Building outside his window had just been switched on, signaling him to pour the first scotch of the evening into his Mets coffee mug. "Is this White Fang?" she asked.

"Speaking." The connection was good. Too good, Chris thought. This time, whatever Graner had cooked up, there would be no escaping it.

"Thanks for the wheelchair. Am I going to need it after this conversation?"

"Merely a fringe benefit, my sweet."

"I appreciate your concern for my well-being. Very heart-warming."

She heard a crackling on the line that she knew wasn't static. Graner had taken the last Camel from his second pack of the day and crumpling the cellophane into a ball, had heaved it across the room at his wastebasket. He always missed.

"Have a nice flight?"

Chris knew such chummy openings were a bad omen, an attempt to soothe her before he lobbed the Molotov cocktail. "For Chrissake, get on with it!" She stopped short, clamping a lid on her annoyance. "Strike that from the record, okay? It's just . . . well, I was sort of hoping I wouldn't be hearing from you for a while."

"All right, so I've been less than frank about the Panaguas assignment."

Chris sighed. "I know. I saw the cover of your blessed

magazine in Bombay.' "

" 'Latin America's Powder Keg.' How'd you like it?"

"Originality was never one of your strong points."

"Cliché? Perhaps. But apt. For a country that's about to blow sky high. The corpses on the cover were a grabber, don't you think? Newsstand sales topped Brand X by four hundred thou."

"When are you going to send me somewhere there isn't a war or a plague or ... I mean, doesn't *peace* ever break out?"

"The Four Horsemen of the Apocalypse. Let's see, Chris, what were they? War ... Famine ... Death ... Fear ... You're the fifth."

"On my salary, I'll have to ride bareback."

"Stop fishing for compliments. You're good, okay? I said it, is that what you wanted? You're indispensable. Jesus Christ!"

"Don't tell me. Let me guess. The hotel assignment is off."

"Come on, Chris, do you think I'd sink that low? Lure you down to beautiful Tierra del Fuego or whatever the hell they call that capital city down there and then pull the plug?"

"Well, wouldn't you? Haven't you?"

"What kind of monster do you take me for?"

"I don't know. What kind of monster are you?"

"Rest assured you have a luxury suite at the El Dorado waiting for you."

"But?"

"No buts. There are just a few ... details ... that I somehow neglected to tell you."

"Such as?"

"Such as the El Dorado's grand opening is a big PR effort by the government to prove that it's business as usual down there."

"So?"

"So we think that makes it an ideal target for the guerrillas."

"That, and everything else in Panaguas that's not nailed down."

His tone changed. "From the information we've come across, the El Dorado's a *certain* target."

"Reliable informant?" she asked. He didn't answer. It was as good as yes.

"Whatever happens," he continued, "we want you there to cover it."

"Sort of like hiring a defense attorney before the murder's been committed."

"We think you'll be the only press. It's practically a guaranteed exclusive."

"You've really got a thing for corpses, haven't you?"

"You'll look good . . . I'll look good . . . The magazine will—"

"I wouldn't rent my tux for the Pulitzer banquet quite yet if I were you."

"So now you know as much as I do. Go ahead. Catch your connecting flight to the El Dorado. Bake your brains out in the sun. Pick up some exotic strain of the clap. Just lie back and let the story happen."

"It's a little hard to get a suntan wearing a bulletproof vest."

"So maybe our tip was wrong. Maybe nothing's going to happen at all. In that case, you've got yourself a paid vacation with my compliments."

Chris didn't dignify Graner's last remark with an answer. His informants were seldom wrong. "I don't suppose it's occurred to you to pass your tip on to the Panaguan government. Save some lives."

"And blow an exclusive?" Graner laughed. "Seriously, Chris, I tried. But I'm afraid the Panaguan secret police are too arrogant to take a tip from a nice Jewish boy from Long Island."

Chris frowned. "They know I'm a journalist. If things are as sensitive as you say, why should the government let me come down to the El Dorado at all?"

"Their tourism is in desperate straits. They need all the hype they can get. A color spread about the opening of the El Dorado would be the first good news to come out of that country in years." He paused. "So you'll go, sweetheart?" Whenever Graner sank to the "sweetheart" level, Chris knew he had reached the part of the conversation he hated. Because for that moment, at least, he was at her mercy. "You'll go?" he repeated, trying to keep his voice on an even keel. Chris allowed the line to go dead for a full minute. She thought she could hear the nervous tinkle of ice cubes as he downed a shot from his mug 10,000 miles away. He added, as an afterthought, "Of course, it could be a bit nasty." Graner knew Chris well. They had played this game for almost ten years now, this ritual of seduction. She felt a perverse smile creep across her face. Graner was dangling the bait like a pusher, and as usual, against her better judgment, she was going for it. She felt the visceral thrill that came from the knowledge she could do a job—an important, risky job. That he needed her.

"Do I have a choice?" she said.

"You sure as hell don't!" Graner laughed, relieved. No more "sweethearts." He was back in control again. "You'd better get a move on. I wouldn't want you to miss your connecting flight."

Chris didn't want to let him off so easily. The little girl in her wanted him to appreciate the risk she would be taking. "I suppose you know Panaguas was listed as one of the ten worst human rights violators by Amnesty International last year."

"Wrong, my dear. One of the *five* worst. Have a nice flight."

When she hung up, the Pan Am representative studied her face. "Is it as bad as that?"

Chris didn't answer. As quickly as the surge of elation had come, it evaporated. She felt more weary than ever, and very much alone. And she knew she was being used. She rummaged in her flight bag for the copy of *View* she had bought in Bombay and turned to the cover story. A black box at the end of the piece caught her eye. "This was our correspondent Neil Lawrence's last report. He was killed in Panaguas last week, a victim of the repression his life in journalism had done so much to combat. . . ."

Chris closed the magazine. She hated reading obituaries. It made it too easy to imagine her own.

3

AS CHRIS STEPPED OUT OF THE AIR-CONDITIONED
terminal onto the apron of the runway, the humidity drenched
her face with sweat. The sleepless hours in transit, the sudden
stress of her assignment left her vulnerable. And the setting
only heightened the tension. She had been whisked inside so
quickly on her arrival that she hadn't noticed the airport was
an armed camp. Troops stood vigil on the rooftop of the terminal, manning machine-gun nests. Half a dozen tanks were
stationed along the perimeter, their 40 mm cannons scanning
the tarmac. Trudging toward the bus that held the other passengers for her connecting flight, Chris had to walk directly
across the tanks' line of fire. As she ran the gauntlet, she could
hear the turret of a tank whine, its cannon following her. A
sadistic gunner, no doubt, watching her squirm.

Normally she would have shrugged off such harassment.
But in her exhaustion, Chris's footsteps faltered. She wished
to God she could have used her camera's lens to distance herself
from this menacing landscape, like a little girl staring down
the wrong end of a telescope. But a sign warned that photography was forbidden, and though she frequently sneaked shots
at airports with similar prohibitions, the hair-trigger atmosphere
today forced her to play this one by the rules.

She followed the grizzled porter carrying her camera case
toward the bus and to avoid withdrawing into her private fears,
she focused on the here and now: the stench of diesel fumes
from the tanks, the bawling of an infant in the shantytown
beyond the barbed wire edging the runway. Ragged inhabitants
of the slum stood on the opposite side of the thorny barrier,
the same poor she had seen the world over. Shoeshine boys,
beggars, a woman hawking cheap straw hats, they thrust their
arms through the barbed wire, clutching at her as she passed.
They would sell her anything to stay alive, even themselves.
Chris could detect a wild glint in their eyes, the fever of revolution. On a wall behind them, someone had scrawled a word:
"Vargas." The name of the rebel leader had been whitewashed

over, but not completely. She knew their longing to escape oppression might be stifled, but still it smoldered. Sooner or later their hunger for change would topple the government. And the next regime, on left or right, would bring only new oppression. Then the dream would wax strong once again, as inevitable as the next full moon.

She spotted what looked like a dead animal lying on the runway. A closer look revealed a mongrel snoring in the heat, its ribs stretching through its hide. There were no takeoffs or landings to disturb its siesta.

Chris reached the bus and rummaged for a tip for the porter. Her change purse held a few Indian rupees, a few French francs, a dollar bill, and her mind seemed just as jumbled in time and space. After slipping the dollar to the porter, she climbed aboard the bus. She searched for a familiar face among the passengers, someone to relieve her isolation.

The wilted Hollywood glamour of the couple sitting nearest to the front helped her get her bearings. The man was dressed in a lime-green silk shirt open to the navel, with the name Irv stitched in silk over the breast pocket. He even wore his Palm Springs tan like an affectation. His companion, a champagne blonde, seemed ready to burst out of a sequined T-shirt stretched over enormous breasts that defied the laws of gravity. She was the kind of woman Graner would have called a Stollywood Harlot. While her escort fanned her with a copy of *Variety*, she chewed gum reflectively, as if analyzing the subtleties of spearmint could answer a much larger riddle. Chris passed them by. They were familiar faces, all right, but not friendly ones.

A thirtyish, bearded man sat behind the couple, his hand resting on the guitar case beside him as if it were his best friend. He radiated a blur of corruption and innocence: a wilted flower child from the sixties, she concluded. His watery eyes matched the washed-out beige of his tunic, reminding Chris of an album cover that had faded in the sun. She kept right on walking.

Across the aisle, a woman in her fifties, clad in a flowered dress much too young for her, fluttered, birdlike. She looked embalmed rather than made up, her eyebrows plucked, then penciled in, the powder that masked her wrinkles so thick it only worsened the damage. Chris cast her as a would-be Hedda Hopper, but one with an ear for strange, unspeakable gossip.

A motley handful, she concluded: sweaty, silent, lobotomized by the heat.

She realized she had overlooked one passenger sitting in the back. In his mid-forties, he had the staid features of a lawyer waiting for the New York to Boston shuttle. Yet he seemed almost deliberately unkempt, his sleeves rolled up, two days' growth of stubble on his chin. His tweed coat, ridiculously hot for the tropics, sat in a heap atop a suitcase strapped to an aluminum trolley. She read the name on the coat's label: "Langrock—Princeton." An overgrown preppie, she deduced. Of the odd little group he was the least intriguing. But he seemed the safest. Or were his vices merely less obvious than the others'? When she stepped closer and smelled the whiskey on his breath, she wondered if she'd made the right choice.

"Plane's late," he said.

"It's better to be down here wishing you were up there"— she shrugged—"than up there wishing you were down here."

He pulled a brochure out of his pocket and read aloud: "'A luxury flight will whisk you from Panaguas's modern capital to the resort's private landing strip.'" His smile engaged her. "I don't know the opposite of 'whisk,' but this is it."

She nodded and glanced back at the other passengers: compared to them, they had something in common.

"Not much of a turnout," he said.

"I'm surprised anyone showed up at all." Chris gestured out the window at the tanks.

He looked away. "They . . . *we* . . . we all have our reasons." His tone was not quite mysterious—she doubted if he could be capable of mystery—but he was definitely hiding something. Of that much she was certain. Before she could pin him down, he shifted his tone: "A pretty Raggedy Andy group."

"En route anyone looks like an unmade bed." She offered her hand. "Chris Latham, unmade bed."

He took it. "Alan Reynolds." He removed a cigar from his vest pocket. "Mind? It's Havana." He rolled the panatella appreciatively between thumb and forefinger, and the wrapper crackled. "This whole country's a goddamn humidor." He removed the paper ring from the cigar, paused for a moment, then tossed it on the ground. "When my wife was alive, I'd always put those paper rings on her finger. Dumb."

"No, it isn't." Chris was surprised by the suddenness of her reply, an instinctive response to the pain on his face.

"No fumar, señor!" A weasel of a man in a dark suit and

sunglasses strutted onto the bus. "I am Señor Gavaldón. I come from the Department of Internal Security, to assist you with airport formalities."

It was no mystery to Chris how this civil servant could afford his Italian suit, alligator shoes, and gold watch on a government salary. Panaguas was a leading supplier of cocaine, most of it smuggled out of the country by air when certain officials of negotiable virtue looked the other way.

"Venga, Enrique." Gavaldón beckoned to a fat guard with droopy trousers to climb aboard. When Enrique wedged his belly behind the wheel, Gavaldón snapped his fingers, and they were off. They cruised along the edge of the airstrip, passing Piper Cubs, Beechcrafts, Comanches, and stopped in front of a hangar where two curtained booths stood like changing cubicles at a clothing store.

"Pasaportes," Gavaldón proclaimed, and the passengers handed them to him as they filed out, the inspector examining the documents one by one. "Dawn Parfait." He read the starlet's name off her passport and, sizing up her endowments, beckoned her into the booth with him. Enrique watched, his revolver weighing his trousers down so that his ass crack showed. He ushered Chris into the other booth. Judging from his expression, he considered her a poor second.

"You got any plants?" he asked, patting her arms, her hips, her thighs. "You got any fruits?" His hands grazed her buttocks, his ardor growing. "You got any *vegetables?"* He groped at her chest to cop a feel. Chris knew better than to resist. Once, in Dakar, she had elbowed Enrique's black counterpart in the gut, and they had jailed her for a week. He was starting to pant, his exhalations reeking of garlic, and it was the aroma that finally drove her out. "Señorita!" Enrique seemed stung by the rejection, wrestling with trousers that sagged like his spirits.

"Hands off, creep!" There was a scuffle in the other booth. Dawn burst through the drapes, stuffing her T-shirt back into her slacks. Chalk-faced, Señor Gavaldón clutched his crotch, where she had evidently directed a shapely knee. *"Dawn Parfait."* He repeated her name with menace, bent on revenge. "Show me your luggages. Now." When she unlocked her leopard-skin bag, an astonishing variety of lingerie greeted him. Chris smiled at Gavaldón's indecision, the inspector torn between the temptation to finger her black lace bras and pink garter belts and his desire to maintain a facade of professional decorum. He chose discretion and, leaving her suitcase in disarray, rummaged inside her shoulder bag.

"What is *this?*"

Before Dawn could explain the purpose of the flesh-colored vibrator, he handed the mysterious device to Enrique, who had been rifling through Chris's suitcase with equal zeal.

"*No sé. . . .*" The potbellied guard shook his head, handing the object back to Gavaldón.

Dawn blushed with outrage. "Don't you know *anything?*"

The inspector turned the handle and was startled by the cylinder's buzzing. Dawn's partner in the silk shirt came to her rescue. "For her *back*," he said, and pressed the humming instrument onto her shoulder blades. Gavaldón's eyes narrowed, but he decided not to pursue the point, for Chris was coughing with what he seemed to fear was stifled laughter. Enrique fished something equally suspicious from Chris's purse: a Tampax. He sniffed it cautiously. "*¿Para fumar?*" He pantomimed puffing it.

"*Exactamente.*" Alan slid the tampon beside the Havana in his shirt pocket. The guard seemed satisfied, and Chris squeezed Alan's arm to keep from breaking up.

"Margot Hampton." Gavaldón read the name off a dog-eared passport tattooed with stamps. When neither of the inspectors took the middle-aged woman into a booth, Margot seemed disappointed. Gavaldón didn't bother to open her suitcase, but rifling hastily through Margot's patent leather purse, he discovered an object he couldn't ignore. Chris strained to see it: a scrap of fur little larger than a rabbit's foot, but with tiny fingers instead of claws.

"A monkey's paw," Margot fluttered. "How do I say that in Spanish? An amulet." Looking over Gavaldón's shoulder at her passport, Chris was surprised to see she was only fifty-two. Margot's stilted speech was that of a much older woman. "Sir, please permit me to explain. It's a good-luck charm." She looked to the others for support. "Oh dear, I do hope he understands."

But Gavaldón did not choose to understand. A bureaucrat had no time for mysteries. He slipped the monkey's paw back into her purse and snapped it shut.

So far, Chris thought, the inspector had managed to dig up embarrassing information about all the guests. What about Alan? As Gavaldón searched his luggage, she noticed Alan's fingers were squeezing the handle of his suitcase trolley so tightly that his knuckles went white. Was it just her suspicious journalist's mind, she wondered, or should she trust her instinct that Alan might be hiding the biggest secret of all? Gavaldón did not share her misgivings. Dismissing both Alan and Irv, the inspector homed in on a more promising target.

"Scott Hershey." He held the overripe hippie's passport to the light to examine the watermark, before he and Enrique frisked the longhair with more than usual thoroughness. A drug bust would, Chris knew, enhance their official records, considering their dubious sidelines. Enrique removed an electric guitar gleaming with gold-flake paint from its case. Poking a finger inside it, he fished out a plastic bag and handed it to his boss. Gavaldón tore it open and sniffed. He broke into a smirk of triumph. "Marijuana?"

"Hey, no way," Scott said. "Granola."

"Granola?"

"Health food, you dum-dum!" Dawn removed a handful and chewed it defiantly. "See?" Gavaldón ignored her. He was about to arrest Scott when a hoarse voice interrupted.

"Lay off him." Another passenger had joined them, one who had not come on the bus. It seemed to Chris that he had congealed out of thin air. The old man seemed drained, skeletal in his white double-breasted suit. His eyes were dark sockets, his teeth yellow. He wore the most obvious toupee she had ever seen. It resembled the stuffed remains of some small fur-bearing mammal. She noticed Gavaldón's posture change suddenly, the way she had seen wolves shift from dominance to submission when facing a more powerful member of the pack. The stranger handed his passport to Gavaldón.

The inspector did not open it, yet she could hear him whisper the man's name under his breath: *"Curzon."*

Oblivious to the stranger's apparent importance, Enrique frisked him. The guard's eyes widened as he pulled a Luger out of Curzon's shoulder holster and gave it to his boss. Gavaldón glared at Enrique for his faux pas. Then, wearing a sickly smile, he handed the weapon back to Curzon. Chris wondered whether even President Zamora himself could have inspired such groveling. Did this stranger derive his authority from a more potent power than the government of Panaguas?

"Terminado." Gavaldón bowed stiffly from the waist. Whatever the reason, Curzon's arrival had shortened their ordeal. With a sigh of relief, the passengers followed a porter in coveralls who pushed their bags along the runway on a

wooden cart. Alan noticed a case of liquor jiggling beside the luggage.

"Things are looking up," he said.

The others agreed, for the porter was leading them toward a Learjet. Irv doubled the pace of his white Gucci loafers. "Now that's what I call class!" Chris, too, was relieved by the sight of the million-dollar aircraft. In countries like Panaguas, with minimal ground radar, vast stretches of wilderness, and violent storms, an ultramodern jet was more than a luxury; it could mean the margin of survival.

Her heart sank when the attendant skirted the aircraft's rakish shadow, moving past it to a potholed corner of the runway. She was certain it was a dreadful joke. It seemed an aerodynamic impossibility that the decrepit DC-3 before her could actually fly. Its dented skin was mud-spattered from jungle landing strips, its wings clashing shades of green, as if the plane had been concocted from the aquamarine taxis that loitered at the airport.

"Terrific!" Irv Florsheim groaned.

Chris sighed. "What did you expect? Air Force One?" She should have known.

Margot knitted her brow. "Do you think it's *safe?*"

The pilot climbed out of the cockpit, a tricky maneuver in his tight jeans and high-heeled cowboy boots, and stood beside the cargo hatch, hands on his hips. A brawny six feet six and the downhill side of fifty, he showed symptoms Chris knew well: the machismo a man displays at the moment in his life when he most fears it will desert him. "All right, folks," he boomed in a southern baritone, "now identify your luggage before you put it on the plane. Safety precaution. And make it snappy." He jabbed a thumb at the glowering sky. "We don't have all day." Chris couldn't see his eyes behind his mirrored sunglasses, but she could tell they were flicking over Dawn's unnatural enlargements. He tilted his weathered Army Air Force cap at a rakish angle and his mouth spread into a grin. "Harley Stokes, at your service."

As he hefted Dawn's suitcase, Chris glimpsed the butt of a Colt automatic in his belt. He slung the bag into the cargo hatch with a grunt. Dawn threw back her shoulders and flashed a smile.

Margot struggled to lift her suitcase into the hold, but the valise toppled back to earth with a thump. "Sir," she asked, "could you provide me with some assistance please?" But Harley's chivalry was in short supply, and he had turned away from the passengers, to watch the ground crew gas up his plane.

Alan helped Margot and Chris with their suitcases, then shoved his own inside. The porter was hauling the case of whiskey on board. "At least"—Alan wet his lips—"we won't die of thirst."

Chris found a seat near the cockpit by a window. It afforded her a view of Harley handing his flight manifest to Gavaldón at the bottom of the boarding ramp. But instead of signing it to issue takeoff clearance, the security officer grabbed the pilot's arm and led him toward the starboard wing. There was a suitcase on the runway that no one had claimed. Though unable to hear their words, she could read the conversation in pantomime. *"¿Qué pasa?"* The inspector ventured a step closer to the suitcase, then backed off. Nothing shook a bureaucrat worse than learning his security precautions might serve some useful purpose. He waved an exasperated hand. *"¿Qué vamos hacer?"*

The pilot shrugged. He glanced at his watch and at the sky. Clouds were bunching overhead like a hundred black valises, posing threats of much more concern to him than this earthly baggage. He held out the flight manifest again and took a menacing step toward Gavaldón. In a timid reflex the inspector scribbled his signature. Stokes clattered up the ramp three steps at a time and swung the hatch shut with a clunk. The engines sputtered to life, belching a cloud of exhaust that obscured Chris's view of the inspector. As the DC-3 began to taxi to the far end of the runway, she caught sight of him again, standing beside the abandoned luggage.

Suddenly the suitcase flew skyward in a burst of flame. The explosion scattered black confetti, gouging a crater in the asphalt. Chris felt a sharp jolt as the plane rocked from the shock wave of the blast. And what of Gavaldón? One moment he had been standing there; the next he was gone in a puff of smoke. Chris was sickened to see shreds of his suit. They spoiled the illusion of a sorcerer's exit. As the plane took a leap skyward, she glimpsed the mongrel below, sniffing Gavaldón's remains. The dog turned up its nose and trotted away, in search of more appetizing prospects.

4

HANS BERGER AWOKE, BATHED IN SWEAT. THE dream. Again. A nightmare spawned by a childhood trauma, set in the old house on Pandorastrasse in Munich where he had grown up. It had been a gloomy presence, that gabled house, with musty drapes and unexplored crannies, as labyrinthine as those war years. But in spite of the house and its veiled threats, compared to the others in the bombed-out rubble of Germany, Berger's family had been lucky. His father, whom the Allies accepted as untainted by membership in the Nazi party, had been awarded a comfortable bureaucratic niche helping the occupation forces, and Hans always had enough to eat and warm clothes to wear. But he was not a happy child. Something troubled him, as if he were living with questions as enigmatic as the locked door in their basement. A door that was kept locked for reasons his parents refused to discuss.

On his tenth birthday, a blustery fall afternoon in 1946, Hans decided he was old enough to find out for himself and tiptoed down the creaky stairs to the cellar. The task of prying back the latch with his pocketknife took him half an hour. He could still remember the click of the lock snapping open, like the hammer of a gun cocking back. The rusty hinges resisted as he forced the door wide enough to slip inside, and even as he entered, he was stricken with a terror that he might never be able to get out. His eyes strained to probe the dark. The stench of sweat and singed hair was overwhelming. But his curiosity compelled him to venture deeper inside. There, lurking in the farthest corner, he discovered it. With its arm and leg straps, at first it looked like a dentist's chair, until he noticed the claw marks on the wooden arms. As he sat down on it, he felt like a black prince, heir apparent to his father's secret throne. But his reign was short-lived. A shadow darkened the doorway, a specter worse than the ghosts of his wildest imagining: it was his father, cursing in rage. He dragged Hans upstairs and beat him with his belt, forcing him to swear never to tell a soul what he had seen.

His father beat him often after that, but instead of fearing for his own safety, Hans feared for his mother. No matter how his father tormented him, in his mind what his father did to her was much worse. Hans would lie awake at night, shivering in the moonlight, and listen through the wall as his father took her by force. He would imagine that her shrieks and groans came from the hidden room below, that his father was torturing his mother in the basement. He hated his father for making her scream like that.

It was not until the early fifties that the truth came out, a truth that he had refused to accept. Herr Berger had, in fact, been one of the Gestapo's most zealous officers, the basement of their house on Pandorastrasse his inner sanctum. Hans felt torn by guilt and shame: guilt, however unfounded, that his discovery of the chair might have led to his father's arrest; shame that as his son he had somehow shared in the crimes.

Was it any wonder, Hans mused, that he had chosen the profession of hotelier, to rule a realm of clean, well-lighted rooms? A safe enough domain, until he went to sleep and found the forbidden basement behind his eyelids. In his recurring dream, he was sitting on the cobwebbed throne, his arms and legs bound so tightly his circulation was severed, his limbs as numb as death. His fingers were scraping claw marks in the wood, his blood staining the leather straps. There were no monsters in his nightmare, only the torture chair holding him captive. Perhaps what terrified him most was that he might be the monster himself.

Hans lay awake until dawn, listening to the raucous chorus of howler monkeys in the jungle, the sweat on his palms as sticky as blood. He was a burly man, powerfully built, but it took all his strength to climb out of bed. For today, he knew, was the climax of his professional life. He had served his apprenticeship at some of the finest hotels in Europe: the Excelsior in Florence, the Alfonso XIII in Seville. He had learned the subtleties: how to obtain, discreetly, a woman for a man who needed one (and vice versa): how to say no with kindness on a rainy night when there were no rooms left. Hans had methodically worked his way up from assistant desk clerk until twenty-five years later, at the age of forty-four, he had won the right to command the El Dorado.

He shaved with a straight razor, wielding it with surgical precision, the steel blade flashing past his jugular. But then, today most of all, he felt prepared for such close brushes with disaster: the El Dorado's first guests were expected this afternoon. In the mirror, under his thinning blond hair, his usually cheerful face was haggard, his blue eyes restless, searching for flaws to be corrected, as if there were a defect within himself he could never quite set right. He dressed quickly for his morning inspection. He knew he wasn't going to like what he saw.

By the time Hans had hurried downstairs to the front desk in his gray silk summer suit and Yves Saint Laurent tie, the digital clock on the wall read 8:22. Through the open door to the back office he could see the shortwave radio, the hotel's only link to the outside world.

Hans straightened the portrait of Panaguas's dictator, Francisco Zamora, that stared arrogantly down at him from its baroque frame. A cylindrical bamboo birdcage dominated the lobby, a spectacular centerpiece shooting thirty feet from the floor to a skylight, alive with parrots, macaws, toucans, and jacamars. The birds twittered, shimmering in sunlight that transformed their bright plumage into a feathered rainbow. He noticed that one of the toucans lay lifeless on the floor of the cage. Another victim of the air conditioning, he mused. But there was nothing he could do. His American guests would demand the thermostat be kept at a meat-locker 65 degrees Fahrenheit. The dead toucan would have to be fished out of the cage, and carefully, to keep the others from escaping. A hotelful of squawking parrots was all he needed.

Hans picked a cigarette butt off the floor and walked past two elevators that had been shipped all the way from Chicago. He climbed the sweeping staircase with its chrome banister and headed along a corridor of guest suites with carved mahogany doors. One of the doors was ajar, and inside, Hans glimpsed a dumpy maid in a black uniform, refilling an Évian mineral water bottle with murky water from the tap in the bathroom. *"Buenos días,"* he greeted her, in heavily accented Spanish. The maid averted her eyes. Hans turned off the faucet and handed her an unopened bottle of Évian from her cart. How could he make this woman understand that the water from the river could make the guests deathly ill? "The staff." Hans wondered if he should dignify them with that name. He had seen a chef with an open sore slicing the filet mignon in the kitchen and had caught another spitting on the floor. What good did it do to warn them of health hazards when they didn't know what a germ was? The El Dorado's employees had been recruited from a remote fishing village fifty miles away. He had to teach them everything: how to make a bed, set a table, uncork a bottle of champagne—not just once, but over and over, in a pantomime they watched stone-faced and, often, uncomprehendingly. Hans handled his duties with outward good humor, but beneath his calculated charm lay resentment that he wasn't dealing with professionals. He felt foolish ordering these sullen people around. If they were his troops, how could he take himself seriously?

But it wasn't just the staff. There was something precarious about the whole place. Even before a single guest had arrived, the hotel seemed to invite disaster, like a luxury liner plying iceberg-studded seas. He scanned the Carrara marble floor that had been flown in, stone by stone, from Italy, the mahogany that paneled the hallways, the cut crystal chandeliers, and wondered whether he had linked his fate to the world's most elegant white elephant. That every pillowcase, every demitasse spoon, every roll of toilet paper had to arrive here by air was, he acknowledged, a monumental feat, achieved only because huge transport planes, American C-130s from the Panaguan Air Force, had been liberally lent to the cause. Funds and building materials had been diverted from school and hospital projects to construct "the ultimate resort" here, of all places, in a scenic but impractical setting.

The bulldozers had carved the site out of the jungle. Taken it by force. Throughout the construction, the government had waved the banner of national pride, but he knew the driving motive was more pecuniary than patriotic. Members of the President's Cabinet, the hotel's stockholders, stood to make a tidy profit.

Now, five years after Generalissimo Francisco Zamora had dug the first spadeful of earth, the El Dorado, still incomplete, was about to welcome guests. Though only a few floors were finished, Zamora had ordered the grand opening in a last-ditch effort to keep tourism in Panaguas alive. The President would not be able to attend, however, for the revolutionaries had vowed to make this, his tenth year in power, his last. Hans expected the government officials who would come in his place to be arrogant and demanding. It did not make him breathe any easier.

He watched as a maid sprayed a dense mist of insecticide into a guest room, a daily precaution against malarial mosquitoes. Though constant vigilance could delay their advance, nothing could halt it. No poison could deter the venomous spiders or the fire ants that seemed to infiltrate, by magic, through cracks in the walls.

His passkey unlocked the doors to the dining room, its stained-glass ceiling aglow in hues of harvest orange and gold. Each table was graced by silver candelabra and leather armchairs that faced out through picture windows onto the palm-fringed beach. He buffed a smudge off a brass serving cart with his handkerchief. Everything still had a patina to it, a gloss which in this climate and with his staff's dubious care would, he feared, soon tarnish. He strode into the bar, its counters inlaid with mother-of-pearl, an elaborate mosaic depicting sun, moon, and stars adorning one wall. The other side of the bar opened outdoors onto the Olympic-sized pool and offered swim-up service with underwater stools.

As Hans stepped out onto the humid terrace, something rippled the chlorinated water. He walked around by the pool's edge for a closer look. Two naked Indian boys shot to the surface and scrambled out, wet and shivering. They crouched on the tile and looked up at him with fearful eyes, but instead of meting out punishment, Hans offered each of them a mint from his pocket. Without a word, they snatched the candy and ran away. For Hans it was one of many awkward encounters with the children of the staff. As if to underline his isolation, a breeze bore the scent of charcoal fires from the hovels behind the hotel where the employees cooked breakfast. Today he would lunch on coq au vin in the dining room, alone.

After traversing the length of the pool, he rounded the far side of the building and approached the diesel generator. He felt like whispering a prayer to this whirring behemoth, for everything depended on it: the lights, the stoves, the refrigeration, and the air conditioning. It was German-made, a Daimler. The contractors hadn't stinted on that, thank God. Reassured by the turbine's drone, Hans followed a flagstone path down to the beach, where peppermint-striped parasols were stacked like cordwood. His mind was overwhelmed with a welter of detail, as glutted as the grid nearby which fried hundreds, thousands of insects. And still more were drawn to the electric coils, clogging it, rendering it useless. He made a mental note that the paste would have to be scraped away. There was no end to his duties, he brooded, no end to what might go wrong.

The path dead-ended in the sand, and he balanced on the final flagstone to avoid sullying his shoes. The sand, too, had been shipped in by the ton, but he noticed that the surf was already starting to wash it away, replacing it with coarse gravel, wave by wave. For a moment the breakers hypnotized him with their persistence as they slammed into the beach, raked back, then assaulted the land with another crash. He eyed the sea distrustfully. It was a dubious ally, quick to anger. But it was the jungle that was his enemy. The jungle, looming behind him, a green tide advancing ever closer, driven by a cosmic hunger. Haunting him like his nightmares. He was convinced that he, his future guests, the very hotel would all be under siege, that the moment his guard was down the vines, the roots and creepers would make their final assault. He had sent the staff out every day to stave off the jungle's advance, hacking away at the vines with their machetes. Even so, their defense had been futile, for fed by torrential rains, the vegetation counterattacked defiantly, tendrils snaking over lawn chairs, grass stabbing between cracks of tile. Hans stopped, facing a freshly painted sign at the forest's edge, his attempt to protect the foolhardy from their own curiosity.

PELIGRO DE MUERTE
DANGER OF DEATH
DO NOT GO BEYOND THIS POINT!

Already, vines had woven a shroud over the word "Muerte," and he tore them away. He knew that tomorrow they would be back.

If a cigarette butt on the carpet affronted Hans's sense of order, then how deeply did this jungle bedevil him? Now that the first guests were about to arrive, he felt doomed. He smiled at the irony of his plight; no doubt the guests would believe they were at his mercy in this godforsaken place. But he was at the mercy of the elements. His career. His life. At the mercy of the snarling sea, the heat, the monsoon winds. Above all, at the mercy of the jungle's hungry green. The anticipation of disaster made him ill. He wanted to be everywhere at once: at the bar, the patio, the pool; in the kitchen, the lobby, the dining room. His strict attention to detail ran him ragged by day, and then, when he collapsed into bed, the nightmare would slither up on him: an impending chaos foresight could not delay, nor reason comprehend. Above the forest's web of branches the sky writhed, black clouds tangled in a rising wind. Somewhere a door was creaking open. He dreaded where that door might lead.

5

THE DC-3 CLIMBED SKYWARD, RISING ABOVE THE outskirts of Tierra del Mar, and Chris watched the shantytown sink without a ripple into a rain forest that stretched horizon to horizon. After the arid brown of India, she found this emerald infinity appealing. The Gir had been a frail sanctuary, but this jungle was all-powerful, a godhead without a single road to scar its face.

Now that she was back in the air once more, Chris wondered if this limbo was the only place she belonged. Why did she find such comfort in it? She conceded that being forever in transit saved her from ever having to come down to earth, from ever having to face the puzzle of her future. In her work she had learned to run many risks, except, perhaps, the most disturbing one: a serious relationship. Men had proposed to her, even some she had loved, but she had avoided marriage, fearing that like one of those lions in the Gir, she would be left with only the illusion of freedom. Yet the gypsy life that had suited her perfectly in her early twenties was, almost ten years later, starting to pall. How much longer could she keep up the pace? Growing old: Chris was, perhaps, most afraid of that. Once she had heard that if you flew in a jet at the same speed as the earth's rotation, the sun would never rise or set, that it would always hover at the same point in the sky. Perhaps if she could move fast enough from place to place, she could halt time completely. No, she admitted, she could never stop herself from growing old. But perhaps she could stop herself from growing up.

She felt a hand on her arm. The fiftyish lady with the overstated makeup had sat down beside her. "Margot Hampton. Pleased to meet you."

"Chris Latham." They shook hands.

Margot's palm was clammy. "Isn't it strange?" Her voice trembled. "I consider myself a devotee of the occult. You see, I've written several books on the subject: *Visitors from Outer Space, Voices from Beyond the Grave, Secrets of Atlantis.*" Chris nodded politely, as if she'd read them all. "I have the ability to make considerable leaps of faith," Margot continued. "But when it comes to believing that an airplane, all these tons of steel, can actually *fly*. . . ." Again the nervous giggle. "Well, I find that a little bit too much to swallow."

Chris noticed that as she spoke, Margot was rummaging in her purse. "This trip!" She pulled out the monkey's paw and squeezed its shriveled fingers. "From the very start it has filled me with . . . misgivings. Portents," she repeated ominously. "There are *portents!*"

Chris had enough doubts of her own about this assignment. The last thing she needed were rantings of doom from an excitable stranger. She unsnapped her seat belt. "Excuse me." Snatching her Nikon, Chris edged past Margot into the aisle. "I've got to take some pictures. It's my job."

"I understand." Margot's Revlon lips froze in an overripe smile. *Click.* Behind Margot, Curzon turned away, denying her his image. In search of a better vantage point, Chris stationed herself near the bulkhead, as her eye roamed, the camera panning from one passenger to the next.

Click. Dawn basked in Chris's photographic attentions. But she pretended to ignore the lens, continuing her conversation with Irv. "God, it was sickening. I mean, yuk! This beggar at the airport had no hands. Would you believe? That was how he made his *living!*" Chris guessed that Dawn earned her living from her twin physical abnormalities just as effectively as the beggar capitalized on his stumps. *Click-click.*

She caught the urgency on Scott Hershey's face as he elbowed past her to the toilet. When he emerged a moment later, his dilated pupils indicated he had accomplished his objective, and grinning, he slumped into a seat across the aisle from Dawn and Irv. "Granola?" Scott offered them a bag. Irv ignored him, shaking dice into a felt-lined box on his lap.

Dawn eyed the Granola disdainfully. "A hundred fifty calories."

"So?"

"I'm very careful about what I stick into my body," she said.

"I'll bet."

Dawn missed Scott's double entendre and took out a pocket calculator with an aloofness that told him his time was up. "I had a ham sandwich at the airport." She frowned and riffled through a book for the calorie count. "Would that be under *H* or *S*?"

Taking one final stab at conversation, he offered his hand. "Scott Hershey." The name had a magical effect, halting her finger on the calculator in mid-ham-sandwich.

"You're kidding. Hey, wasn't there a rock star named . . . ?"

"There still is." He stretched his lanky arms as if to confirm beyond doubt that he did, in fact, exist, but Dawn looked as though it would take more than that to convince her. Chris remembered Scott's name from the sixties, when she had been assigned to *View*'s L. A. bureau. In an era of protest, Scott's music had been surprisingly bland, the secret, perhaps, of his success.

"I thought he died," Dawn said. "OD'd or something. I mean, didn't he?"

"No such luck," Scott said. In his wistful smile, Chris detected that death may have once seemed an attractive alternative to his slippage on the charts.

Dawn cocked her head coquettishly, her golden hair teasing his shoulder. "Like, I used to have this apartment on the Strip. I mean, every day I'd see you out my window on this billboard." Her tone warmed. "You were big. You were *real* big." She took a handful of Scott's granola as a concession to fleeting fame.

He accepted her compliment, despite the past tense. "Well, you know, after the platinum records and all, I just dropped out for a few years to get my head together." A lie, Chris knew, but a forgivable one. She could read his recent flops in the wrinkles under his eyes.

Dawn had taken a liking to Scott, Chris decided. Was it his tarnished glory or that he discreetly avoided staring at her chest? My God—she stopped herself—what is this? Am I so horny that eavesdropping turns me on? Even watching the lions screwing in the Gir was better than this.

"Coming down to soak up the rays?" Scott asked Dawn.

"Well, business and pleasure, I guess you'd say." She wriggled to keep his question from pinning her down. "Apples and oranges. A little bit of both." Whatever her secret "business," it was delicate enough that when Dawn opened her mouth, Irv looked up from his dice with a grimace, as if they had taken a bad roll.

"Irv Florsheim." He forced a smile through capped teeth and reached across Dawn to clasp Scott's hand in both of his.

Scott flinched from the jagged edge of Irv's Florentine gold ring. "Nice to meet you."

"You used to be dyna-fucking-mite. So what happened?" The barb was aimed with malice, and Scott squirmed.

"Like I was telling Dawn..." he began, but to his relief, before he had to mount a defense, the seat belt sign flashed on. "Better get back to my seat."

The plane slammed into heavy turbulence, and after framing Dawn, Irv, and Scott in one final composition, Chris could no longer keep her balance in the aisle. Peering through a window, she knew they would soon taste much worse, for they were flying straight toward a black squall line. The next time the plane shuddered in an air pocket, she plopped down beside Alan.

"I got a look at your passport at the airport," he said. "You've been around."

"Work," she said simply.

"I don't know why anyone in their right mind would want to go to Bangladesh...."

"Who says I'm in my right mind?" She smiled. "I'm a correspondent for *View*."

"I'm a journalist, too," Alan said.

"Really?"

"I write a column for *Travel World* magazine."

Chris was relieved. Alan's presence wouldn't spoil her exclusive. *Travel World*'s idea of journalism was sending a writer ten thousand miles to criticize the El Dorado's béarnaise sauce.

"I'm glad to see that even a publication like *View* isn't above sending its reporters on a junket now and then," he said.

"It's nothing like that. I pay my way."

"Sure. We all do."

"What's that supposed to mean?"

"Nothing. Just that they'll be getting their money's worth, one way or the other."

"Who?"

"The hotel. The Panaguan government. Nobody's doing anybody any favors." She didn't answer. *"La mordida,"* he continued. "The quid pro quo. Am I right?"

She looked at him hard. "We've all got problems. Being on the take isn't one of mine." She resented his bitterness and his self-pity, common afflictions of middle-aged men, especially middle-aged travel writers who feared they had squandered their lives. All too often, they had.

Alan withdrew into his thoughts, pretending to stare out the window. He seemed angry, but not, Chris guessed, at her.

Angry at himself, perhaps, for choosing the role of whore. "Excuse me." He unsnapped his seat belt and squeezed past. "The *mordida*. Time to collect."

The plane was fighting a stiff headwind, and to keep his balance, Alan clutched the seat backs for support, weaving up the aisle as if drunk. When he reached the entrance to the cockpit, he turned the handle, but the door stuck. Chris could see the case of liquor was blocking it from inside. Harley Stokes was sipping from a fifth of scotch, as if to fortify himself against the impending clash with the gun-metal sky. A pilot drinking on the job was bad enough, Chris thought, but in *this* weather? Harley had removed his sunglasses, and his eyes smoldered in the gloom. "What do you want?"

Alan glanced at the case of Johnnie Walker Red. "I thought that was for us."

Harley looked as though he would slam the door in his face. "Forget it," he said, but Alan didn't budge. The plane took a malicious jolt, upending the case of whiskey. Harley handed Alan a bottle as grudgingly as if it contained his own blood. "Get back to your seat, and strap yourself in." He jabbed a thumb at the horizon, which had darkened another notch. "Haul ass. We're about to go through a Beaufort niner."

Clutching the bottle, Alan staggered down the aisle and sat in the empty row in front of Chris. He leaned over the seat to face her. "What the hell's a Beaufort niner?"

"Wind," Chris said. Growing up in Chicago and sailing on Lake Michigan, she had learned to measure its moods. "Nine on the Beaufort scale means a strong gale."

"Motherfuckingshitasssturds!" Curzon shouted from across the aisle. His invective seemed aimed at no one or perhaps at the universe, a volcanic eruption as they bucked into the storm. "Goddamn guerrillas down on the ground, and Harley Stokes up in this flying shithouse! Harley Stokes, licensed SOB and number one cheapskate!" It was Chris's punishment to be the only one sitting close enough to receive the brunt of his tirade. "Look for a barf bag, why don't you? The bastard even steals them!" Checking the seat pouch in front of her, she found that the old man was right. "Know *why* Harley Stokes was late?" Curzon raved on. "A few extra bucks for a milk run to San Ignazio. Flying a planeload of whores to the wildcatters. Damnation!" A blast of thunder punctuated his words, and rain shot through a poorly caulked window, its cold spray catching Chris by surprise. "I hope he rots . . . I hope he dies! May the devil eat him on the half shell and blow him out his ass!" Lightning split the sky in two, echoing his wrath. His fury spent, Curzon closed his eyes and dozed off, spittle flecking his mouth. He didn't even flinch when the next lightning burst exploded in a direct hit.

For an agonizing moment the electricity flickered, before the lights glowed bright again. Fighting panic, Chris tried to focus on the others. Margot popped a peppermint lozenge into her mouth and closed her eyes, the monkey's paw slippery in her palm. Scott Hershey had been humming softly to the engine's drone, but when the right prop snagged like a stuck record and began to miss, he gulped a downer. It was too rough, by now, for Dawn to punch the numbers on her calculator. Instead, she gripped Irv's left hand, while his right kept tossing the dice in a nervous reflex, as if his life were riding on the next throw. And the next. And the next. The plane was hurling the dice now, for as it lurched, the cubes bounced out of the felt-lined box and rolled off under the seats. The outcome—win or lose—was hidden from him, but Irv didn't dare bend down for a peek. Instead, he squeezed Dawn's hand, like a child on a roller coaster clinging to his mother.

When Chris glanced at Alan in the seat in front of her, his calm surprised her. She pointed to the bottle of whiskey, in which he had already made a sizable dent. "Must be damn good stuff."

"It's not the booze," he said. "Maybe I've just learned that sudden catastrophes aren't so bad, compared to the other kind. The kind that creep up by inches."

The plane plummeted 100 feet in a downdraft, dealing the passengers a blow to the stomach. Chris tried to concentrate on their conversation. How easy it was, she thought, to talk about the most intimate matters when things were touch and go.

"I watched my wife die," he said simply, and the last word sounded obscene in the stuffy cabin, as if he were somehow invoking their own destruction. "I watched her die of cancer. . . ."

His voice trailed off. She wondered if the reason Alan didn't fear death was that part of him had already died. Was he too numb to feel pain ever again? Though his outward calm might look like courage, she suspected it came closer to paralysis.

The plane nosed downward in a steep dive, and Chris instinctively shielded her cameras. They were her babies, burnished by loving use over the years, until the blacking on the lens barrels had been worn off by her touch. But she found no salvation in her cameras now; the critical elements of the moment were invisible: the vengeful wind; the stomach-churning roll of the fuselage. The vomit smell of fear.

Then, magically, the clouds dissolved. The vista that opened before her was hardly reassuring, for neither the hard green of the jungle nor the armor-blue steel of the sea in the distance offered the least assurance of happy landings. They were sinking fast now, sinking too fast to reach the water, plunging toward a forest that, like the ocean, had its own unfathomable depths. Raindrops flooded the windows, and the plane lurched in a haphazard descent through the downpour, as if it were being piloted by a malevolent child. Chris could see nothing resembling an airfield, only a quicksand of green, opening its jaws to swallow them up in a gulp. As the earth rushed up to meet them, the plane teetered, first left, then right, until the wings were no higher than the mangroves of the forest. Chris closed her eyes and braced her body for a crash landing. But just when she expected the shock of impact, she felt the gentle thud of the landing gear as the wheels splashed and skittered through puddles on a muddy field.

Harley revved the engines up to maximum rpm before he cut the power and the whirling blades died, slashing at the rain. Chris studied the passengers as the blood drained back into their faces. Irv was scanning the floor for his lost dice, as if to reassure himself that he had, after all, won the throw. Scott hummed a grateful tune, wildly off key. Alan absentmindedly slid on his tweed coat, though in the fetid cabin he was soaked with sweat. Dawn teased her hair with a brush, as if primping to meet a swarm of *paparazzi*. Curzon smacked his lips, and patted the pistol that bulged like a tumor under his arm. Margot tucked the monkey's paw away with satisfaction, the value of her amulet proved.

They piled out of their seats to crowd down the aisle toward the hatch. When Harley pushed it open, they were greeted by a tropical deluge that threatened to dowse the flickering smudge pots marking off the landing strip. The vista of rain and muck was hardly inviting. But facing the sodden wall of green, the passengers beamed.

"As a wise man once said"—Alan sighed—"I must get out of these wet clothes and into a dry martini." He turned to Chris.

"In my column, should I call this picturesque spot 'sun-drenched' or 'sun-baked'?"

"Sun-drenched," she replied as the rain thrashed the landing strip. "At least then you'd be telling half the truth."

6

IT WAS ONLY A FEW YARDS FROM THE PLANE TO the waiting minivan, but by the time Chris ducked inside she was soaked to the skin. She brooded that she was doomed to spend her life on the ragged edges of the earth, a female hybrid between Clark Kent and Tarzan. All right, so maybe they wouldn't serve goat at the El Dorado, she conceded. Maybe they would serve goat under glass. Any way you sliced it, that bastard Graner had her number. How stupid of her to think for a moment that he might send her somewhere that wasn't a haven for leeches. Wake me when it's over, she thought, and I'll fly back to New York and give it to the SOB with both barrels.

The others had already piled into the van and she watched as they assessed the damage. Irv mourned his mud-spattered loafers; Margot tried to shake the water out of her Bulova. Curzon patted his toupee, fearing perhaps that it might come unglued in the damp. Chris heard a thump as, with more strength than brains, the driver slammed the trunk shut, mashing their suitcases into the luggage compartment. The stocky Indian with secret eyes had introduced himself as Fernando. A gruff, impassive welcoming committee, she mused, as he slid behind the wheel in his torn T-shirt.

Harley Stokes jumped in beside him, and they were off, fleeing the storm's black limos that rumbled in pursuit overhead. Fernando's fists wrestled the steering wheel as they sloshed through the mud gully that passed for a road. The metronome of the windshield wipers swept the rain away just long enough for a subliminal glimpse of the muck, before the next watery sheet blinded them. It baffled her how Fernando could see, until she realized he couldn't. "Whoa!" Harley Stokes cringed as Fernando careened around a fallen tree trunk before skidding back onto the rutted road. Let Harley sweat, Chris thought. Poetic justice.

The minivan slammed into a pothole, with enough force to bump their heads on the ceiling. Looking up after the jolt, Chris was startled to see the giant that loomed ahead. The El

Dorado glistened white in the rain, a monolith seemingly planted in the wilderness by a benign intelligence. It towered, serene, above the palms, a citadel jutting over the ocean. To Chris the building had the perfection of an act of nature rather than a creation of man. Her eyes met Alan's. They had both been wrong. The brochure wasn't hype. It was understatement.

"Not bad," Irv said.

"Amazing!" Margot exclaimed.

Scott moved his lips but no sound came out, the uppers and downers gumming his speech. Finally: "Far out!"

They had all turned their heads toward the white monolith. All, Chris noticed, but one. Curzon was gazing in the opposite direction, staring intently into the forest. He seemed to draw strength from the wilderness, his shoulders raised ramrod-straight, his eyes gleaming brightly, as if he were admiring a long-lost love.

Chris lost sight of the building for a moment as they swept under tall mahogany trees, and skirted a leafy stockade of bamboo. They rounded a clump of mangroves, and there it stood, a pristine vision of marble, glass, and chrome: the cool thrust of reason surrounded by green chaos. As the van's muddy tires rolled under the archway of the entrance, Chris wished life could be as simple as the movies—that she could cut straight to her suite's clean sheets and a nap to the lullaby of rain.

Through the window, she noticed a man standing in the lobby. He had a military bearing, as if he were waiting for the guests to be piped aboard his flagship. His face came back to her from the brochure: "Your attentive host, Hans Berger."

"That guy looks vaguely familiar," Alan said.

"*All* hotel managers look vaguely familiar," Chris replied. "They're okay, if you don't mind a little fawning."

"After my last assignment," she said, "I'll take all the fawning I can get."

Two bellboys in red jackets with gold braid met the guests with umbrellas as they stepped from the van. Awkwardly they held open the double doors under Berger's critical gaze.

Shivering in her soaked khakis, Chris was the first into the lobby. Floral wreaths had been placed around the room to celebrate the grand opening. They reminded her of a gangster funeral. The other guests seemed to share Chris's misgivings. "Where *is* everybody?" Dawn asked Irv. "This place is a morgue. A goddamn morgue!"

"Probably just taking siestas." He gave her a squeeze. "How about it?"

The porters carried in the luggage, and as the guests hastened to claim it, Chris edged away from them. Pretending to browse in the postcard rack, she eavesdropped on a sotto voce exchange between Berger and Stokes.

"Is this *all?*" Berger seemed shocked.

"What you see is what you get." Harley shrugged.

Berger laughed, a brittle laugh, as if the pathetic turnout were the punch line to an elaborate practical joke. "After all the millions, the weeks of planning . . . *this?*"

Harley didn't reply. Chris realized both men knew full well the reason for the pitiful turnout: Vargas. The guerrillas.

Berger glanced at the freight manifest Harley handed him and at the baggage cart. "I thought you were bringing us a case of scotch."

"Scotch?" Harley scratched his belly innocently. "The monkeys must not have loaded it aboard."

"They must not have." Berger eyed him suspiciously. Chris wondered if he could smell the whiskey on Harley's breath.

"You owe me." Harley extended a meaty hand, and Berger gave him a wad of cash. The pilot counted the bills. "Hey, just a goddamn minute! What is this?"

"Half your fee. When you return on July fourteenth to take them back, I'll pay you the rest."

"Now you listen to me . . ." Harley began. But the hotel manager met the pilot's cold look with one of ice. Harley pocketed the cash, his bluster deflated. Chris liked Berger for that. "July fourteenth," Harley puffed. "I'll be here."

He turned on his heel and left, following Fernando back to the minivan. Chris noticed a wisp of a smile on Berger's face as he watched him go. It broadened into a professional grin as he hurried behind the front desk, where the bedraggled guests had lined up for their rooms. "How delightful our first visitor should also be our most lovely!" Dawn blushed when he kissed her hand and gave her a gold-plated key, the medallion of the room number embossed in silver.

But Dawn's companion was not so easily satisfied. "I want a corner suite," Irv snapped. "I've *got* to have one." Chris guessed his request was rooted in Hollywood mythology, for the status symbol in the Black Tower at Universal was to be able to view the smog out of two sides of the building at once.

"No corner rooms have been completed as yet, sir." Did

Chris detect an extra politesse in Berger's voice, the solicitude of a postwar German toward a Jew? "However, I can assure you that you and your lovely companion will find the Bridal Suite exquisite."

"The *Bridal* Suite?" Dawn nudged her breasts against Irv persuasively. "Can't we take a peek? Please?"

"All right. We'll *look*." Grudgingly, he took the key.

"Very good, sir." Berger tapped the bell on the desk. "Front!" As a bellboy led Irv and Dawn away with their bags, Chris saw Hans slip a plastic tab beside their room number on the switchboard: hotel shorthand for "special handling required."

When Berger turned to face the next in line, he blanched as if a gun were leveled at his chest. It was only Scott Hershey's guitar case, but Chris knew the sight could terrorize even the bravest hotelier. Rock stars, abetted by their hangers-on, could reduce a suite to a shambles overnight. Berger stuck a flag on the switchboard beside Scott's name, too.

"I'm afraid my room simply won't do." Margot's rouged face was a mask of determination.

"But you haven't even seen it."

"That won't be necessary."

"I beg your pardon?"

She handed him back the key to Room 206. "I couldn't possibly stay in a room that has two even numbers in it. Out of the question."

"It is?"

"Numerology. It's a very exact science. Perhaps you're familiar with my book *The Magic Numerals of Destiny*."

Berger pretended that he was. "Would this be more suitable?" Like a jeweler displaying a gold bracelet, he placed another key on the front desk.

Margot studied the number 415 on the medallion. "That will do quite nicely, thank you." As she trundled off, Hans frowned and slipped a tab beside her name as one to watch.

The manager squinted to read the next admittance card, filled out in the scrawl of one addicted to a typewriter. "Mr. Alan Reynolds." Hans delivered a stiff bow. "Mr. Reynolds, I feel like a playwright on opening night meeting his severest critic."

"Haven't we met before?"

"Perhaps," Berger frowned, as if he didn't want the American to remember.

"It must have been nine or ten years ago. The Alfonso Thirteenth in Seville, wasn't it?"

"My *Götterdämmerung*." Berger winced. "Yes. The morning you arrived the hotel's chef quit. That afternoon we lost our electricity!" Though he managed a chuckle, clearly the wound still smarted. "I don't believe I shall ever forget your article: 'Sangria should be the color, but not the temperature, of blood.' I also believe you had a few words to say about the gazpacho." He tried to change the subject. "But where is your lovely wife?"

Alan took the key. "She . . . died."

Berger's regrets were genuine. "I'm very sorry."

"Yes . . . well . . ." It was Alan who was struggling to change the subject now. "Anyway, forget about the Alfonso Thirteenth thing. I know that the only experience worse than staying in a hotel at a time like that is having to run it."

"I was only assistant manager then," Berger corrected him. "Here I'm in charge. I trust you will find things considerably more to your liking." When the porter led Alan away, Chris saw Berger tab his name, too. The hotel manager wasn't the kind of man to undergo a roasting from the same critic twice.

It was her turn to check in, and Chris realized she had neglected to claim her bag on the luggage rack near the door. On her way across the lobby she stopped cold, noticing something totally unexpected—something more unlikely than the cageful of birds dominating the room, more out of place even than the El Dorado on this jungle promontory.

Wearing a searsucker suit, a woman in her early sixties with short gray hair was sitting on the far side of the lobby, sipping tea. She was certainly no ghost. The mud soiling her sneakers was real enough. But how had she come? And why? Chris detected something in the stranger's manner that set her apart from the others—a melancholy, perhaps, a longing. Her down-to-earth bearing seemed so out of place amid the pretense of the other guests that to convince herself the woman was real, Chris felt compelled to take her picture. She slipped out her camera silently, as if to photograph a rarer bird than those caged nearby. The stranger was dunking a lump of sugar in her tea, watching the liquid impregnate the tiny cube, and as she looked up for a moment, her eyes met Chris's uncertainly, before she returned to her tea and her reflections. Chris rested her shoulder against the bars of the bamboo birdcage to steady her camera arm. She pressed down her index finger. *Click.*

All hell broke loose.

Behind Chris, the cage exploded, the birds shrieking and flying at her, their impact against the bamboo bars loud as gunshots, talons clawing, beaks slashing in fury.

"God!" She staggered backward, and Alan rushed over to her.

"You all right?"

There were no bloodstains spattering her blouse. But Chris had the impression she had been wounded nonetheless. It must just be injured pride, she thought. "I'm okay." She smiled. "I guess I've—I've got a way with animals." She laughed nervously, trying to make light of it. "Last week I almost got eaten by a lion."

"Well, if they bother you again," Alan whispered, "I'll wring the little buggers' necks personally."

Chris noticed that the birds had settled back on their perches, ruffling their feathers with what she took for disappointment.

Hans hurried over from behind the desk. "My apologies. It must be the storm. The thunder and lightning—it has a strange effect on them."

"I was just taking a picture of the lady over there. . . ." She pointed in the direction of the settee. "I guess the sound of the shutter—" Chris stopped herself. Berger was looking at her strangely. The lady was gone. "I guess the commotion must have scared her away," she added, but Berger seemed anything but satisfied.

"Madam. . . ." He phrased it as delicately as possible. "There is no 'lady.' There are no other guests registered at this hotel but you and your friends."

"Maybe I just. . . ." Chris trailed off. She might be punchy from exhaustion, but she wasn't insane. She had seen *someone*. When her film was developed, it would offer proof. But—and here her fatigue undercut her levelheadedness—what if the roll turned out to be blank?

"You must be tired," Berger said, as he escorted her to the front desk for a room key.

"Of course she's tired," Alan piped in. "All she needs is a decent night's sleep."

But somehow sleep didn't seem so inviting to Chris now. She didn't know where her dreams might lead or whose faces might be staring down at her as she tossed in bed. She left the front desk and hurried into the elevator.

When the doors slid shut, she realized someone was standing

inside, waiting for her. "Miss Latham!" Margot's face was aglow, grinning with compassion as if in Chris she had discovered a kindred spirit. "I didn't actually *see* the lady myself, you understand," Margot said. "I didn't *see* her. But I felt the presence." Beneath the mascara Margot's eyes widened. "You are not mad, my dear. You are gifted! Blessed with the power to see. It is the others who are wrong. The others who are blind!"

7

AFTER SHE RAN BACK FROM THE LOBBY AND DOU-
ble-bolted the door to her suite, the stranger kicked off her
muddy sneakers and hung up the jacket to her seersucker suit.
She would have been the first to admit the irony that she should
be hiding here—*here* of all places. But in this room, for now
at least, she would be safe. She paused to study her face in a
gilt-edged mirror, like a homely black-and-white snapshot that
had been extravagantly misframed. Her gray hair had been cut
sensibly short, and she wore no makeup, for she was enough
of a realist to know her plain face would probably not have
profited from it anyway. She was a woman who, above all,
despised illusion. No jewelry adorned her age-spotted hands.
It would only have "gotten in the way," as she would have put
it. Everything about her bespoke sensible decisions.

Everything but her desperation. She chewed on a fingernail,
but it was already bitten to the quick, so she ran a palm across
the headboard of her bed, tracing the mottled grain of the
walnut as if following the map of what had been, and what
had to be. Her agile mind was moving too fast for her body,
which was, after all, no longer young, and she groped for one
of the books that filled her suitcase. They had, in the past,
assuaged her loneliness. But not this time. Her hands trembled
on the book's spine, and the footnotes blurred with tears. She
tried to wipe them away with the back of her hand. She dis-
approved of this "display," as she would have called it. It was
definitely *not* sensible. Like so many of those who had set a
grand mission for themselves, she refused to accept her own
frailty. In the past, she had prided herself on her ability to
hold her feelings in check, to get the job done without senti-
ment. But under this crushing emotional weight, she had no
choice but to surrender. Collapsing on the bed, she sobbed in
grief, and weariness, and pain.

Stop this blubbering at once, she commanded, for she was
always hardest of all on herself. And stop she did, sniffling as
she searched for a handkerchief among the books. That afternoon, in her loneliness, when she had heard the guests arrive,

she had been unable to resist the temptation of human contact. She remembered one guest in particular, a young woman in the lobby whose face had hinted that she would listen and understand. Couldn't she allow herself this one sympathetic ear? No, she must speak to none of them. It had been a mistake to allow the guest even to lay eyes on her. Perhaps, a fatal mistake. There must be no more such slipups. She would, by choice, be a prisoner in her suite until the moment of departure. For now she must rest and build her strength. Sleep, she ordered herself, but in its troubled state, her body flouted her commands. Sleep, she coaxed. Sleep. Tomorrow the need for secrecy will be over.

8

HANS STUDIED HIS WATCH; THE COUNTDOWN HAD
begun, the interval between the guests' check-in and their calls
to complain about their rooms. With this group, he predicted
it would take a matter of seconds. Sure enough, a light on the
switchboard was already flashing. Suite 415: "There's a *thing*
in my room!" Margot's voice was shrill. "It has *legs!* Thousands
of them! Come quickly, *please!*" Hans raced upstairs and
rapped on her door. When there was no reply, he unlocked it
with his passkey. Margot was too involved in spraying a can
of insecticide at a centipede on the floor to look up. The creature
seemed to be suffering no adverse effects from the bombardment.

Hans flushed it down the toilet. "Nothing to worry about."
He noticed she had changed from her flowered dress into a
flounced robe. She had been caught in the act of taking off her
artificial lashes, and she wore only one, the other sitting on
the dressing table like the centipede's cousin.

"It's so kind of you to come up and handle this personally,"
she fluttered, and he wondered whether the "menace" had only
been a ploy to see him alone. "This place must be frightfully
remote, for someone as...cultured, as *continental* as yourself." She batted her single eyelash at him, and he was startled
by the cyclopean effect. To fill the dead air, she blurted out,
"You see? Numerology does have its practical side. If I'd stayed
in 206, I bet that little bug would have been a *tarantula!*"

"Quite right." He managed to keep a straight face. "Is everything else to your satisfaction?"

Impulsively she handed him a book: *Visitors from Other
Worlds.* "It's my latest. I hope you find it enlightening."

"Thank you very much. I'll read it with great...interest."
And bowing slightly, Hans left the room. Whoever sent out
the invitations to the El Dorado's grand opening, Berger mused,
they really must have been scraping the bottom of the barrel
to invite Margot. But he had no time to ponder her bizarre
behavior. More calls flooded the switchboard, enough for several times this number of guests. Room 405: Scott requested

a pitcher of orange juice, then sent it back when he realized it wasn't fresh-squeezed. Room 428: Irv called down to ask if they did one-day dry cleaning (they didn't), then rang back demanding more towels. Room 415: Margot called again, anxious to know if her toilet had been "sanitized." Something about a paper band across the seat. Hans hadn't the foggiest idea what she was talking about, but he said yes.

Then, abruptly, the fireflies on the switchboard twinkled out, and the place was as quiet as if there were no guests at all. While they unpacked, Berger knew he would have barely enough time to check that all preparations for tonight were in order. He lit a cigarette, the first he had found time to savor all day, and blew a stream of smoke toward the lobby's picture windows. Outside, the deluge had slackened like the guests' demands, calmed to a secretive sky that concealed just where the storm ended and the approaching night began.

A nudge in the ribs startled him. Where had this old man with his obvious toupee hidden since the others' arrival? There was no time to ask. The cutting edge to the stranger's voice said he hadn't come for chitchat.

"I want a room. And it's got to be facing thataway." He hooked an arthritic finger toward the jungle. The request seemed even more ludicrous than Margot's hocus-pocus. Hans wondered whether he was into numerology, too. Or maybe he was just drunk. "But, Mr.—"

"Curzon."

"Mr. Curzon, all our rooms face the ocean. Each has a lovely view, and...." Hans felt Curzon slip something into his hand: a U. S. $100 bill.

"The customer is always right. Right?" The old man cocked his head and squinted at Hans slyly.

Hans handed back the bill. The man was treating him like a headwaiter. "I'm afraid you don't understand. There simply *are* no guest rooms facing inland. The hotel was designed that way. Only the storage and linen closets and a few of the staff quarters are on the land side."

"You're on."

"But that's impossible, sir. Those rooms are tiny. They're not even air-conditioned, and—"

Curzon jabbed a thumb at a bellboy and started toward the elevator. Hans had no choice but to follow. In an hour, shouting instructions in clipped Spanish, he managed to have a room cleaned out, furnished with a king-size bed, an armchair, a dresser; the small washstand in the corner was provided with guest towels and soap. "Son, you know shit from shinola!" Curzon jabbed him in the ribs with a jocular cackle. Rubbing his hands with satisfaction, he eased into an armchair, and stared down at the servants' shanties near the ragged mouth of the jungle.

Hans was quick to take his leave. The world was full of crazy people, he mused as he closed the door, and most of them were Americans. On his way down the hall, Hans realized Curzon had slipped the $100 bill back into his pocket. This time he decided to keep it. He had it coming. Judging from the demands of Curzon and that woman Margot, to say nothing of the others, he wasn't running a hotel. He was running an asylum. Slipping the bill into his wallet, Hans wondered if perhaps Curzon's request was really so unreasonable after all. The ocean might hold painful memories for the old man, and Hans knew how distressing such memories could be. After all, in his mind the undertow of Pandorastrasse was even fiercer than the surf that gnawed at the El Dorado's beach.

Hans returned to the front desk and scanned the switchboard. He realized there was one guest who had made no requests. Strange, he thought, remembering how demanding Alan Reynolds had been at the Alfonso XIII, years before. But today he hadn't even called for a bucket of ice. Not a word out of Reynolds this time. Nothing at all.

9

ALAN WADED INTO THE DEEP-PILE CARPETING OF his suite, grateful to be alone. He ached to sit down, but the suede armchairs facing the picture window repelled him; he feared that if he touched them he might become just another part of the fatuous furniture himself. Despite his thirst, he ignored the bottle of Piper Heidsieck on the coffee table, and though he hadn't eaten since a stale ham sandwich in Tierra del Mar, the box of Godiva chocolates on the nightstand turned his stomach. They were *mordidas*, bribes in return for the rhinestone adjectives he despised—"fabulous" ocean views, "sun-drenched" beaches, and "intimate" candlelight dinners. He leaned over to sniff the long-stemmed roses in the crystal vase by the bed, hoping their scent might calm him. But the petals were as odorless as if made of wax. For Alan the embalmed roses, like the room's other refinements, bespoke the artifice of a burial chamber: ritual preparations to divert the dead.

He shed his coat, and his sweat-stained shirt as well. A look at his reflection in the window told him he had subjected his once-athletic body to the same neglect he had leveled at the other facets of his life. He shivered from the breath of the air conditioning against his chest. I must make a note of this arctic ventilation, he told himself, and this decor which manages to be ostentatious without achieving elegance. But reaching in his pocket, he realized he had lost his note pad. No matter. Each article he wrote propped up the same sagging adjectives, like a hooker changing push-up bras.

He leaned over his battered valise, the canvas damp from the rain, and unstrapped it from the metal trolley. Then, sitting on the king-size bed, he set to work unscrewing the trolley's aluminum tubing. It was no easy task, for the metal had swelled in the humidity and was slippery in his grasp. He removed the towel from the champagne bottle and wrapped it around the stubborn aluminum. One strong twist, and it opened. A few more, and the trolley slid apart. He stepped over to a rosewood desk and tipped the hollow tubing. A dozen steel pieces tumbled out onto the tabletop—fragments of what, exactly, it would have been impossible for an outsider to say.

But Alan knew, and the knowledge made his fingers tremble as he worked to assemble the recoil spring, plunger, and slide. He had never been adept with his hands. Perhaps, he thought, that was why he had first chosen to work with words. They were so much more easily twisted than these steel elements that just wouldn't fit. A greased rod slipped from his fingers and clanked onto the desk, scratching the rosewood. He swore at his clumsiness and snatched it up again. Though he had performed the assembly before, practiced dozens of times, today the pieces seemed to resist, as if the device knew the end for which it was intended and opposed it.

Alan's devotion to his task astonished him, for in the eight years since his wife's death, he had been anything but conscientious. Grief had driven him to commit a cardinal sin, allowing the word "travel" to attach itself to "writer" like a parasite, and as a "travel writer" he had found himself transformed from an aspiring novelist into a hack. It was safer to crank out trivia than risk failure at ambitious goals. But he was risking failure now. More than anything he had written in years, the stubborn construct in his hands demanded all his concentration. And yes, he conceded, it demanded courage as well.

In the end, Alan's determination won out over his clumsiness. The assembly was far enough along so that there could no longer be any doubt what the puzzle was: the tubing of the luggage trolley had worked admirably to conceal the pieces of a compact Budischowsky automatic. He had taken a perverse satisfaction in smuggling it right under the noses of airport security. At JFK, he had even let the armed guard hold the trolley for him as he had stepped through the metal detector. But that trip seemed like years ago. He stared at the gun with amazement, as if he hadn't been the one to smuggle it here at all, as if it had assembled itself. That he should have gone to such lengths for *this*. . . . He had never killed anything before.

The assembly was finished too quickly. From a handful of disjointed elements the gun had become an organism with a life of its own. He hesitated before inserting the final screw. It would be easier to leave the weapon incomplete, to cut it short as everything else in his life had been: his college education, by war; his marriage, by death; his novel, by the paralysis of grief. He stared out the window at the sky, as flat as a headstone. Somehow the sight convinced him he had no alternative now. This would resolve all the other incompleteness, finish everything with one masterstroke. He tightened the final screw with a twist of his Swiss army knife, turning the blade as far as it would go, until the tip bit into the metal.

Then he took a deep breath and looked up to survey the room once more. There was a calculated elegance to the decor of polished wood, glove leather, and chrome that annoyed him, perhaps because it was every bit as calculated as his own efforts to smuggle the weapon here, to prepare for this moment. He noticed the push buttons on the console beside the bed—buttons for the electric curtains, the digital alarm clock, the tensor reading lamp; buttons to summon the valet and maid. A push-button life, he thought. He looked at the pistol cradled in his hand. Push-button death.

The task was complete, but instead of opening the champagne in celebration, he retrieved the bottle of mineral water from the bathroom and succumbed to one of the Danish armchairs. Time for the test. Picking up the pistol, he slipped his finger onto the trigger and squeezed. The firing pin slammed into the empty chamber. *Clack.* Alan Reynolds had, for once, completed something.

His eyes seized on one last switch on the bedstand console, and impulsively he pushed it. The roar of waves flooded the room, transmitted by microphones he saw implanted along the beach. Piping the ocean in like Muzak was a frill not even Alan had seen before, and he smiled in spite of himself. "*Shhhhh....*" He hoped the surf would jam the conflicting signals in his mind with a final calm. "*Sssssshhhh:...*" He turned it up loud, painfully loud, but not even the ocean could drown out his uncertainty. With a sigh of defeat, he flicked it off.

It was so quiet now that he could hear his own breathing as he slid the cap off the mineral water bottle. The act he was about to perform would require a mind as lucid as the liquid tumbling into his glass. He took a sip and tried to console himself that a clear head and a loaded pistol were all he would need.

Staring out the window, he was startled to see the clouds had writhed alive, slithering silver like the belly of a snake. As if to arm himself against the sky, Alan reached for the nuggets of brass and lead that lay on the bedspread, glinting with the luster of jewels.

10

CHRIS OPENED HER EYES, BLINKING IN THE NO-
man's-land between sleep and wakefulness. Lying on her back
in bed, she stretched her arms toward the ceiling, fists clutching
at thin air as her mind groped to recall where she was. One
look at the crystal chandelier, and it all started to come back.
No ceiling fans, thank God, no mosquito netting, and the air
conditioning worked. She climbed out of bed, clad in bra and
panties, and flexed her muscles in her drowsy ritual of ballet
pliés, humming a Chopin accompaniment. With the perspective
of an hour's nap, she could consider the most outrageous of
possibilities: that this might turn into a vacation after all. She
squeezed the shag carpet between her toes like spring grass and
padded into the bathroom, across the hand-painted tile to the
bathtub. The water gushed on, and she stared at the cloud of
steam in wonderment. But instead of diving into her first decent
shower in months, she summoned up the nerve to face the
mirror and assess the damage. Her skin was chapped, her eyes
bloodshot, and the circles under them would defy even the
heaviest of Revlon cover-ups. She tugged at her hair like a
fright wig. Wash the mop first, she ordered herself, and rejoin
the human race. She would take an hour-long shower. No,
make that a week-long bubble bath.

She rummaged in her toilet kit and stopped humming. In
the time warp of her jet voyage, she had found no time to get
shampoo, not to mention a tube of toothpaste. But though she
groaned at the thought of dragging her carcass downstairs to
buy them, the errand had its appeal. It had been a long time
since she had been able to shop for small indulgences. She
slipped on her khakis for what she swore would be the last
time. She vowed that the moment she set foot in the room
again, she would put them to the torch.

As Chris descended the stairs and hurried through the empty
lobby, she realized, too late, that she had no Panaguan cur-
rency. She would have to charge it to her room. Or—a smile
played across her lips—just let them try and give her a hard
time. Right now, for a tube of Crest she'd shoplift.

Beyond the lobby, the bright fluorescents of the souvenir shop announced it was open, and the display cases were stocked with a tidiness that told her she was the first customer. From the look of it, the "local crafts" had been manufactured at the same factory that cranked out kitsch for resorts from Mount Rushmore to Mount Fuji: straw hats, key rings, alabaster ashtrays, and the inevitable menagerie of polyester dogs with soulful eyes.

She spun the postcard rack and selected a glossy portrait of Panaguas's strong man, Generalissimo Francisco Zamora, looking suitably constipated. Graner had it coming. Her hand twirled the postcard rack again, a blur of obligatory scenes: the El Dorado by the surf, a couple hand in hand on a deserted beach, a donkey in a sombrero. But whom could she send them to? Her maiden aunt in Albany? Her mother in Chicago? She winced at the thought that until a fresh prospect materialized, the only male in her life was her boss.

It was a relief to see that his magazine was nowhere in sight. Just a stack of *La Independencia*, the state paper, its front page featuring a three-column spread on the El Dorado. Though her Spanish was rusty, Chris could translate the banner headline: HUNDREDS OF CELEBRITIES ARRIVE FOR GRAND OPENING. She smiled. Panaguan journalism had sunk to new depths. Beside the stack of papers, a paperback rack leaned heavily toward the horror genre, including *The Accursed*, *The Exorcist*, and *Carrie*—books from years ago. Life was horrific enough, she thought. Why spoil the few serene moments with mayhem?

"*Gott in Himmel*. . . . And where is María?" Berger's voice startled her as he stepped behind the counter, looking for the attendant. From his sigh, Chris concluded this was not the first time his staff had let him down. "These people!" He shook his head in exasperation. "They learn quickly, yes? Just one day on the job, and already they know the art of—how do you say it? The kaffeeklatsch!"

Chris smiled. "I just need a few basics . . . toothpaste . . . shampoo."

"Certainly. . . ." He scanned the shelves. "I see a dozen different brands of suntan cream, but toiletries. . . ." He shook his head. "*Ach!*" He snapped his fingers, remembering. "Stokes was supposed to deliver a shipment on your flight. María must not have put them on the shelves yet." He disappeared into a storeroom and started rummaging through cardboard boxes.

As Chris waited for Berger, she stared into the cigar humidor, its sliding glass doors displaying Don Diegos, Montecristos, Flores de Havana. At least the travel writer would be happy, she thought.

"I'm still looking!" Berger's voice boomed as the rummaging in the storeroom grew more frantic. She turned back to face the picture window, and her bare arm brushed against a texture that caught her by surprise. It was only a cluster of imitation shrunken heads. Molded from gray vinyl, they dangled from the souvenir rack by nylon hair, and glued to the bottom of each was a label: "Made in Hong Kong." A grotesque novelty item, Chris thought, sold on Times Square, the Ginza, or the Place Pigalle along with plastic noses and whoopie cushions.

The rubbery heads, each about the size of a peach, swayed as she raked her fingers absentmindedly through the nylon strands. Her fingers stopped moving. She felt the pulpy consistency of something hidden beneath the fibers, an alien texture she did not yet dare identify. She hesitated, but an impulse—perhaps a presentiment of danger, perhaps sheer curiosity—compelled her to spread the shroud of nylon hair to see. A split second later she shut her eyes, but it was too late. Though she had glimpsed the sight so quickly that the image barely registered on her retinas, the shock lingered. She gasped in horror.

Beneath the nylon strands were three shrunken heads subtly but profoundly different from the others. They dangled from her trembling hand like a cluster of poisonous fruit, eyes sewn shut to sleep the slumber of the dead. And no neat label saying where they had been shaped or by what power. Beneath the stench of scalded meat, she thought she detected the odor of some strange spice, incense perhaps, as baffling to her as the crucible where the heads had been transformed. Their coarse hair had become enmeshed with the nylon fibers of the imitations on the souvenir rack, but somehow Chris managed to untangle them, to separate the real from the fraudulent. Each of the three trophies was the size of a human fist, and though altered by death and the shrinking itself, they were human still. There was no sign of decay; rather the flesh had been artfully preserved. It seemed they retained the breath of life.

Though the sensation of the clammy flesh nauseated her as she held the three baubles in her hand, she was too fascinated to let go. Her eyes were drawn to one of the faces. Its features had warped like wax melted by the heat of a flame. Its eyes had been reduced to slits, the eyeballs evidently gouged out along with the skull. A scar, which she judged in life must have disfigured the victim's cheek, had been so diminished in size by the shrinking that it was hardly a blemish at all. It rubbed against a second head that seemingly belonged to a younger, fairer-skinned victim, for even the charcoal massaged into its flesh could not fully disguise its original pallor. A china doll's face, she thought, but a doll no child would dare to fondle. The third head's metamorphosis struck Chris as the strangest of all. For the face had shrunk irregularly, and the corners of the sewn lips, perhaps dried with the red-hot blade of a machete, puckered upward into a caricature of a smile. She held it at arm's length, scrutinized it suspiciously as if this one were not yet quite dead. As if it might be leering at her through its closed eyelids, sneering at her with its sewn lips. She was seized by the terror that this third specter might, at any moment, open its jaws with such force that not even the tautly knotted threads could seal them shut when its shriek finally burst forth.

"Apparently our intrepid Mr. Stokes 'mislaid' the toiletries along the way," Berger said as he returned behind the counter empty-handed. "I'm terribly sorry to have taken so long. . . ." She didn't answer. Time seemed of no consequence in the thrall of these artifacts, which, like death, were somehow beyond the pale of time itself. They reminded her of the gruesome Spanish relics enshrined in crypts in Andalusia—the teeth of a saint, the mummified hands of a martyr—and she suspected that yes, to someone, even these most profane of artifacts were sacred, too.

"Miss Latham. . . ." Berger noticed that Chris was mesmerized by the shrunken heads. "These trinkets . . . well, I'm afraid they're what most tourists have come to expect." She didn't respond. "Plastic monstrosities." He laughed. "They certainly *look* real, don't they?"

In reply, Chris handed the three gnarled objects to him by the hair. Now that they were no longer in her grasp she felt free of their spell, objective enough, at least, to watch Berger's reaction: a look of shock as he realized the relics in his hand had once been alive.

"A practical joke. . . . A cruel practical joke," he thought aloud as he studied them. "It has to be Harley's doing." He shook his head with disgust.

Chris realized that Stokes made an easy scapegoat for the

annoyances plaguing the hotel, but she was anything but convinced that he was behind this. She realized it would be pointless to press the issue. Now that Berger had delivered his verdict, he considered the matter closed.

"A practical joke," he repeated, and patted her on the shoulder. "I'm sorry if it upset you.... But I'm forgetting you're a journalist. You must have *answers*. Well, when I find out what led to this bizarre mixup, I will tell you. I promise." He smiled. "Think of it. You come down here to buy toothpaste, and you leave with an exclusive!"

Succumbing to Berger's charm, Chris returned his smile in spite of herself. She took her leave, but as she walked back toward the lobby, she couldn't resist stealing a glance over her shoulder. Berger's rigid posture had slackened, and his shoulders were stooped. He looked as though he had aged years in a span of minutes. Mopping the sweat from his brow with a handkerchief, he eyed the shrunken heads in disbelief. Dangling from his hand by the hair, they struck Chris as marionettes in some bizarre, as yet unfathomable drama.

11

"SUPPOSING HE DOESN'T COUGH UP THE MONEY . . ."
Irv shouted to Dawn in the shower. There was no answer. She
must not have heard him over the rushing water. But the question had ricocheted so often in his mind that firing it at a blank
wall didn't bother him. Sprawled out on the king-size bed, clad
only in a towel, he fingered the platinum razor blade on the
chain around his neck. He could feel the edge against his
jugular, a sliver of ice, and with a shiver stood up and walked
over to the stone fireplace that dominated the Bridal Suite.
The flick of a switch, and gas jets engulfed artificial logs with
blades of flame. As a child growing up in Brooklyn, he remembered, fires had thrilled him. A good blaze was like a
Hollywood extravaganza, all blood and thunder, and because
they had lived close enough to a fire station to hear the alarm
clanging the firemen out of bed, Irv and his father had made
a game of chasing after the red hook and ladders in their decrepit
Ford. But one night, thirty-five years ago, a night he would
never forget, it hadn't been a game. After trailing the engines
to a three-alarm blaze in a shoe factory in Manhattan, they had
followed the fire company on a second call. The pursuit led
Irv and his father on a frantic chase, running red lights, screech-
ing around corners, until they found themselves in a familiar
neighborhood, on a familiar street. The road had been blocked
off, and he had fought his way through the crowd to see. He
remembered that already he had been crying, though he didn't
know whether it was from the smoke or from the growing
awareness of what he was about to discover. His house was
an inferno, his room, the kitchen, the basement, all flailing
gaudy streamers of flame, and under the glare of flashing red
lights, firemen were carrying a stretcher out of the building.
Even before they lifted the blanket from her face, he knew it
was his mother. Irv felt that same shock, that same horror,
today. He was careening around the corner now, hot on the
sirens' trail, and fear gripped him that he had come all this
way, only to discover his own life in flames, his own body on
the stretcher, charred beyond recognition. He stood up in a

sweat distilled of stale memories and fresh forebodings and bent down to turn the gas log off.

Stepping out of the shower, Dawn was bathed in the glow of the heat lamp, and Irv admired her full breasts, her supple thighs. The decor in the bathroom gave him the jitters. The onyx paneling, the gold-plated fixtures, the complimentary Chanel No. 5, reminded him just how far he would fall when it all came crashing down. He collapsed on the bed, as if the thought had decked him. Christ, he mused, sneaking another peek into the bathroom, will you get a load of that? They even fold over the goddamn toilet paper. Origami to wipe your ass.

Who was it who had said, "There's no deodorant like success"? If that was true, he brooded, he stank to high heaven. In the past few years he had managed to pyramid a few penny-ante films into the chance for a big feature. Well, he had gotten his crack at the blockbuster—shot it, edited it—and now he couldn't get the turkey released. All right, so it wasn't *Gone with the Wind*. But he had brought it in under budget. How bad could it be? In Hollywood they don't judge a film on its own merits, he concluded. In the City of Angels it's who you know and who you blow. You could get Birns and Sawyer to allow you deferred payment on equipment rentals if they really believe in you. Once. You could convince the stars to accept points in the gross instead of paying them up front. Just once. But if the deal flopped, if the picture wound up on its ass, and you wanted to ask more favors, make more deals, forget it. They wouldn't even return your calls. His whole life was about to blow away—poof! His house in Beverly Hills was leased, his Mercedes was leased, his thirty-foot Chris Craft at Marina del Ray was leased. And what about Dawn? Would she stick with him through hard times, or was she leased, too?

"Say again?" Dawn pulled a towel off the heated rack and buffed her body pink.

"I said, supposing he doesn't come up with the money?"

"If anyone can make him, sweet pea, you can."

Squirming on the bed, he studied his naked body, perhaps to convince himself that he could live up to Dawn's expectations. His torso was still firm, but his chest hair was flecked with gray, as if from a killing frost. He could see himself in a few years, an old fart on a stool at the Hollywood Orange Julius, reading the producers' obituaries in *Variety*, grateful only to have outlived the bastards. His hands slid down to his sides, and he imagined he was a corpse. After his turkey had been buried six feet under, Irv had looked for independent financing. He had tried zipper magnates in Jersey and proctologists in Beverly Hills. He had tried the Mafia. He had tried anybody alive enough to draw fog on a mirror. And still nothing. This maneuver at the El Dorado was the end of the line. Unless he got the money now. . . .

Dawn emerged from the bathroom, the light from the window softly modeling her in green as if she were a mermaid floating toward him underwater. He watched her hips sway, her breasts bobbing as she leaned over her suitcase. But when she selected a frilly negligee, he cried out in protest. "Hey! The other one!"

"Silly!" She laughed but pulled out the prop he demanded, old-fashioned, utilitarian; even dowdy. It took a moment for her to slip the cups of the nursing bra over her breasts, before she climbed into bed beside him. He could smell the scent of the hotel's complimentary Chanel on her neck, more subtle than her usual musk fragrance. Hardly had she straddled him than he unsnapped the front flaps of the bra cups and pulled her gently toward him by her exposed nipples. To suck. And suck. He did not bite them but teased her nipples with his lips; the droplets of milk tasted sweet and warm, calming him as no drug could. He unhooked the bra, letting her breasts swing free. They were so enormous that as she sat on his belly, he could not see her face, just the huge orbs, part tanned, part white, with the pink nipples jutting straight out. Each breast was big enough for him to clutch in both hands, and he squeezed and sucked in rhythm, as if sipping nectar from an exotic fruit.

Soon after they had met, Dawn had confessed to him the reason for her unusual gift: she had given birth to a son two years before and quickly put him up for adoption. But she still had a need to suckle, perhaps out of guilt for having given up the baby. It was that need that had attracted him. She had never parceled out her favors like the other starlets he knew.

Cradling his head in her hands, Dawn pressed his face so tightly against her breast that he could hardly breathe. "Baby . . . baby . . . baby . . ." she murmured as she suckled and rocked him, and he drank his fill, the anxieties dissolving in his mind like smoke. Irv was erect and hard, hard as her nipples, and she straddled his hips, allowing him to slide deep inside her. She rode him, her firm thighs aquamarine in the light from the window, his hips thrusting, his mouth drawing sweet sustenance from her body. As he squeezed her breasts harder, she let out little sighs as the milk squirted out in ever more lavish jets. Her dripping nipples flushed from pink to red from his sucking, and their soreness excited her, keeping pace with the fever building between her thighs. "Baby . . . baby . . . *baby*!"

The spurts of milk that dribbled onto his chest lubricated their bodies as she shimmied against him, belly warming belly, moist with a creamy fragrance that drowned out the scent of Chanel. She was jiggling so fast now that her breasts bounced out of his grasp, the milk trickling down the corners of his mouth. Hungrily he slid his hands down to her buttocks, taut and hard-muscled where her breasts had been malleable, and squeezed her haunches so hard that in the final seconds she cried out: "Baby . . . baby . . . *BABY*!"

She toppled over onto the sheets and kissed him once, but not on the lips. On the forehead, like a mother bidding her little boy good night.

Dawn tried to close her eyes but found sleep impossible, and leaning on one elbow, she massaged Irv's shoulders, trying to piece her thoughts together. "Irv . . . you know . . . sometimes I think a long time from now . . . like what if I *meet* my kid . . . ?" She hesitated. "I mean, in twenty years or something, let's say I'm at this bar and I pick him up by accident. And I mean, what if, you know, we *made* it? I mean, suppose I did the tit thing with him, like I do with you, and. . . ." She said nothing more, but from her expression the fantasy brought her a strange satisfaction. As if, when she nursed her grown child, then it would all make sense at last. "Irv," she asked, "do you think . . . ?"

But he didn't answer. Curled in a fetal ball, he was sleeping soundly for the first time since he had left his water bed in Beverly Hills.

12

THE RAIN STOPPED, AND THE STORM CLOUDS FLED, leaving the sky a dead-letter white. Margot had secretly hoped the deluge would continue, for now that it was over, she knew that she could delay no longer. She checked to make sure she had everything: the pen and notebook and jackknife. Above all, the monkey's paw. Her choice of clothes would have seemed more appropriate for an autumn outing in Vermont: rubber boots, jeans one size too large, rolled up at the knee, and a zip-up windbreaker. God forbid anyone should see her looking like this, she fretted. What would it do to her image? She fastened her hair into a bun and replaced her contact lenses with horn-rims, an elastic band holding them in place. She wished things could be battened down as securely inside her. She was, she acknowledged, a timid woman, but timid or not, she was forced to act boldly for the first time in her life.

She stepped stealthily from her suite into the corridor. As if to compensate for the drab garb, her makeup was even heavier than usual, a mask of lipstick and mascara that projected fear at twenty yards as she hurried down the hall. She pushed a button for the elevator but was too impatient to wait for it and headed for the staircase. She hoped that the other guests were still in their rooms, that the staff would be too distracted to notice her, galoshes and all, squishing down the steps to the lobby.

"Can I help you, Miss Hampton?" Berger's voice startled her, echoing off the marble walls. "Is everything all right?"

"Absolutely!" She tried to reshuffle her expression into one of nonchalance.

He was staring at her clothing. "Going for a walk?"

"I thought I would," she said, and fumbled for the brochure in her coat pocket. "I even thought I would take a look at *this*." An illustration depicted a heap of weathered slabs: *"Stroll into yesteryear to visit the colorful ruins of an ancient civilization...."*

"I gather it's just a stone's throw away," she said, fearing he wasn't buying her charade of disinterest.

"It's half a kilometer at least. I wouldn't recommend it. The storm may have passed for the moment, but the weather is unpredictable and...."

"Oh, don't worry about me. I can handle it." She feared her show of self-confidence only made her look absurd. She started toward the patio.

"Wait!" His voice was more urgent now, and he was no longer smiling. "Why not wait until tomorrow? I'll organize a group of the others and take you there myself."

"Quite right," she agreed, a little too readily to be convincing. "Absolutely right. I'll take a stroll along the beach instead."

As she walked toward the patio, Berger hesitated, seemingly debating whether he should follow. Finally, he spoke, as much to convince himself as his stubborn guest. "The El Dorado isn't a prison, Miss Hampton. I can't put you under house arrest. But I strongly suggest that as far as the jungle is concerned...."

Margot let out a girlish giggle. "The jungle is *verboten*. I understand."

"I'm sure you do," Berger replied, but from his tone she knew he didn't believe her.

She stepped out onto the flagstone terrace and found that the storm had brought no relief from the oppressive heat. The swimming pool was littered with bamboo leaves, its edge slippery from the rain, and she rounded it cautiously. She had never learned to swim. In the humidity, her windbreaker was stifling, but she kept it tightly buckled. The familiar texture of the waterproof canvas was comforting. She shaded her eyes with her hand, her nail polish pink against penciled eyebrows, and squinted up at the sky. Glinting through dense clouds, the sun seemed like a blade trying in vain to hack its way through a wall of ice. She lowered her eyes from the sky to face a green wall, every bit as threatening.

DO NOT GO BEYOND THIS POINT!

The sign was all that stood between her and the jungle, but it did more to discourage her than Hans's admonitions. There was something terribly official about such warnings. To deny them meant to trespass. She wavered. Her fear was real enough, her palms shiny with sweat. But there was a gun at her head. Her publisher in New York had complained her books were selling poorly, that they were a rehash of others' work. Carve out fresh territory of your own, he had warned, chart a new Bermuda Triangle, or we terminate your contract. Her very survival was at stake, and her choice of the El Dorado as a base camp for her quest had seemed a shrewd one. Where else could she find unexplored ruins a short stroll from a luxury hotel? She could inject firsthand adventure into her book while taking a minimum of risk. It had all seemed so tidy, until she stood on the threshold of the labyrinth. But she had no choice. She had to go alone. That way, if she were forced to "enlarge" on the facts a bit, no one would be the wiser. She cast a backward glance toward the hotel to make sure Berger wasn't watching, then struck out along the trail into the jungle.

At first the grass was ankle-high. Flies buzzed around her, a swarm as drab as the frown lines creasing her face. An annoyance, nothing more. But soon her resolve started to unravel. For, scarcely a dozen yards into the jungle, the workers who had hacked out the path had been forced to sheathe their machetes and yield to the inevitable. The undergrowth rose to her waist.

She waded into the thick of it, and the leaves whispered a language she did not know, shadows rustling as drops of water filtered down from the mangrove trees into lower, spiny palms. Like a mountain climber on a sheer wall, Margot tried to concentrate only on her next step, eyes searching for a foothold. The summit, if it existed at all, was a distant abstraction. Instead of dwelling on the route she would take to get there, she tried to manipulate her mind to block out all thought. But this was no place for someone with Margot's rich imagination. She ran the gauntlet of her fears. Another step, and she was certain the sole of her boot had landed on something alive. Pray God it wasn't a bushmaster. She had read that these deadly South American pit vipers hunted in pairs. Kill one, and its mate would track you down. No more thoughts, she promised herself, but with her next step she wondered if even stranger creatures lurked just beyond her field of view, behind the next tree trunk, or straight ahead, in the path of her hesitant boots.

She felt puny, walking along the floor of this green chasm, a solitary target. She had been lonely much of her life, but all those years of solitude did nothing to prepare her for the isolation today. Was this how it felt to be dead? She was ill-equipped for jeopardy. For years her mother had locked her in her room with books, to "protect" her from men, until finally Margot started locking the door herself. When at last she emerged at thirty, it was with the pathetic pretense of a little girl playing dress-up for the first time.

She spotted a clump of bougainvillea, pink against the green, as out of place as the rouge on her sallow cheeks. Margot ran her hand to her lips and was startled by the red that daubed her fingertips. The thought raced through her head that it was blood, until she realized it was only Revlon Apple of Sin. Her mask was peeling off, leaving her vulnerable. Groping her way among the peperomia vines, she clutched her flat bosom, as if to keep dark forces locked in her breast. She wondered if they had, at last, arrived at their natural home, to run amok.

A black widow spider crept across a shimmering web in her path, and she gave it a wide berth, taking a detour through stalks bristling with thorns. The most dangerous penalty she had ever risked before was an overdue fine at the library. A bookworm, they had called her, and as a pariah she had been drawn to the dark corners of the stacks, to dusty tomes on subjects that repelled others: banshees, vampires, the undead— the myriad powers of the universe—perhaps because they were the only forces she knew that were as overwhelming as a spinster's longings.

For a moment she looked back toward the hotel, but the jungle had swallowed it whole. Her pace faltered. It struck her that she was being transformed by the jungle. Her hands were the sickly shade of algae, and her windbreaker glistened like the leaves in the damp. Too much green, she concluded, and shook her head. Definitely too much green. She wished that she had worn gloves, to save her from the jungle's clammy touch.

The latticework of ferns and philodendrons, their leaves as shiny as the paint on a hearse, existed only to conceal. And what lurked there? The vaulted cathedral was an abattoir. Only the jungle knew the secret hiding places: the nest of a million army ants, the lair of a jaguar, or . . . ? She remembered reading that scientists believed this habitat harbored whole species of creatures that had yet to be discovered, alien predators whose very existence was beyond the ken of the human mind.

Squawks and howls filtered down from the branches 100 feet above, echoing the cacophony of Margot's thoughts. The shrieking in the treetops seemed the repertoire of a mad ventriloquist, a chattering screamer-beast with a thousand tongues. Was it watching her?

Glimpsed through the macramé of tree ferns and bromeliads,

the ruins were at first a disappointment. The sketch in the brochure had made the stone outcropping seem imposing, but from where she stood the jungle dwarfed it. Perhaps, she thought, the ruins had sunk into the moist earth and would keep right on sinking until they were swallowed up. The stone blocks, blotched with moss, had tumbled helter-skelter, like dice in a game where the stakes were annihilation. Margot's research had revealed that the ruins were of unknown origin, and archaeologists had thus far been unable to decipher the meaning of the rock carvings. Had this once been a temple? If so, it had not been built to gentle gods. She tried to imagine the high priests, their bodies adorned with quetzal plumage, their hands clutching obsidian daggers. Their shrine had collapsed under the weight of centuries, engulfed by liana tentacles. But had the gods died? Or had they masterminded the temple's destruction with wind and fire? As if reading the fine print on a will, Margot peered over her steamy glasses at the wall carvings: human skulls, thousands of them, chiseled in geometric patterns. They reduced death to a decorative diversion, the glyphs a perverse indulgence, like tattoos on an old man's chest.

The birdlike woman picked her way among the toppled blocks, groping for handholds, her rubber boots slipping on the rain-slick surfaces. Although the outer buttresses had fallen on the ground to form a rugged obstacle course, she could see that the walls of an inner sanctum still stood, in a U open at one end. She hesitated at the threshold.

Obeying conflicting orders from her mind, Margot kept her feet firmly planted outside the sanctuary walls, while she craned her neck to peer inside. But the contortion didn't accomplish her objective. The interior of the shrine was still hidden from her. She gulped a nervous breath and slid her right boot from the stalks carpeting the temple's outer court into the shadows of the inner sanctum. When her foot touched earth, she noticed that the shrine had somehow been cleared of undergrowth. Not cut back by machete. Scorched by fire. She had been holding her breath and once inside the hallowed place, found herself hyperventilating, as her eyes adjusted to a dazzling brightness. For the sun shot through a cleft in the branches fifty feet above to spotlight a simple stone altar, its surface hollowed into a bowl. And squinting at the altar in its circle of brilliance, Margot *saw*.

Blood overflowed it—dried blood, clotted brown. Rivulets

had trickled down the gutters on both sides of the chopping
block and congealed. How recently had the blood been shed?
From the dying flies mired at the stone's sticky rim, she could
see it had not been long. It had to be goat's blood, she told
herself. Or sheep's blood. Yes, that must be it. She had read
that animal sacrifices were a common practice among the an-
cients. But when she remembered the distinctly *human* skulls
carved on the surrounding stones, her eyes widened. It seemed
as if all the raindrops filtering down from the jacarandas were
rust-red from some awesome sacrifice. She had stumbled across
the aftermath of a ceremony both sacred and profane, a baptism
in unholy water.

Margot advanced cautiously, fearing she might be the next
victim. She was close enough now to see the altar was nicked,
the sacrificial knife descending over decades with such fury
that it had scarred the stone. She extended her hand to the altar,
hesitant to place the whorls of a single fingerprint against the
mottled grain of the granite. When, at last, she touched it, the
stone was warm, as if the blood had heated it to life.

Suddenly she felt a blast of hot air, like the heat from a
furnace, that raised the hackles on her neck. She heard a deep,
rhythmic breathing, the inhale and exhale of someone or something watching her. But when she turned, there was no one.
The granite was as enigmatic as ever, the skulls chiseled in
stone were mute, and the pool of blood reflected only a few
drowned flies.

But she could sense the presence, feel it prickle her skin.
More intensely than at any séance she had ever conducted,
more vividly than in any haunted house, she felt a spirit hovering, descending from the attic of this lofty mansion. And this
time there were no others to share the moment with her, no
loyal coven of believers to hold hands and pray. The giddy
anticipation of something at once wonderful and terrifying
evoked the night at age thirteen when she had seen her own
blood, staining her sheets, and learned that yes, she was a
woman.

And still it grew, the breathing ever louder, the presence
close at hand. She had prayed for such a discovery, something
terrible and awesome. But now that it was taking place, she
wished she had never set foot here, that she had stayed home
in Philadelphia behind bolted doors. Anything but this inescapable moment. The breathing swelled so loud it drowned out
her own, and in panic Margot fumbled for the monkey's paw

in her coat pocket. It felt alien, as if it were conspiring against her, the tiny fingers in league with giant unseen forces. She stuffed the monkey's paw back into her pocket. It could not be trusted.

She knew she had to move, and quickly, but fear sapped her legs of the strength to escape. Instead, with trembling fingers, she took out her pencil and notebook and started to make a rubbing of one of the carved skulls on the inner wall. An absurd task under the circumstances. But the effort steadied her, distracted her from her terror as, bit by bit, the death's head loomed through the paper.

She gasped. Pad and pencil flew out of her hand as something exploded past—man or beast, or something in between, hurtling by so quickly she couldn't identify it beyond the certainty that it was alive. As it bolted past, it struck a granite block perched at the entrance to the shrine and sent it crashing to earth in a feat of superhuman strength. The scorched ground shook from the impact, and the air went dead, as if crushed under the weight of stone.

She was rooted to the spot, the blood pounding in her ears. Then, belatedly, her body responded, a jolt of adrenaline shooting into her paralyzed knees. She scrambled away, running out of the inner sanctum, falling, stumbling back up again until on the perimeter of the ruins she hit the path to the hotel. Choking on hysterical sobs, she tore back along the trail, her heart pounding like a schoolgirl's. She felt a wild exhilaration, as if she had just received her first kiss, the adolescent embrace that had, in her teenage years, been denied her. This creature wasn't a product of her hyperactive imagination. It *lived*. From her split-second glimpse of it, she guessed it was eight feet tall, but the truth was she had no idea of its size, only that it had dwarfed her. And though she had seen just a blur, she was certain "it" was a male.

If only she had seen its eyes. They would have told her so much more. It walked on its hind legs, she thought, trying to place her experience in scientific terms. As she caught sight of the hotel's swimming pool through a veil of branches, she wondered whether she should commit herself and call this monster a South American subspecies of Bigfoot. No, it was much too human for that. Too benign to be branded a monster at all. She wouldn't label her discovery yet. She would merely call it the El Dorado Mystery. She chose to ignore the implications of the altar of blood. To ponder its meaning might rob her of the surge of warmth she felt from her jungle encounter. She had known too few such moments in life to deny herself this one.

By the time Margot stepped out from among the branches, squinting into the late-afternoon sunshine, she was wearing a giddy smile. Her cheeks were flushed, and bathed in perspiration, her face had a glow that came not from rouge, but from within.

Making his rounds on the patio, Hans Berger was startled to see her emerge from the forest. "Good God! What happened?" Her legs were bloody from insect bites, her knees bruised and grimy from her escape.

She stared out from the smeared mascara with wild eyes. *"Marvelous!"*

13

THE PISTOL LAY ON THE TABLE BESIDE THE CHAM-
pagne and chocolates, like one more amenity supplied by the
management. The jewels of lead and brass had disappeared,
five slotted into the clip in the pistol's handle. One in the firing
chamber.

Alan slumped in his chair, staring out the window at the
clouds as they churned from black to white, nimbus pitted
against cumulus, as if, like his mind, the sky were fighting a
last-ditch battle with itself. His gaze shifted focus from infinity
back to the plane of the picture window. A ghost was staring
at him. It was not the first time he had seen the apparition. He
knew its face as well as he knew his own. Their first and only
meeting had been in Manhattan, at the Sherry-Netherland,
weeks before, when he had been awakened in the middle of
the night by a tapping on the window of his suite. Switching
on the light, he had seen a man, gray-haired, distinguished,
a face which might have been that of Alan himself, twenty
years hence. The stranger had been standing outside on the
narrow window ledge, his nose pressed against the glass, stark
naked except for his gold Rolex. A cold wind ruffled his thinning hair, his flesh pale against the night, as he balanced on
the cornice of the fifteenth floor, teetering above Fifth Avenue.

Alan had tried to beckon the man in, but it had been no use.
There was no time to fling open the window. The stranger
winked once over his shoulder at Alan, then stepped out into
infinity with the self-assurance of an executive entering a pent-
house elevator. For one fleeting moment the body stood taller
than the glittering skyline, before it plummeted into the chasm
of the street below. That night, after the police wrote their
cursory report, Alan had lain awake, haunted by the expression
on the man's face. What was it that had impressed him so? It
was almost dawn before Alan realized. In the instant when the
stranger had turned to him, his face had registered pure bliss.
Alan had asked himself how long it had been since he had felt
such joy.

The next morning the desk clerk had handed Alan chits for

two free drinks at the hotel bar as compensation for the "inconvenience." He had used them, then bought several more rounds of his own, and hunched there at the bar, he had plotted the act. An act which he was convinced would make up for years of hypocrisy in one decisive moment.

Alan peered down through the picture window. Pastel tablecloths blossomed on the patio. The staff was rolling out chafing dishes for the evening's "get-acquainted" cocktail party and buffet. He composed an RSVP: "Regret unable to attend due to previous engagement." It was the appropriate thing to say. The enduring lesson of his patrician upbringing had been to do the "right" thing, and he judged there could be no more fitting launching pad to oblivion than this hotel, a setting as remote as he felt from himself. "We're only on this earth for a hot minute," he remembered his wife saying. Well, he was hurtling toward the finish line. How much tidier it would have been if he had just gone down in the plane. How much simpler if the storm had pulled the trigger.

But even the storm had abandoned him now. The sun filigreed the clouds with gold, the rays cascading down to shimmer the ocean like foil. Picturesque, he conceded wearily, romantic. But after all this trouble, he wasn't about to let anything so banal as a sunset stop him. He knew that the night too had its loveliness, even the starless night of death. The thought prompted him to reach out for the weapon, but he couldn't bring himself to touch it, as if it concealed a powerful electric charge. As an abstraction, the pistol had attracted him, but now that he was about to clutch it in his hand, now that all it took was a flex of the finger, he balked. Would this, his last act, also be his most foolish? Like an amnesiac, he looked around him, trying to remember whether he was in South America or South Jersey. All the hotel rooms in his life merged into one labyrinth, with infinite adjoining baths. But what, he wondered, would accommodations be like on the Other Side? A single by the elevator, no doubt, and American Plan: Spam, mashed potatoes, and twenty different flavors of Jell-O.

Only one group would profit from his death. By the immutable law that any PR is good PR, the suicide of a travel writer might be just the ticket to hype the El Dorado's grand opening. If it were a slow news day, it might even land the hotel a mention in the *Times*. Strange, he thought, how in death he would still be giving the El Dorado its quid pro quo.

Alan knew his mind was stalling, buying time to delay the

inevitable. How, it teased him, would the other guests take the news of his demise? Would there be a moment of respectful silence before they descended on the Swedish meatballs? The debate of life against death paralyzed him. He studied the clouds, as if seeking a forecast of his verdict, but found that black and white had merged into inscrutable gray.

A knock at the door. Like a teenager caught playing with himself, Alan stuffed the pistol under his pillow. "Who is it?"

"Chris." He opened the door. She was still wearing her khakis. "Did I wake you?" she asked.

"Not at all. . . ." Alan was surprised to see her and more grateful than he would like to admit.

"I know this is one hell of a romantic opening"—she smiled—"but I need my Tampax back." He drew a blank. "The one you took at the airport . . . ?"

"You're right." He beckoned her into the room. "It is one hell of an opening." He fumbled in his coat among his cigars. "You're in luck." He handed it to her. "I haven't smoked it yet." Alan could feel Chris studying him with that damned journalist's eye of hers. He considered apologizing for his rumpled appearance but decided against it. She had already seen quite enough of his self-pity.

"You're sure I didn't wake you?" she asked. She had noticed his disarray, he realized, and was trying to make some sense of it. But if she felt sorry for him, she kept it to herself, nodding out the window at the flurry of preparations: "I'll see you later then . . . at that cocktail thing."

"Sure." When the door clicked shut, he was alone again with the nagging steel question mark. He almost wished he had left the pistol in plain sight to prove he was in desperate straits and win her sympathy. What did she really think of him? "Did I wake you?" she had asked. Perhaps, he thought, perhaps she had awakened him after all. Somehow, after their ridiculous exchange, he found his appetite for self-destruction had dwindled. Not that it was gone. It had just receded a bit, a remission of hours or minutes. Was this change of plan an act of wisdom or cowardice? Maybe he wouldn't have to use the gun at all, so long as he carried it with him, like the prophylactic he had kept in his wallet as a teenager for years before ever having the chance to use it. A symbol of possibilities unfulfilled. The rubber and the gun, he thought. They book-ended his manhood, one to mark its beginning, the other to bring it to an abrupt close. It took courage to use either, and courage was a quality that was, he suspected, rarer in his life than Beluga caviar.

His mind drifted from the pistol to the question of which shirt to wear for cocktails that evening, as if they bore equal weight in his life. He hesitated between a Lacoste and a Cardin. Delay the decision, he concluded. Delay the shirt decision as you delayed the gun. He went into the bathroom to shave, reassuring his haggard reflection in the mirror that he still intended to end it. The reflection seemed skeptical, and he avoided its glance, injecting a new blade into his razor. His hands were shaking. For as his suicidal impulse slackened so did Alan's cerebral calm. He had neglected his body, and now that he acknowledged it once again, he was besieged by countless minor complaints. He was suddenly annoyed by the stubble on his chin, his bad breath, and his need to urinate. He stepped over to the toilet and zipped open his fly. If anyone had told him that pissing could be a life-affirming act, he would have laughed, but now, as the stream arced into the toilet bowl, he felt strangely at peace.

Returning to the bedroom, Alan noticed a Montecristo that had slipped out of his coat pocket onto the bed. He rolled the cigar between thumb and forefinger, and the leaf crackled like a crisp dollar bill. After biting off the end, he lit the tip. The cigar's aroma replaced the gun-metal taste of desperation, the smoke curling through his nostrils, lingering in the hollow of his mouth. He slid the gold paper ring off the moist end, and for the first time in years, the first time since the death of his wife, in fact, instead of throwing it away he slipped it into his shirt pocket.

Did he really have Chris to thank for his sudden change of heart? A few words from a stranger, and he would spare himself? Melodramatic, he concluded. Ridiculous. No, maybe it was just that she brought up a possibility he had ignored—that there *were* possibilities, that a chance meeting could inject the unexpected into a hackneyed script. In a sense, she did bear the credit—or the blame—for his reprieve. But did she know the Oriental rule that whoever saves a life is responsible for that life forever after? Chomping the cigar between his teeth, Alan picked up the bottle of Johnnie Walker Red Label, Harley Stokes's grudging gift, and placed it on the bedstand before slumping down on the mattress. He called room service and requested a bucket of ice. Berger took the order himself. The hotel manager sounded relieved, Alan thought, to hear from him. Or was Berger only echoing the relief in his own voice?

A few more comforting puffs, and Alan closed his eyes. The whole room smelled of cigar smoke, the drifting pollen of some dark and manly flower. He opened his eyes again and stared out the window. The ghost had leaped out of sight.

14

LIKE A GIANT MANTIS BRED OF THE JUNGLE, THE attack chopper burst out of the wall of green, looming in menacing silhouette against the turquoise of the ocean. Then, just beyond landfall, it turned, swooping back toward its gleaming target, diving arrogantly close to the marble façade of the El Dorado. As it swept over the patio, full bore, the gust of its whirring rotors sent waves sloshing over the side of the swimming pool, a hundred cocktail napkins fluttering into the water like drowning butterflies. A moment later it was gone, but the drone of the engines lingered in the distance, hovering over the jungle.

The chopper was crammed with men, their eyes glazed, faces blank, like robots that had been deactivated until the moment when they would be required to perform a lethal task. They sat, their guns across their knees, their camouflaged khakis sweat-stained. Their uniforms were identical, but their weapons were a matter of individual preference: Garand and M-16, Mauser and pump shotgun; an arsenal of hand grenades, hunting knives, and bayonets—badges of a warrior profession. The pilot spotted the brown patch of the landing strip in the green expanse. Reducing speed, he eased up on the stick to start their descent. The mercenaries registered no curiosity at their destination. They were being paid. That was enough.

Only the man in the silk suit seemed impatient, squinting out the starboard gunport into the late-afternoon glare. Jorge Lopez strained against his shoulder harness. It had been a choppy four-hour ride from the capital, hedgehopping at 4,000 feet. A Learjet would have been faster and more comfortable, but then he would have been unable to bring his escort. He studied them with pride: his palace guard. He had recruited men for whom violence was a matter of preference. For some of them, he knew, it even brought pleasure. He would take this seasoned platoon of 40 over 500 Panaguan regulars any day. They would remain loyal as long as he continued to pay them well. It was the only loyalty he trusted. The other kind, bred of idealism, was folly. Strictly for the enemy, he thought—

Vargas and his guerrillas, a band of fanatics.

He glimpsed the hotel out of the gunport and congratulated himself. Every inch had been bought at a high price, and not just in time or money. At a high price in lives, a secret few knew. But the cost had been worth it. The hotel was a monument to his vision. And since he had given all the members of the Cabinet a piece of it, it had won him support for future plans that might someday lead him to the pinnacle.

As the helicopter rotated in its descent, he lost sight of the hotel. The briefcase on his knees shifted suddenly. He gripped it as gingerly as if it contained a bomb, perhaps because the information it held was devastating. Even if he had not wanted to pore over its details, he would have taken it with him. The information was too valuable to entrust to anyone else.

Lopez tugged the chain on his wrist, pulling the satchel closer to him. Sensing his impatience, the khaki-clad man beside him stood up and wrapped a meaty hand around the handle to the exit hatch. Lopez eyed his majordomo: Torres's face was a clenched fist. He displayed his brutality for all to see, like a beetle that wears its armored skeleton on the outside. It didn't bother Lopez that Torres followed him everywhere, for Torres's coarseness only enhanced his own elegance and charm.

The chopper lurched, throwing Lopez against the steel bulkhead, where someone had taped a poster of Generalissimo Francisco Zamora: proof of allegiance to the chief of state in times when even the loyalty of the military was being brought into question. Lopez frowned. The poster annoyed him. His own darkly handsome features looked so much more impressive than that old walrus. It should have been a poster of him. Someday, it would be.

The chopper hastened its descent, hurtling to earth as decisively as his thoughts. Smoothing out his jacket for his arrival, he felt a bulge in his trousers pocket and removed a scrap of paper. The dispatch had been ripped off the telex at the Internal Security Communications Center and handed to him as he boarded the helicopter. He reread it: a warning from the editor of a New York newsmagazine reiterating rumors of trouble at the El Dorado's grand opening. Lopez sensed the editor's concern for the woman reporter he had assigned to cover it. He smiled. She must be his mistress. A woman who could make a man squirm like that would be worth meeting. He crumpled the warning into a ball. No public event went by without gossip of trouble from the guerrillas. He studied his men with satisfaction. If someone wanted trouble, they were ready.

The porthole was obscured by a cloud of dust as the chopper touched down on the landing pad, its wheels sinking to the axles in red dirt. The blades whined down, and the haze thinned to reveal a minivan parked thirty yards away. By the time Torres wrenched open the hatch, Berger was jogging over to greet him.

Lopez emerged smiling. "A pleasure to see you."

"Welcome to the El Dorado." Berger shook his hand. It was a correct greeting, but without warmth.

Shouting gruffly, Torres ordered the mercenaries out. Lopez could see that Berger was appalled by these uninvited visitors.

"I wasn't told about this," the German said, controlling himself with difficulty. "Why have you brought them? Are you expecting trouble?"

Lopez smiled reassuringly. "I want our guests to feel secure."

Berger seemed to have many questions. He came out with only one. "But where will they *stay?* Only a handful of rooms in the hotel are complete, and—"

Lopez dismissed the objection with a wave of his hand. "I will worry about that. Your job is to look after our guests." Berger said nothing in reply, but as he led the way to the minivan, Lopez sensed that the German was furious. That was unfortunate. He admired Germans for their combination of efficiency and ruthlessness. They had a lot to teach his people.

Torres shouted to Lopez from the chopper: "Your mares. . . ." He beckoned toward the rear compartment, where the troops were already emerging. "Where do you want them?"

"Let them walk," Lopez said. "Let the mares walk with the men."

Berger seemed baffled by the exchange, but Lopez said nothing to enlighten him. The German reached out to take Lopez's briefcase from him but, noticing it was chained to his wrist, opened the door to the minivan for him instead. He slid behind the wheel and switched on the ignition. Already the mercenaries were marching down the dirt road toward the hotel, their weapons slung over their shoulders. Berger gunned the engine and roared past, smothering them in a cloud of dust. Lopez could see that the German took a perverse pleasure in that.

"Is everything at the hotel in order?" Lopez asked. Berger

nodded. "How many guests?" Berger twisted the wheel sharply, as if to evade the answer.

"I saved the Presidential Suite for you."

Lopez nodded approval. Berger had followed the proper protocol—Lopez was, after all, the President's representative—but the gesture also showed that Berger recognized him as heir apparent. Relying on an outdated power base of the church and the landed gentry, Zamora was obsolete. After the guerrillas were crushed, Lopez judged the time would be ripe for a new order, based on resources like oil and tourism. And he would lead.

Rounding a bend, he glimpsed the hotel through the trees, as lofty as his own expectations. The grand opening of the El Dorado was his personal triumph.

As they rattled up to the entrance, he repeated to Berger, "How many guests are there?"

This time Berger was forced to tell him.

The two nude women fondled each other on the bed, one black, the other white, their lithe bodies so alike that in the candles' glow, it seemed like one woman caressing her shadow. They stroked each other with skilled fingers, the full lips of the black nibbling the pale breasts of the blonde, who repaid the attentions with her tongue. The dark one turned and plunged her head between the thighs of the white woman, melting into the sheets.

The illusion of passion was perfect, except for one detail: their flesh was cold. Their sex act was *only* an act, performed for the benefit of the man who watched with jaded eyes. Usually the sight of his "mares" aroused him. But tonight, as he sat in an armchair, naked under his silk bathrobe, his lust had not yet begun to stir. Instead, he felt an icy rage. *Only seven guests.*

When he had heard the news of the pathetic turnout from Berger, he had sought someone to blame. But the invitations had been mailed from the capital, from his office. If Panaguas was anathema to travelers, they could hardly be expected to flock to the El Dorado. There was no ready scapegoat. None, that is, but himself.

"Enough," he said, and the women stopped their caresses, breathing hard. From their excitement he sensed that they had forgotten the charade, that the passion was real. It only made him angrier. Their enjoyment interfered with his own, turning him into a voyeur instead of their master.

"Fight," he commanded. They hesitated, and their reluctance pleased him. "Fight," he repeated, lifting a pendant from the pocket of his robe, a sapphire set in gold filigree. The two women eyed the prize. Then, muscles flexing, Rima grabbed Inez by her blond hair, forcing her down to the mattress. Squealing, Inez raked her nails across Rima's ebony back. Lopez's pulse quickened as he watched the women bite nipples they had caressed, spank bare buttocks they had massaged ever so gently.

The mock battle had turned into a full-fledged scrap. Rima screamed with real pain as her opponent mauled her breasts and dug a sharp talon into Inez's crotch. He felt his penis rising under his silk bathrobe, stiffening as the black trapped the white woman in a hammerlock that forced her face into the mattress, her nose dripping blood onto the sheets. "No!" She pleaded for mercy. Seeing Rima was about to break the arm of her opponent, he called the victor off, dropping the pendant into her outstretched hand.

"You are my tigress"—he smiled—"eh, Tigrita? And now that you have won, you get another reward...." He lifted one of the candles, the hot wax dripping onto her breasts, and led her to the bed. As he pulled her down onto the sheets, he was hard as only violence could make him. And the news of the humiliating turnout charged his hips with a vengeance. As if to punish her for his failure, he stabbed his penis between her thighs, lunging so violently in the moment of orgasm that she cried out.

He rose off her, spent, the anger for now lifted from his face, and with a charming smile said, "You are tired. You must rest." Rima attached the clasp of the gold pendant around her neck so that the bauble dangled between her breasts. Admiring the prize, Inez rubbed her sore arm and pouted.

"You are both my pets," he said, handing Inez an identical pendant. "Now go make yourselves beautiful. I want you to look like my mistresses, not my whores."

He watched the women disappear into the adjoining room. They were perquisites of power, like his estate in the capital or his Rolls-Royce. But he was tiring of them. He hoped to find others at the hotel, to play out new fantasies, and his mind ticked off the meager guest list Berger had shown him. He lingered on the name of the American woman: Chris ... what was it? Chris *Latham*. The name stuck with him, perhaps because of her editor's exaggerated concern for her well-being—

or was it Berger's expression when her name was mentioned which had telegraphed that she was the one the German preferred? He smiled. He had seduced the international press before, in spirit. It would be a pleasure to seduce one of its more alluring representatives in the flesh.

In the bathroom, he removed a razor from a pigskin pouch and began to shave off his five o'clock shadow. His was, he knew, a mobile face, capable of shifting suddenly from charm to menace, a skill essential in the interrogation basements of the Department of Internal Security, where he had begun his career. Strange how those twelve years rising through the ranks of the secret police had prepared him for the role of lover. Charm and torture were, he had learned, two equally valid means of manipulating the human animal, and he had become adept at both. Perhaps, he thought with pride, only those who knew how to inflict pain with his consummate skill could ever truly understand how to bestow pleasure.

15

HALF AN HOUR AFTER RETURNING TO HER ROOM from her disturbing trip to the souvenir shop, Chris received a package of toiletries, sent up with Berger's compliments. She had her long, hot bubble bath after all. And when it was over, when she was shampooed, talcum-powdered, and perfumed, she made herself a promise. Tonight, for once, no camera. Tonight she would lock the albatross in her room and relax for the first time in months.

But as she slipped into her Indian batik dress and clasped a necklace of amber beads around her neck, she felt anything but relaxed. Her photographer's fever persisted, the hangover of a brutal work schedule. It was a compulsion she knew Graner banked on: her guilt at placing her own pleasure ahead of the Almighty Assignment, even for a single night.

She finished her makeup and then, feeling like a negligent mother abandoning her babies, slid her camera case under the bed. She turned out the light to her room and stepped into the hall, but she couldn't slam the door. She felt naked without that damned albatross. With a sigh of defeat, she ducked back inside and slid the braided leather thong to her Nikon around her wrist. Oh well, she sweet-talked herself, the sooner I get the photo coverage out of the way, the sooner I'll *really* be able to enjoy myself. She stuffed five canisters of High Speed Ektachrome into her shoulder bag, followed by a telescoping aluminum tripod, a telephoto lens, and an electronic flash. She slammed the door behind her. Who was she trying to kid? That camera might as well be grafted to her. The only way she would ever rid herself of the tumor would be to cut her arm off at the elbow.

When the elevator doors slid open in the lobby, she was grateful she had brought her albatross. For suddenly she needed the sense of protection only a camera could give: a dozen soldiers were posted around the room. Unlike Panaguas's awkward recruits, the troops wore their khaki uniforms arrogantly, hefting their automatic weapons as if hungry for targets. They were members of a tribe she knew well—men who killed for profit—and in her experience, their mere presence bred violence. She felt a twinge of *déjà vu*, recalling the mercenaries from her past—in Rhodesia, Vietnam, Mozambique. Had those dark legions tracked her all the way here, she wondered, infesting the lobby of this hotel like worms in an apple? Avoiding their gaze, she walked quickly past, down the tiled corridor to the patio.

Outdoors, jasmine-scented air replaced the smell of sweaty uniforms. Under the canopy of stars, the mercenaries were, for the moment, forgotten, like the ocean that had receded into the shadows. Alone on the patio, she could almost convince herself she was vacationing on the Riviera, that beyond the hotel's warm circle of light lay highways, restaurants, churches. But when she turned toward the jungle, the black tangle of vines brought her back to the El Dorado: the shrunken heads she had discovered that afternoon, and the mercenaries' threat of violence. Was it merely paranoia, or professional savvy, that convinced her there was a mystery here, one she had better unmask before it reached out to throttle her?

She gazed into the swimming pool, shimmering under the torches that surrounded it. An ice swan sparkled like an idol to forces of darkness, and she could hear the scraping of steel blades on whetstone as Indians in starched white uniforms sharpened carving knives. She felt that she was witnessing the preliminaries to a primitive rite of human sacrifice, that before the ring of kerosene torches burned out, blood would flow.

Sweating in his tuxedo, Berger helped two waiters set out an iced magnum of champagne, pantomiming how to open it with a towel so the cork wouldn't go flying.

"Thanks for the care package you sent up," Chris said.

He looked her up and down. "You seem to have made excellent use of it."

She eyed the roast turkeys on the buffet, encircled by orchids and embellished with tulips of cheese and prosciutto. "I'm impressed."

"Thank you. . . ." Berger took the compliment reluctantly, as only a perfectionist could.

"You've laid out enough food for a hundred people," she said.

He nodded. "German overkill." He scanned the buffet and frowned. "I hope the guests come down before the swan melts."

"Did I get here too soon?"

He studied his watch. "You're fifteen minutes late. By Panaguan time that makes you an hour early."

She strolled the length of the buffet, past sculpted foie gras and diadems of caviar to a mosaic of French pastries. She could feel the onyx eyes of the Indian staff following her—as though they knew that her every move in tonight's drama would be crucial. The roar of waves drew her to the balustrade. Beyond it, under a rising moon, a handful of soldiers stood against the luminescent surf, guns at the ready.

"I'm afraid they do somewhat spoil the view." Berger hovered behind her.

"Mercenaries . . . ?" She tried to draw him out.

"For a certain class of men"—he shrugged—"money is the best . . . the *only* inducement."

"When did they get here?"

He hesitated, then lowered his voice. "They came with Lopez."

"Jorge Lopez?"

"The Minister of Tourism. Of course, his actual duties are much more far-reaching."

She nodded. She knew of Lopez's pivotal importance in the government. "I'm surprised he's here. I thought he'd have his hands full in the capital."

"Don't underestimate Lopez's pride in the El Dorado," he said. "The grand opening isn't just another ceremonial occasion. It's a major propaganda coup for him."

"I look forward to meeting him," she said.

"May I ask why?" There was a sarcastic edge to his voice.

"Would I have visited Nazi Germany and passed up a chance to meet Martin Bormann?" For a moment, realizing Berger's nationality, she regretted what she had said.

To her surprise, he nodded appreciatively. "Touché."

"Why did he bring all the men?" He didn't reply, dipping a crab leg in a bowl of sauce. He frowned and added a dash of lemon juice. His resistance tantalized her. "Does he expect trouble from the guerrillas?"

Berger was studying a platter heaped with exotic fruit. He picked up a spoiled mango and hurled it beyond the patio, into the darkness. "When I first came here," he said, "I thought that all kinds of fruit grew in the jungle. Delicious, exotic things." He turned back to her. "But I learned that none of them do. Guavas, papayas . . . they all have to be flown in from countries

thousands of miles away. Here in Panaguas, things only rot."
He tapped his forehead. "In Panaguas, things rot up here,
too. . . ." She was about to press her questioning when he cut
her off with a charming smile. "Enough. It's time for you to
stop playing journalist and for me to start playing host. Let me
have Jesús make you a drink."

He led her to the bar, where a short Indian with a shiny
pompadour toyed with the gold braid on his uniform. She
hesitated, and he added, "If it's the ice cubes you're worried
about, they're made with distilled water. They're perfectly
safe."

"It's not the ice cubes. I just think I'll wait."

"As a favor to me?" He lowered his voice. "Jesús needs the
practice."

But she was already adjusting her Nikon's built-in light
meter, testing the reading she got from the torches. "I'd better
take a few mood shots first. You know, the ultimate tropical
resort awaiting its first visitor. The calm before the storm."
She scanned the patio with a professional eye. The magazine
would shy away from head-on shots of the guests. But the
lavish buffet set against the dark infinity of the evening—the
elegant but somber mood—offered a fresh perspective, and
she decided to go for it.

"I need a bird's-eye view of everything . . . the pool, the
patio. . . ." She spotted a steel ladder leading to the roof of the
two-story restaurant pavilion. "What's that for?"

"The air-conditioning maintenance. The units are up on the
roof." He read her mind. "I'm sorry. I can't let you go up
there." He shooed away a fly, to keep it from perching on a
pâté rosette—apparently an equally forbidden spot. "The roof
will be slippery after the rain. And in the dark. . . ." He shook
his head and clamped down a silver lid as the fly buzzed away.

She wasn't so easily discouraged. "I'll take a chance."

"No." But before he could admonish her, he was interrupted
by a terrific crash. One of the waiters had dropped a case of
champagne, and he hurried over to direct the mopping-up.

When, minutes later, the staff had whisked away the last
shards of broken glass, he returned to the balustrade where
Chris had been standing. She had disappeared into the dark.

The steel ladder was sweating in the humidity. Chris struggled for a grip, her dress billowing in the wind, her sandals
precarious on the slippery rungs. A drumbeat was ringing in

her ears, and she realized with relief that it was only the electric generator throbbing in the shadows below.

One final step, and she swung her body up onto the roof. Against the far wall, twenty feet away, the central air-conditioning unit hummed at a shrill pitch. The high-rise monolith of the main building towered above her, blocking out the stars. Damn, it was dark. She tested the roof with her toe: a flat veneer of tar paper, solid underfoot.

"Come down!" She heard Berger's shout.

"I'm okay," she shouted back, unable to glimpse him over the side. He said nothing more. He must have been called away to solve some new disaster. It would leave her free to pursue her work uninterrupted. She started across the rooftop, threading her way among the puddles left by the rain, but before she could reach the edge, she discovered something else: piles of excrement. She had lost her delicate sensibilities long ago, but this sight in so unexpected a location shocked her. The feces appeared human in origin, but with a reddish cast. They reminded her of the droppings of the big cats of the Gir after they had feasted on raw meat. As her eyes adjusted to the light, she saw that the heaps of excrement were not randomly placed, that they had been positioned in a semicircle facing the moon, and she wondered who or what would do this. Could it be that this territory had been marked off, as she had seen wolves mark off their private turf? It frustrated her that her camera could do nothing to capture the eerie atmosphere of this place. The foreboding that the roof was inhabited.

Vultures, perched on the cornice, flapped away as she moved cautiously to the edge. They were the first scavengers she had seen since her arrival. Did they roost here to feed on carrion in the hotel's garbage pits, or were they waiting, with that abominable patience of theirs, waiting for something to die? She looked down and realized the cornice offered a perfect view of the patio, the pool a vast eye gleaming beneath her in the glow of torches.

She removed the telescoping tripod from her bag and, after positioning it on the edge of the roof, set the shutter speed of her Nikon for a time exposure. Squinting in the dim light, she concentrated on fastening the shutter release cable to the camera. She loved the precision of her work. It was her one true relaxation, her one true escape. She peered through the viewfinder to frame her composition: the staff in their white chefs' hats stood behind the buffet table, as if offering a feast to unseen creatures lurking in the jungle night—predators which, traveling on Panaguan time, would arrive only when they saw fit.

Balancing precariously near to the edge, she pressed the cable release. But instead of the familiar click of the shutter, a sound erupted from nowhere—the flapping of wings, perhaps, the skittering of clawed feet. She had no time to decipher it. Someone—or something—lunged at her from behind. It caught her off-balance with a shove that sent her over the edge, one leg thrashing in thin air. Only the thick leather strap of her shoulder bag, snagged around a metal post, saved her from plummeting thirty feet to the flagstones below.

She tried to cry for help but could manage only a gasp, a shrill intake of breath that was both scream and sob. Below, there were no witnesses. Berger and his staff had stepped back into the kitchen, out of earshot. It took all her strength to pull herself up with one arm, before she could kick out with a leg, get a foothold, and scramble to safety.

Trembling from the jolt of adrenaline, she crouched on the edge, huddled on the dank roofing. She realized that whatever it was, it had not bumped into her by accident. The attack had been deliberate. She braced herself for what she felt certain would be the second, decisive lunge.

It never came. She looked around her. No sign of her attacker. Whatever it was, it had vanished. She wasn't about to wait for its return. Stuffing her camera into her shoulder bag as if to smother it, she clambered over toward the ladder, on unsteady legs.

By the time she set foot on solid ground she was already trying to arrive at a rational explanation for the incident. Could it have been a nearsighted vulture, swooping in for a landing? No, she thought, as she eyed the soldiers on the beach, the culprit was decidedly human. When there was no blood to shed, she had known mercenaries to concoct such malicious practical jokes out of boredom.

Berger was positioning the chafing dishes with the precision of field artillery as she slumped into a chair nearby. "You know that drink you offered me? You're on."

He could see she was pale and shaken. "What happened?"

"Something exotic, with rum. In a pineapple." Berger translated her order to Jesús, who set to work. "I fell...." She continued cautiously. "I *almost* fell."

"I told you," he said. "The roof is wet. It's hard to see in the shadows."

"I didn't slip. Somebody pushed me." They exchanged a look. "I've seen mercenaries bayoneting babies in the Congo," she said. "They're capable of anything. . . ."

"You forget. I'm German." A seeming non sequitur, but one which told her that he agreed with her verdict: impersonal cruelty could as often be a motive for murder as private vendetta. *"Voilà!"* With a flourish, he handed her the bartender's concoction.

Her hand was shaking as she removed the little paper parasol to lift the pineapple to her lips. She took what she hoped would be a steadying gulp, then spit it out. "This is bourbon!"

But Berger wasn't listening. He winced as though he, too, had a sour taste in his mouth, and she followed his gaze. Entering the patio from the lobby, the stranger wore an old-fashioned double-breasted suit, his bald head reflecting the torches' glow like a chunk of raw meat. He reminded her of a thirties gangster, right down to the bulge under his armpit.

"Torres," Berger murmured. "Lopez's right-hand man." He gestured toward the mercenaries on the beach. "He keeps the hired help in line." He hurried to finish before Torres came within earshot. "Lopez doesn't like to get his hands dirty. That's Torres's job." Quickly Berger donned his professional smile. *"Buenas noches,"* he said to him.

"Noches. . . ." The phrase escaped in a gravelly voice as coarse as his pocked face. Torres was carrying two large fishbowls, one in each hand, over to the buffet table. He placed them atop a raised chrome centerpiece. Beneath it, gold letters read in English, PANAGUAS—LAND OF BEAUTY AND ENCHANTMENT. A closer look revealed that the bowl atop the word BEAUTY held a gaudy angelfish. A school of larger silver fish swam in the bowl above the word marked ENCHANTMENT. It was an unimpressive sight, and she was surprised that Berger tolerated Torres's dubious contribution. Maybe the hotel manager was simply grateful Torres hadn't done something worse.

"¡Momentito!" Berger called to him as he made his way back into the lobby, and Torres turned ponderously, barely acknowledging him. Berger asked a question in wooden, deliberate Spanish.

Torres seemed surprised at the words. *"Repetirlo,"* he said, and Berger repeated himself. Torres shot a glance up at the roof of the restaurant pavilion, then eyed Chris with contempt. He rattled off a brusque reply and disappeared inside.

Berger hesitated before he turned to Chris. "Torres says he didn't station anyone up there. He was most insistent." He handed her a fresh drink, and she was grateful to sip the sugarcane sweetness of rum. She studied the two glass bowls—the angelfish in one, the metallic swarm in the other—as if gazing into crystal balls to probe an uncertain future.

When she looked up, she saw that armed guards had climbed the ladder to the restaurant roof. Their flashlight beams scoured the shadows.

16

A MARIACHI ENSEMBLE FOUGHT ITS WAY THROUGH "Feelings," but their rendition struck Chris as painfully off key, each stanza ending on a note that was somber, if not downright funereal.

Slowed by the humid air, her mind tried to discern a pattern in the day's bizarre events: the woman glimpsed in the lobby who Berger insisted didn't exist; the shrunken heads discovered in the souvenir shop; finally, her harrowing close call on the roof. Each might be of little importance in itself, perhaps, but together. . . . She smiled. Graner always accused her of constructing conspiracy theories out of thin air. But this time. . . .

She studied the guests who had assembled on the patio. They sipped their drinks without exchanging a word, isolated each from the other like chess pieces in a stalemate: Margot, the eternal wallflower, ungainly in her strapless magenta cocktail dress, was sniffling as if allergic to her orchid corsage. Clad in a brocade caftan, Scott seemed as casual as Margot was ill at ease. His golden beard, the silver coke spoon dangling around his neck like a crucifix, gave him the aura of a fallen disciple. Grinning as if arriving at a world premiere, Irv Florsheim, his gut sucked into a powder-blue leisure suit, swept Dawn out onto the patio, her shoulders thrown back in her hot-pink shift to show off her cleavage to best advantage. Chris wondered whether the shadowy outskirts of the patio were peopled with hidden visitors, like the rooftop where, without warning, the intruder had so suddenly made its presence known.

The guests seemed as awkward as teenagers to her, and Margot broke the ice, like a debutante broaching spin the bottle. "What sign are you?" she asked Irv.

He squirmed. "Jewish." The others laughed until Margot took a shot in the dark and guessed he was a Taurus. After she guessed correctly that Dawn was a Virgo and Scott a Sagittarius, the little group clustered in an attentive circle around her.

"I'm going to do a horoscope for each and every one of you," she bubbled, and scrawled their birthdates down on a cocktail napkin. When Margot turned to Chris for her birthday, she surrendered it reluctantly and left the group.

As the ocean breeze slackened, her thoughts grew oppressive, like the humidity, and she was drawn to the buffet. She heaped caviar, shrimp, and pâté onto her plate and sampled each, but they did nothing to satisfy her. She needed other nourishment—she needed answers. But she couldn't even put her questions into words yet. The mystery was too elusive for her to know if it *was* a mystery.

She felt a tap on her shoulder. It was Alan, in a Lacoste shirt and blazer, clean-shaven for the first time since they had met. A definite improvement, she thought, and from the way he smiled at her, he had noticed her transformation as well.

"Some spread." Alan scanned the buffet. "It looks like the prom decorations committee did a swell job." His tone changed abruptly, the sarcasm replaced with gratitude. "I want to thank you for barging in on me this afternoon... I was at a pretty low ebb...." He paused awkwardly and laughed at his inability to express himself. "Anyway, thanks."

But she was staring over his shoulder at the sentinels on the roof, her mind trammeled in riddles.

"You didn't hear a word I said."

"I'm sorry." She managèd a smile. "It's been a strange day... a very strange day."

"Really?"

For a moment she debated whether to share her misgivings with him. She decided to proceed with caution. "Since you've been here have you noticed anything... *unusual?*"

He shrugged. "After a while these resorts all blend together...." He paused, "No.... You're right. There *is* something unusual at this hotel. You."

She ignored the compliment. She was in no mood for flirtation. He couldn't offer what she needed—answers to the questions that baffled her. She put down her plate and raised her camera. "Work to do...."

"Sure." He managed a smile as she headed toward the pool to frame a group shot of the gathering. Alan's response to her gentle brushoff was to head for the bar. He was too vulnerable, she thought, much too easily floored by rejection.

The guitars strummed out a fanfare, and a man in a silk suit and tie entered with a woman on each arm. It had to be Lopez. Tanned from the Panaguan sun, he was a picture of vigor, befitting his title of Minister of Tourism. He had the mien of a bullfighter, she decided, but not the face of the matador who kills with merciful swiftness. Rather, he evoked the mounted picador, the lancer who builds his career on his skill at inflicting pain.

She admired the women at his side: the black in a stunning white sheath, the peaches-and-cream blonde in black velvet. Lopez was the kind of man who had to have more than one of everything—whether lovers or thoroughbreds. And from what she'd heard, he treated his polo ponies more humanely than his women.

When her eyes met his, she could tell that he was a man who took beautiful women for granted. He seemed vain enough to assume that her interest in him went beyond professional curiosity.

Berger offered champagne to Lopez, who handed the crystal goblets to his women before taking one himself. A command from Berger, and champagne flowed for the other guests. Lopez raised his goblet, speaking in fluent English. "Ladies and gentlemen, I wish to propose a toast. To all of *you*, our guests who have come so very far to visit us." He looked directly at Chris. "If there is anything we can do to make your stay more enjoyable, you have only to ask me.

"I hope that while you are with us, you will take a second look at our land, one of democratic freedom, like your own, and cheerful, friendly people. . . ." Chris stole a glance at Torres's men and at the staff. No one looked either cheerful or friendly. No one, that is, but Jesús, who was secretly killing a bottle of champagne at the bar.

Lopez beckoned the guests around him as he stepped over to the glittering centerpiece. "Ours is a land, above all, of the exciting and the *unexpected*." He lifted the bowl that held the angelfish and, scooping it out with his palm, dropped it in with the metallic swarm of fish in the other bowl. The mariachis struck up on cue as the water blurred. He had combined two volatile elements to spark an explosive chain reaction. The struggle whipped the water into a froth, reducing the angelfish to a scrap, a tail without a head to guide it, swimming in a final spasm of life.

The guests' sudden hush magnified the sound of the water sloshing in the bowl. Lopez had a rare gift, Chris realized— to appeal to the brutality within even the gentlest guest. He manipulated violence like a weapon—to "entertain"; to terrify; always to exploit it for his own ends. If he found this an amusing opener, what new charades did he plan for the days to come?

"Piranha." Scott broke the silence. "I saw them in a movie once. . . . They ate Victor Mature's horse." At the sound of his voice, Rima and Inez whispered to each other, like breathless teenagers. Though Scott Hershey hadn't had a hit in the States for five years, Chris concluded that in Panaguas—running on Panaguan time—he must still be a star.

As the two women rushed over to ask for Scott's autograph, Irv saw his opening. "Irv Florsheim." He pumped Lopez's hand. "Did you get my letter?"

Lopez nodded with cool politeness. "I found your proposal . . . intriguing."

Irv presented the woman on his arm as if offering dessert. "This is Dawn."

"Delighted." Lopez kissed her hand, then, to Irv's chagrin, turned to Chris. "You must be Miss Latham. . . ."

Chris was both complimented and suspicious that Lopez should prefer her to Dawn. But then, she had something more alluring than her body to offer: favorable publicity. "The El Dorado's quite a place," she said.

"Miss Latham—shall I call you Chris?—I think that's the first kind word an American reporter has ever said about me *or* my country." He gestured for Jesús to refill her champagne glass.

"Do you think fear of terrorism is what caused the low turnout?"

Lopez seemed unruffled by the blunt question. "We wanted to have a few selected guests. A dry run, as I believe you say, to make sure the hotel is working properly. Terrorism had nothing to do with it."

"Then why the tight security? Should we take it to mean that—"

"Take it to mean"—he cut her off with a smile—"that we believe in making our guests feel secure. Now if you will excuse me"—he nodded to Torres nearby—"I must return to my room. I have business to attend to. I hope you enjoy the evening."

"Thanks."

"Until tomorrow, then. . . ." He started toward the hotel, surrounded by a retinue of mercenaries. He was a true politician, Chris mused. She knew even less after talking to him than she did before.

A skyrocket flew over the ocean, and garish flowers blossomed, bouquets exploding at the moon. In the strobe of the fireworks, the jungle shifted from fiery red to the blue of a forest in Atlantis. Then darkness, as the staff on the beach reloaded their launchers. In the light of the next burst, she noticed a new arrival. Curzon had appeared out of nowhere. As he helped himself greedily to the buffet, he looked wilder than before, his chin stubbly, his suit stained.

"Good evening," Berger greeted him.

Curzon heaped his plate in such haste that turkey, ham, and caviar dripped onto the ground, his eyes glued to the jungle. "No room service," he snapped. "There's no fucking room service!"

Berger was rattled by his ferocity. "But . . . we were expecting you to join us."

Curzon ignored him and stared into the darkness. "I can't stay down *here!*" He almost laughed at the absurdity of Berger's statement. "Are you out of your gourd? I have to stay up *there!*" He stabbed a finger at his room. "I may already be too late!" He grabbed a bottle of bourbon from the bar. Berger gestured for a waiter to help him with his plate, but Curzon was in too big a hurry for that and strode off.

Chris hurried after him. Curzon was the most unapproachable of the guests, yet she sensed he might be the only one who knew enough to help her. Before she could catch up with him, he entered the lobby and slammed the door in her face.

"Help!" Dawn squealed, and Chris turned in time to see the starlet leap into the pool with her clothes on. Chris didn't even lift the camera to her eye. She wasn't about to waste film on such stunts. Dawn shot up to the surface, gasping for breath. "Come on in!" she cried, and Scott took the plunge, followed by Inez and Rima, who shrieked with delight as they hit the water. Chris turned away from them, toward the beach, convinced the answers to the questions that plagued her lay not in that chlorinated pool, but somewhere out there in the shadows.

The fireworks burst sporadically now, like heat lightning, and she decided to make the most of them. Snapping on her telephoto, she used the viewfinder to pan the outer reaches of the patio, ending with the balustrade fronting the beach. Her hands froze. She strained to bring an indistinct silhouette into focus. She was certain it wasn't one of the mercenaries. Except for the handful on the beach, they had all left with Lopez. And it couldn't be one of the guests; they were clustered around the pool. She considered telling Alan her discovery, but there wasn't time. She didn't intend to let *this* apparition get away.

Chris stepped into the shadows. Drawing a bead, she snapped a picture of the ill-defined figure to convince herself she wasn't imagining things, then walked resolutely toward her target. The fireworks ended, and plunged her into darkness. She edged toward the balustrade, and wondered if she was making a gross miscalculation to confront the intruder face to face.

With just five yards to go, she stopped, and strained to hear a telltale sound above the waves. As if to reassure herself that she wasn't alone, she glanced back toward the pool. The mariachis were playing "How Dry I Am" as Scott and the women climbed out of the water.

"Did you ever see such a bunch of damn fools in your life?" The voice, a woman's, rang out of the darkness. As Chris spun around, her jaw dropped. Standing before her, outlined against the night sky, was the woman she had glimpsed in the lobby on her arrival—the "phantom" Berger had insisted didn't exist. The specter Margot swore was a ghost.

17

THE STRANGER TOOK TWO STEPS FORWARD, EMERG-ing from the shadows of the balustrade: a broad-hipped, sixtyish woman in a seersucker suit. She was stout without being fat, her thick legs planted firmly on the ground. Disarming blue eyes winked at Chris through metal-rimmed spectacles, and before either had exchanged a word, Chris felt an enormous sense of relief. Fearing the woman might disappear as suddenly as she had that afternoon, she felt compelled to speak.

"I'm Chris Latham," was all she could manage, and in her excitement the three words left her breathless.

The woman's reply was self-confident, almost manly in its timbre. "With *View* magazine. I know."

"You do?"

"Ever since Berger told me you were a reporter, I've been meaning to talk to you. I've got a story for you."

Chris was stunned. "When I told Berger I'd seen you in the lobby, he insisted you didn't exist."

"And it's a good thing he did." The woman chuckled, as if enjoying a private joke. "You see, my dear, I'm not one of the invited guests. Berger would lose his job, or worse, if anyone knew I was here. And if Lopez found out, what he would do to me would be. . . ." She shook her head. "Well, we won't discuss the possibilities." Chris was puzzled. It made no sense that anyone could see this unassuming woman as a threat.

The stranger offered her hand. "Dr. Eleanor Tobias." Chris knew the name: an anthropologist famed for her studies of primitive tribes. Tobias's warm handshake calmed her.

"Tell me . . ." Chris said, fumbling for a line of questioning. "I don't understand why. . . ."

"Slow down." Tobias laughed. "As the Masai in Kenya say, let's rest a moment, to allow time for our souls to catch up with our bodies." She beckoned Chris back into the shadows, where a table overlooked the surf, and tilted a teapot in her direction. "Camomile? It's the best thirst quencher in the tropics. Won't bloat you like beer or give you the runs like booze."

"No, thank you." Chris was only thirsty for answers.

They were interrupted by shouting and giggling from the pool. Scott was sharing a coconutful of rum with Inez, Rima, and Dawn. Tobias sipped her tea and studied them. Chris noticed that she covered her teeth with her lips when she smiled. It transformed her expression into one akin to pity—as though Tobias thought the guests were a tribe more endangered than the Masai. The anthropologist set her teacup down on its saucer without a sound, then looked up at the high-rise hotel, looming like a monument to unknown gods. She seemed to be in pain. She spoke slowly, as if what she was about to reveal were hard to believe, most of all for herself, as if only by saying it aloud could she convince herself that it was true. "This used to be jungle," she said. "Just ten years ago this was all green and growing." She spoke with a gentle lilt, as though telling a fairy tale to a small child. "The forest used to come all the way up to the promontory where we're sitting now, right to the edge of the beach. And with all its creatures it was an infinitely more complex web of life than this world of glass and chrome— more complex and more delicate. . . ."

Chris started to ask a question but stopped herself, realizing that an inner compulsion drove the woman to tell her story, that it would unravel in her own good time.

"Oh, I think most talk of racial superiority is bunk," Tobias said. "Black or white or yellow, we all have our strengths and weaknesses, and *vive la différence*. But the Warak—the Warak were special. The marriage of what is perfect in nature and in man: the courage of wild beasts, wedded to human intelligence and sensitivity."

"The Warak . . . ?"

"The Warak were not like the Dogon of Mali," Tobias said, "who fire their weapons at the heavens out of wrath at the gods' injustice. The Warak were at one with their gods. And at peace with themselves." She hesitated, as if she knew that her next statement would startle her listener: "I regard them as the ultimate fulfillment of the species *Homo sapiens* on this planet."

Chris was skeptical. She had seen enough primitive tribes in her work to know that the "noble savage" was usually just malnourished and ignorant. They had often evoked her pity— never her awe. "How can you say that?" she asked. "For a primitive tribe—"

"Not primitive," Tobias corrected her. "Anything but primitive. So advanced that they didn't need technology to make them feel safe or clean or happy."

"But . . . how do you know so much about them?"

"Years ago I conducted a study here. It was my privilege to observe them." Abruptly her tone shifted. She was speaking lyrically again, as though recalling the summers of childhood. "They didn't know the meaning of guilt. Their lives alternated between love and murder, between sex and the hunt. They were at once the most ruthless and the most gentle of peoples. In fact, women of other tribes were eager to be enslaved by the Warak in the tribal wars. For the Warak didn't resort to the barbaric practice of the other tribes: clitoral excision—the amputation of the female's clitoris to assure faithfulness. The Warak saw the sex act as pleasure for both men and women. You see"—she sipped delicately from her cup—"they were said to have other gifts as well. . . ."

"I . . . I don't understand."

Tobias sweetened her tea with another lump of sugar. "The penis sheaths of all the other tribes in this region are made from the slender kumai stalk." She paused significantly. "But the physical endowments of the Warak . . . required their penis sheaths be hollowed from a fully mature sugarcane. And their physical gifts didn't end there. Where the other tribes of the Amazon are short of stature, the Warak grew to considerable height—taller than the average American. And they performed fears of strength which I would never have believed if I hadn't seen them with my own eyes. I've seen them stalk a jaguar armed only with a machete, break the neck of a peccary, a kind of wild pig, with their bare hands. . . ."

Chris tried to remain skeptical, but Tobias was utterly disarming. Chris had an eerie sense that the legends of the Amazon had come to life in this tribe. "Where did the Warak *get* their powers?"

"I looked for the secret of their virility, their potency and strength. Was it diet? My research revealed that, like countless lesser tribes, it consisted mostly of the raw meat of fresh-slain prey. The mineral properties of their sacred spring perhaps?" She shook her head. "There is no fountain of youth, no magic formula. No, their prodigious gifts came from this jungle, what it *demanded* of them." The mariachis had stopped, and the cries of unseen creatures began to insinuate themselves into the conversation. Tobias stared out into the darkness, seemingly debating how much she could reveal before the jungle punished her.

She turned to Chris and lowered her voice confidentially. "If you believe, as I do, that strength comes through adversity, consider this fact: the Panaguan coastal jungle is the dark opposite of Eden. It has the heaviest concentration of predators on earth: the jaguar; the deadly constrictors like the anaconda; the carnivorous bats; the venomous spiders. And others," she said, as if she didn't dare utter their names, "*others* much more deadly. There was only one way for a tribe to endure in this hostile environment for thousands of years. They had to become the ultimate predators themselves. Not out of evil. But to survive. It took generations of struggle and bloodshed for the tribe to conquer this domain. But it emerged triumphant—*Homo sapiens rex*, master of all. For once, a ruler living in harmony with nature, a god among gods."

She stopped as a mercenary swaggered toward them along the beach, an automatic rifle in the crook of his arm, the ember of a cigarette glowing against his face like a single eye. She leaned back deeper into the darkness. "The Warak weren't peace-loving people," she said. "Peace isn't the jungle way. They could kill anything that walks. As predators perfected for the hunt, they lived in a perpetual state of war: first to subdue other fierce tribes, then to resist the government's encroachment. They waged a war against Generalissimo Zamora's troops, striking quickly, then melting magically into the forest. When they were driven to the ocean, to this very spot, they made their last stand." She seemed relieved when the mercenary disappeared into the darkness.

"Even the Warak were not invincible," she said. "Even angels can fall. An AR-15 can penetrate six inches of planking at a hundred yards. Imagine what it can do to bare flesh, even the body of a Warak warrior." She glanced at the surf. "Beachfront property is, after all, pretty valuable real estate. Deals were made."

"Deals?"

"Lopez masterminded the whole thing. Ten years ago the mercenaries came and did their job. Massacred men, women, and children. I gather that by Panaguan standards, it was quite efficient. They burned the Warak's longhouses to the ground to make way for this monstrosity. Neither the tribe nor the game they hunted live here now. . . ." Flies had swarmed around the bowl of sugar cubes, and she waved her hand to dispel them. ". . . Only insects."

Chris was riveted. Those murders left unpunished—perhaps their eerie resonance explained her own uneasiness about the El Dorado.

"After the mercenaries left, the work crews came," Tobias continued. "They bulldozed the corpses under, buried them in cement. So you see, the hotel was built from their flesh and blood. Señor Lopez has, unwittingly, constructed for the Warak a gaudy tomb." She sipped her tea delicately and made a face, then sweetened it with another lump of sugar as if to dispel the bitterness of her thoughts.

Chris glanced up at the roof of the restaurant pavilion and noticed that the vultures had come back to roost. She wondered if those gargoyles had acquired an appetite for human flesh years ago, feeding on the bodies of the Warak. How long, she asked herself, would they have to wait for their next feast?

"Are you telling me," she asked, "that the entire tribe was wiped out to build this hotel?"

"Apparently a few survived," Tobias said. "They're a long way from here now, on the upper Marañón, I'm told. And they're desperate. When they were forced to leave their ancestral grounds, they became more . . . human? At least, more like the rest of us. Prone to infection—smallpox, influenza. Subject to malnutrition, too. And despair. When I learned what had happened, I told the authorities. They wouldn't lift a finger. I told my university, but they were content to embalm them in the pages of books, like pressed butterflies. I decided I had to save them—that they were *worth* saving. I invested what little money I had in drugs: penicillin, erythromycin. Tomorrow I'm going in after them. I want to show them that someone from the outside cares." She stopped to catch her breath, a smile revealing she knew she was on the brink of a sermon. "I do tend to ramble on," she said. "An occupational hazard of academia, aggravated by old age."

She squinted out over the ocean with the melancholy of a much older woman, as if surveying her life. "I've lived with a lot of tribes, from Quinana Roo to the Serengeti," she said. "They're mostly gone now. Killed with bullets or, worse, with 'kindness.' Turned into pets to amuse the tourists. But this tribe—the Warak—must survive."

Dr. Tobias reached over to pour more tea, but only a few drops trickled out. When she put down the teapot, Chris was shocked to notice that the index finger of Tobias's right hand was missing, leaving a ragged scar, as though the amputation had been performed with a blunt-edged blade. Tobias had evidently paid a price for her commitment, yet that didn't seem to discourage her from the risks of the trek ahead.

She stood up, and Chris realized her interview was over. Her mind was swimming with questions, but one took precedence over all the others: did the Warak perform the ritual of shrinking human heads? Was that most grisly of ceremonies somehow at the core of their power? "To your knowledge, did the Warak ever..." she began, but before she could finish, Tobias caught sight of the mercenary again, walking back toward them along the beach at a brisk pace.

"Past my bedtime," the anthropologist said. She shook Chris's hand warmly and melted into the shadows.

But for Chris to allow this woman to slip through her fingers was unthinkable. "I've got to talk with you again."

"Impossible. I leave at dawn."

Chris played the one card she had left—the reason, no doubt, why Tobias had confided in her in the first place. "How can I write the story if I don't know more?" she asked. "I need proof—proof of your allegations against Lopez."

There was a long pause, as if Tobias were turning Chris's words over in her mind. "All right. You've got a job to do, too. I have documents implicating Lopez. You can have them."

"When?"

The mercenary had slowed his pace. He was standing a few yards away from them now. Tobias's voice subsided to a whisper. "Six A.M. Room 302. Use the documents as you see fit. They won't do me any good where I'm going...."

From her tone, she was bequeathing her most precious possessions. Perhaps, Chris thought, the anthropologist didn't expect to come back from the trek. She lost sight of Tobias in the darkness.

But, she heard her voice once more from out of the shadows. "What I know puts me in jeopardy." Tobias paused significantly. "Make no mistake, it puts you in jeopardy, too."

Dr. Tobias waved her four-fingered hand in farewell. Then she was gone, like a benign spirit.

As she strode back across the patio, Chris felt the breathless high that had first attracted her to journalism, the exhilaration of discovery coupled with danger. She had found secrets that revealed a seemingly innocuous resort in a shocking new light.

The hotel, which had seemed so banal at first, had its own shadowy past, its own secrets, its own saints and demons. A hotel built on the bodies of its victims—and she would be the one to tell the tale to the world.

She tightened her fingers into a fist. She could still feel the coarse scar tissue of Dr. Tobias's mutilated hand, and it brought home to her the price of the knowledge she had so suddenly acquired. If Lopez found out what she knew, this would be her last assignment.

As if wounded by the fireworks, the moon had begun to list toward the horizon. Chris walked back past the buffet—what was left of it. The ice swan had melted into a glassy skull. Judging from the turkey carcasses on their silver platters, the guests had eaten voraciously.

"Miss Latham. . . ." Berger appeared at her side, his face drawn. "Something has come up. One of the guests . . ."

Chris looked around her. The patio seemed deserted, except for Jesús, who was carrying an armload of empty bottles into the kitchen with an unsteady gait. Then she glimpsed a figure at a far table. Margot was sitting bolt upright in her chair, in what looked like the rigor mortis of a drunk. The major casualty, it would seem, of the evening.

"She's been like that for half an hour," Berger said. "She refuses to go up to her room. Could you have a word with her?" He hesitated. "Sometimes women, they know how to speak to each other from the heart."

Chris nodded. In her experience, spinsters grew morose with alcohol. But heading over to her, she was surprised to see that instead of empty glasses, Margot's table was littered with papers.

"Are you okay?" Chris asked.

"Wonderful!" Margot sniffed, blowing her nose into a lace handkerchief. Her eyes were misty with tears; her makeup was smeared. Chris noticed that in her distress she had pulled the petals off her orchid corsage, leaving the dismembered flower strewn on the table.

"Would you feel better talking about it?"

Margot shook her head and, pressing her lips into a taut line, returned to her computations.

Chris could smell liquor on Margot's breath, but the woman seemed stone-cold sober. Something had terrified her enough to clear her head. "Tell me," Chris said, "tell me what's wrong."

Margot's facade crumbled. "It's these *horrorscopes!* I promised I'd do them for everyone . . . I gave my word. . . ."

"It's hard to figure out a horoscope," Chris comforted her. "I know. I've tried."

"Oh, that's not it." Margot frowned. "I've *already* figured them out. And I've checked and double-checked it all, but. . . ."

"I don't understand."

"*Look.* This is Scott, and Dawn, and Irv, and here's me." She showed her an indecipherable list of figures, with a sigh of despair. Chris drew a blank. Margot squinted into the sky, gazing up at the constellations as if they had betrayed her. "Don't you see?" She was indignant that Chris couldn't recognize the obvious. "All these people . . . all of them. According to my computations, they're doomed to some terrible misfortune. Now isn't that ridiculous? Isn't that just absurd?"

A month ago, a week ago, Chris would have said yes. But that was before she had discovered the shrunken heads, before her misadventure on the roof, above all, before Dr. Tobias's revelations. She placed a hand on Margot's shoulder. "Don't take it all so . . . seriously," she managed, and gave what she hoped would look like a reassuring smile. She wondered what Dr. Tobias's horoscope would have been if Margot had computed it tonight, on the eve of her trek into the jungle. And that thought prompted her to ask a difficult question, one to which she didn't want to hear the answer: "Did you figure out *my* horoscope?"

Margot nodded and closed her eyes. When she opened them, they were red and worn, as if they had witnessed some unthinkable disaster. "I won't tell the others about their charts. There's no reason to, is there? I mean, astrology is a terribly inexact science, and. . . ."

"Of course it is," Chris answered dutifully.

A breeze riffled through the papers, as if to verify the prophecy, and Margot gripped them more tightly, to keep the wind from stealing them away. "We mustn't take it too seriously. We *mustn't.*"

Margot's panic was contagious, and Chris experienced the same vertigo she had felt on the edge of the roof just hours before: the dizziness before a sheer drop. "You didn't answer my question," she prodded. "What about my horoscope?"

Margot fumbled among the papers until she found one with Chris's name scrawled at the top. "If you're going to *believe* all this"—she tossed it off with a nervous twitch of her head—"then the odds are that . . . that you'll never leave this place alive."

18

CONCHITA UNCORKED THE BOTTLE OF JOY AND took a sniff. It smelled of flowers, like the rosewater in the church of San Juan Campostella where she had grown up. The fourteen-year-old maid didn't dare touch a drop to the nape of her neck. If Berger smelled the scent on her, she would lose her job and would be sent back to her poor fishing village, where only the undertaker had perfume, to sprinkle on the dead. With the delicate essence still fresh in her nostrils, she wistfully replaced the bottle among the other crystal decanters on the service cart, beside the pillowcases, towels, and chocolate mints.

Conchita loved her job. Her prim black uniform with its starched white apron allowed her to peek into the private lives of the rich, to observe a glittering world she found as intoxicating as Joy. But tonight her work was drudgery. Berger had assigned her to make up the suites while the rest of the staff was downstairs at the party serving the guests. It didn't seem fair that she should be the one condemned to make the rounds, walking the empty corridors to turn down the guests' beds for the night. She was the prettiest of all the girls on the staff— the waiters had told her so—and she longed for the chance to flirt with her admirers, her dark eyes flashing as the music played in the moonlight.

Just one more guest room, and she would be able to go out on the patio herself. The final room was apart from the others, under a staircase in a hallway that wasn't even air-conditioned. Why would a guest select this fetid spot over one of the luxurious oceanfront suites? She stepped cautiously into the shadows of the stairwell, where she knew poisonous spiders spun their webs.

Conchita knocked on the door. There was no reply. The guest was downstairs, she brooded, enjoying the party like everyone but herself. She inserted the passkey into the lock and the door creaked open. Overwhelmed by the stink of whiskey and cigarette smoke, she pushed the door wide open for air. She flicked the wall switch, but nothing happened. The light bulbs had been removed from the crystal chandelier. She squinted to adjust her eyes to the dim light from the window.

A greasy dinner plate and a bottle of· bourbon sat on the chest of drawers. And something on the bedstand beside it riveted her gaze: a hairy form six inches long. At first glance, she thought it was a jungle rat. But it was too large for that. A closer look revealed it was a scalp of human hair. She had never seen a toupee before, but she knew the guests resorted to many strange practices. Two rooms earlier, she had mistaken a woman's false eyelashes for a tarantula.

Her gaze traveled to the coffee table on the far side of the room. There were three passports on it, one Panaguan, one American, and one South African. In all the other rooms, each guest had only one passport. She wondered why this guest had three. Was he three times more powerful than the others?

She removed a glass of water from beside the bed to exchange it for a clean one. Something was floating inside it, spinning as she turned the glass in the half-light. It was a human eyeball. Before she could recoil from the shock, a hand reached out of the darkness and plucked the tiny sphere out of the water. She whirled around and stared into a skeletal face: Curzon. He deposited the glass eye in his left socket and leered at her, his teeth gleaming mother-of-pearl in the twilight. *"Buenas noches."*

She backed toward the door. *"Buenas noches."* Her voice trembled. As she edged away, she could see he was wearing wrinkled white trousers, held up by red suspenders, and a stained white shirt. He had deep lines around his mouth, like the nun at the convent school in San Juan Campostella who had always smiled before she beat her. He wasn't just any guest. She had heard murmurings among the staff that he was, in his own way, more powerful, even, than the government officials. She understood no English, but when he spoke to her in that unfamiliar tongue, she was too fascinated to run away. She hovered with one foot in the corridor, just in case.

"I seen you down there," he said, gazing out at the shanties, their kerosene fires flickering in the darkness. "I liked what I saw. The other girls all look like they got hit with an ugly stick. But your skin is as fresh as a Georgia peach. You've even got all your teeth."

She didn't understand his words, but the way he looked at her—she had seen that hunger often enough on the faces of men in the shanties. She averted her eyes shyly and turned to leave.

"Quédate aquí," he said. "Stay." But she shook her head, her long black hair rippling down her back, and started to pull the service cart out of the room. She was surprised when he spoke in rapid Spanish. "If you don't stay," he said, "I'll tell the manager I caught you stealing from my room." She hesitated, then stepped back inside. "Now close the door," he continued in Spanish. She did so. He must not complain to Berger. The manager had caught her stealing chocolate mints from the cart today. He had warned her: once more and she was out.

"Sientate." He beckoned her to the chair next to his. She hesitated, then perched primly on the edge.

"You're going to be a perfect listener." He chuckled and lapsed back into English. "You don't understand a blessed word. That's the way I like it. That's the way it's gotta be. 'Cause I'm the only one knows what's coming. Oh, it's worth waiting for, all right. If I live long enough." He handed her the massive binoculars resting on his lap. "Here, have a look. *Mira."* She tried to steady the heavy binoculars before her eyes. When she looked through them, the darkness outside the window was transformed into bright relief, a fiery vision of red trees against a purple sky, light as day.

"Infrared binocs." He chuckled. "Pretty nifty, huh?" She didn't understand. But he had whetted her curiosity. What other toys did he have to show her? Maybe he wasn't going to hurt her after all. Maybe he was just lonely. She had heard the older women in the shanties say that a girl who knew how to keep a rich man company could be handsomely rewarded.

He reached into the cart and took out a handful of mints. "Here's something to tickle your fancy," he said. "Go ahead," he coaxed in Spanish, handing them to her. "Help yourself."

"No, gracias." She feared Berger's wrath.

"Why not?" He winked. She hesitated. She *did* love candy. She unwrapped one, rolling the silver foil into a bright bauble, and placed the mint on her tongue like a communion wafer. She sucked it slowly to make it last. When she looked up at him, she could see that he was staring at her lips. He disappeared into the shadows by the washbasin and emerged with the hotel's complimentary bottle of Joy. She quivered as he uncorked the bottle and dabbed the perfume at the base of her neck. It was worth the risk of an old man's hands for her to receive the gift she coveted. Enraptured by the scent, she allowed him to unbutton her uniform and slip it down over her shoulders as he drenched her in the perfume.

"Doctor," he murmured softly, *"médico,"* and from his gentle touch, she believed him. The old physician who had visited her fishing village once when she was sick with the fever had given her pills that had made her feel good. Maybe this stranger would make her feel good, too. She felt his hand graze her breast and wondered if she should scream. But why? He wasn't hurting her. He was being very, very nice. Maybe if he liked her, he would adopt her, take her to faraway places even more elegant than the hotel.

Her fear yielded to excitement, and her body grew taut under his caresses. She had never slept with a man, and the few whom she had allowed to touch her body had been much rougher with her than he was now. He ran his hand over the contours of her buttocks, along her budding breasts, shaping the soft curves of her hips like a sculptor, his touch feather-light. Her breathing quickened as the dress dropped to the floor.

"Just because you're a little Indian girl, no reason you can't have nice things, too," he murmured, and her eyes widened in amazement as he grabbed a second bottle of perfume from the cart and emptied it over her, until her torso glistened, sticky-sweet from the scent. "That stuff ain't cat piss," he said. "Sells on the open market for fifty bucks an ounce." She closed her eyes, too intoxicated by her perfumed body to move.

"Nothing wrong with being naked," Curzon said. "Better than that tacky old maid's uniform. Why, I bet when your folks lived in the jungle just a few years back, they was naked as jaybirds themselves." He was starting to sweat, as he ran his hand down her belly to her torn panties. "These here your only pair? Why, you poor thing!" He pulled down the panties to reveal a mist of pubic hair.

Once more he ducked into the darkness to rummage in his suitcase. She stood there nude, sucking the chocolate off her fingers. Already she was imagining how she would tell the other maids of her adventure. They might not believe her, at first. But they would envy her.

He returned with a container that looked like one of the black tins of caviar from the kitchen. Another exotic treat. But when he unscrewed the lid, she saw it was shoe polish.

He stuck his finger into the paste and daubed ocher lines on her cheeks, chuckling to himself. "All my life I been out there in that forest. Lined my pockets good, but I never found me a jungle beauty like you, all gussied up in war paint. All I got was jungle rot." He put down the can and admired his handiwork.

The scent of shoe polish drowned out the perfume. For Conchita, the daydreams were over.

He unzipped his fly.

"No!" She lunged for the door, but he tore her wrist from the handle. She felt the touch of steel against her belly: the barrel of his Luger.

"No sweat. I'm not gonna pop your cherry. I wouldn't want to spoil your chances to get a handsome *caballero*."

He dragged her toward him with the strength of a much younger man, and she couldn't wrench herself free. He forced her to her knees. "You don't know how," he said, "but I'll teach you real good. Pretty soon you'll be an expert. Then all the boys'll like you. You'll see."

She resisted even now, until he pressed the gun against her head. He forced himself inside her mouth. "Don't bite it, honey," he instructed her in Spanish. He was limp at first, but her mouth was so childlike that even before he was erect, he filled it. "There, that's good. Use your tongue. . . . Oh boy . . . !"

Gagging, she tried to squirm free, but he held her head tightly to his crotch. She made a small terrified sound. "Go ahead, whimper," he said. "Natural thing for you to be afraid." He smiled, stroking her hair. "That makes your mouth all hot and dry. Even nicer for me, don't you know." He was hardening as he spoke and cackled with an old man's pride. She tried to pull back, but he only forced it deeper, into her throat.

"Macho, eh? Muy macho!"

She was moving her lips up and down his shaft, sucking in a desperate reflex. "Now ease up a bit. . . ." He pushed her shoulders back and forth to move her head in the rhythm he longed for. "Good girl! You're a hard worker, you surely are!"

She was suffocating now, and her mind swarmed with images of writhing albacore, choking on the hook that murdered them.

"I'm the big man," he roared. *"El numero uno!"* A death rattle of orgasm shook his body. He pushed her away, and freed at last from the tube of flesh, she inhaled a few quick breaths that sounded like sobs.

"Yo soy amigo de Lopez," he said. *"No diga nada a nadie.* Don't tell a soul." A tear ran down her cheek.

* * *

Conchita pushed the service cart along the corridor away from Curzon's room, tears smearing the makeshift war paint. Her mouth no longer tasted of chocolate—it was sour, like brackish water. Her uniform clung to her sweat-soaked body. And her mind punished her, as unforgiving as the windows that perched like crows in the doorways of San Juan Compostella. She longed to grow old and ugly, to mourn what she had lost.

She maneuvered the cart carefully at first, to keep the bottles of perfume from rattling as the wheels glided along. But something caught in her throat. Gagging, she doubled over and threw up on the impeccable beige carpet. Even the smell of vomit was a relief from the salty substance that had nauseated her. Her pace grew more self-assured now, as she pushed the cart to pick up speed, shoving it faster and faster until it clattered down the hallway. She reached the far end of the corridor and, after kicking open the door to the servants' stairs, sent the cart careening down them. It tumbled end over end and crashed to the ground. The smashing glass was drowned out by the laughter of guests on the patio.

She looked down at her handiwork with satisfaction, inhaling the scent of Joy wafting up from the dank stairwell. When she reached the servants' shanties, she washed off her body with muddy water.

Orgasm had offered no magic for Curzon, only relief. The rage at his forced vigil was replaced by a satiety that enabled him to stay at his post. He took out a cassette and inserted it into his tape recorder, then pressed the button. "Lou Gehrig at bat, bottom of the third. . . ." It was the '36 World Series, Yankees against Giants, and he knew each hit and strike by heart, each time the crowd would rise to its feet with a roar. "Ball three, strike two . . . full count. Here's the windup. The pitch. . . ." The words were his lullaby, one he had listened to a hundred times before. It comforted him to know who would bobble the ball and who would cross home plate in glory. In the time capsule unspooling before him, there would be no surprises. He wished to God he understood his own game as well, a game unfolding so treacherously. True, the risk was great, but if he pulled it off, he'd be able to have his own box at Yankee Stadium. Hell, he'd be able to *buy* Yankee Stadium.

"*A home run. . . .!*" The crowd's roar drowned out the announcer. That game was more than forty years ago, he mused. How many in that throng were dead? In the silence, their cries resounded like a chorus of ghosts. Yet he preferred those phantom thousands to the night outside his window. Only after sunrise would he be free to rest.

He swore at himself for letting his gaze stray from the window during his few seconds of orgasm. Had he missed the signal? When he had gone downstairs for food—in that three-minute interval on the stairway—had it come then?

He took a swift snort of coke from an envelope in his pocket, using the edge of a fingernail to insert the powder into his nostril. Energized by the rush, he forced the binoculars to his bloodshot eyes and scanned the darkness. He had spent most of his life trespassing. And in all those years, the jungle had begrudged him a just reward. Tonight he had offended the jungle, humiliated it in war paint, raped it. Witnessing his act of defiance, would the jungle punish him, force him to wait even longer?

His wrists ached from the weight of the binoculars. It was going to come soon—but *how* soon? The hours of vigilance had stiffened his back, and in his pain, he realized he had been wrong to think that he had been raping the jungle all these years. The jungle had been raping him: sapping his energy, sucking out his life.

19

DESPITE A POTENT BLEND OF RUM, CHAMPAGNE, and exhaustion, Chris lay awake most of the night, turning a decision over and over in her mind. Staying at the hotel had little to offer. There was no hope of prying any information out of Lopez or his men. The real story led into the jungle on a trek to the upper Marañon with Tobias—to learn the truth from the Warak survivors—to capture a photo essay of a people exiled from their homeland.

She felt confident that Graner would want her to go. This was what he called a "getting the serum to the baby" story, the kind that grabbed readers by the throat. When she returned with her coverage, he would be thinking Pulitzer. And right now, giddy from the prospect, she was thinking Pulitzer, too.

Of course, she would have to persuade Tobias to let her join her forced march into the jungle. But that didn't worry her. She had scars to prove her endurance—the marks of leeches in Sarawak, the wound of a pungi stick from the Ho Chi Minh Trail. Tobias might protest at first, but on so grueling an expedition she could use all the help she could get.

In the final analysis, impulse, not reason, sealed her decision. For the hotel gave her a mounting sense of claustrophobia, while the jungle offered escape. It would be easier to face wild creatures than the fears spawned within these walls.

The electronic chirping of the digital alarm woke her at five-thirty. Outside her window, the sky glowed faintly. She was relieved to find that her khakis and T-shirt were still in the wastebasket where she had heaved them the day before. They stank from the sweat of India. No matter. They'd be soaked with fresh perspiration by the time she was ten yards into the jungle. She laced up her boots and strapped the pouch of insect repellent, antibiotics, and Lomotil to her belt, grateful she'd kept the pills with her from the Gir. What she didn't use for the rigors of the hike, she'd give to the tribe.

She stepped into the corridor. Berger had given Tobias a room on the story below all the other guests, in an alcove near the fire exit. When she neared it, she could hear the room's radio was playing a cheerful mariachi tune. She knocked on the door. No answer. She tried the handle. It was unlocked, and swung open to her touch.

"Good morning." The words froze on her lips. The room had undergone a convulsion. She staggered backward, as if in its chaos the floor were spinning, throwing her against the wall from centrifugal force. It was inconceivable that a human being could wreak such havoc. Only an earthquake, a tornado could destroy with such ferocity. The furniture had disintegrated into splintered fragments; the mattress had been torn to shreds. And on the wall, like the signature of the victim, a smear of blood clotted rusty brown—the imprint of a four-fingered hand. It was the only trace of Dr. Eleanor Tobias. A power of unthinkable intensity had been unleashed in the room, yet there was no sign of violent entry. Had Tobias felt secure with the murderer, and opened the door unwittingly? Or had the lethal energy somehow seeped inside—under a window, through a keyhole—like a potent strain of nerve gas? Murder was etched into the shambles, as on the pavements of Hiroshima, where after the blast, shadows were seared into the stones.

Her boots crunched over the broken glass that littered the floor, the shards sparkling in the rising sun. It was the medicines, dozens, perhaps scores, of broken bottles. Tobias's gifts had been squandered, and so had the Warak's chances of survival.

Chris turned off the radio, as if music in this grim setting were a crime. She reached for the phone but realized it had been severed from the wall. On unsteady legs, it was all she could do to climb up the flight of stairs to her room and call Berger.

She didn't tell him what had happened, perhaps to delay her own realization. She only asked him to come—at once—to Tobias's room. Then, she grabbed her camera and hurried back there herself.

Standing at the threshold, she hesitated before taking a single picture. She possessed the same incriminating knowledge that had cost Tobias her life. Did the murderer realize that too? Harley Stokes's plane would not be coming back for another three days. Until then, she was a likely target.

She started sifting through the wreckage, convinced that clues were hidden here, if only she could identify them. The lock to a battered leather suitcase had been pried open, she judged, by a hunting knife. Its contents—books on anthropology by the likes of Margaret Mead—littered the floor. From the modest possessions strewn helter-skelter—reading glasses, hiking boots, a toilet kit—she could see that the anthropologist was a woman of austere tastes. And just as she had suspected, there was no trace of the documents Tobias had promised.

Something gleamed among the debris: a gold pocket watch. On the back was an inscription: "With appreciation for thirty years of dedicated service—American Anthropology Association." It surprised her that the watch was still there. Mercenaries were a greedy lot. In Uganda she had seen them pry the gold fillings from the mouths of corpses. She turned the watch over in her palm. Its face was smashed. The hands had stopped at 3:43.

Berger appeared in the doorway in a velour bathrobe and slippers, breathless from a dash up the stairs.

"*Gott in Himmel!*" he gasped. The blood drained from his face, and he leaned against the door.

"I came in to see her," Chris said in a monotone. "The door was open . . . I found this. . . ."

"You came here at six in the morning?" His tone was accusatory.

"Tobias was going into the jungle," she said. "She was going to take me with her."

Reluctantly, he seemed to accept her explanation. "I let her stay here," he said. "I gave her this room. It was my fault."

She was surprised at how quickly his shock had turned into guilt. His hands fluttered, attempting to tidy up his thoughts, a task as hopeless as it would have been to tidy up the room. He sighed. "I knew what they would do to her if they found her, but I let her stay. I as good as killed her."

She put a hand on his arm. "Dr. Tobias was grateful for all you did."

He nodded grimly. "I bent the rules, and this is what happens."

"Do you know who did this?"

"I have no doubt," Berger said.

"Then let's contact the authorities."

He laughed bitterly. "They *are* the authorities!"

She didn't reply. She had found a grim trophy and lifted it, without a word, for him to see: a bathrobe, its collar sodden with blood. She felt the onset of tears. Why did the loss of this stranger affect her so deeply? Was it because in the lonely, adventurous old woman she had seen what she herself might become? She stared at the bloodstained garment. Only a jugular wound could bleed like that.

"She knew she was going to die," Chris said.

He nodded. "She was ready for it." There was anger in his voice, as if Tobias had sabotaged his tiny world. "But when she started to involve you, that was quite another matter." His blue eyes met hers. "I saw you talking with her at the balustrade last night. For your sake, I hope to God Lopez's men didn't see you, too."

Chris struggled to remember: the mercenary who had passed them so nonchalantly on the patio last night—had he recognized her?

"Stay out of this," Berger warned. "No one can help Dr. Tobias now." He waved a hand around him. "You see what these people can do. Don't get involved."

But she ignored his warning. "What have they done with the body?" she asked.

He was already leaning into the bathroom for a look. The room was immaculate, the tile gleaming, the mirror over the sink intact. He opened a closet. It was empty. He shook his head.

"We'll never see her again," he said. "They have a way of disposing of their victims that is . . . most efficient. Sometimes they let the corpse drift out to sea, to feed the sharks. Or they just drag it a few yards into the jungle. After the scavengers get at it . . ."

But Chris couldn't stop her mind from descending down twisted paths: was the jugular wound that had drenched Tobias's bathrobe with blood the first step in an ancient ritual? She wondered what Tobias's face might look like, shrunken to the size of a fist, her skin leathery from the scalding pot, her lips sewn shut, her common sense replaced by an eternal wisdom. Chris felt a sudden chill and started toward the window to catch the warmth of the rising sun.

"Wait!" Berger stopped her in mid-stride, stepping to the window himself.

She peered down cautiously at the patio. "Great!" It was the mercenary from last night, staring up at Tobias's suite with binoculars.

"Go back to your room," Berger said. "Go back to sleep." He led her into the hall, slamming the door behind them as if locking the event into the past.

"Please," he pleaded, "do not mention this to anyone. I will see that the professor's belongings are disposed of . . . properly. Her remains, if and when they are found, will be handled with respect. *Just stay out of this.*" He was squeezing her arm tightly now, so tightly it hurt. "For what happened to Dr. Tobias, I take a large measure of responsibility. But if you choose to disregard my advice, I cannot, I *will* not, be responsible for your life."

20

DRESSED IN A BIKINI, CHRIS STEPPED INTO THE glare of the patio. Her mind remained locked in the blood-spattered room. Was Margot's prophecy coming true? The waves raced each other to shore as if, like events, they were rolling too fast for her to keep up, each breaker violently canceling out whatever meaning the last might hold.

As she walked across the flagstones, the sun beat down with a vengeance, forcing her to bow her head like a penitent. She needed a hat to shelter her from the heat but wasn't about to venture into the souvenir shop to buy one. Was she afraid of finding Dr. Tobias's head dangling among the souvenirs?

The sight of the couple sitting on the patio stopped her in her tracks. Margot was chatting with Curzon, and her frilly sundress, his white suit made the couple seem oddly Victorian. Chris couldn't resist the temptation to discover what had brought them together.

"You see?" Margot called to her. "You see *that?*" She waved a piece of paper. "A ray of light, Miss Latham. A ray of hope! I just double-checked my computations, and according to Mr. Curzon's horoscope, everything is going to work out splendidly for him."

"I'm... I'm glad to hear that," Chris said, but she feared she didn't sound convincing. A rosy future for someone as unsavory as Curzon boded well for no one else. He was dozing off in his chair, but even his snoring failed to deter the spinster, who lingered at his side, perhaps in the hope that his good luck might rub off on her.

Chris approached the mercenaries positioned along the balustrade cautiously, as if nearing a wall of barbed wire. A grim substitute for beach boys, she thought. Yes, they would have been capable of anything, even the destruction she had seen this morning.

The guests were sprawled on the sand like victims of a firing squad: Inez and Rima lay face down, their bikini tops untied, glistening with suntan oil; flat on his back, Alan nursed a drink in a coconut; Irv and Dawn fiddled with a transistor radio that picked up nothing but static.

Nearby, squat as a toadstool, Torres picked his teeth at the foot of a palm tree. He watched the sweltering guests with satisfaction, as if he had stoked the furnaces himself.

Chris helped herself to a beach umbrella and a towel. Anything beat staying alone in the hotel. The sand scalded the soles of her bare feet, but she kept walking past the other guests, along the lace hem of the surf. She couldn't bring herself to lie down in the sun. To bare her throat, expose her seminude body to the insidious power at large was more than she was willing to risk.

An object in the sand blocked her way—something the size of a large coconut—and she stumbled over it. Quickly she averted her eyes, as if the image were one she had dreaded— and expected—all along. When she finally forced herself to gaze down at it, her heart stopped: *a human head in the sand*. The head of Scott Hershey, his eyes glassy, his tongue lolling from the side of his mouth. The head looked as though it had been freshly severed, color still flushing its cheeks. Chris's knees wobbled.

Suddenly the head winked at her and burst out laughing. "Stay cool," Scott chortled. "Stay cool!" and like a corpse rising from the grave, he pulled himself out of the hole in the sand where he had been buried and trotted into the water. Chris leaned on her beach umbrella for support.

"Easy now. . . ." It was Alan, wearing a boxer swimsuit and a straw hat one size too small. She felt like telling him everything. But what could he do? She couldn't afford to involve someone who knew even less than she did—and who might be even less able to handle it.

"It's just the sun, I guess," she said, and continued walking.

"Here. Take this." He placed the hat on her head. "You know what they say about mad dogs and journalists." He raised a hollowed coconut containing a ruby-red brew. "Would a slug of this help? It's guaranteed to destroy all the right brain cells."

She shook her head. "I'll be all right."

His eyes searched hers. "Whatever it is, I'm here if you need me."

"I'll remember that." Though she pretended to be comforted by his offer, it did nothing to help.

She wandered off down the beach, until she could walk no

farther, and collapsed. It took all her energy to rake her fingers through the sand. The glittering grains reminded her of glass spattered across a highway after a wreck. A conch shell lay nearby, and she started to lift it to her ear, but threw it back in the sand. She couldn't bear to hear the sinister murmurings of its hollow chambers. In her agitated state, the violent moments of her career came back to haunt her, and she relived a *grand guignol* of images she had repressed: a leper in Sri Lanka; a living skeleton from a famine in the Sahel; a ten-year-old prostitute in a cage in Bombay; a Cambodian "enemy of the state" who was buried up to his neck, until, with one clean sweep of a sledgehammer, the executioner sent his head rolling across the ground. *Heads....*

She heard shrieks from a hundred yards down the beach. Dawn was splashing through the surf in a string bikini, giggling as she ran. Lopez trotted after her on an Arabian mare, stripped to the waist, his hairy chest bathed in sweat and sea foam. Dawn's thighs flashed white in the spume, her blond hair catching the sunlight, streaming like the thoroughbred's mane as she ran. When her bobbing breasts bounced free, she yanked off her bra and threw it behind her, racing along the water's edge. Lopez scooped it out of the waves and, laughing, spurred his horse into a canter, its hooves shooting up a wall of spray. Suddenly he reined the mare in, and the horse reared out of the water. Lopez looked around him. No sign of Dawn.

She burst to the surface. "Better luck next time!" She skipped out of the water, cupping her breasts in her arms. Irv wrapped a terry-cloth robe around her, like the manager of a boxer who had won an opening bout.

Looking like a bedraggled hound after the fox had given him the slip, Lopez spurred his mare out of the water. When he found himself facing Chris, he brightened. "The chase." He grinned, assuming the role of a good loser. "My horse Alcazar and I have run many together. And of all the creatures we hunt, women are the most elusive prey."

"Oh?" Chris wondered just how elusive he had found a certain anthropologist to be. She controlled her anger. "I didn't realize you had invited Dr. Tobias here," she said, to gauge his reaction.

"Who?" His face revealed no flicker of recognition.

"Dr. Eleanor Tobias. I suppose you might describe her as one of your enemies."

Lopez laughed. "I have a few friends. It's easy to remember their names. But do you expect me to know the names of all my *enemies?*"

"An anthropologist," she continued, her adrenaline pumping.

He snapped his fingers, as if remembering. "Tobias . . . a *señora* . . . an American. Yes, I remember now. I know of her work. You have an expression for her in English, I believe. A bleeding heart."

"Is she bleeding thanks to you?"

Her frontal assault failed. His face betrayed no hint of guilt. "Are you making a joke?" he asked. "In any case," he continued, less warmly, "I can assure you that there is no Dr. Tobias staying at this hotel."

Alcazar was fighting the bit, as if sensing his rider's impatience to leave. "Enjoy the sun." He pointed at a single white cloud teetering on the horizon. "The storm will be here sooner than you think." He nodded curtly and spurred his horse into a canter, its hooves spitting sand.

She frowned as he raced off along the beach. She had assumed that in a confrontation he would give himself away. But the longer they had spoken, the less sense it all made. What troubled her was not that he denied knowledge of Tobias's stay at the El Dorado. What scared her was that she suspected he was telling the truth.

21

BY NOON A FINE CLOUD LAYER COVERED THE SKY, like the white ceramic coating inside a kiln. Chris lay crucified in the blinding glare. Her skin was roasting under the suntan oil and she dreamed that her head was shrinking, shrinking, to a shriveled lump. The heat sapped her strength, and it was all she could do to prop herself up on one elbow to study the others, sprawled like driftwood on the beach.

Rima and Inez were joined at the head like Siamese twins. Scott appeared to have passed out, though whether from the heat or from some exotic drug, it was impossible to tell. Alan snored, using an empty coconut as a pillow. And Irv squatted beside Dawn's supine body, a landlord with his property. The producer was engaged in what was certainly the most strenuous activity on the beach—sculpting two large mounds of wet sand which bore a startling resemblance to Dawn's breasts.

Like a warning bell on an overheating oven, a gong rang from the patio. In slow motion, the guests mobilized themselves for lunch. All but Chris. She had lost her appetite in the blood-spattered room.

"Lunch?" Alan beckoned for her to join him.

"I'll pass," she replied. He managed a smile as he joined the others. She could see how each of her rejections hurt him. But he had no one to blame but himself for coming back for more.

She was alone with the mercenaries now, and their hostile gaze from the patio felt harsher than the sun's glare. She turned away from them, and squinted at the bottle-green sea. It seemed calmer than the land, free from human complications. It promised a place to think, to unravel the tangled doubts plaguing her; a place to escape the mercenaries' prying eyes.

She found an air mattress by the parasols and dragged it down to the water. The cool surf soothed her as she waded in up to her waist. Launching the rubber raft into the waves, she had to fight the undertow to keep from being dragged off her feet. But as soon as she paddled beyond the breakers, the raft rocked her with surprising gentleness. Even the sun seemed benign.

At first, she thought she had shed the fears that had haunted her since her arrival—and that had turned to panic with To-bias's death. But it was too late. The fears nibbled at her mind like rats. She stopped paddling and lay on her back, her eyes shut, her mind groping to understand the morning's events. Yet the harder she tried to concentrate, the more her thoughts wheeled restlessly, like the gulls circling overhead.

She leaned on an elbow and peered into the water, but instead of the clarity the calm surface had promised, the water was clouded, obscured by crosscurrents. She couldn't erase from her mind the image of Scott's head in the sand. Somehow the childish prank held a crucial relevance. Was it a link with the grisly trophies in the souvenir shop? Was it a prophecy of the future?

She was pushing herself too hard. To keep pawing over the memory of Tobias's murder would be necrophilia. She needed to catch her breath, to regain her strength for the quest that would resume the moment she set foot on dry land.

From her vantage point in the water, the hotel seemed dwarfed by the sea and sky, no longer an oppressive presence. It was easier to place it in perspective now. She had survived many dangers. "This, too, shall pass."

The violent moments of her life receded. In her world travels, she realized, she had seen much that was joyful: she had tasted the exquisite ices sold on Paris street corners; seen colors as radiant as the peacocks of the Gir. Swept along on gentle currents, she allowed her mind to drift into the gardens of the Alhambra, to inhale the scent of orange blossoms, and the honeysuckle and rose petals that floated in reflecting pools. Her dream, if she could ever find a man, was to spend her wedding night in those fragrant gardens, under the yellow lantern of a Granada moon.

Water sloshed against the side of the raft, and she opened her eyes in time to see a dorsal fin knifing through the water. But instead of running at attack depth like a shark's, it arced playfully out of the water. A porpoise was watching over her, escorting her with maternal care. She trailed her arm languidly

in the water, and her face relaxed into a smile. Rocked by the
waves, drifting with her memories on the rubber raft, she soon
forgot where she was, lost in the limbo of the deep blue sea.
For others, perhaps, an uneasy state. But to Chris Latham, the
eternal transient, a taste of peace.

At first, Chris thought it was all a dream, for it had a
nightmare's wrenching suddenness. But the salt water that
choked her was real. Even before she awoke, her arms and
legs were flailing, fighting for her life. The storm had struck
with sudden force, as if the elements had waited until she dozed
off, until she was at their mercy. The raft had been swept away,
and from the pressure on her eardrums she knew she was more
than ten feet deep—soon to be entombed in indigo waters. She
looked up. The glimmer of the surface seemed higher than the
El Dorado. She could feel the air bubbles streaming from her
nostrils, like strings of pearls, but much more precious. *My
God, I'm drowning!* She lashed out with her arms and legs as
if to scramble up a sheer cliff. *I'm drowning!*

The salt water that had once buoyed her up now imprisoned
her. Her hands and feet were going numb, as with a desperate
kick she shot to the surface. Sound exploded on her: the moan
of a gale. She gasped for breath, but the ocean forced down
her throat an unholy brew of salt spume and heavy rain. She
searched for a landmark, but there was no way to see the shore
above the mountainous whitecaps. One breath was all she got,
before the waves swept her under again, thrusting her so deep
she knew she would never be able to fight her way back up.

There was only one way out now: to accept the invitation
and sink into the abyss. To let her watery murderer cradle her
for eternity.

All the close calls from her past suddenly ended with a
twist. The lion in the Gir completed its attack lunge, tearing
her limb from limb. Harley Stokes's DC-3 crashed, blossoming
into flame. And she toppled off the hotel roof onto the patio,
her skeleton shattered on the flagstones.

She could no longer resist. The tide was toying with her,
and she drifted at its whim, helpless as a sea anemone. Her
eyes no longer saw. Her body was numb. Her whole life was
reduced to a single sensation—something gripping her leg,
with enough force to wrench it from its socket. She wondered,

in her final delirium, if death had seized her. At least now she *had* an enemy, a focus for her rage, and she lashed out at it. If only she could fight free from its grasp, she might live. But though she struggled fiercely, its hold over her grew.

"God!" Tears filled her eyes, droplets as puny in this briny infinity as her own life. She flailed her arms in one last desperate lunge. There was a sharp blow on her head, and it was over. Her lips, closed so tightly to block out the inevitable, opened at last, to drink.

Drifting back to consciousness, Chris floated in a starless void. There her senses revived, one by one. Her mouth tasted of seaweed and bile and vomit. It was painful to breathe, almost more painful than drowning—or *had* she drowned? No, she could feel wet sand against her skin as the earth shook with the impact of waves. She could smell sea cucumbers and squid that had been hurled ashore in the storm's frenzy. Her arms and legs were too sore to move. Though she was out of the ocean, water still engulfed her, rain pelting down. Where was she? Squinting through wet lashes, she could see the El Dorado's beach, a sodden gray in the deluge.

A figure hunched over her, breathing hot air from its mouth into hers. From the taste of the lips, she knew it was a man. His body was wet, and it smelled of the sea. With their lips joined, their faces were too close together for her to tell the stranger's identity. She opened her mouth to speak, but pain stopped her. She raised a hand to her bruised jaw.

"I had to hit you," the voice said. "You were pulling me down, too. We both would have drowned." She started, queasily, to sit up, and realized her breasts were bare. He wrapped a towel around her, and she huddled under it. "You almost didn't make it. I was ready to give up on the artificial respiration."

Chris wiped the salt water from her eyes. After hearing such excellent English, she was surprised by the face—an Indian in his mid-thirties, clean-shaven, with solemn, intelligent eyes. And oddly familiar. She'd seen the face somewhere before. His perfect English meant he wasn't a member of the staff. Was he a mercenary? None she had ever met would save a life. She tried to speak, but her lips couldn't shape the words.

"You saved my life," she said at last, her teeth grating on sand. He didn't reply. Her skin had broken into goose bumps.

Shivering, she closed her eyes and managed to stop her teeth from chattering long enough to fill her lungs with another gulp of air.

When she opened her eyes, he was gone.

22

CHRIS TRUDGED WEARILY UP THE BEACH. THE MER-
cenaries had deserted their posts in the driving rain, yielding
to a slimy contingent of sea slugs and giant snails. The waves
continued their bombardment, the green surf slithering up the
sand, nipping at her heels. She picked her way over a dozen
scattered beach umbrellas. The wind had strewn them like
jackstraws to foretell the future, but as with so much else here,
Chris thought, she had yet to crack the code.

She had heard that those who reached the cold frontier of
death and came back were supposed to have a serene acceptance
of it, but her own brief journey into oblivion had brought no
insights—only the determination never to totter on the brink
again. Her resouer's identity was a riddle. He joined the other
unseen powers haunting the hotel. She hurried to her room.

After a hot shower her outlook brightened. By the time she
dressed in slacks and blouse the only aftereffect of her ordeal
was what she feared might become a bad case of the sniffles.
The benign spirit that had plucked her from the waves—would
he be capable of more? Would her new ally understand the
mystifying forces at work here? Tracking him down was her
top priority.

She stepped into the corridor, her trigger finger itching, a
loaded Rollei SLR hanging from her wrist thong. It was 2 P.M.,
the siesta hour, and both the guests and the staff were in their
rooms, dozing behind closed doors. She conducted a hasty
inspection of the lobby, the hallways, the bar. All were deserted. Life in the hotel would not revive for a good two hours.
It would be pointless to continue her search.

On the way back to her room she peered into the restaurant.
A few busboys were clearing away dirty dishes in the dim light
from the window facing the rainswept beach. Alan lingered,
nursing an espresso and a snifter of Rémy Martin. She tried
to avoid him. What she wanted now was the strength of the

guardian angel who had saved her, not Alan's small talk. But he beckoned her over, and there was no turning back.

"So! You accepted my invitation to lunch after all," he said. She could barely manage a smile; his persistence was wearying. "Chris!" She had come close enough for him to get a good look at her, and he seemed shocked at the sight. A glance at her reflection in the silver coffee pitcher told her why: her skin had the color, her hair the consistency, of seaweed. He eased her into a chair, and she was grateful for the small kindness. "You look like hell! What happened?"

She sneezed, and he wrapped his tweed sports coat around her. "I went swimming and got caught in the storm. Dumb."

"It came up like someone flipped a switch," he said. "You were lucky."

"That's debatable." She didn't want to discuss her close call any further. The ordeal was an embarrassment—she had no one to blame but herself.

"Here." He poured her a slug of cognac. "Medicine." He pointed into the shadows. "You came just in time for the floor show."

She followed his gaze over to Torres, sitting alone at a table with a floral centerpiece. He looked as ill at ease as if he were being forced to eat the tulips. He held a menu upside down, and the waiter didn't dare point out the oversight. Torres pretended to read the name of each dish to himself, then had the waiter describe it to him aloud.

"I don't think he's up on the fine points of haute cuisine," Alan said as Torres speared a roll with a salad fork. "They ought to just throw him a slab of raw meat." Alan struck a match to light a cigar, but one queasy glance from her, and he blew it out. He handed her a menu. "Eat. You'll feel better."

"Maybe some soup or tea. . . ."

"I'd recommend the consommé," he said. "A nice chicken stock." She looked at him skeptically. "No, really!" He picked up the morocco-bound wine list. "Then I know a velvety Côte du Rhône which should help thicken your blood. 'A naïve domestic burgundy,' as Thurber said, 'but I think you'll be amused by its presumption.'" She slumped back in her chair, too weak to reply, and he stared at her with fascination. "I think you're one of the most intriguing women I've ever met. Either you're in total control, or you're a basket case."

"Please pass the basket." She smiled, and he handed her the

pannier. She selected a roll and nibbled the crust. It sank in her stomach like a rock.

He fiddled with his cigar, obviously reluctant to broach the subject. "I don't know what's been happening, what you've been going through since you got here, but whatever it is . . . maybe you'd feel better if you shared it. Is there something I can do?"

She nodded. "Order the soup."

"*¡Camarero!*" He waved to the waiter. Chris found her gaze drawn to one of the busboys. She recognized the intelligent Indian face. The mouth that had breathed life into hers. He was carrying a trayful of dirty dishes when their eyes met. As he darted into the kitchen, the tray went flying, and the dishes crashed to the floor.

She ran after him.

When she burst through the swinging doors into the kitchen, he had vanished. There were only two ways out of the steam-filled room—one past the stoves to the pantry, the other leading outdoors—and she gambled on the latter, elbowing past two chefs who were busy trussing a suckling pig.

Outside, the rain had stopped, but the rumble of the electric generator turbine drowned out the sound of fleeing footsteps. Damn, she swore. She had lost him.

She leaped down the stairs two at a time, past a spilled garbage can he had apparently knocked over in his escape, and ran across the patio. Beyond the steel grating of the turbine enclosure, she found herself among the servants' shanties, crazy quilts of caviar boxes and canvas, champagne crates, and corrugated tin. The rain had soaked the ground to muck, and the smell of damp charcoal and sewage overwhelmed her. Here, too, it was siesta hour, and all but a few stragglers were swinging in their hammocks, asleep.

A toothless hag was scavenging chicken bones from a garbage pit, gnawing the scraps of meat clinging to them. Another crone was pouring the dregs of discarded wine bottles into a jar. The old women eyed her with distrust. She was on their turf now. A stroll among the rambling shacks yielded nothing. She had already turned back toward the hotel when she heard a steady thudding, steel chopping into wood, and was drawn to its source.

The shanties beside the jungle were engulfed in vines. Crouched there, a slender adolescent girl, her dress smeared with mud, was hacking open coconuts with a machete. Chris's arrival made the girl attack the next coconut with heightened ferocity, one blow of the blade splitting the husk in half.

Chris turned and saw the busboy standing with his arms crossed in the doorway of a tin shack. "You look like you've been expecting me," she said.

The stranger didn't answer. He was watching the girl's machete arc through the air, as if the murder on her face expressed his own rage. "Her name is Conchita," he said. "One of the guests used her...the way he wanted." Chris was amazed by his accent—North American and college-bred. He beckoned her inside his shack, slamming a door made from orange crates.

His face revealed as much pride in the hovel, as if it were an elegant suite and she were an intruding maid. "They say this new hotel helps the common people," he said. "How did it help her?"

She didn't reply to the rhetorical question, struggling to decide who the stranger was, what he was doing here. The shack was barely big enough for the two of them, and they stood wedged between a rope hammock and a pasteboard trunk. Water dripped from a crack in the roof. She was surprised to see books scattered everywhere. The books, his fluent English didn't gibe with the squalor.

She offered her hand. "Chris Latham." He gave no name in reply. "I wanted to thank you for saving my life."

"You'll have a chance to return the favor."

"I don't understand...."

"You didn't think I just *happened* to be on the beach, I've been watching over you since your arrival. I couldn't have allowed anything to happen to you, now could I?"

Chris was stunned. "Who *are* you?" she blurted out. "What are you doing here?"

He yanked the cork from a bottle and handed it to her. She suspected it was the brew of the old crones in the garbage pits. "Peasant wine," he said. "After we talk, you'll need it." She took one sip, and that was enough. The wine had already turned, as acid as his words. "Do you find this all very picturesque?" he asked. "Quaint customs of the natives?"

She was angry as she could only get when her curiosity was thwarted. But she could see he had no intention of answering her directly.

A smile played across his lips, hinting for the first time that he saw her as a woman. He pulled off his waiter's coat and threw it onto the hammock. She admired his brown torso, lean and muscled. Like his mind, his body was strong, with no flab to hide its force. There was a boldness, an independence about him that under other circumstances she might have found appealing. But the way he withheld key information from her was nothing short of sadistic. "If you don't explain what's going on," she said, "I'll leave."

"You won't leave until I tell you to." The arrogance of his reply scared her. Its harsh tone jogged something in her mind. Suddenly she understood why his face seemed so familiar. She struggled to recall all she had learned about him in her *View* briefings: born in Panaguas, educated in America at Berkeley, then deported after being convicted of complicity in several terrorist bombings. He soon became the protégé of pro-Castro factions and was indoctrinated at Patrice Lumumba University in Moscow. Blooded with Marxist guerrillas fighting in Angola, he returned to his native Panaguas and. . . . She tried to separate the flesh-and-blood human being standing before her from the poster revolutionary. How could it be? Here? Why would she risk discovery? No, the idea was too farfetched.

But she said it aloud, just the same: "You're Manuel Vargas."

He didn't answer.

"Why are you here? What are you going to do?"

"I'm here," he said calmly, "to watch what *you're* going to do."

She was speechless.

"You see, it *had* to be you. You were the only photographer who came. Of course," he said, "it's dangerous work. I would have preferred a man."

His words rankled her. She suspected they were meant to. Her patience had been strained to the breaking point, and he must have read it in her eyes, for he nodded. "All right, now it must all come out. It comes down to this. . . ." But before he could continue, a shadow flickered under the door. He edged over silently and yanked it open. Conchita had been eavesdropping. She looked up at him in terror. He rested a hand on her shoulder like an understanding parent and walked her outside, speaking to her gently.

In the few seconds she was left alone, Chris had to find out more. She lifted the lid to the battered trunk. Inside was an automatic pistol. And she caught sight of something beside it that was much more terrifying: a photograph of herself. Suddenly she realized that she had not pursued him here at all; he had lured her to this remote spot. She was his prisoner.

23

"THE PISTOL IS RUSSIAN." VARGAS'S VOICE GAVE Chris a start. He had caught her in the act, but her snooping seemed merely to amuse him. "It's not much of a weapon, really—intended for poor Latin countries. The same kind of junk that Americans offer, but at least the Soviets gave it to me free." He handed the weapon to her, but she didn't take it, her eyes lingering on her picture in the trunk.

"What do you want from me?" she asked, unable to hide the fear in her voice.

"You're part of the plan. A very important part."

"What . . . plan?"

"It's simple enough," he said matter-of-factly. "A theft of information. But no objects can be physically removed. A task which makes someone with your talents especially valuable. . . ."

"I don't understand."

He studied her camera. "You own a couple of cheap ones like that—a Rollei and a Mamiya Sekor . . . am I right?" She nodded reluctantly. "But you're most adept with the Leica and the automatic-drive Nikon FTN. You work in close to your subjects. Catch them before they have time to flinch. Pictures grabbed against the clock—quick-draw, you would say." He added, as an afterthought, "The same qualities demanded of a good assassin."

She found his knowledge of her working style unnerving. Whatever his scheme, she wanted no part of it. "I have an exclusive contract with *View*," she said. "No free-lance work."

"Your contract runs through next July," he said. "Am I right again?" Chris was burning. "I hope you live to renew it."

"If you know as much about my life as you seem to," she said, "then you must also know how I feel about terrorism."

"How you feel," he said calmly, "has nothing to do with it."

She considered her only way out: agree to anything, then go to Lopez. Vargas was one step ahead of her. "If you betray me," he said, "I'll kill you."

She realized her first impression of Vargas had been wrong.

He didn't look at her the way a man eyes a woman. He looked at her the way he studied the automatic in his hand: as a weapon that would get him what he wanted. She felt the same resignation she had felt when she was drowning, and there was no choice but to yield to the undertow. "And if I go along with this?" she asked.

His tone changed. He was ready to plunge into the details. "You will be required to photograph certain . . . documents," he began. The ploy was familiar to her, a common practice for the KGB: enlist an innocent bystander through threat or blackmail to commit a crime. Then, if the amateur is killed in the act, nothing can link him to the instigators.

"But even if I take the pictures you want," she said, "what good would they do you here?"

He opened the footlocker again and held up a small canvas sack. She had seen several like it in Vietnam, a minidarkroom for developing film. Once he developed the negatives, he would be able to analyze the data with a magnifying lens.

"Suppose I don't get the documents," she asked. "Suppose I *can't.*"

"I saved you from drowning because I needed you," he said coolly. "If you can't"—he weighed the pistol in his hand like a threat—"you'll be no worse off than if you'd drowned."

No, she thought resentfully, he was wrong. If Lopez or Torres caught her in the act, what they would do to her would make drowning seem humane by comparison.

"When . . . is all this supposed to happen?"

"Tonight."

"Give me time," she pleaded. "I need more time." If she could stall him for a day, put it off until tomorrow, perhaps she could find a way to get out of it.

He shook his head. *"Tonight."*

24

MARGOT REALIZED IT MIGHT BE A TERRIBLE MIS-take. But after the ominous horoscopes, and the night of foul dreams, and the morning of merciless sun on the beach, she was certain it was her only choice.

She had packed the Tarot in her suitcase for the gravest of emergencies. She avoided using the cards because they foretold too much, just as she avoided glancing into the magnifying mirror on her dressing table, which ruthlessly revealed the crow's-feet attacking her face. And now, as the gypsy cards were turned up, shuffled, turned over once more—suits of wands and cups, swords and pentacles—the cards' verdict resounded: The Reaper. A grinning skull with a scythe, fore-telling a lethal harvest.

Astrology might fall prone to errors of computation. Palmistry might lie. But Margot believed in the Tarot. The Tarot spoke the truth.

And Many Would Die. . . .

The skull was smiling, but the hollow sockets of its eyes were as cold as craters on the moon.

And it was a Force beyond pity. . . .

The executioner's bony fingers wielded the scythe with a vengeance.

And there was no escape. . . .

Death had registered at the El Dorado. The Guest of Honor.

She collected the cards again and carried them into the bathroom, where she flushed them down the toilet, like a nest of spiders. Then she donned her hiking garb and headed for the door. She left her note pad behind. Ideas for her next book, issues of financial survival, were meaningless now.

Perhaps her antennae had been the first to detect danger because they were more finely attuned than those of the other guests. Oh, she knew that Chris Latham sensed it, and Berger—yes, the ravages showed on his face as well. As for the others, let them live in a fool's paradise. Knowledge of their fate would do them no good. If anyone could save them, Margot thought, she was the one.

She stole downstairs and across the hotel patio. Eagerly she stepped into the green shadows and waded onto the trail. In the hotel's corridors, her fear had become a palpable, breathing thing, so much more forbidding than the benign spirit she had confronted in the jungle. Could the mystical being offer salvation now? Could its magic combat the Reaper? In a spasm of panic, she had vowed to track down the forest presence. And as she set off into the jungle, she wore lipstick and mascara, to seduce.

The trek that had seemed so terrifying yesterday was now a leisurely stroll with a certain destination. For she was convinced that the presence knew she was coming, that it would be there waiting for her, just as it had been waiting before. She could endure the mosquitoes buzzing around her broad-brimmed straw hat, drawn to her heavy perfume. Even the howling in the treetops no longer terrified her. This was *its* domain, and the unseen creatures—goblin, troll, or griffin—were only the spirit's minions. In this jungle where so few human laws applied, she dared hope the Tarot, too, would be false, and that other more benign laws would prevail.

She groped for the monkey's paw in her pocket and gave it a squeeze, as if she were leading a small child by the hand. The jungle took on a rhapsodic glow, and she could almost convince herself it was enchanted, a shrine to the power she had come here to court.

She caught her first glimpse of the tumbled granite slabs through a web of tree ferns and peperomia vines. The sight of the skulls carved in stone reminded her of the Tarot card she was escaping. The Reaper with its crater eyes had multiplied by thousands, like poppies in a meadow, scented to kill with slumber. Yet the more fretful she became, the more tenaciously she clung to her fantasy. The benign spirit had not harmed her before; it had filled her with wild elation. Now it could save her when all else was beyond hope. Stepping into the clearing, she moistened her lips, as if expecting a lover to sweep her into his arms.

The snap of a twig. She heard it distinctly. *Footsteps.* They were coming closer, a shadow flickering across a stone wall. She took a few hesitant steps forward to meet it—but stopped and backed away. The footsteps were coming from the inner sanctum.

She froze in alarm. *Curzon.* He was clad in the same rumpled shirt and white trousers he had worn on the patio that morning. And he had been watching her. His face looked skeletal, as if he bore a family resemblance to the stone carvings. He spit on the ground, his boot smearing the skull carvings with mud. She wished he would show the shrine more respect. If he offended the gods, she didn't want to be the one to suffer their wrath.

"Afternoon." He winked.

"What . . . what are you doing here?"

He shrugged. "Catching the air. Yourself?"

When he lifted his arm from behind the granite slab, she took a panicked step backward. He held a shotgun. As he raised the weapon to his shoulder and pumped a cartridge into the firing chamber, an apocalyptic vision tore through her mind: the Tarot; the monkey's paw; the blood-filled altar in the inner sanctum. Then she realized she wasn't his target at all. He was firing into the forest, and with each squeeze of the trigger he seemed to relax a notch, discharging an explosive unit of tension.

"Just a little target practice." He ejected the smoking cartridge and slotted another into the chamber. "Want to try?"

Margot didn't reply. She gazed along his line of fire, but saw no target—only a green tangle.

"Shooting my wad. Just ten more rounds to go. It'll be sundown in an hour. Then it's back to the room for the night."

"But . . . why?" she asked. It was his turn not to answer. As he fired again, she could see leaves shivering under the spray of buckshot. She wondered whether he was venting his frustration at having to stay in his room after nightfall.

He lowered the gun and cradled it in the crook of his arm. "Sorry if I gave you a scare," he said. His apology startled her more than the shotgun blasts. In their talk on the beach that morning, when she had figured out his horoscope, he had been barely civil. But even then she hadn't given up. In the lonely mathematics of spinsterhood, she had reduced the guest list to a solitary prospect: Curzon.

"Please stay," he said. "It's been too long since I had honest-to-God feminine companionship." He pulled the trigger again, peppering the foliage. Perhaps, she thought, perhaps this was all meant to happen. Wasn't this a place for unlikely assignations? Like the jungle presence that had lured her here, Curzon, too, stood for good luck. Hadn't his horoscope been the only one that had promised success? "Stay awhile," he repeated.

"Perhaps I will. . . ." She dawdled, pretending to study the skulls carved on the weathered rock, hoping to scrutinize Curzon's motives just as closely. He was somehow different from all the other guests—somehow like her. Others might regard him as "strange," but in that very strangeness he resembled many of the magical people in her life—mystics, mediums, psychics. In exchange for the bizarre behavior that branded them pariahs, they partook of awesome powers.

He lowered the gun, and studied it philosophically. "The diversions of a single man . . ." he mused, and shook his head. "After a while all you want to do is settle down." She was complimented that he was confiding in her. "You fight all your life to be able to support the right kind of woman," he continued, "but by the time you reach my age all the good ones are spoken for." He studied the blue veins on his wrists. "And now, I'm too damn old."

"No, you're not." There was a quaver in her voice she had not intended.

"How come a woman of your refinement never got trapped all these years?" He winked at her, and Margot realized she was blushing. Could it be that he might actually find her attractive?

As he turned once more to blast away at the forest, her heart was pounding. Could the magical stones of this shrine spark a romance? For Margot, such a possibility was more wondrous than any poltergeist.

When the shotgun blasts stopped, she felt compelled to fill the awkward silence. "You certainly seem very *adept* with that," she said.

"Belongs to the hotel. Berger keeps 'em for the guests, to shoot clay pigeons."

She reached out to touch the barrel of the weapon. The steel was so hot it burned her hand, and she pressed a finger coquettishly to her mouth. "I do admire marksmanship. I admire finesse of any kind. . . ."

His eyes met hers. "And I admire a good woman."

She glowed from the compliment, like a dormant jungle flower which could blossom in a single ray of sunlight. For fear that he might continue with something even more personal, she started chattering. "You have no idea how it relieves me to see you indulging in target practice. It's so much more civilized than hunting."

"Needless slaughter of God's creatures." Curzon nodded solemnly.

"Reverence for life," she agreed. "It's the only thing that separates us from the wild beasts. Where," she asked politely, "where *are* your targets?"

He pointed the gun muzzle at the edge of the clearing, but the granite slabs of the temple obscured her view. Awkward in her galoshes, she walked toward the spot where he had been aiming. Vines and branches had been sheared off by the volleys of buckshot, and on the heap of fallen leaves lay his targets. Her eyes brimmed with tears at the sight: half a dozen howler monkeys were writhing in death agony, pathetically human in their spasms of pain.

"You . . . murderer!" she shouted. "You've killed them!" She picked up one of the mangled bodies in her arms, cradling it in a bizarre *pietà*.

Curzon was laughing so hard he turned purple. "Reverence for life!" he cackled. "I did 'em a favor, putting 'em out of their misery!" He slotted in two more cartridges and brandished the shotgun at her. "Maybe I oughta put you out of *your* misery, you shrunken old bag!" Still clutching the dead monkey, she ran down the trail, but the vines tore the corpse out of her arms.

"Monster!" she shouted over her shoulder at him, between sobs. *"Murderer!"* But he had vanished, along with the ruins, behind a curtain of green. She stumbled down the trail toward the hotel, scrambling over rotting tree stumps and twisted lianas. She had taken the risk of opening up to him and had suffered for it. Her mother had been right all along, and in her loneliness she had foolishly ignored her teachings: men were beasts.

Breathless, she reached the patio and, choking back sobs, rushed inside to the front desk. Two mercenaries blocked the doorway to Berger's office, with an arrogance that made her wonder whether they were protecting him or holding him prisoner. Even in the late-afternoon shadows, they wore sunglasses, like night creatures who could only see in darkness.

"Mr. Berger!" she called out. "Please help!"

Grudgingly, the mercenaries let her enter his office. Berger didn't greet her with his usual smile. His face was ashen, his necktie askew. He was sitting at the glowing dials of the shortwave radio console, twisting the frequency-selector dial idly, as if there were nowhere to turn for help. The sight of fresh blood staining Margot's dress brought him to his senses. "What happened?"

Her voice was shrill. "There's a *maniac* out there killing endangered species! And he's using one of your guns!"

Berger seemed too numb to be rattled by her hysteria. "You would be referring to Mr. Curzon?" he answered in a monotone.

"Well? Aren't you going to *do* something? Don't you even care?"

"Of course I care, madam. But . . . the problem you refer to is not likely to recur."

"What?"

He gestured toward a mahogany cabinet in the corner, its lock split in half, its glass doors ajar. She stepped over for a closer look. The cabinet was empty.

"It happened less than an hour ago," he said, and nodded toward the mercenaries. "As you can see, I'm not the only one who's upset." Margot caught her breath, her indignation squelched by the despair in his eyes. "Except for the gun Mr. Curzon borrowed," he said, "all the shotguns, and all the ammunition, have been stolen."

She ran a hand over the mahogany panels of the plundered cabinet. Its message was exactly the same as her Tarot cards. The Reaper was loose. His scythe was sharp, ready for the harvest, and as certain to descend as the next breaker guillotining the beach.

25

CHRIS OPENED HER DOOR A CRACK, TO VIEW THE presidential suite across the hall, as if lining up a target in her camera's viewfinder. Now, at least, her task was straightforward: to reach an objective behind a locked door. The penalty for failure was equally direct. And severe.

She felt her Leica on its thong, a shackle on her wrist. That damned albatross. . . . She glanced at her watch: 11 P.M. The signal should have come by now. She glanced back across the hall. The "Do Not Disturb" sign hanging on the double mahogany doors to the Presidential Suite seemed superfluous, considering the armed guard at the threshold.

She could hear the squeaking of wheels from the direction of the service elevator. A waiter in a white coat was pushing a cart with two ice buckets of champagne. The guard nodded coolly and unlocked the door, watching with his finger on the trigger as the cart was wheeled into the suite. When the waiter emerged seconds later, Chris could see his face: Vargas. He walked past her door and gave two quick taps: the go-ahead.

Poised on the brink, she wondered why she was going through with this. It wasn't just Vargas's threat. It might have been possible to tell Lopez and get him to arrest the revolutionary. But she would never have done that. Maybe her real motive was strictly personal. Her late friend Neil Lawrence, the *View* journalist, had been a victim of the "official hospitality" of Lopez's police. But no, she swept such noble motives aside. There was something childish in her decision to take the plunge. Like a skier facing a virgin slope, she was a junkie for danger. The time had come for her fix.

Her thoughts skidded to a stop, as the guard's walkie-talkie crackled alive. He snapped it up and listened intently. She didn't need to decipher the rapid-fire Spanish. Vargas had explained what it would say: the identification code of the mercenary commander, followed by an order to report to the patio. The guard asked the question she had been primed to expect: "Should I wait to be relieved at my post?"

"Negative," was the reply. "Come now."

He took off down the hall, lowering his M-16 into firing position as he ran. Vargas had told her she would have twelve minutes from the moment he left to do her job—twelve minutes for the guard to reach the patio, search the beach, realize the command was fraudulent, and dash back. But after testing the route herself at a rapid clip, she had narrowed the time to a mere ten minutes. She glanced at her watch: 11:04. She had to be out by 11:14. By then the place would be swarming with troops. But if she did her job right, *if*... they would find nothing.

As she stepped across the hall, she was surprised by her exhilaration. Maybe what Graner had always said in jest was true. Maybe she really did have criminal tendencies.

She inserted the key into the lock. A copy, and a crude one at that, it fitted poorly. She twisted it first left, then right, before it caught with a click. The door creaked open. Even now, standing with a key in Lopez's door, she might have convinced a guard that she had made an innocent mistake. She stepped inside and closed the door behind her. If they caught her now, no alibi would work.

In contrast with the hotel's modern suites, the darkened room was decorated in rococo style, with a damask-canopied bed and gilt-framed pseudo Fragonards on the walls. She was startled by the sound of laughter. My God, she thought, *someone's in the next room!* Vargas had promised the suite would be empty. Had she been led into a trap? She edged across the thick carpeting and peeked through the slats of the French doors to the bathroom. In an enormous sunken tub, Lopez, Inez, and Rima lounged naked in the water, drinking champagne. As he pawed their soap-slick bodies, the girls splashed and giggled. Chris knew she could never attempt her assignment now. They might be out of the tub and into the bedroom any moment. She had to escape immediately.

But when she tiptoed back to the hall door and gripped the knob, she stopped herself. She could see a shadow under the door, hovering in the corridor. Could the guard have made it back already? Had *another* taken his place? She released the doorknob and turned back into the darkened room. She was a prisoner here. Her gaze wavered, then came to rest on Lopez's black leather briefcase, standing out boldly against the white coverlet, its chain locked to the bedpost. She decided to proceed with her task.

Vargas had given her the combination and the briefcase snapped open easily. Damn. The sheaf of documents was much thicker than he had said. She should have expected that. She had chosen a Leicaflex for the job, instead of her Nikon FTN, with its noisier shutter release. It was already loaded with Tri-X, pushed to ASA 800, and she tightened it to a telescoping aluminum tripod. With the camera locked in position, she wouldn't have to frame each shot—just turn the pages and press the button. She aimed the tensor reading lamp at the bedspread, ready to feed the documents into the pool of light one by one.

Click-click. She became a machine, her left hand triggering the camera's automatic drive, her right flipping the pages. As she worked, she shut her mind off, functioning on reflex alone. No time to read the papers she was photographing. Vargas had hinted at their contents: the names of government informers seeded into the ranks of the guerrillas; maps of key airfields and munitions dumps; the troop strength of elite army units. *Click-click*. She was careful to replace each document in the direction she had picked it up, to conceal any hint of tampering. *Click*.

Laughter, and the splashing of water in the bath, blocked out any sounds of Chris at work. Inez poured a glass of champagne over her breasts, and Lopez licked it off. To do her one better, Rima held her breath and ducked below the surface, between his legs. Lopez let out a sigh, his hands stroking her head underwater, and for a moment his eyeballs rolled upward in ecstasy. He forced his hands down hard on her head.

Click-click. Mechanically Chris turned endless pages of names. *Click-click*. Whatever Lopez was doing to the women in there, she hoped he wouldn't stop. *Click-click*.

Rima was struggling to come up for air now, but Lopez held her head under the water with both hands. She was suffocating on his penis, and as a few bubbles trickled up from her nose, he laughed at her desperation. Finally, when it seemed she could hold out no longer, he grunted in orgasm and released her. She lunged to the surface, gasping for breath.

For a second, as she continued to photograph the documents, Chris glimpsed the cruel tableau through the French doors. She was revolted—furious at Lopez, but angry at Inez and Rima, too, for allowing him to humiliate them. *Click-click.* She fired her camera again and again, with mounting satisfaction. Apart from squeezing the trigger of a gun, this was the best way to hasten his destruction.

Damn. The shutter release stuck. She had run out of film. Rewinding the spent roll and slotting in another, she stole a glance into the bathroom: Lopez had climbed out of the tub and was wrapping a towel around him, walking toward the bedroom. Chris had to escape, but her only way out was blocked; the figure still lingered outside in the hall. Lopez pushed open the French doors. Chris barely had time to flick off the lamp. She froze in the shadows.

But before he could set foot into the bedroom, Inez threw her arms around him. She whispered something in his ear. He nodded and climbed back into the tub.

Chris breathed a sigh of relief. It caught in her throat. For without warning Inez pushed open the French doors and ran into the bedroom. The briefcase was open—papers strewn on the bed. Would she *see?*

Inez padded, nude, across the deep-pile carpeting. Chris held her breath. Abruptly Inez faced her. For a chilling moment, their eyes met. But instead of calling to Lopez, Inez placed a finger to her lips. Then she grabbed a vibrator off a shelf and hurried back to the bathroom to join the others.

Chris hesitated, then flicked the lamp on again. Why had Inez kept her secret? There was no time to ponder her motives. For Chris had only a few more documents to go.

Click-click. Finished. The lens had taken its sweet revenge. On an impulse, she aimed through the slats of the bathroom door and snapped a picture of Lopez with the two naked women. *Click.* If Vargas wanted to use it for blackmail, more power to him. She slipped the papers back into the briefcase. After twirling the combination, she placed it on the bed exactly as she had found it.

The figure still hovered outside in the hall, a shadow blocking out the light. She had to wait for it to pass before she could leave, but it wasn't moving. Was it waiting, too—waiting for *her?*

But she had to escape now, even if it meant meeting the figure face to face. For Lopez and the two women were toweling off, walking toward the bedroom. She reached for the doorknob. Her mind scrambled for a ploy. Impulsively she opened the top buttons of her blouse and rumpled her hair. She took a deep breath. Twisting the knob, she stepped into the corridor.

Torres. . . .

He was surprised to see her and toyed with the handle of his automatic, sizing her up. Seemingly flustered, Chris started to button up her blouse and primp her blowsy hair. She gestured toward the door. "Lopez and I. . . ." Torres smirked. He knew Lopez's lusts well. Would he see her as one more of his conquests? Or was he shrewder than that?

She pressed her hands to her sides to keep them from shaking and waited for his next move. Finally, with the contempt she had seen men show to whores, Torres dismissed her with a sneer. "Go!"

26

CHRIS EASED THROUGH THE SWINGING DOORS INTO
the darkened kitchen. It was the last spot she would have chosen
for their meeting, but her own room was out of the question,
and here, at least, they would be alone. She stepped into the
moonlight that filtered through a window, glinting off the pots
and pans. Strange, she thought, how this rendezvous had taken
on the aura of a lovers' tryst. Ironic, for she would be meeting
with a man she hoped to never see again. She walked around
the massive butcher-block table. It reeked of blood.

The clock on the wall read 4:17. Why wasn't he there? Had
they caught him, she wondered, and if so, did that mean they
would catch her, too? She clutched the two rolls of film in her
hand, clicking the canisters together. They were wet from her
sweaty palms. It was too risky to hold onto them more than
a few minutes longer. If he didn't arrive soon, she would throw
them into the garbage, with the fish heads.

Why, she wondered, did she always find herself risking her
life to please an ungiving man? What made her gravitate toward
a tough, demanding Graner or an aloof Vargas rather than to
the charm and friendliness of an Alan Reynolds? Maybe it was
easier to risk her life for a withholding SOB than to risk failure
in a real relationship.

A figure emerged from the meat locker, sculpting itself out
of the dark. Silhouetted there, Vargas seemed even more remote
than before. He had changed out of his waiter's uniform into
the khakis she recognized from Wirephotos. "Did you get
them?" he asked, his voice as cold as the moonlight.

She handed him the two canisters with a trace of pride,
remembering his taunt that he would have preferred a man for
the job.

"Did they see you?"

"Torres saw me leave. I think he thought I was sleeping
with Lopez." Vargas frowned, but said nothing. He zipped the
two rolls of film into his pocket. Bastard, she thought. He can't
even thank me for risking my life.

But as he turned to go, Chris thought she detected something

151

on his face beyond the acknowledgement of a debt paid in full. Respect, perhaps, the special respect that can exist between a man and a woman and that, under different circumstances, could have led to friendship or even something more.

Near the door he stopped. "I'm leaving. You must also leave."

Chris managed a bitter smile. "The plane doesn't come for two days. Where the hell do you expect me to go?"

He shrugged and pointed toward the jungle. "Even that would be safer."

"But . . . why?"

He cut her off. "This hotel. They should never have built it *here*. . . ." For the first time she detected fear behind the guerrilla's mask. "I believe in the class struggle," he said. "I believe in our movement. But there are *other* forces at work here. Forces I don't understand. Leave quickly, before those other forces . . . explode."

The kitchen lights flashed on, blinding them. Chris gasped, as the door from the dining room burst open, and half a dozen mercenaries poured in. The men pinned her against the wall at gunpoint.

But Vargas wasn't so easily stopped. He whipped an automatic pistol out of his belt and dived for the back door. When he yanked it open, three more mercenaries were waiting for him outside. A blade of flame shot from his pistol, and the tallest of the three toppled backward. Vargas dashed into the night toward the patio, the other two men chasing after him. She could hear their boots ringing on the flagstones, their footsteps suddenly muffled as the chase led onto the beach.

Torres seemed torn whether to join the pursuit or to stick with his prisoner. He switched off the lights and squinted out the window toward the ocean, trying to catch sight of his men. He could see nothing. "*¡Pendejo!*" he swore in frustration, and rushed to the wall console which controlled the Muzak for the dining room.

He switched a dial to SURF and strained to listen. The microphones on the beach picked up the thunder of crashing waves, but Chris could hear something else, faint against the ocean's roar: the mercenaries shouting for Vargas to stop. Then the crackle of pistol rounds, followed by the rattle of automatic rifles. He would make an easy target, silhouetted against the jungle in the moonlight. His chances of escape were poor. And what of her chances? In the eyes of the men who held her prisoner, she was guilty of conspiring with an enemy leader. She struggled not to yield to panic, trying to remain rational: Torres must have spoken with Lopez. Then he had shrewdly followed her here, waiting to trap her with Vargas.

Breathless, the two mercenaries trudged up the cement steps into the kitchen. The rage on their faces said Vargas had escaped. She felt no relief for the rebel leader, only a sense of betrayal. He had gotten what he wanted, and now she would pay.

One of the mercenaries had been wounded in the chase. His arm dripped blood onto the butcher block as he lurched toward her and raised the muzzle of his AK-47 to her head. She closed her eyes and listened to the surf over the loudspeakers, praying that it would not all end with a single explosive tidal wave.

"Can I kill her now?" the man asked Torres in Spanish.

"Más tarde," he growled. Later.

They dragged her out of the room, and as if swept off by a riptide, she didn't resist. She felt, once more, as if she were drowning, sinking into the depths. And this time Vargas was not there to save her.

27

FOR ALAN, VISITING A BAR IN THE MORNING WAS distasteful, as if daylight and alcohol weren't meant to mix, a clash as offensive as brushing one's teeth with bourbon. But today he found himself entering the El Dorado's cocktail lounge at nine, as the sun's rays sparkled off the bottles, refracting tiny rainbows onto the dark wood of the bar. His pistol would have been a braver solution to his feelings of worthlessness, he thought. But at least the bottle took off the hard edges, just as the bar's stained-glass skylight burnished the morning glare into an amber glow.

He eased onto his usual stool at the oak bar. So far he was the only customer of the day. Under normal circumstances, he respected bartenders, the sages who ministered to the walking wounded of life, but this one looked as friendly as a hangover. A brawny mercenary in khakis, he studied Alan with beady, suspicious eyes. Alan's arm was sticky from leaning against the bar. The soldier hadn't bothered to wipe it down, and Alan could see rings staining the wood, all that was left of last night's boozy euphoria.

He mused that his infatuation with Chris had proved equally transitory and lit a cigar, puffing up a smoke screen to obscure the mercenary from view and perhaps to hide Chris from his thoughts as well. She was independent and strong and had refused to lean on him even when she needed it, even though he had offered his help. But then, he had a habit of leaning on crutches: on his wife when she was alive; on his self-pity after she died; on the sauce. The bottles shimmered like the skyline of some distant and unattainable Oz. His life had run out of such glittering destinations. Even death no longer held allure. His failure to commit suicide was merely one more decisive act aborted.

The mercenary's face loomed above the cigar smoke. "I'm wise to you, Ichabod," Alan said, drumming his fingers on the bar, waiting impatiently for his drink. "I've seen you sneaking a slug of this and that, refilling the bottles with water. Knock it off. My taste buds can tell."

The mercenary missed the meaning of the words but understood the mocking tone. As if in reply, he unhooked two hand grenades from his chest and stashed them among the liquor bottles.

"Where the hell is Jesús when I need him?" Alan asked. "That's his real name, believe it or not, Jesús. It took me three hours to teach that short little Indian how to make a decent Bloody Mary. Then Torres gets the bright idea to transfer him to the scullery and hire you." The mercenary shifted uneasily, rattled by Alan's banter, his pistol butt clinking against a bottle of Galliano. "You know, Ichabod," Alan continued, "old Jesús was sullen and surly, but you make him look terrific."

Seemingly to prove Alan's point, the soldier slapped a meager glass of tomato juice and a jigger of vodka on the bar. "Mixology is an art, Ichabod." Alan frowned. "It's not simple, like pulling a trigger. It calls for subtleties. A dash of bitters . . . a soupçon of Tabasco. . . . Watch." He leaned behind the bar, helping himself to the ingredients. The mercenary eyed him distrustfully, as if suspecting he might reach for the hand grenades. "So why am I here, you may well ask, if I find associating with you so unappetizing?" Alan sloshed the vodka into the tomato juice and raised his glass in a mock toast. "Simple." He gestured toward the glittering Mecca of bottles. "Because it's there."

Alan swizzled his concoction and took a sip. The drink seemed to have more bite than anything else in his life right now. He had to face the fact that learning how to make a superior Bloody Mary had been his only creative achievement in the past eight years.

A voice boomed over his shoulder. "The Spanish have a saying: *Si bebes para olvidar, pagues antes de empezar*. If you drink to forget, pay the bill before you start."

Alan stared at Hans Berger. "I can't believe it! Hans hitting the schnapps!"

The German reached behind the bar and poured himself three fingers of brandy, but he didn't raise it to his lips. Berger hadn't come here to drink. He had come to talk. Alan tried to make it easy for him. "If you're worried about what I'll write about this place, don't. There are bound to be foul-ups the first few days, getting the bugs out. Considering what you're up against, I'm impressed."

His reassurance did nothing to calm Berger, who lit a cigarciie, inhaling deeply, his mouth twisted downward as if he were stifling a sob.

"What is it?" Alan asked.

"There's been some . . . unpleasantness." The hotel manager slipped an American $20 bill onto the bar. The mercenary stuffed it into his shirt pocket and slouched away to the far side of the room, where he slumped down in a chair out of earshot.

Berger turned back to Alan, tightening his necktie like a noose. "One of the guests"—he spoke haltingly, as if it pained him to pronounce the words—"one of the guests has been arrested by Torres. . . ."

Alan's first reaction was to back off. Oh, during his wife's illness he had played the role of rescuer, all right. He had searched from clinic to clinic, from specialist to specialist for some way out. But after her death, afflicted with a sense of his own failure, he had vowed never to accept responsibility for another human life again. Very softly he asked, *"Who* did they arrest?"

Berger drank the cognac like castor oil, in one painful swallow. "Chris Latham."

It was as if one of the hand grenades on the bar had exploded. "Chris! But . . . why?"

"They say she was involved with Vargas, stealing government secrets. . . ."

"Manuel Vargas was *here?*"

"That's what they say."

"But . . . the whole thing's absurd."

"Certainly. But when you've worked in Panaguas as long as I have, you *expect* the absurd."

"Where is she?"

Berger sighed. "On the thirteenth floor, under heavy guard."

"And Vargas?"

"Escaped. They think Chris knows where he went."

"My God. . . ." They shared an ominous silence. Whether or not she knew anything, Torres would torture her. Alan felt old muscles starting to flex, stirrings in a part of him that he thought had died long ago. Just a twinge at first, for his sense of commitment was sluggish from disuse. "We can use the radio-telephone to call the American Embassy in Tierra del Mar," he said. "I know the chargé d'affaires there. He can help."

The hotel manager glared in the direction of the mercenary. "Torres's men control the radio. I can't get near it. Even if I could, it only feeds to the Office of Internal Security. And they're the ones who *arrested* her."

Alan was surprised at the excitement building within him. How long had it been since he had been forced to pit himself against so formidable an obstacle? He glanced toward the mercenary, the *mordida* visible in his pocket.

Berger read his mind. "They think Chris has priceless information. They would hardly be dissuaded by a few hundred dollars...."

Berger's resistance only made Alan scrabble harder for a plan. "I have a pistol in my room," he whispered. "You could distract the guards. Then I'd sneak up with the gun...."

"Fantasies," Berger said, and filled the brandy snifter a second time. "There are forty heavily armed men up there. They'd cut you in half before you even laid eyes on her." Berger's tone grew bitter, as if Alan's naïveté were an insult. "Suppose you rescued her by force ... where would you escape to? You would not survive one day in the jungle."

Alan scanned the bottles as if their labels might provide answers. "Suppose I made it to one of those fishing villages up the coast. I could telephone the American Embassy from there...."

Berger shook his head. "It's fifty miles through thick jungle, or if you take the hotel dinghy, it's a fight against riptides and reefs. No, the only way out is by air. But Mr. Stokes won't be here for another day. By then...." The cognac was starting to take its numbing effect, and he found it easier to rationalize. "It's beyond our power to help her. Maybe we just have to accept that." Berger placed a hand on Alan's sleeve. "Don't get involved. One guest lost is bad enough."

Alan ignored his words. The German had no idea of the low value Alan placed on his own life. If he lost the gamble, it was a price he was willing to pay. He eyed the mercenary. Right now, to Chris, those men must seem as inescapable as cancer. He had failed with his wife, but at least with Chris he might be able to reason out a cure if he acted in time. How much time did he have left? Was he already too late? Whatever his plan, if he didn't act quickly, there would be no point in acting at all. He stood up from the bar and started toward the door. The intoxication he felt was of an unfamiliar sort, an elation replacing the paralyzing effects of vodka.

Berger watched Alan leave, surprised to see that he had left his drink untouched.

28

TORRES PACED IMPATIENTLY IN HIS SWEAT-STAINED
suit. *"Where you first contact Manuel Vargas?"*

"I never contacted him," Chris's reply was proof that she
still clung to her professional composure. Sitting bolt upright
on the wooden stool, she summoned all her willpower to keep
from falling apart. She had learned that men like Torres could
sense terror in their prisoners the way a lion smells the spoor
of fear.

"What you do with film you take in Lopez's room?"

"I didn't take any film in Lopez's room. . . ." Her cameras
had gotten her into this mess. They sure as hell couldn't get
her out.

She scanned the shadowy expanse where she was being held
prisoner. The thirteenth floor was still under construction, and
the space had yet to be partitioned into rooms. A row of cement
pylons divided the space in two, casting bold shadows across
the floor. Beyond the hanging tarpaulin that marked off the
interrogation area, she could see the mercenaries, an infestation
on the dusty floor. One soldier urinated beside a glittering
room-service cart that seemed as out of place as she felt.

"Why Vargas come?"

"I don't know. . . ."

Window glass had not yet been installed along the façade
facing the ocean, and the morning sea breeze revived her like
a dose of smelling salts. From the shadows of a pylon against
the wall, she guessed it was well past nine. That would mean
six hours since her capture, six hours of interrogation by Torres,
his meager English grating against her even more wretched
Spanish. The mercenaries had stopped paying any attention to
her hours ago. With masturbatory intensity, they sharpened
their knives, rubbed the barrels of their guns with grease.

"What you do for Vargas?"

"Nothing."

His meaty hands fluttered as if they were impatient with the
tedious progress of the interrogation. Though in the hours of

questioning Torres had learned little from his captive, she felt she had learned much about him. The Department of Internal Security in the capital, like other secret police forces she had known, had two units—investigative and punitive. Torres must have worked his way up as a bone crusher in punitive. She wished to God it were Lopez doing the questioning; he might be vulnerable to charm, to persuasion—even to seduction. But the last thing Torres would do was contact Lopez now. For if he went to his boss and recounted the night's events, he would be in serious trouble for letting Vargas escape. He had to have the guerrilla leader in his clutches before he told Lopez anything.

"*Who else in hotel work for Vargas?*"

"No one . . . I don't know. . . ." She could do nothing to escape—her threats to contact the American Embassy had been dismissed with scorn. Nor could she exonerate herself—she was already judged guilty as charged. The last thing she would do was tell the truth. Her complicity with Vargas, even under threat, was evidence enough for a death sentence. All she could do was keep Torres talking. For if the talking stopped . . .

"*How you know Manuel Vargas?*" He started it again.

"I *don't* know him. . . ."

"*Why you go Lopez's room?*"

"He invited me to see him. I saw he was busy. I left."

"*What you steal from Lopez's room?*"

"Nothing."

The questions varied, but they always climaxed with "*Where is Vargas now?*"

"I told you. I don't know."

Torres rolled his eyes, like a teacher with an idiotic student. "You do not answer my questions. You *will* answer them."

For the first time in hours he stepped beyond the tarpaulin and walked toward the soldiers lounging in the shadows. Nothing he said could have terrified her as much as this sudden departure. But though he had left her alone in the interrogation area, she made no effort to flee. "Killed while attempting escape" was a favorite cover story for murder.

The conversation between Torres and his men ended abruptly. The mercenaries slotted ammunition into their rifles. For a moment she thought they were to be her firing squad. Impossible. There was no need to dispose of her so ceremoniously. All they had to do was hurl her out a window into the jungle. She would be dead before the vultures even spotted her.

She was relieved when Torres came back alone. "I have something for you," he said, placing a large box on a table nearby. She hoped that it contained something to eat.

He reached inside the box and pulled out a glass tank. Inside it, a dozen piranha gleamed like knives. The fish spun in the water, like a hypnotic art form, a steel mobile as volatile as quicksilver. Torres regarded the predators like tools of his trade: thumbscrews or the rack. How could such tiny jaws wreak such destruction? She knew the answer: hunger was a more lethal force than TNT. And yet her fascination with the piranha outstripped her fear. She had witnessed death in its many forms, sometimes even courted it. But this time, was she actually meeting her own murderers face to face?

"Three days, no eat," Torres said. *"Tienen hambre."* He chuckled. "Hungry." He grabbed her wrist and her hand started to tremble. He let it drop back into her lap. "Now you tell me all things, yes?"

The piranha spun silver, cutting impatient circles in the water. She had heard how they could cleave through bone with such surgical precision that the victim only discovered when he *saw*.

She wished she had a cyanide pill concealed in a cavity, the spy's key to a hasty exit. But no, she would never be capable of that. She would choose mutilation over death—anything to postpone the end. She would cling to life, even if it meant the lingering agony of bleeding white.

But . . . it was absurd. She had covered the towering events of her time—Vietnam, the space race, the Mideast wars. Now would the curtain drop in this two-bit banana republic? To be executed for a cause she didn't believe in, for loyalty to a man she didn't even *like?*

Torres allowed her ample time to contemplate the piranha, to imagine the water blossoming from delicate pink to deep crimson, darkening until it became opaque with blood.

"These help your mind work, yes?" He leaned over and leered through the fish tank at her, the water grotesquely distorting his face. She remembered how doomed English nobles would tip the executioner before their beheading to assure a swift, painless death. She watched the piranha spin, like a bribe of silver coins. Yes, she should definitely have tipped the executioner.

"You think," Torres said, and tapped his shiny head. "Maybe you think good now."

She clutched her hands into fists as if to deny the piranha the food they sought. Her fingers were chapped, the nails broken, but they were delicate and feminine. She would rather have her face disfigured, rather lose a leg, than lose them. For it would mean giving up the work she loved. She stuck her hands in her mouth, bit down on them hard. She started to shake, as if the piranha were already gnawing her fingers—and her sanity—to shreds.

Like a clock spinning faster and faster, driven by a mainspring of gluttony, the piranha sped with accelerating force. It seemed that soon the tank would no longer be able to contain their mounting frenzy, that they would smash through the glass and fly out at her.

"Tell me now . . . where is he?"

"I don't know!" Chris stammered, her voice reduced to a childish whimper. Her hands were numb, as if they had already been sheared off at the wrist. She raised her eyes from the tank to Torres and was surprised by what she saw: a mirror of the fear that lined her own face. For if Chris refused to reveal Vargas's whereabouts, when Lopez found out that Torres had let the guerrilla leader get away, Torres's *own* fingers would end up inside that tank.

He nodded to two soldiers who grabbed her by the shoulders, and dragged her toward the fish tank as she clawed to break free. It was no use. Her hand trembled in their grasp as they lowered it toward the water. One foot . . . six inches. . . . The piranha rose expectantly to the surface. "Now," Torres said, *"speak."*

A scuffle outside the canvas wall interrupted them. The mercenaries released their hold on her, and she slumped back on the stool. It was Alan. Had they arrested him, too? No, he was barging his way through the soldiers, holding Jesús by the collar of his stained hotel uniform. The closer they came to Torres, the harder the Indian kicked and fought. The mercenaries blocked the way, but Torres waved Alan through. Alan lifted Jesús off the ground, his prisoner's feet flailing in midair, and dragged him up to the interrogator.

At the sight of Torres the little man bowed his shiny cowlick submissively. Alan started to speak. A few of the soldiers shouted him down, but Torres overruled them. *"Habla,"* he said.

The American spoke to Torres in tolerable Spanish that was slow enough so Chris could understand. "This man knows where Vargas went. . . ."

Torres's eyes narrowed. Jesús was staring, transfixed, at the piranha. He tried to back away, but the mercenaries prodded him with their guns. He looked desperately to Alan for help.

"This man, Jesús Alvarez, is afraid you'll hurt him if he talks." Alan gestured toward the piranha. "I promised you'd do him no harm."

Torres gave Jesús a sickly smile of reassurance. "In Panaguas we do not resort to such measures." Grudgingly Torres waved Chris from her stool and placed the fish tank on the floor. "Nothing will happen," he said to Jesús.

"We have your word?" Alan asked.

Torres nodded reluctantly as if the vertical movement of his head were choking him.

"I was talking to Jesús today," Alan began. "He boasted that he knew where Vargas went."

Torres pursed his lips suspiciously. "Vargas has many sympathizers among these people. How do I know he isn't lying?"

Chris was astonished to see Alan remove a Budischowsky automatic from his pocket. "Jesús didn't want to come with me," he said. "I told him if he didn't talk, I'd use this."

Torres cocked his head to one side. "And why would *you* do this?" he asked. "Do you care so much for the regime of Generalissimo Zamora?" Alan cast a glance over at Chris. Torres smirked. "She is your *puta*—your whore?"

Alan said nothing, but Chris was quick to speak. "I am his woman." Torres seemed satisfied with Alan's motives. He turned to Jesús.

"You know about Vargas?" Clearly he resented the implication that a servant could obtain better intelligence than he could himself. *"How* do you know?"

Alan stepped in. "He hates Vargas more than you do." Torres looked skeptical. "Vargas slept with his wife. When he found out, Jesús beat her until she told him everything. He was ready to go after the guerrilla himself."

Jesús was quivering with humiliation, and Chris could see that Torres relished his discomfort. "So your wife chooses Vargas over you in bed, eh? Vargas is a *maricón*," Torres hissed. "If you are a worse lover than Vargas, you must have no cock at all." The mercenaries laughed scornfully, but Torres turned dead serious. "Why was Vargas here at the hotel? He did not come all this way to screw your slut of a wife."

Jesús shook his head. *"No sé."*

Torres took a deep breath. He had reached the punch line. *"Where did Vargas go?"*

Jesús managed an answer, in halting Spanish, barely above a whisper. "His men were waiting for him in the jungle."

"How *many* men?"

Jesús hesitated, uncertain, looking at the mercenaries. "As many as you have...."

"And where is he *now?*" Torres kept his voice on an even keel, but Chris could see his hand tighten around his pistol butt, as if to throttle it.

"Montaña de los Ciegos," Jesús blurted out, and he winced, as if now that he had said the words, his usefulness were over.

Torres snapped his fingers, and two mercenaries spread out a map on the table. Chris strained to read it over their shoulders—a vast green expanse sprinkled with names and ruled into military sectors. Torres squinted at the paper but couldn't locate the target. One of his lieutenants found it, far from the blue of the ocean, and Torres read the name slowly: "Montaña de los Ciegos." He repeated it again, to himself, as if he had discovered a magical incantation. "How far?" he asked one of his men.

The mercenary studied the map. "Three days, four, each way."

Another broke in: "But if we take the helicopter to Alicante, we can stop them before they reach the bridge at Puente Fuego."

Torres seemed to be juggling the logistics in his head. "If we ambush them there . . . we could catch up with Vargas before dark?" His eyes burned with excitement.

The men nodded. Chris edged toward Alan, but Torres gestured for his men to stop her. She waited for an agonizing moment, as Torres weighed his alternatives. He gazed down at the piranha in the tank on the floor, as if scrutinizing his own violent core. She knew Torres's options were limited. He could torture her, with no guarantee of success, or he could believe Jesús and give chase. It was a decision on which his survival depended, and he knew it.

Chris could almost see his mind at work: to tell his boss that Vargas had escaped would cost his life. But if he secretly left now with his troops, he could still capture Vargas in time to return a hero. Torres picked up the map. He seemed relieved that the time for thinking was over—that the time for action was at hand. He ordered all his men to prepare to leave. *All* his men, she noticed. He didn't intend to let Vargas get away this time. She imagined the interrogator was already planning what he would say to his boss when he presented him with the guerrilla's head.

Torres waved for Chris and Alan to leave. The Americans were an annoyance now, distracting him from the hunt. He glanced at Jesús. "*¡Fuera!*" A guard herded him out with the others.

The elevator doors sealed shut, and Chris watched as the floor numbers ticked by on the console. But the sinking feeling in the pit of her stomach didn't come from the elevator's descent. She slumped against a wall, shaky from an overdose of adrenaline. Her mouth was parched, her blouse soaked with sweat. She felt mutilated, as if those teeth had torn her apart after all. All she could manage for Alan was a polite "thank you."

"You're welcome," he said. She sensed he had expected more, but she hardly felt like throwing her arms around him. Paranoia was epidemic in the tropics, and she had been infected with a virulent dose. She even suspected Alan's motives now. For he had changed drastically after confronting Torres. He stood straighter and seemed younger, more masculine and self-assured. The transformation made her uneasy, as if he had been deceiving her before. She could still see the bulge in his pocket, the pistol that he had used to bully Jesús. The weapon distanced him from her, reduced him to one more fragment in the El Dorado's riddle.

Out of desperation, she had told Torres she was Alan's woman. Would Alan hold her to it? She was grateful for his rescue but feared what price might be attached. After all, Vargas had saved her life but had forced her to pay back the debt. Would Alan make even greater demands?

When the elevator jerked to a stop, he turned to her. "You look like you could use some lunch."

She broke into a smile of relief. "Okay," she said. "I'm buying."

29

CLAD IN A CORAL SILK KIMONO, DAWN CLOPPED down the steps in her wedgies, turning her back on the morning sunshine as she descended from the patio into the basement. The dank cement gave her the shivers, for the jungle permeated the earth under the hotel with the scent of rot. Her watch read 9:30. Lopez was staying in the Presidential Suite. Why couldn't they have met there? She frowned. It was always like this with the powerful men who wanted her. She was their secret vice, condemned to sleazy assignations.

She reached the foot of the staircase and hesitated at the door to the sauna: vines had snaked underground from the jungle, intertwining the hotel's rusty pipes; roots engulfed electrical cables. The subterranean forest echoed the green tangle aboveground, and was every bit as threatening. Instead of the screeches of howler monkeys or the cries of toucans, this thicket had other, even stranger noises: shrill twitterings; eerie electric hums. Eager for the security of the sauna, she pulled open the heavy redwood door with both hands.

Inside, the air was oven-hot, a red glow from the rocks in the corner keeping the temperature at 120 degrees Fahrenheit. Where was Lopez? Had he overslept? She knew how hard it was to get up at this hour. Morning usually didn't exist for her, and only because Irv had impressed her with the vital importance of this meeting had she forced herself to put on her makeup, throw on a robe, and come down.

The sauna door slapped behind her, with the finality of a safe sealing shut. After all, she thought, money was why she was here. She still didn't understand all the financial details— that was Irv's department— but from what the producer had said, it boiled down to one thing: Lopez could make them rich. If he showed up, it meant tacit approval of the deal Irv had discussed with him. Then, after her dalliance with Lopez, the three of them would meet for lunch. Irv would explain how the same government money that had been diverted to build this hotel could be used for international productions. How the same highly placed Panaguan investors could cash in by their involvement in his motion pictures.

But why wasn't Lopez here yet? She had teased him at the party and on the beach. Had she failed to arouse him? The two women he kept were certainly tough competition. As if to reassure herself of her seductiveness, she shed the silk kimono and reclined nude on the bench. The tropical sun had darkened her Palm Springs tan into a rich mocha, except for a single creamy triangle. Languorously she extended a leg into the air and inspected her shocking pink toenails. She had painted them this morning, just for him. She ran her hands along her belly, already moistening from the heat. So smooth. She had shaved her legs, shaved under her arms, even delicately shaved her pubic fluff. She had daubed perfume everywhere, and as her flesh warmed, like an exotic sachet, her body yielded the scent of musk.

Beads of sweat trickled down her cleavage. Yes, thanks to her breasts, she was in a class by herself. Right now, they were so full of milk they hurt.

The heat was overpowering, but though it sapped her strength, it didn't help her to relax. Too much was riding on this. If Lopez stood her up, the trip to Panaguas would have been wasted, and soon Irv would find another companion.

The sauna door creaked open without warning. A figure lingered outside in the darkness. "Who is it?" She leaned up on one elbow and, suddenly vulnerable, covered herself with her kimono.

Lopez entered, dressed in a crimson robe, and closed the door behind him. "I have stationed my men at the door," he said, "to make sure we are not disturbed."

"You're late," she breathed flirtatiously. She sucked in her belly and threw her shoulders back, allowing the kimono to tumble to the floor.

"I had trouble getting away," he said. "I promised Torres, my chief of security, that for safety's sake, I wouldn't leave my room. I had to bribe my men to escort me down here." He laughed. "I don't know if you remember what Señor Torres looks like—but there are few things beautiful enough to make me risk his wrath." He leaned toward her and kissed her hand. "You are one."

Dawn basked in his praise, her body glowing in the heat. "You'll be glad you came."

With childlike curiosity, he ran a hand along her thigh,

gliding it past the pink fold between her legs. "You know how to make a man hungry," he murmured, lifting up her breasts so that they stood straight out. "Do you also know how to satisfy him?"

He pulled off his bathrobe, and Dawn admired his body. His torso was more powerfully muscled than Irv's. This tryst would be both business and pleasure. She eyed his penis; it was uncircumsised, an intriguing change of pace. She was impressed to see it stiffening already, despite the heat, and remembered a song she had heard once, that only the devil could screw in hell.

She held a breast in each hand, and he leaned to suck them. She didn't resist. She would let him hurt her, if he wanted, for Irv's sake, to seal the agreement. But she squirmed as he squeezed harder, biting her nipples. "Please . . . ! Stop . . . !"

Her squeals of pain seemed only to excite him, and instead of lingering over her breasts, as most men did, his hands clenched her buttocks, spreading them wide. He turned her over on her belly and mounted her canine fashion, reverting to Spanish in his fever. "*¡Mamacita, te quiero!*" He was greedy to possess her, and he probed her forcibly from behind. She cried out, but he lunged deeper. She struggled to writhe free.

"So you fight, eh Tigrita?" He laughed.

"I'm not some goddamned chippie!" she cried, but he pulled her roughly on top of him. She had no choice but to hold on, like a rider on a runaway horse, to hold on for dear life until, frothing at the bit, the steel would spend itself.

In the shadowy basement, three mercenaries hunched outside the redwood walls of the sauna, indifferent to the sounds of struggle inside. They were grateful to have been spared sentry duty in the glare of the sun. As far as Torres was concerned, they were still in the Presidential Suite with Lopez, for they had promised to keep him safely under lock and key in his room. Lopez's bribe had changed that. Cradling an M-16 in his arms, one of them lit a Gauloise. The others reached out and he dealt a cigarette to each of them.

While they leaned over the match, while their guard lowered ever so slightly—in that millisecond, it struck. It lunged out of the forest of pipes and electrical cables so swiftly that their fingers didn't have time to flinch on their triggers. It was as swift and sudden as a thunderbolt, but an electric force that came from the earth instead of the sky—an awesome voltage harnessing the power of the jungle.

The mercenaries' bodies slammed against the walls. Their cigarettes had fallen to the ground, and smoke still curled from them, rising up the stairwell into the sunlight, ascending the morning brilliance like their ghosts.

The hinges didn't squeal, the floorboards didn't creak as it entered the sauna, as if the steel and redwood were in league with the intruder. The door that had taken such exertion for the others to open *it* opened effortlessly. Dawn felt its presence in the room. At first she feared it was Lopez's men who had come to join him, to inflict more pain. But no. . . . Her jaw dropped open. How could this be? She had come here to offer her body, not her life.

The blade whipped through the air imbued with the power to transform life into death with a single flourish. Lopez couldn't withdraw before the machete separated their embrace, severing his genitals from his body so that he left them inside Dawn as he staggered away with an effeminate gait, blood gushing from between his legs. In spite of the wound, his will to survive gave him strength. He groped for the pistol hidden in his bathrobe pocket, but before he could clutch the weapon, the blade hacked again, slicing through his esophagus and windpipe, crunching through his spinal cord. His head thudded to the floor.

The machete gleamed in the sauna's red glow like a tongue of flame. Blood, not milk, was spurting from Dawn's breasts now as she stumbled toward the door. Her feet slipped on the red-slick planking as she grappled for the handle, but she couldn't wrench the door open. A scream lodged in her throat, ready to escape, but the sound was sliced in half by the severing blade.

As she fell, the machete caught her from behind, chopping again and again, a shower of blood sizzling on the hot rocks in the corner. Blow by blow, the steel struck with such impact that it lodged in the wood. It had to be wrenched loose, splinters flying, before it slashed again, the blood clotting quickly in the dry heat. And again it struck, and again, long after life had passed from the bodies, driven by a compulsion that even murder could not satisfy.

30

IN THE DINING ROOM, SITTING ALONE AT A TABLE
set for three, a smug Irv Florsheim was buying champagne for
the house. Though the gilt-edged plate before him was empty,
he had the look of a man who had been served a feast. Dawn
and Lopez were almost an hour late for lunch, and their tar-
diness was cause for celebration. Proof that Dawn had sealed
the deal. In the afterglow of such passionate lovemaking, Lopez
would no doubt settle the final details without a quibble. Irv
was confident his multipicture financing package would be
wrapped up with the Panaguan government in a matter of days.
He would tear up their coach-class tickets back to Los Angeles
and, with the signed contract in hand, fly back first class. The
moment they touched down he would open a charge account
at Gucci's. He would pay off the right people to get his own
star on Hollywood Boulevard. Cantor's Deli would even name
a sandwich after him. Money couldn't buy happiness, he
mused, but it sure helped to wipe those tears away with a $20
bill.

He removed a velvet box from his pocket and placed it on
his plate. He had gone into hock to buy the engagement ring
at Van Cleef and Arpels in Beverly Hills. The platinum band
sported a diamond big enough to choke a horse. He had vowed
that if this junket worked out, he would ask Dawn to marry
him. She had proved her loyalty by sleeping with another man.
He swore that as his wife she would never have to make such
crass use of her attributes again. He admired the dining room's
glittering crystal, the bouquets of roses, the radiant stained-
glass skylight, and imagined the Las Vegas wedding chapel
where they would marry. On their honeymoon night they would
do the two things he loved most—screw and shoot craps.

Chris's knife sliced through a filet of fish, as though she
were wreaking revenge on the piranha at last. As she ate, her
generosity returned along with her strength. She raised her
glass in a toast to Alan. "For what you did. I won't forget it."

He smiled. "The things a guy has to do to take you to lunch."

They clinked glasses, but her hand shook as she lifted the goblet to her lips. She didn't feel like sipping the champagne and, instead, ran a finger along the tines of a fork, feeling them prick her like the realization: she hadn't received a reprieve, only a stay of execution. Torres would probably return well before Harley Stokes's plane arrived tomorrow. Then he would continue his interrogation with renewed ferocity.

"When Torres gets back...." Her words trailed off. "I'm only safe till then."

"I wouldn't worry about it," Alan said. "They'll be awhile."

"If they catch Vargas the way they plan to," she said, "they could be back *tonight*." Alan didn't reply, and she resented his unconcern. "It's easy for you to stay calm," she said. "It's not your neck."

He looked up from his plate and spoke to her as if she were slow on the uptake. "You really believe that?" But before he could continue, Jesús walked over to their table and flashed a broad smile. *"¿Todo fué bien?"*

"Muy bien," Alan replied, reaching into his pocket for his wallet. Chris was amazed to see him count out five $100-dollar bills and hand them to Jesús.

"What's that for?" she asked, but she was already beginning to understand.

"I'll tell you one thing," Alan said. "It's not for making the world's best Bloody Mary."

"Gracias." Jesús pocketed the bills. He winked at Alan, bowed his shiny pompadour toward Chris, and scuttled away.

"You mean the whole thing...?" She stammered. "So Vargas *isn't* going to that place... Montaña de Whatsis?"

"How the hell should *I* know where Vargas is going?" Alan laughed.

"But Jesús's wife...."

"Jesús is too ugly to *have* a wife."

She paused a beat, impressed. "I owe you for that *mordida* you gave Jesús," she said.

"Forget it."

But the puzzle still didn't make sense. "Even for that much money," she said, "to get Jesús to go up there and run that kind of risk...."

"You're right," Alan said. "Jesús didn't just do it for the

money. He wanted his old job back. I convinced him the only way he'd get it was to get rid of the mercenaries." She could see Jesús in the cocktail lounge. He had changed from his greasy scullery jacket into his bartender's coat, and threw his chest back proudly to display its gleaming gold braid. He poured himself a whiskey and sipped it greedily.

Alan grinned. "You see, Jesús had become addicted to his job's fringe benefits." He turned serious. "Anyhow, the point is Torres won't dare show his face back here without Vargas. And by the time he realizes he's on a wild-goose chase, we'll be long gone. Remember," he said, "the son of a bitch does everything on Panaguan time."

She raised her glass in a toast. "To Panaguan time." She felt giddy as she sipped the champagne, but it was Alan's revelation, not the Piper Heidsieck, that was going to her head. She felt relaxed enough now to watch the other diners. Berger was serving Scott Hershey a chocolate mousse from the pastry cart. The singer had ordered three desserts, heaping them with whipped cream, and the hotel manager seemed appalled. Scott must have a bad case of the munchies, she thought. When her glance met Berger's, she read guilt on his face. Was it because he had done nothing to help her?

His look drove home the fact that her rescue had been Alan's initiative—an Alan who suddenly intrigued her. She watched as he lit a cigar and puffed away with relish. Was it a comment on her own childishness that she was more attracted by his talents as a con man than by his more solid virtues? An afterthought nudged her, and she pushed her goblet away. "What about Lopez?"

Before Alan could answer, Berger stepped over to her, as if to redeem himself in her eyes. "Lopez—" he lowered his voice confidentially—"is upstairs with three bodyguards and his women. He asked not to be disturbed, and Torres seems to have no intention of doing so." Berger pointed outside the picture window, where the mercenaries were lining up, forty-pound packs on their backs, automatic rifles slung over their shoulders. He raised a glass of champagne. *"Auf Wiedersehen."* Torres, clad in green fatigues, led his men down the dusty road toward the airstrip.

Chris had finished her fish and drained her goblet by the time the chopper rose above the jungle. It hovered there a moment, then vanished into the green. Feeling the urge to celebrate, she picked up the champagne bottle and refilled Alan's glass. But when she turned to offer some to Berger, she was surprised to see he was on his way out of the room. From his urgent pace, she suspected he had a secret rendezvous of his own.

31

BERGER'S NERVES WERE SHOT, AND THERE WAS only one way to soothe him. Not sex or champagne—but a diversion which better suited his ascetic bent. He descended the basement steps to the sauna. True to form, he could even turn that pleasurable experience into an exercise in Prussian discipline. For instead of lolling in the heat, he preferred to alternate the sweltering with icy showers from the spigot outside the sauna door. Today he hoped the masochistic regimen might purge him of his sense of guilt, stop him from blaming himself for all that had gone wrong.

He knew the way downstairs to the basement by heart and didn't bother to flick the light until he stepped onto the cellar floor. His shoe slipped on something wet. A leak, he concluded, perhaps a serious one. He swore as he stared into the maze of pipes. It might take hours to trace the problem to its source in that rusty thicket.

Then he realized that the viscous liquid wasn't coming from the pipes at all. It was seeping out from under the door to the sauna. And it was red.

Suddenly the minor task of opening the door became a burden. He gripped the handle and hesitated. Then he pulled. When the door creaked open a few inches, a blast of scorching air stopped him. The sauna thermostat had been twisted out of kilter. A gauge on the wall revealed the temperature: 250 degrees. The heat was so intense that it was all he could do to lean in.

"Oh, no . . . oh, no . . ." he murmured over and over, shaking his head at the garbled image, as if to overrule brute reality with reason. He slammed the door shut, but it was too late. The image was printed indelibly in his mind.

The sight induced a wave of nausea, a spasm of anguish that brought his childhood trauma back to him: he was suddenly in the basement in Munich where he had discovered cruelty in its most virulent form. He feared he had brought the German seed of evil with him, that the virus of Auschwitz and Dachau had now taken root in alien soil.

He struggled to remain objective, to remember the sight exactly as he had glimpsed it: a confusion of corpses, some naked, some clad in khaki. His fevered brain couldn't sort the orgy of mutilation into separate victims, each with his own identity. Instead, the severed limbs all seemed part of one monstrous creature—as if in this blast furnace, arms and legs had fused together, clustering squidlike, into a hybrid even more horrific than man.

32

IT WAS THE SIESTA HOUR, AND CHRIS YEARNED TO
go upstairs and collapse, but Alan took her firmly by the arm
and steered her out of the dining room onto the patio. "There's
something you have to see," he said. "There's something I've
got to show you." Though wary of new revelations, she let him
lead her onto the beach.

In the midday heat the sand was scalding, but he strode with
a purpose away from the hotel, along the surf, and her curiosity
whetted, she hastened to keep up with him. She realized that
with Alan she had made a photographer's mistake—to assume
that the surface revealed all. He was turning out to be as strange
a bundle of contradictions as any of the other guests. With his
every action she understood him less and less. And she guessed
he held even more surprises.

He didn't stop until they had reached the end of the beach,
where the sand melted into the jungle. They were beyond earshot of the hotel, she realized uneasily, as isolated from the
El Dorado as they could get without entering the wall of vines.
When she caught up with him, his back was to her. A hot wind
blew from the ocean, sending up a stinging barrage of sand,
and he was squinting into it, staring out to sea, as if to make
out something on the horizon. After rescuing her, it would be
easy for him to assume that she was his. She hoped that he
hadn't brought her here for a romantic overture.

But when he turned toward her, she realized she was wrong.
He held a gun. She started to back away.

"You really *are* paranoid." He laughed.

"Guilty as charged." She managed an uneasy smile. Somehow, at the El Dorado, they were all potential murderers.

He turned the muzzle of the gun away from her, toward
himself. "I needed you here as a witness," he said. "It was a
way of making sure I'd go through with it."

"Go through with what?"

"It's taken me a long, long time getting here," he said
cryptically. "But sometimes, like they say, the long way 'round
is the shortest way home." He wrestled with the best way to

continue. "I came to Panaguas on a one-way ticket," he said. "And I brought *this* with me to fire one bullet."

"You're not going to. . . ." She tried to snatch the weapon away, but he held onto it.

"Don't worry." He laughed. "I still have problems. But I'm through thinking a bullet can solve them. You see, this morning on the thirteenth floor, what I did with Torres. . . ." He groped for the words. "It was all very selfish, really."

"I thought it was very . . . *un*selfish," she said.

He shook his head. "Self-hatred. . . . It's like this damn heat. Each day it saps your strength a little more." He was staring at the gun with disgust, as though the worst part of him had hardened into that lump of steel.

"After trying to drink away my guilt for all these years . . . guilt about my wife's death . . . it had reached the point where if anything was going to snap me out of it, it had to be something sudden. Something drastic. I have you to thank for that."

"Me?"

"You were the most independent of the guests—the strongest. I was the weakling of the group. When you were suddenly a helpless prisoner, it . . . well . . . it gave me the kick in the ass I needed. Oh, it didn't work perfectly. There's still a lot of guilt. But it worked well enough for me to ditch this"—he looked at the gun—"this part of me." She read pride on his face. "So you see, it was very selfish of me, really. Because it wasn't your life I was saving. It was mine."

He wrapped his fingers around the pistol and swung his arm back, to hurl it into the ocean. "I guess this is like when the President throws out the first pitch to start a new baseball season. I'm *ready* for a new season." He added, "I wanted you to be here. To hold me to it." His bicep tensed, and he was about to snap his arm in the throw when something compelled her to stop him.

"Don't! We might need it!"

She grabbed his arm but he wrenched free, surprised at her response. "I know you've been through a lot," he said, anger creeping into his voice, "but don't go paranoid on me. I have to do this."

"Wait!" She reached for his arm again, but it was too late. He had hurled the gun with all his might into the ocean.

The pistol glinted in the sunlight as it skipped across the water, then sank like a stone. She feared they had lost their last weapon to the invisible enemy. And she blamed herself.

She should have told Alan everything. Perhaps, if confronted with the El Dorado's mysteries, he would have understood. But where to begin: with the mishap on the roof? Tobias's death? It would be pointless to retrace the past for him now. It would be a waste of breath.

She felt her helplessness sour into resentment. No, even if she had confided her misgivings, he wouldn't have believed her. In his world of elegant restaurants and resorts, there was no place for the horrors that a combat photographer knew. He had sacrificed a precious tool for their survival on a personal whim. Well, this wasn't a self-awareness weekend in Big Sur, she thought bitterly. It was a bloody gauntlet they were running together.

On their way back up the beach they passed Margot, strolling along the water's edge in her flounced sunsuit. She had stopped to stare at a dead moray eel that had washed up on the beach. Fascinated by its leering gaze, its gaping jaws, she gave the slimy carcass a poke with her parasol. An ugly discovery, Chris mused, foretelling other ugly surprises ahead. She avoided a dozen more eels scattered along the beach, bloated with seawater, their gill sacs pulsating. Though the creatures were dead, she was convinced their eyes were following her. She had never liked this beach, she realized, not since she had seen Scott's head buried here, mocking her.

When they reached the patio, neither wanted to speak, yet neither could bear to be left alone with his thoughts. Chris forced herself to stare out into the ocean, squinting at the rapier-blade horizon, blue as Toledo steel. She avoided looking into the jungle, where she sensed something unspeakable was lurking.

As if spawned by her foreboding, a figure emerged from the stairwell to the basement: Berger, his face as pasty as if he had lived his life underground. When he stepped into the sunlight, she saw his sleeve was drenched in blood.

"Lopez..." he stammered. "Dawn...." He staggered to the door leading to the lobby.

Alan put his arm around Chris, but it was not to shelter her. It was to lean on her for support. "My God...."

She didn't respond, lost in her private horror. Vargas must have murdered Lopez, she thought. He would have been capable of it, even capable of the murder of an innocent bystander like Dawn if she got in his way. Had all the riddles since their arrival been part of this assassination plot? She wanted to believe that it was so, that the swath of murder had ended—that it had all been spawned by political motives.

But she suspected the murderer was something much more monstrous—a force which would not end its rampage with one life, or five, but which had to have them all. She felt certain that the murderer was not human, that it was spawned of the jungle. Yet somehow it was intelligent as only a human could be. She felt a gnawing conviction that the El Dorado was the tip of some sinister iceberg. Hadn't Vargas warned that this place was in itself a peril? Hadn't the late Dr. Tobias called it hallowed ground? Sacred or profane, she feared the terror she had experienced so far would be only a prologue for what was to come.

They had been foolish to rejoice in the mercenaries' departure, she realized that now. It had left them defenseless, as helpless as those moray eels stranded on the beach. The timid and the weak—those least equipped to survive—were doomed to fend for themselves until Harley Stokes's plane arrived tomorrow. Whoever or whatever was waiting for them, she brooded, the time for it to strike was now.

33

A CRUST OF ECZEMA CONSUMED CURZON'S CHEST, as if the vigil were mortifying his flesh, aging him into an invalid with brittle bones. He sat bare-chested in his armchair, his scaly skin so tender he could no longer wear his shirt. He had neither eaten nor drunk since the meal filched from the patio buffet, and he felt as if he were drying up, his mouth too parched to speak. The infrared binoculars weighed heavy in his trembling hands.

Even before the setting sun had impaled itself in the mangrove trees, he had been at his post. The chiaroscuro of the tangled foliage had teased him with its hieroglyphics, until the hours blurred together like raindrops on a window. He had cursed the jungle, and fought it, and, abusing Conchita, even raped it, and now it had humbled him into unconditional surrender with its ultimate weapon: time. It was past midnight. It seemed night had descended years ago.

Curzon rubbed his eyes and blinked in disbelief. After the hunger and the thirst and the crusty growth ravaging his body, had he started to hallucinate? He couldn't believe the image dancing in the sky. It was no meteor shower, no comet to mark a new millennium. To Curzon, it was something much more miraculous: a flare hovering neon-red against the night before it plunged into a sea of mangrove trees.

In the darkened room the flare tinctured his pupils like a drop of blood. His hands knocked over an empty whiskey bottle, sending it crashing to the floor in his haste to snatch up an optical range finder. Just in time to gauge the distance and compass heading of a second flare against the stars. *South-southeast and five to seven miles away.* His lips parted in a stifled prayer of thanks to dark powers which scorned prayer. His faith had been rewarded.

There was much to do, but as he lowered the range finder from his eyes, they were misting over. Tears ran down his cheeks and he wept with gratitude that he had been freed from his imprisonment.

Ignoring the pain from his blistered skin, he slipped into a bush jacket and buckled on a holster: his Luger, with an extra bandolier of cartridges. He strapped on his machete and pocketed a waterproof compass. Then, after donning a hard hat with a light attached like a miner's helmet, Curzon sneaked into the hall and down the back stairs.

Moments later he reached the border between the patio and the encroaching night. It was the hour of the hunt. The jungle stirred from the paws of the jaguar, rustled from the condor's beating wings, shivered from the hiss of the anaconda. All stalked in darkness, yet Curzon didn't hesitate to enter their domain. He was one of them.

At first, he used the hard hat's light to find his way down the trail. But soon he switched the lamp off. His pupils dilated to warn him of creatures too wily to be caught in a flashlight's beam. He allowed his aching muscles to flex at last, as he vanished among the leaves.

34

"I'M SO GLAD YOU COULD COME!" WEARING A
black lace dress and blood-red lipstick, Margot beckoned Alan
and Chris inside the sauna. The firm grip of Margot's handshake revealed a strength Chris hadn't seen in her before. Her
hostess didn't even apologize for summoning them to a room
which scarcely twenty-four hours before had been a scene of
murder. Chris could see that the walls had been swabbed clean,
but bloodstains still stood out on the floor.

The sauna had undergone an eerie transformation. Flickering
tapers in silver candlesticks dripped wax onto the redwood
planks, and Margot had brought in vases of gardenias to drown
out the smell of disinfectant. The floral scent was funereal,
Chris thought, only rivaled in its cloying fragrance by Margot's
perfume. In fact, it seemed that Margot had decorated the room
the way she adorned herself—to disguise the reek of death.

As her eyes adjusted to the candlelight, Chris recognized
Irv, clad in a blue blazer and a white silk shirt, sipping a drink
in the shadows.

"Thanks for coming!" His eyes were red from crying. She
noticed that both a Star of David and a crucifix dangled around
his neck. Extra insurance, perhaps, against tonight's dangers.
"Hey, I really appreciate it, you know?" He pumped Alan's
hand and gave Chris a stage kiss. "I bet if Dawn was here
tonight, she'd thank you, too."

"Who knows?" Margot smiled enigmatically. "Maybe she
will be here tonight."

"Let's hope so." Chris feared her skepticism was showing.

Irv took a nervous sip of his Chivas. "I'm a gambling man,
right? I mean, what have I got to lose?" But he looked to Chris
like a man who had already lost.

"Positive thoughts!" Margot spoke with the voice of authority. "Remember, attitude is everything!" Her lips twitched,
her impatience growing by the minute, as if she were already
tuning in to murmurings from beyond. She beckoned to the
benches around the circular onyx-inlaid table that had been
moved inside for the ceremony. "Please be seated. We have

no time to lose." Chris and Alan sat side by side. "There is only one person who can tell us who was responsible for Dawn's murder," Margot continued, "Dawn herself."

If she hadn't known Margot took it so seriously, Chris would have considered it a cruel joke. She shot Alan a glance, and Margot picked up on it. "Doubting Thomases can make our task difficult, even impossible. I hope you'll both keep that in mind." They nodded, but evidently Margot didn't believe them. She separated the couple, positioning Alan on one side of her, Chris on the other. Irv faced Margot across the table.

"The sauna is where Dawn's spirit stepped from this world into another, more perfect one," Margot said. "It's the only place to make contact with her." She removed the monkey's paw from her pocket and placed it in the center of the table. In the candles' glow, its fingers cast a spidery shadow across the wall.

"I hope you will respect my wishes, Chris, and not use a camera here. *They*"—she looked into the room's dark corners—"they wouldn't appreciate it."

With a twinge of guilt Chris cocked the shutter of the Leica concealed under her shawl.

A sudden buzzing jarred them. Margot pressed a button on the travel alarm beside her. "Midnight. The hour when two worlds kiss. The new day and the old. This life and the happier one beyond." She stood up and pushed the sauna door ajar to admit a humid breath of air. Chris could hear a high-pitched hum from the deepest recesses of the basement. Margot sat down again and grasped Alan's fingers with her right hand, Chris's with her left. Alan and Chris both held Irv's hands. They could feel his fingers tremble.

"Now let's close our eyes," Margot said, "and sweep our minds clean of impure thoughts. Reach out to commune with the spirit world!" Chris peeked through her closed lashes at the others: Alan skeptical; Margot intense; Irv hopeful. "Enter a realm where there are no unkind words or evil acts, where the best in all of us will live on for eternity."

With Margot's sharp nails digging into her left hand and Irv's gold ring squeezing her right, Chris felt like a prisoner. Margot's bizarre behavior no longer fascinated her. She tapped her foot impatiently. This hocus-pocus by candlelight was absurd.

"I'm getting disruptions." Margot frowned. "Someone isn't concentrating." Chris closed her eyes. "There . . . that's better."

Margot's face stopped twitching, and she breathed deeply. "Good . . . good . . . no more interference. Now try to concentrate on Dawn as we all knew her . . . her face . . . her personality. The things we cherished. The things that will endure for eternity."

Chris could feel Irv's hand tense up, like an athlete lifting a great weight.

"We are crossing into the beyond!" Chris could feel Margot's hand break into goose bumps. "The lines of resistance are parting to enfold us!" Margot grinned, triumphant, tilting her head back to face the ceiling. "We are reaching out to a poor departed soul, known in this life as Dawn Parfait. *Dawn Parfait!*" She repeated the name distinctly, as if addressing a multitude. "Dawn Parfait. A lady of beauty and taste and sophistication. A budding Thespian, whom fate saw fit to remove from us before the fullness of her years. Though she has shed her earthly coil, we still love her for the acts of generosity she performed on earth." Margot took a deep breath. "Oh, disembodied spirit, bless us with your presence!"

Irv's whiskey glass rattled, the ice cubes tinkling like spirit bells. That's impossible, Chris thought. How could he have lifted it to take a drink if they were holding hands? She opened her eyes. The onyx-inlaid table was starting to vibrate, as if from an earth tremor.

But while the others shrank back, Margot pressed her breasts against the surface of the table, flushed, as if the energy that infused the onyx were coursing through her body. She inhaled the suffocating darkness like fresh mountain air, running her tongue along her lips until they glistened in the candlelight. "Yes," she whispered, "I feel the presence!"

Chris stared at the monkey's paw in amazement. As if responding to Margot's words, the tiny fist unclenched its fingers, releasing whatever it had clutched so tightly all these years, to let it float free in the room. The vibrations must have caused the shriveled muscle fibers to loosen, Chris concluded, groping for an explanation. *Unless. . . .*

"The jasmine blossoms in moonlight!" Margot recited. "The soul rises heavenward! The spirit is manifest in all things. It has the power to imbue dead stone with life, to kiss dead flesh with the spark of love. The petals open! The lotus reaches to the sky. Behold!"

The table lurched violently, sending Irv's drink skittering to the floor with a crash. Chris thought she saw cracks appearing on the onyx surface of the table and feared that from its volatile energy, the stone inlay might fly apart. Then, as quickly as it had started, the vibration stopped. Slowly, steadily, the table rose inch by inch until it hovered a foot in the air.

Irv gaped. "Holy shit!"

Margot's eyes were brimming with tears. She had summoned proof no one could deny. The others looked on in horror, waiting for the table to come crashing down. But it descended slowly, settling so gently onto the planking that it didn't make a sound.

Margot groaned. The force that had seized the table gripped her now. Her teeth chattered, and she shook like a rag doll. As her eyes rolled upward, her arms and legs stiffened. Her grimace softened into the subtlest of smiles.

The guests rejoined hands in a gesture of self-defense. "What the hell's going on?" Irv whispered.

But Margot didn't hear him, lost in her reverie.

"What do we do now?" Irv's voice quivered, like the flickering candles. With no reply from Margot, he squeezed Chris's hand. His palm was slippery, his body drenched with sweat, as if the sauna's heat had been turned on high. He licked his lips with a parched tongue. "Dawn...." Irv whispered the name and tried to smile, but his jaw muscles froze. *"Dawn...?"*

An icy pillar of air glided through the sauna's open door, whirling from Chris's left shoulder to her right, circling the table once, twice, prickling the hairs on the back of her neck. It returned to the door, and the redwood slab slammed shut. As if from the breath of a hundred tiny lips, the candles blew out.

Sealed in pitch-blackness, Chris was overwhelmed by the smell of scorched wax, the heavy scent of gardenias. She could feel Margot's hand stroke hers in a bizarre caress.

"Tell me...Tell me...Tell me...Give me...Give me... Give me..." Margot chanted, her voice rising in a crescendo. *"Tell me...Tell me...TELL!"*

Liquid spattered Chris's bare shoulder in the dark. At first she thought it must be Irv's drink, but hadn't his glass already smashed on the floor? She tugged her hand out of Margot's grasp to touch the droplets: sticky and warm. She heard a rustle of movement and whipped out her camera. She fired off the flash.

For a split second the burst of light revealed a hulking form behind Margot. Then the cubicle plunged back into a darkness more total than before.

"Turn on the light!" Chris screamed.

"No!" Margot growled. "It has so much to give!"

"The light!" Chris shouted.

"Please . . . no!" Margot whimpered, grasping Chris's hand so tightly it hurt. *"I command you!"*

Chris tried to wrench her hand away to grope for the light switch, but she couldn't free herself from Margot and Irv's grip. Alan flicked his cigarette lighter and relit the candles.

Chris *saw*.

"No!" The sight knocked the breath out of her, jolting her with the impact of a rifle bullet: Irv Florsheim's head was gone, sliced off with surgical precision. Blood gushed from his severed throat, spurting onto his chest, trickling across the tabletop like spilled wine. His hand was still warm, his grip on her fingers tightening in death.

It took all her strength to wrench free. As she pulled away from him, his body toppled onto the redwood floor with a soft thud.

Chris's head swam on the green verge of nausea, the sickly sweet smell of gardenias clashing with the scent of blood. She clutched the edge of the table to keep from keeling over.

Margot looked around her, dazed. Then her face grimaced into a ghastly smile. She primped her hair and patted her sweat-drenched forehead with a handkerchief. In the flickering light she peered under the table, scanning the floor. Then she riveted Chris with her gaze.

"What have they done with the head?" Margot asked. *"What have they done with the head?"*

35

SCOTT, INEZ, AND RIMA SKIPPED THE SÉANCE, POL-
ishing off a saddle of lamb bouquetière in his suite. Just one
more day before the plane, Scott thought as he scooped the
raspberry mousse from his bowl. How many more gourmet
meals before he had to fly back to reality? Once he returned
to his wretched apartment below Sunset Strip, he brooded, he'd
be living on food stamps. He tried to imprint on his mind the
two elegant women in their low-cut cocktail gowns sitting
across the table from him. He knew he would savor this moment
for years to come. Staring out over the moonlit surf, his companions listened enraptured to a tape of his old hits on a cassette
player. But the music only reminded him of all that he had
lost. When the tape ended for the fourth time, he jerked it out.
"Enough!"

Inez grabbed the cassette from him playfully and slotted it
back into the tape deck. "Just once more, okay? We hear your
music, and we see your face. It's a real cool trip, man." Scott
smiled at her outdated slang. No doubt she'd picked it up from
old Hollywood movies that were just now being released in
Panaguas—along with his own stale songs.

They smiled flirtatiously, and though he found their attention
flattering, it was a bit unnerving as well. Had they already
forgotten that their lover had been murdered today? Inez finished licking the Grand Marnier sauce off her spoon and
stretched, allowing the hem of her gown to ride up to her hips.
When Scott saw the bruises on her thighs, he guessed what
might be the reason for the women's lack of grief.

He felt a nudge under the table. Both women were rubbing
their legs against his. He conceded that their adoration was due
to more than his charisma. After Lopez's death, Inez and Rima
needed someone new to keep them. He wasn't about to tell
them that he was flat broke. Broke, that is, except for the
$1,000 bill he kept in his pocket for moments like this. He
rolled it up, then, bending over the table, used it to snort a line
of coke. Slipping it back into his pocket, he went over to lounge
on the bed. Inez flicked on *Scott Hershey's Greatest Hits* again.

"Hey, c'mon," he groaned. "Enough's enough!"

Inez laughed. "Give us a chance, okay, man?"

Rima flicked off the chandelier and focused a lamp against the wall. Swaying in the makeshift spotlight, the women started to strip in rhythm to the beat. They posed nude, thrusting out their breasts, shimmying so that their nipples bounced and shook. When the song ended, they leaped, giggling, on top of him, yanking off his belt and sliding down his jeans.

Scott laughed, high from the coke. "Hey, I can dig it . . . Dessert!"

They were fighting for him now, vying for his favor. Rima tongued Scott's penis, and jealous, Inez shoved her aside, her mouth slippery and warm, sucking in rhythm to the song that throbbed over the cassette player.

Rima pushed Inez away roughly. "Hey, take it easy." He laughed. "There's enough for everybody."

"Oh, baby, it tastes so *good* . . . !" Rima murmured.

Inez glared at her. Dividing up the spoils of Scott's body, the two friends obeyed an uneasy truce. They worked until their lips and tongues were sore, their bodies slippery with sweat. And as their breathing quickened, their rivalry grew. "Hey, man, fuck me. I be good for you," Inez whispered, reaming his ear with her tongue. Rima spelled the same message with her nimble fingers between his legs.

Scott rolled over weakly. The thought of giving all this up was more than he could bear. "You girls've got to come back to the States with me. Be my backup group, OK?"

"You take us to America?" Their eyes widened.

"You want it, you got it."

Once they were back in L.A., he'd find something for them to do. Women like them knew how to get by. Maybe they could even support *him*.

Inez and Rima went for his penis again, as if to convince him he'd made the right decision. He groaned and tried to fight them off, but the girls toyed with him hungrily. Lost in their love play, the women ignored the loud crash in the neighboring suite. But Scott heard. His penis wilted.

"What's wrong, baby?" Rima heard a clatter beyond the wall. "What's that?" Again the shock of impact, with such force that the pictures in the room were knocked out of kilter.

"Beats hell out of me." Scott cocked his head to listen. Next door something huge—perhaps a sofa—was hurled against the wall. The tremor sent the painting over Scott's dresser crashing to the floor. "Jesus Christ! Either someone's trying to bust into Chris's room—or bust out!" But who could *lift* something that heavy, much less hurl it across the room? he wondered. And *why?*

"Silencio!" Inez strained to listen, pressing her body tightly against the wall.

"The revolutionaries!" Rima whispered, her eyes wide. "They kill Lopez. Now they kill us!"

"Hey . . . No . . . Cool it." Scott climbed out of bed and double-bolted the door. Chris Latham was downstairs in the séance, out of harm's way, he thought with a pang of envy. But what about *them?*

Rima fumbled in her purse and handed Scott something. He looked at it as if he'd never seen one in his life. A switchblade. "You *muy macho* man, yes?" she said. Reluctantly he pressed the button on the handle, and the blade flicked out. After proving himself as a lover, he wasn't about to reveal himself a coward. But how could he defend them when he didn't even know how to defend himself? He caught a glimpse of his face in a mirror and read the terror in his eyes. Then the mirror shattered as something slammed into the other side of the wall.

Inez screamed, and with the next tremor, the tape deck flew off the bed, Scott's song reduced to a death rattle.

He snatched up the phone and dialed the front desk with trembling hands. "No answer!" He slammed the phone down, and tried to steady his voice to an even keel. "Let's keep cool," he whispered, his heart palpitating as he wedged a chair under the doorknob. Inez clutched a crucifix, Rima a steak knife snatched from the room-service cart. It angered Scott that they looked so much calmer than he felt.

A fresh shock from next door rattled the windows. Then, abruptly, the pandemonium ended.

In the eerie silence, Scott felt vulnerable in his nakedness and pulled a caftan over his head. Rima and Inez were dressing, too. The three of them sat on the edge of the bed and held their breath.

Something was moving across the debris-strewn floor of the adjoining suite, out into the hall. Who could destroy a room like that? Scott wondered. Who could have the *strength?* It could be nothing human . . . nothing *mortal.* Had a demonic spirit lured by Margot's séance come here by mistake? He snatched up the phone and frantically called the front desk again, the dial grating loud in the room. The line was dead. He slumped down on the bed and slipped his arms around Inez and Rima, their sexual link replaced by a deeper bond.

Teetering on the brink of panic, Scott feared that he knew the intruder all too well. On bad trips, his mind enflamed by hallucinogens, he had seen its face: a creature that slithered and crawled and crept, a hybrid, three-headed beast—hyena, squid, and anaconda—with thick, vile-smelling fur and scaly tentacles. But this time it wasn't just perched in his brain. It prowled the corridors, and its claws drew blood.

He struggled to blot out the image. "Maybe"—he tried to summon hope—"maybe it's over."

Rima clapped a hand over her mouth.

The doorknob to their suite was twisting, first left, then right. They froze. The knob stopped turning. Scott strained to hear the sound of receding footsteps, some clue that they had been spared.

God! A force slammed into the door with the impact of a battering ram. *The monster has come!* he thought.

Another sledgehammer blow. The girls screamed. He gasped as if he had been punched in the stomach. *The monster knows we're here!*

The brass hinges groaned, the interlocking blocks of mahogany creaking from the stress. Again a hundred fists pounded the slab of wood.

The women left the bed to press their bodies against the door, to keep it from breaking in, but before they could reach it, Scott held them back. For he saw the flash of steel, hacking through the wood. The blade hypnotized him as it spewed a shower of splinters into the room. It was a machete, and whoever, *whatever* grasped the weapon, wasn't tiring. The fury of the chopping was *building*, shearing off the wood in chunks. Three more blows, and it would be inside. Two more blows. *And then?*

With Rima and Inez beside him, Scott edged away in terror. Plaster dust snowed down from the crumbling ceiling. There was nowhere to run. Their backs were pressed against the picture window.

The machete completed its task with brutal efficiency. First the top, then the bottom hinge popped loose, the chair wedged under the doorknob buckling from the stress.

The door fell in with a deafening crash.

Silence. Glimpsed through a haze of plaster dust, the threshold was a gaping mouth. They waited for one minute . . . five. Still no sound from the hall. Crunching debris underfoot, Scott risked a look into the corridor.

"Nothing."

"Gracias a Dios!" With a trembling hand Rima downed a glass of flat champagne in a gulp.

Though Scott hadn't raised his voice above a whisper, he realized he was hoarse from the screams that had caught in his throat. Inez and Rima threw their arms around him, but his rubbery knees could barely support his own weight, and the three of them collapsed onto the bed. Their faces were clown-white from the plaster dust, like performers in a minstrel show of fear. Scott wished to God there were some magical elixir of uppers and downers that could purge him of his dread. But the monsters in his mind had escaped. He swore he could see a clawed foot sticking out from under the bed. No, it was only his shoe. But what of the serpentine shadow in the closet and the way the shower curtains shivered in the hiss from the air-conditioning vent?

Scott looked at Inez and Rima, and at the void beyond the threshold, and burst into tears.

36

WHEN HE STEPPED INTO THE SAUNA, BERGER HAD the doubly stunned look of a man who had witnessed lightning strike twice in the same place. Leading him into the basement, Alan had tried to explain what had happened, but nothing could have prepared the hotel manager for this. Spattered with blood, Margot and Chris sat frozen in shock, like survivors from a game of Russian roulette. Something rooted them here—grief perhaps. Or was it simply the fear of stepping out into the basement? Berger's arrival did nothing to rouse them from their inertia. It was as if their bodies had turned to onyx, like the bloodstained table.

Alan slumped down beside Chris. Neither of them spoke. They didn't have to. Berger just followed their eyes. "This is horrible...horrible!" he said, and knelt down, shining his flashlight at the headless corpse. On the floor beside the body, Irv's Mogen David and crucifix glinted in the candlelight. Berger slipped them into his pocket. He started to stand up but stopped himself, scanning the floor. *"The head...?"* he murmured. The word hung heavy in the air. To Chris, it seemed less a question than a statement. After what had happened to Lopez and Dawn, had he expected this?

Berger noticed a spot of blood on his sleeve. He spent a long time trying to wipe it off with his handkerchief, but the stain seemed as indelible as his horror. "Let's go upstairs," he said. Nobody moved. The séance had turned into a wake.

Berger eased Chris off the bench and led her toward the door. But Margot wouldn't budge. The spinster was conducting a conversation with the decapitated corpse. "Don't you worry, sweetheart," she murmured. "Don't you worry about a thing."

Berger approached her with the same dismay he had shown toward Irv's body, as if she were a victim instead of a survivor. "Miss Hampton...It's time to go." He took her arm gently. "Miss Hampton?"

She turned her eyes up to him. "He's going to be all right. He's going to be all right, isn't he?"

191

Berger waited a polite moment. Then he offered his arm. "May I escort you to your room?"

With deranged logic, Margot took out a lace handkerchief and draped it over Irv's severed neck. Then she picked up the monkey's paw from the table and accepted Berger's arm. "Why, how thoughtful. Have we met?" Her lips grimaced into a coquettish smile. She let him lead her out of the room.

Chris hesitated at the threshold and looked back into the sauna. There were two spirits hovering in that tomb now, she thought. Though it was not the way she would have wished, Margot had brought Dawn and Irv together, after all.

On shaky legs, Chris climbed the stairs to the patio. She took a deep breath. Outdoors, the air seemed as stifling as in that bloodstained cubicle. The night had soured, the smell of brine from the beach mingling with chlorine from the swimming pool. Beyond the balustrade, the waves had hurled the carcasses of countless sea creatures onto the shore, as if the ocean itself were dying.

Margot and her escort crossed the flagstones at a funereal pace. The patio furniture stood out starkly in the moonlight, like a reminder of those whose stay at the El Dorado had already ended—Tobias, Lopez, Dawn. And now Irv. Chris looked up at the building that towered into the night and counted the few illuminated windows. The lights were going out, one by one. How many passengers would be left to board Harley Stokes's plane tomorrow?

She felt betrayed, as if the victims had gone over to join the enemy, to conspire against the few who still survived. Steam was rising from the pool and, lit by underwater spotlights, a sea gull with a broken wing thrashed for its life. But it was too late for her to save it. The bird was drowning. Perhaps, she thought, it was too late to save any of them.

She stepped into the air-conditioned void of the hotel lobby, as numbing as a plunge into the deep.

They rode the elevator in silence. Its wood-paneled walls reminded Chris of the sauna, and she longed for them to reach their destination. At last, the doors whooshed open—to reveal chaos.

The hallway was littered with splinters of mahogany, shattered glass and the limbs of smashed furniture, as if the rooms had exploded. A pall of powdered plaster hung on the air. The same tornado that had turned Tobias's room inside out had been unleashed here, Chris thought, but on a much more monstrous scale.

"What have they done?" Berger clutched at his chest.

Ironically the very devastation which stunned him brought Margot back to her senses. "Irv is *dead!*" she murmured. "Someone chopped off his *head!*" She punched the "Door Close" button, as if to switch to a less threatening channel.

But Chris held the elevator doors open. *"My cameras!"* Berger tried to stop her, but she forced her way past him, rushing toward her room at the far end of the hall. Alan and Berger each snatched up a chunk of wood and followed her.

Their feet crunched over the debris. They would give ample warning to anything lying in wait, Chris thought, as she picked her way down the devastated corridor. Only the occupied rooms had been destroyed, proof that the force had been guided by reason. A strategy which, she feared, was just beginning to unfold. Her pace slowed to a walk, as if the hallway were booby-trapped.

She gasped. A bushy head popped from one of the doorways. It was Rima, covered with plaster dust. She ran out and threw her arms around Berger, stifling sobs. Inez joined her and hugged the hotel manager, who stood there, awkward in their embrace.

Scott peered cautiously from behind the doorjamb, then swaggered out. "Where the hell *were* you?" he shouted. "We could've got killed, for Chrissakes!"

Berger seized Scott by the shoulders and shook him. *"Who was it?"*

"How the fuck should I know? All hell was breaking loose. Our door was locked... until he... *it* smashed it in with a *machete*. Sonofabitch! The door falls in, then we look outside, and it's *gone!*" He stopped himself, like a child spouting a tall tale, convinced his parents would never believe him.

But when Chris saw her room, she believed. The Danish armchairs had been torn apart, the glass table crushed, and mattress stuffing gaped from a slash up the middle of the bed. The mirror hung crookedly on the wall, reduced to a silvery mosaic, like a relic from a bombed-out fun house. But those details eluded her. She teetered on the threshold and choked on her words, as if she had discovered a corpse. *"My cameras!"*

The Haliburton case had been pried open, and her equipment was smashed, shards of lens glass scattered across the floor.

She knelt down beside her cameras in grief. A fragile part of her had been violated. The delicate instruments had been as familiar to her touch as old friends. They had survived the most dangerous moments of a dangerous career. She had worn them over her heart at Khe Sanh, in Zaire and Mozambique. More than once, when one of them had slipped from her grasp in a dash across a battlefield, she had risked her life to scoop it from the crossfire. She ran her fingers across the fragments of metal and glass. They left a void in her life that couldn't be filled by going out and buying newer, shinier models. She had learned the idiosyncrasies of each of her cameras, and she even believed they had learned hers as well.

Her hands cradled the only one of her glass menagerie to escape destruction—the Leica she had taken downstairs to the séance. It was her monkey's paw—all the magic she had left.

As she turned away from the wrecked cameras, her eyes began to mist over. How strange, she thought, how perverse. After all the blood of the past few days, she hadn't cried. But now the sight of these scraps of metal and glass blinded her with tears. Images unreeled mercilessly in her mind, specters she had managed to avoid facing head-on ... until now: Tobias's slaughter, Torres's brutal interrogation, Lopez, Dawn, Irv.... Her cameras had made it through the most dangerous moments of her life, but they hadn't survived *this*. How could she expect to survive the ordeal herself? The awareness overwhelmed her, and she collapsed in convulsive sobs.

Alan was there to cling to as she cried. "It's going to be all right." He hugged her to him. "Everything's going to be all right." She wrapped her arms around him as if she had known him all her life, as if this man were the one known quantity in a sinister world. "It's time to sleep," he said.

"But ..."—she squinted through her tears at the floor—"my cameras...."

Berger took out his passkey and led them to a suite that had been spared from the onslaught. Alan tried to help Chris inside, but even on the verge of collapse, she insisted on walking in under her own power.

Berger was having trouble coming up with reassurances. The best he could manage was: "This will be your last night at the hotel. The plane comes tomorrow."

"*If* it comes." Chris and Alan exchanged a skeptical glance.

"Good night," Berger said, with a stiff bow, instead of his

usual charming smile. "Try to sleep."

Alan and Chris found themselves alone in the room. "Is this the last night before Harley Stokes gets here?" she thought aloud. "Or is it the last night . . . period?"

"I never should have thrown that gun away," he said.

Chris shook her head. "We didn't know we'd need it." Clutching her last camera on its wrist thong, she lay down on the bed.

It seemed that she had fallen asleep. Then she opened her eyes. Alan had double-bolted the door and was wedging a chair under the knob. Empty precautions, she thought. Her lips formed the thought that was on both their minds. "You know what would be the worst part? Even worse than not making it through all this? To never know what hit us. . . ."

"We'll know," Alan said with grim certainty. "We'll know soon enough."

"When I shot off the flash in the sauna," she said, *"I saw."*

Alan was riveted. "Saw . . . *what?"*

"It was alive," she said, struggling to bring it into focus.

"Was it . . . human?"

"It was . . . enormous." She closed her eyes, as if studying the image imprinted on her retinas by the blinding light. It was no use. The specter had retreated into her subconscious.

Her gaze drifted to the door, and she tried to imagine how any living thing could drive a steel blade through four inches of solid mahogany. The realization was growing. It had been in her mind for a long time, but this was the first time she had dared to say it aloud. "The . . . Warak . . ." she whispered.

"The Warak . . . ?"

"A primitive tribe. They used to live here before the hotel was built. Lopez had his men wipe them out."

"How do you know this?" His voice echoed her excitement.

"I know . . ." was all she would say.

"But . . . if all of them were wiped out . . . ?"

"No, not all," she said, and their eyes met. "There were survivors. *There must have been survivors."* Could one Warak, alone, have been capable of this? She knew the answer had to be yes. Hadn't Tobias said they were more than human, if only in their capacity for revenge?

"But . . . how do you know all this?"

She was too impatient to explain the details now. What mattered, *all* that mattered, was her certainty. *"It's one of them,"* she said.

"But you've got to tell me. . . ."

She shook her head. She wouldn't mention the extraordinary strength of the Warak, their stalking skill, their will to vengeance. That could wait until tomorrow. He had seen the devastation with his own eyes. To inflict more on him tonight would only breed nightmares.

Though she ached for sleep, she couldn't close her eyes. The darkened chandelier mesmerized her. In the half-light, the dangling shadow looked like one of the shrunken heads, the trophies which, she knew, could only belong to the Warak.

Alan saw her staring up at the chandelier and switched on the light, as if to dispel the specter. He turned to leave. She could see that he was angry that she wouldn't confide in him. But wasn't she doing him a favor? He had unbolted the door when she sat up in bed. "Stay," she said. He nodded, and locked the door again. He seemed as relieved as she was that they would be spending the night together.

She lay back on the bed as he walked over to the window and held a match under a cigar, puffing until it glowed alight. She inhaled deeply. The aroma of tobacco replaced the lingering stench of gardenias and spilled blood. He was a comforting presence, and as he sat down in a chair facing the night, she closed her eyes at last.

In the free-fall between consciousness and sleep, she found no escape. For at the El Dorado, the very walls were her enemies. The Warak lurked within them, surrounding her. Like fossils, their bodies were embedded in the cement floors, entombed in the ceiling and facade. The building was infested with their corpses, silent and eternal guests.

Their wrath imbued them with a fierce new life. She could feel them reaching out through crumbling walls to snatch her with onyx fingers, arms snaking up from under the bed, heads twisting out from behind the drapes to snap at her with sharp teeth. She looked up and screamed. Leering down at her from the ceiling, a warrior came burrowing through the plaster to leap on top of her. She ran into the bathroom and locked the door. Hands burst out of the tiled floor, clawing out to grab her ankles. Icy fingers pulled her down, to seal her inside cold cement. A guest for eternity.

Then the vision died. Like a dark blade, sleep felled her with merciful swiftness.

37

BERGER'S FEET CLATTERED DOWN THE MARBLE steps to the lobby. What calm he had been able to muster for the guests had been only a sham. The decision he faced, he would have to make alone. And it terrified him. At the foot of the stairs he dimmed the lights in the lobby and headed toward the front desk. His pace slowed as he neared the cageful of exotic birds, stark against the night. He hesitated before them, as if seeking counsel from creatures closer to life's mysteries than he was himself. But if they had any such wisdom, they withheld it. Perched in silhouette, they were a tribunal sitting in judgment over him.

He heard their verdict. Guilty. Guilty of negligence. After Lopez's assassination he should have contacted Internal Security. But the murder of a man he considered evil, and who had himself probably been guilty of killing Eleanor Tobias, had not seemed sufficient reason to cut short the gala opening of his hotel. He had planned to wait until the guests left. Then he would have reported the death and allowed the place to be overrun with police.

He had delayed, and he recognized now that it had been a terrible miscalculation. It had spawned Irv's death, the mayhem in the rooms, and. . . . He swore at his complacency for assuming Lopez's murder had been politically motivated, for not realizing the magnitude of the danger.

Guilty. The birds condemned him with piercing eyes, sentenced him with sharp beaks. *Guilty.* No, he confessed, it hadn't been concern for his guests that had delayed his summoning help. It had been selfishness. He knew that once he contacted Internal Security, they would blame him. The hotel was his responsibility, and he would be the scapegoat. It would even come out under interrogation that he had harbored Dr. Eleanor Tobias, an enemy of the state. He feared that in the basement of the Panaguan central prison, there was a chair like the one he had discovered in his cellar in Munich years ago. They would torture him as in his worst nightmares.

But tonight he would have to take that chance, if he were to save . . . whoever *could* be saved. Facing the cage, he clicked his heels together as if accepting a necessary but suicidal order and stepped quickly behind the front desk. There was only one way for him to redeem himself. If it wasn't too late.

He threw open the door and, without switching on the light, bent over the shortwave radio. He knew the routine, for he'd sent reports to the capital every day since he'd taken charge of the hotel. When events had started to go awry, he had confined his dispatches to details of hotel housekeeping, hoping to handle the crisis by himself. But now he would tell them everything. He had to convince the authorities they couldn't wait one more day. With luck, a detachment of heavily armed Panaguan Rangers would arrive by helicopter in three hours to evacuate them. His troubles would just be starting. But at least the guests would be safe.

He twirled the plastic knobs—frequency selector and volume control—and switched to 573.2. The Department of Internal Security. He picked up the mike. *"Cuatro Dos Dorado . . . Cuatro Dos Dorado. . . ."* There was no reply. He checked the frequency-selector knob and tried again. *"Cuatro Dos Dorado. . . ."* He flicked his thumb off the mike button, stopping in mid-sentence. The usual glow didn't light up the dial. He snapped on the overhead light to check that the radio hadn't been unplugged. Then he noticed: its circuitry of wires and transistors had been disemboweled, as if in an act of hari-kari.

He closed his eyes and buried his head in his hands to regain his equilibrium. It afflicted him with childhood specters: the troops he had seen returning from the Russian front, their faces frostbitten into masks, men who had lost their limbs to blizzards and shrapnel. Snowblind.

He turned to the shotgun rack on the wall. The weapons, he remembered, had been stolen days before. He realized now that far from being disjointed or irrational, the incidents at the El Dorado had been guided by a master plan. The calamities had been orchestrated to toy with the guests first, to manipulate them, then to reduce them to whimpering terror. Somehow their tormentor even knew that the radio would be their final hope, and had waited until now to dash it.

He looked at the accounting books lining his shelves, petty records of profit and loss, useless now. He had made the bureaucrat's classic mistake, too bogged down in insignificant detail to grasp the enormity of the menace. He looked at the cashbox on his desk. It could easily have been plundered by the intruder, but it was untouched. The killer didn't want money. It was greedy for their lives.

He grieved for the hotel as for the guests. This haven for strangers, this behemoth he had breathed to life, was dying before his eyes. A cancer was invading it, room by room, and he was doomed to watch it perish. Now that his office, the nerve center, had succumbed, they were defenseless. Another bitter memory from his childhood struck him: the German teenagers who in the last days of the war, when the Wehrmacht was a shambles, were forced to fight Russian tanks with rocks. Tonight he understood their desperation.

Cursing his impotence, he turned into a monster himself, railing at the forces that had thwarted him all his life. He grabbed armloads of accounting books off the shelves and threw them to the floor, then overturned the desk with a crash. His fury building, he scooped up the shortwave radio in his arms and hurled it against the wall. Breathless, he leaned against the door, his demon spent.

Suit rumpled, necktie askew, he surveyed the room, disappointed in his destructive powers: a puny job, indeed, compared to the devastation upstairs.

Through the open door he could feel the birds watching him, hear their derisive cackling. They knew the futility of his rage. The tanks were rumbling at attack velocity, their cannons leveled at him, and the thought of resistance was folly.

He slammed the door to shield himself from the birds' gaze and stared at the shambles he had created. His muscles ached as he stood up, gathered the books off the floor, and replaced them on the shelves. He turned the furniture upright and hefted the radio onto the tabletop, stuffing its mangled innards inside. He even straightened his tie and combed his hair. Soon both he and the office were neat once more. The violence that had erupted was as carefully concealed within the room as was the rage beneath his well-groomed exterior.

He opened the door to the lobby and looked outdoors, through the picture window. Grudgingly he conceded that the night was an even greater master of concealment. The moon was failing, fading like a palpitating heart. The moon would be the first to die tonight, he thought. They all would follow.

38

"BY DAY, THE TOWNSFOLK LIVED PEACEFUL LIVES. But when night fell, they hurried home, to bolt their doors and hide...." Margot tried to blot the words out of her mind, but they uncoiled against her will, strident and unstoppable. *"When night fell...."*

Now that the moon was sinking, now that the jungle and the night had coalesced into a seething ocean outside her window, the old bedtime tale took on an ugly ring.

"When night fell, they hurried home to bolt their doors and hide!" Margot had spent an hour checking and rechecking the bolted door to her suite in an obsessive ritual of fear. But she couldn't lock out the dark. Since her suite had been destroyed and she had been forced to move to this new one, death had slithered inside, a lascivious roommate. To protect herself, she felt compelled to shed her seductive trappings. Her red nail polish was the first adornment to go. It fostered too many queasy associations: the tigress with bloody claws; echoes of her guilt for accidentally engineering Irv's death. Long after she had wiped off the stain with polish remover, she scrubbed her hands in the sink. Lady Macbeth, she brooded. *"All the perfumes of Arabia will not sweeten this little hand."* But she knew she was too weak to fit the role. Instead of the murderess's evil strength, she was filled with self-loathing. If she had been an unwitting accomplice in Irv's murder, it had been from the most desperate of motives: to be loved.

Margot mopped off the rouge that blushed her cheeks and smeared cold cream on her face. Unholy powers had toyed with her, used her, then discarded her. The jungle had played a malicious joke in its courtship, like the boys who used to give her the wolf whistle on the way home from school, then run away laughing.

The masquerade was over. She erased the rosebud lips, leaving a fish mouth criss-crossed with age lines. When she washed the blue eye shadow from her lids, crow's-feet seized hold with talons. She feared that her dabbling in the occult had unleashed dark forces that had led to Irv's murder, and it rendered her unclean. The dream of someday leading a normal life, with a husband, a family—a dream she had clung to so tenaciously—was dead. It was time to join her own kind, the netherworld of whispered incantations. The brotherhood of the monkey's paw.

She stepped into the shower, hoping the roar of the water would drown out the voice in her mind. But the words cut through, like thunderclaps through rain. *"For they knew it came tonight on dark and mighty wings."* She twisted the faucet as far as it would go, turning the water scalding hot. Cremation, she thought, that would be a fitting end.

She bowed her head in the shower and the water rushing in her ears gave her a moment's peace as she washed out the auburn rinse, russet aging to gray.

Margot climbed out of the shower cold and wet. The full-length mirror had misted over, and bravely she wiped it off, scrutinizing herself under the harsh bathroom light. One long look at her withered breasts, her legs laced with varicose veins, and she understood why she wasted so much time on small deceits. The water's heat had failed to flush her pale skin, powerless to imbue her body with the glow of life.

Barren, she thought with revulsion. Breasts that would never hold milk. A womb that would never bear fruit. *Barren.* It was an obsolete word, but then, Margot felt obsolete herself. Ancient, like a mummy in a crypt, so shriveled that its sex was now a mystery, so desiccated that a breath of air would crumble it to dust. The mirror was fogging up again, protecting her from the truth. No wonder, she thought, no wonder she preferred the dark.

"When night fell," the voice in her brain repeated, *"they hurried home, to bolt their doors and hide!"*

She shivered under the air conditioning, and wrapped herself in a towel. Then she uncorked her vials of perfume and poured them one by one down the toilet, mingling musk, oil of citrus, and attar of roses. She knew now why she had steeped herself in those scents for so long. She knew why she had clung to the girlish laughter, the coyness of bedroom eyes, the sickly-sweet corsages: to disguise the stench of rot.

"By day, the townsfolk lived out peaceful lives. But when night fell, they hurried home, to bolt their doors and hide. For they knew it came tonight on dark and mighty wings."

Her mother had started the bedtime story like that, more

nights than Margot dared remember. Her mother, consumed with the hatreds of a lifetime, had taken a ghoulish delight in the telling of the tale. Before the little girl of ten had heard of poltergeists, before she knew of exorcism or the undead, the tale had lurked in her brain. She would lie in her bed in the cold attic, watching shadows slink across the wall, and shiver as the words seeped into her mind: *"No head had he, nor eyes nor teeth, but rode the stormy winds of night to kill and maim both weak and wise—death to all who could not cleanse the darkness from their eyes. . . . The headless horseman rode, and sliced his sabre through the air to ghastly vengeance wreak. . . ."* She would wake up in tears long after midnight, certain she could hear the hooves of the black stallion outside, striking sparks on the pavement. She would pull open the window and lean her head into the night, too late to glimpse it as it charged by, faster than a graveyard wind.

The headless horseman rode, and sliced his sabre through the air to ghastly vengeance wreak!

Each night, in the cold attic, by the time her mother was through telling the tale Margot *believed* in the headless beast. Without a brain, it acted from a primal impulse: an instinct for murder. Headless, it would behead others, as Irv had been beheaded. And once mutilated, once transformed, the victims, too, would join in the rampage.

"With passion deep, and boundless hate, no head need guide the arm that wields the blade!" Eyeless, it stalked its quarry. Voiceless, it bellowed in triumph. Tonight, the horse and rider had returned.

She was sweating as she fumbled through her books on astrology, remnants salvaged from her wrecked room. She vowed she would prove the augury wrong. She would create a new horoscope, a new vision.

But though she scribbled down her computations, she didn't dare read them. Lighting a match, she burned the prophecy, holding it until the flames scorched her fingers. She was a witch, she brooded, and they burned witches.

Yet her sorcery was dwarfed by the magic that surrounded her. She looked out the window, over the waves that frothed like an evil brew. The moon had sunk into it long ago, a luminous drop in the potion. She watched the whitecaps bubble and foam, wondering what spell was being cast, and who was stirring the caldron.

39

CHRIS AWOKE IN A SWEAT. FOR A MOMENT, IN THE darkness, she thought she was back in New York, that she had left the El Dorado thousands of miles away. Then she felt the camera on her wrist thong, reminding her she was a prisoner.

A lighter burst into flame, revealing Alan's face as he lit his cigar, and it all rushed back on her: the séance, the blood, the devastated rooms. She sank back onto the pillow and looked at the clock: 3:24. Damn. She had hoped her sleep had devoured more of the night than that. Outside, she could see the cutting edge of the surf rushing toward the beach. She felt a compulsion to talk. She had been alone with her terror long enough.

"Alan . . . ?" He didn't answer, and she strained to probe the silence: did she detect something stirring in the devastated rooms?

"Are you awake?" he asked.

"I never thought I'd spend my last night . . . like this," she replied. "I always thought it would be in a foxhole with gunfire, explosions, all hell breaking loose. This silence is worse. Much worse. . . ." The silence was as threatening as bullets whining overhead. If only she could understand its meaning. . . . She stared across the room to reassure herself that Alan was still there. It seemed they were a great distance apart, separated by the dark and all the questions that it held.

"I was watching you sleep," he said at last. "It reminded me how I'd sit up with my wife in the hospital, waiting for dawn to come. Waiting to see if she'd make it through the night."

"Will we?" she asked. It was an intimate moment, but he made no attempt at physical intimacy, and she was grateful for that. She felt that the gentlest act he could perform now was to keep his distance.

"That tribe," he said. "The Warak . . . Please . . . tell me about them."

But she hoarded the information to herself. To confide her horror would leave him feeling even more vulnerable. To invoke the tribe's name now, to describe their mystical strengths when one of their warriors might be nearby. . . . Could it even invite an attack? "When morning comes," she said. "Then I'll tell you everything."

"Morning?" She heard the hint of a laugh. His voice lowered, as if to remind her of a painful fact they both would rather ignore. "Tomorrow Stokes picks us up. If there's going to be a bloodbath, tonight's the night."

"In the morning," she repeated stubbornly. *"I can't now."*

"Chris. . . ." But he stopped himself, and instead of pressuring her, tormented the tip of his cigar with the lighter's flame. "I always thought the worst way to go would be in a mine disaster," he mused. "Sitting there, trapped in a pitch-black mine shaft, not knowing whether there's enough oxygen to last for days . . . or whether it will all end like that"—he snapped his fingers—"with a cave-in. That damned uncertainty. . . ." He hesitated. "That's how it feels now." He flicked the lighter again and puffed on his cigar like an opium pipe. "The things I've been afraid of," he said, "the fears I've had to face. . . . They were all cave-ins. The fear of things collapsing inside me."

After a long silence she opened her eyes. Alan had slumped into an armchair. Had he drifted off to sleep? She hoped not. "This waiting. . . ." She bit her lip. "It's unbearable. We've got to *do* something."

"Berger's radioed for help by now. What else *can* we do?" From his annoyance, she guessed he had been asking himself the same question. Then his tone softened as if he were asking her a favor that he couldn't put into words. "After being close to death as often as you have in your work, you've probably learned how to face it. . . ."

She shook her head. "No matter how close to death I get . . . no matter how often . . . I'm just as scared. Sure, you learn how to bury the fear deeper inside you. But sooner or later it always rises to the surface." She squinted out the window at the waves. Like the hotel, the ocean seemed deceptively tranquil, as if at any moment a serpent might rear out of the surf. "I guess you do learn a few tricks after a while," she said. "You have to. When it all gets to be too much for me, I focus my mind on . . . a place."

"What place?"

"The gardens of the Alhambra, in Granada."

He nodded solemnly. "I went there . . . with my wife."

"It's the most beautiful spot on earth," she continued. "Right out of the *Arabian Nights*. Just thinking about it calms me."

"Did it work tonight?" he asked.

She frowned. "I guess my mind is too far gone. This time when I thought of the gardens, all I could picture was the way the caliph, when he was angry . . ."

"The caliph . . . ?"

She hesitated to confide her nightmare. "The Moorish king. . . . When he was angry, he'd execute the wives in his harem who no longer pleased him." She dropped her arm onto the bedclothes, rigid as a scimitar. "He used to *behead* them."

She could feel the tension in the air. It imprisoned them each in their separate terror.

Alan thrust his arms into the darkness, as if it took physical effort to get the conversation started. "Strange," he said. "Life used to mean so little to me, I would gladly have ended it. Now, I can't bear the thought that it's all going to be taken away."

"Life is habit-forming," she said. "I've seen a lot of the world in the last ten years, more than most people see in a lifetime. But it doesn't make me any more willing to leave it all behind. It only makes me greedy for more."

"One thing about dying," Alan said, "there won't be a lot of loose ends for me. No kids. No relatives to speak of. No complications."

She could detect regret in his voice. They had much in common. Perhaps she had avoided him because they were *too* much alike, just as she might avoid a mirror because of the blemishes it reflected. Strange, she thought. After all their efforts to keep a conversation going, the result had been to make them feel more alone.

Alan sat on the bed beside her. It was a move which, she knew, took courage. He placed his hand on her shoulder.

"You're strong," he said. "I don't know how you do it."

"It's not enough to be strong," she said, and pulled him to her with an urgency that surprised her. "I need you." Even now she listened for a telltale sound, watched for the hint of an intruding shadow. But somehow the terror that had kept them apart, was bringing them together at last.

They collapsed into each other's arms. She felt tears on her face, but were they hers or his? They were both crying now, crying with relief. They had traveled thousands of miles, only to find themselves prisoners. Now to escape, neither would have to travel any farther than the distance between their lips.

40

SUNLIGHT STREAMED THROUGH THE PICTURE WIN-
dow, slicing Berger in half. Splayed out on the bed in his suit,
he blinked and rubbed his eyes. His watch read 8:15. Was it
possible? Had they been spared? With the joy of a shipwrecked
sailor waking up on the beach, he stretched luxuriously and
stood up, peering out the window. The sun glinted off the
waves, more benign than on any day he could remember. He
ran his hand through his disheveled blond hair. He was badly
in need of a shower, yet somehow he felt cleansed. He could
see the palm trees were nodding in a stiff breeze. With this tail
wind, Harley Stokes might be arriving earlier today than expected.

It was too good to be true, he warned himself, so he tele-
phoned the guests, one by one. They answered drowsily. All
of them had slept through the night without incident. To celebrate, he'd have the staff bring them the El Dorado breakfast-
in-bed, a treat he'd devised himself: eggs Benedict, but made
with Beluga caviar instead of Canadian bacon. Accompanied
by a delicate Sancerre, it would provide a cheerful sendoff
before their return flight.

As he unlocked the door, he felt a twinge of fear, but a
glance down the corridor reassured him that all was well. In
the sunlight, the debris from last night no longer seemed so
forbidding. Even nightmares had to end, he thought, sealing
the terror in his mind as decisively as he locked the door behind
him. The hotel might outlive these grotesque birth pangs. So
might his career. Now that he was convinced the danger was
past, he felt his appetite returning, and pictured the Boursin
omelet he would have the chef prepare for him. He descended
the staircase to the lobby with a bounce in his step.

In the morning, the parrots, toucans, and macaws in the
huge bamboo cage usually greeted him with a raucous welcome. But today they were sound asleep, as immobile as if
stuffed. He reached the foot of the stairs and realized why.
Esmerelda had failed to perform her noisy morning routine of

vacuuming the carpets. He would have to discipline her for the oversight.

A slug was crawling up one of the door handles at the lobby entrance, leaving a trail of slime. He plucked it off with his handkerchief and threw it outside, into the bushes. Where was Maria? Why wasn't she polishing the brass fixtures? As he headed toward the patio, he could hear flies buzzing in the hallway, the drone rising to a shrill pitch as he passed. The maids hadn't sprayed their early-morning mist of insecticide. Why? He would not tolerate such neglect. Even a few chores left undone might endanger the fragile fabric of the hotel. He jogged down the corridor, past the souvenir shop and dining room, and burst outside.

The patio appalled him. A column of driver ants entwined the leg of a table, devouring a scrap of steak from the night before. Palm fronds in the swimming pool revolved slowly, like the hands of clocks. A drowned gull slapped against the tiled edge, as the wind rippled the water. Berger was furious. This was worse than disobedience. It was mutiny.

He ran past the generator, his heart pounding with the turbine's driving pace. Gasping for breath, he smelled a salt breeze, another ominous sign. The morning air was usually tainted by wood fires as the staff cooked their breakfast.

A closer look at the shanties confirmed his suspicions. The wind rustled cardboard shutters, rattled walls of corrugated tin. Not a soul. Pottery jars, colored cloth, straw mats—everything of value had been taken. So little remained, in fact, that the crows hadn't even descended to pick the shanties clean. He kicked the ashes of an abandoned cooking fire. The coals were still warm.

Standing alone among the huts, he could feel his flesh crawl. For he sensed that when the servants had left, something else had moved in to take their place. Something alive. But what? He had watched the staff face poisonous snakes without a hint of fear. What would it take to make them flee? His staff might not have known how to open a bottle of champagne, but when it came to jungle survival, their judgment was astute.

He heard a shriek, and edged around a rusty tin wall, toward the source of the cry. Its eyes wide with terror, a scrawny monkey was bawling like a baby, straining at the end of its tether. It seemed as stunned as Berger by its abandonment, and as he untied the rope from the monkey's neck, it snarled at him. He offered it a piece of papaya. The creature sniffed the fruit, dropped it and then scurried toward the jungle, as if it knew the hotel's grounds were condemned.

Berger watched the monkey disappear into the undergrowth. Now that the gardeners had fled the battle lines, vines and creepers overran the hotel's defenses. The warning sign was already engulfed in weeds, and only one word could be read through the web of green: "MUERTE."

The minivan had been abandoned on the road beside the patio. Its hood was raised, its engine cannibalized for parts. He knew that in the fishing villages up the coast, a battery or spark plug would bring a high price. He slammed the hood shut. Desertion was the most contemptible of crimes, he brooded, as he strode back toward the hotel. By the articles of war, his staff had earned a firing squad. But why had they decided to leave today when the plane was due and the danger past? What discovery could have forced them to give up a month's pay? And why had they not told him of the danger? Were they so full of hate that they would leave the guests at the mercy of . . . God knows what? Overwhelmed with rage, he squinted into the sky. The sun was wedged between a vise of two dark clouds, as if past and future were closing in to crush the daylight.

He entered the hotel cautiously, peering into the shadowy corridors. To combat a surge of fear, he felt compelled to take inventory of their supplies and rushed to the kitchen. The room had been stripped to the walls. The Waterford crystal, the Christofle silver, the Villeroy and Boch china, even the pots and pans—all had been stolen. The food, he wondered, had they taken that, too? Every crumb. The freezers were empty. Even the bins of flour and sugar had been cleaned out. They had done a much more thorough job as thieves, he thought bitterly, than they had ever done for him. But his next discovery was much more alarming. The knives, the meat cleavers— anything with a cutting edge, a sharp steel point—were gone. He threw open the door to the utility closet. The machetes, rakes, and shovels had also been stolen. They were defenseless.

Berger licked his lips. Whatever had terrified the staff, would it strike before Harley Stokes's arrival today? He studied his watch: 9:07. The guests would be expecting breakfast. He would have to explain that it was out of the question. But before he could face them, he needed a drink.

He hurried to the bar and was relieved to find the bottles were intact. At least the staff had been generous enough to leave the alcohol behind. He slumped onto a stool. As he pondered momentous decisions, the choice between vodka and scotch stymied him. He settled for three fingers of Stolichnaya, and downed it in a gulp. It seared his throat, but it didn't bring the numbness he sought. He leaned over to pour himself another shot, and his jaw dropped. Two feet were sticking out from behind the bar. Cautiously, he took a closer look.

Jesús, the bartender, lay flat on his back on the floor. Berger was saddened by the sight. Of all the staff, Jesús had tried the hardest to please. Now, it seemed, he had paid for his loyalty. He bore no visible wounds: his head was still attached to his body, and the expression on his face was one of pure bliss. Rigor mortis hadn't set in yet. How long had the bartender been dead? Berger wondered. Six hours? Seven? He lifted his glass in a farewell, but he couldn't bring himself to sip the drink, as if it had been contaminated by the nearness of death.

"*Ach!*" he gasped. The bartender's mouth widened into a leer.

"They want to take your whiskey, but I protect it, yes?" Jesús lifted an empty Chivas bottle in his fist and patted his belly. "They go." He winked a drunken eye. "They *all* go. But I stay."

Berger wondered whether Jesús had stayed out of loyalty to him or to the booze. What mattered was that he *had* stayed. Jesús was the only link to the mystery. Berger helped the bartender up onto wobbly legs, then downed his second vodka before asking the question. "*Why did they leave?*"

Jesús winked drunkenly and placed a finger to his lips.

"Damn it, tell me why!"

"*No importa.*" He shrugged.

Clutching Jesús by the scruff of the neck, Berger slammed him into the bar.

"Tell me," he said. "*Now!*"

Jesús beckoned for the hotel manager to follow him as he weaved drunkenly out of the bar. Instead of leading him into the lobby as Berger had expected, the bartender pushed open the swinging door to the kitchen. He switched on the fluorescents and walked across the room at a pompous pace, seemingly reveling in Berger's suspense. Finally, he stopped at a china cupboard in the corner. Berger studied the self-satisfied little man and the wooden cabinet. He fought a surge of dread, hesitating to open the door. Then he heard a footfall behind him.

A shadow hovered in the doorway. It was Chris, in her khakis and T-shirt. "What the hell's going on?" she asked. When she saw both men were facing the china cupboard, she turned toward it.

"Don't!" Berger blocked her path. "Don't go near it! Go back to your room!"

It whetted her curiosity. Defiantly she stepped past him. Before he could stop her, she pulled the ceramic knobs. The door creaked open, and light slashed into the dark cubicle. "Oh, my God," she gasped. *"My God!"*

Dangling from the teacup hooks by their knotted hair, the two shrunken heads swung toward her, as if lunging for her face.

"No!" She took a panicked step backward. She had discovered *them,* but in her shock it seemed that they had been lying in wait, that they had ambushed her. The heads quivered, dangling from their hooks. They were sightless, voiceless, and yet, she feared, all-powerful. Totally comprehending.

The blood drained from her face, and she thrust a trembling hand toward the grisly trophies, as if she had to touch them to understand. She felt the rubbery texture of their flesh, and pulled away in horror. Strands of hair still clung to her fingers, as coarse as straw. It took a moment for her mind to make the leap, for her to recognize the shriveled heads. *That,* Chris thought, was the most revolting thing of all. For even now, dangling in this makeshift shrine like two enlarged testicles, each had retained its human personality. They seemed to gloat in their metamorphosis, as if in the shrinking they had found their salvation in evil.

"I know you," Chris murmured. *"I know you!"*

41

HIS SKIN RUBBED WITH BARK, LOPEZ'S FASHION-
able tan had acquired a negroid hue. From the taut line of his
mouth, his appetite for inflicting pain had been repaid in full.
But instead of humbling him, it seemed that death only made
him more vindictive. Chris sensed that he had not only joined
the forces of darkness. He had dominated them.

The caldron's crucible had reduced Dawn's bleached blond
hair to ratty brown and had purged her of lipstick. Threads of
the kumai palm stitched her once-sensual mouth shut, puck-
ering her lips in a final obscene kiss. Severed from the body
that had been her blessing and her curse, Dawn's head seemed
to possess a malevolent wisdom, as if another fifty years of
life had wizened it into this crone's shriveled mask.

Had this been their evil core all along? she wondered. Was
this same monstrous essence concealed within all of them—
even herself? She tried to shut the cupboard door, to lock away
the grisly sight, but even that effort was too much for her.
Nausea welled up, and she turned away and vomited.

"*Tsantsa,*" Jesús said, riveted by the dangling trophies.

"*Tsantsa,*" Berger repeated. "The Warak word for shrunken
heads." She was surprised, and troubled, by Berger's knowledge. And by his calm.

"When I found the headless corpses . . . Lopez and Dawn . . .
and Irv . . . I suspected *this,*" Berger murmured. "I didn't want
to believe it. Now I must."

"The Warak. . . ." Chris blurted it out. She didn't like the
way the word cut through the silence. Or the way Berger reacted
to it.

He spoke mechanically, as if reciting by rote. "A tribe of
the deep jungle, known for its ferocity, driven to the coast by
expanding settlement. Presumably related to the Jivaro. The
ceremony of decapitation and shrinking of the human head was
at the core of the Warak culture. They believed that by their
removing the skull and sewing the eyes and lips shut, their
enemies' avenging souls would not be able to escape. The

Kakaram, as the warriors were known, would carry their *tsantsa* into battle, the hair tied to their breechclouts, convinced that the dead would whisper words of blessing when the killing began. . . ." He paused, obviously embarrassed by his knowledge—and by his fascination with the subject. "Of course, the last of the Warak were believed to have been wiped out years ago. . . ."

His voice took on a confessional tone. "When I first arrived here, I had heard stories from the staff . . . about a powerful force of the deep jungle . . . a tribe that was more than human. I dismissed them as idle legend. . . . Then I met Dr. Eleanor Tobias."

"She told you about the Warak?" Chris asked.

"During her . . . all too brief stay here, I spoke with her about the tribe a good deal. Blame it on my origins," he said with a hint of shame, "but I have always been fascinated by the idea of a master race. After Dr. Tobias's murder, I read the books that were left in her room. And the more I learned about the Warak, the more I wanted to know."

"But," Chris said, "Dr. Tobias believed any survivors had fled to the upper Marañon."

He gestured toward the shrunken heads. "Apparently Dr. Tobias was wrong."

"Vengeance . . ." Chris murmured.

"Yes, vengeance, but on a scale so brutal, so barbarous, it is beyond our comprehension." It chilled her to see that his words both terrified and exhilarated him. "You have to understand," he added. "For the Warak, murder was love. They glorified their enemies with the ritual of the shrinking."

Chris shuddered. "An honor I could gladly do without."

Berger leaned so close to the cupboard that his head was almost inside the doors. He studied the *tsantsa,* as if to quell his fear with clinical objectivity. "The shrinking called for a subtle and complex technology. It took young Warak warriors, young Kakaram, years to learn the secrets of embalming, performed with herbs and roots gleaned from the jungle. The Kakaram used bone needles so sharp they could pierce the flesh without scarring it. Dr. Tobias said it took tremendous skill to knot the threads around the lips in the prescribed way and to shrink the heads in scalding water." He touched one cautiously. "Once they are preserved like this, they can last . . . decades. Perhaps centuries. No one knows how long." He was spewing out the words with a passion she had never seen in him before.

He was obsessed with the *tsantsa*. Perhaps, he was obsessed with death itself.

"Consider the achievement," Berger continued, an unholy gleam in his eye. "A sculpture in a substance more precious than gold." He was staring at what was left of Dawn, and he seemed more infatuated with her now than he had ever been while she was alive. "Grotesque to our eyes, I grant you. But perhaps man's most eloquent monument to death. For it is the only monument crafted in a substance that is itself mortal."

She looked at the heads, unable to view them as more than trophies of slaughter. Berger saw her revulsion. "The *tsantsa* were their work of art. Of course, for us their beauty is impossible to see," he said. "For it lies in their permanence."

"But . . . it doesn't make sense," she said. "If these . . . *tsantsa* . . . were so precious to them, then why would they leave them here, in a kitchen cupboard?"

He hesitated, "Dr. Tobias explained it. There was only *one* time when they would leave the *tsantsa* among strangers. She called it 'the Planting.'"

"Planting . . . ?" She held her breath.

For the first time, it seemed that Berger's fascination with the Warak had soured into horror. He lowered his voice, as if afraid the shrunken heads would overhear him. "The Warak would journey into enemy territory and hide their *tsantsa*, for their next victims to discover. It seems they had a sophisticated understanding of the human mind. With the Planting, their prey would experience the terror of anticipation. The Warak wanted those they had condemned to have all hope drained away before they. . . ."

Chris stared at the heads like a death sentence. It took all her strength to tear her eyes away from them and turn back to Berger and Jesús. The bartender's drunken smirk had vanished. Chris realized he was the only one of the servants she had seen this morning. "Did the staff find *them?*" she asked. Berger nodded. "Then . . . they're gone," she added with certainty.

"They understand the meaning of the *tsantsa*," Berger said. "The peoples of this region had been terrorized by the Warak for decades. In fact, the reason the Indians of the coastal villages converted to Christianity was to protect them from the tribe. . . ."

They had been sadly deluded, Chris thought, to believe that a religion preaching love could prevail over the machete and the shrinking pot. "Isn't there some way to placate the Warak?"

she asked. "Some way to throw ourselves on their mercy?"

"Mercy?" Berger shook his head. "I doubt the tribe even had a word for it."

"But . . . even wild animals have some kind of ritual of submission," she said, "some way to allow the defeated side to surrender without a bloodbath. . . ."

"In many of their skills," he replied, "the Warak resembled wild beasts. But when it came to their ruthlessness, I'm afraid in that respect, they were all too human."

She had learned more of the Warak's mysteries than she might have wished. Her next words were less a question than a plea. *"Why us?"*

Berger seemed stricken by his awareness of their peril. "Once the machine of vengeance is set in motion, it doesn't matter *why*. If *just one* of them were killed in a blood feud, they would wipe out the population of an entire village in revenge—men, women, children." He stared deep into her eyes. "The Warak tribe was liquidated to build this hotel. Just imagine. . . . If one Kakaram survived, to what lengths would he go to avenge *that* crime?"

She turned back to the gruesome trophies. "Victims," she said dully, and wondered whether she was glimpsing a premonition of her own fate. Would this be her final earthly form—her lips sewn shut, her eyes narrowed to slits, her face smaller than a newborn infant's? Would she leave this world as shriveled and blind as when she had entered it?

Berger started to close the cupboard, but she stopped him. She raised her camera and shot a flash picture of the heads, dangling like crucifixes of a vindictive religion. She had hoped the photo would safely lock the image away on film. Instead, the burst of light branded it in her mind.

If only Dr. Tobias hadn't died. Of all the deaths, hers had been the most costly. For that oddly comforting figure with her scarred four-fingered hand, her rumpled seersucker suit, would never be able to save them with her jungle wisdom now. Without Tobias, their hopes were reduced to one: Harley Stokes. His plane was due today. But she feared that like so much else in the jungle, its arrival would be subject to the whim of the Warak—and their perverse, all-knowing *tsantsa*.

42

AS IF PACKING WOULD HASTEN THE PLANE'S AR-
rival, Chris stuffed her clothes into her suitcase. The clasps
had been torn off in last night's rampage, and she lashed it shut
with a khaki belt. She kept repeating to herself that Stokes
really was coming today, that her biggest problem would be
making her connecting flight in Bogotá. But she wasn't convinced.

Her mind reeled from the discovery in the cupboard. She
feared that the shrunken heads wouldn't stay locked behind the
wooden doors for long, that, even if she escaped thousands of
miles away, the *tsantsa* would haunt her in the dead of night:
that she would open a closet and find them dangling in the
dark; that drugged with sleep, she would slip her hand under
her pillow and feel the touch of their flesh. Had they slithered
into her suitcase? No matter. They had already taken root in
her mind.

Sitting on the bed, Alan studied her with a troubled gaze.
She had explained all that she knew about the Warak, and now
he too bore the burden. Strange, she thought, how they avoided
discussing it. But then, after she had described her gruesome
discovery in the cupboard, what *could* they say?

She scanned the leaden clouds outside the window, as if she
could conjure up the DC-3 by sheer willpower. The prospect
of the plane's arrival was the single hope that staved off paralysis. She glanced at the digital clock. It still read 11:54.

"It's not broken," Alan said, reading her mind. He shifted
uncomfortably on the bed. "Time is just passing . . .
very . . . slowly."

"How much longer?" How many times had she asked the
question?

"Stokes is supposed to show up about three o'clock," he
repeated wearily. "That makes three more hours."

"Three, Panaguan time," she corrected him. Three more
hours, when she couldn't stand to stay cooped up in the room
for three more minutes. But what were her options? Outdoors

the glowering sea and sky were even more uninviting—a study in gray, like a picture etched by acid on steel. Why did Stokes have to arrive so late in the afternoon? It gave him no leeway. The airfield lacked electricity, and once night fell, a landing would be impossible. She frowned. The sky was darkening. With the thick cloud bank, night would arrive even faster than usual tonight, black sky and black ocean clamping shut like the jaws of a trap.

She slumped onto the bed and tried to place the few hours that lay ahead into the perspective of the rest of her life—anything to keep her from seeing them as its climax. "I'm always catching the last plane out of town," she said. "You know . . . the fall of Saigon, that final day? I was up there on the U.S. Embassy roof, climbing into the last chopper." She set down her suitcase by the door. "Angry mobs, monsoons, revolutions, you name it. It seems like after every assignment, it's always a hair's-breadth escape. I call it my Saigon exit."

"The point is," Alan said, "the last plane out of town always makes it. And it will today, too."

But she rejected his comfort. Why did he have to act so self-assured? She had preferred last night, when they had both admitted their terror. Why did daylight rekindle the need for bravado?

"It sounds crazy," he said, "but in spite of everything, I'm going to be sorry to leave this place." She looked at him as if he *were* crazy. "Of course," he continued, "this is scaring the hell out of me. But at least I feel *alive*. When I leave the enchanted forest"—he gestured toward the jungle—"what then? Will the handsome prince turn back into a toad again?" He put his arm around her, but she squirmed away. It was too late for that now.

As always, to comfort herself when all else failed, she opened her Haliburton case. She had placed the shards of glass from her broken cameras inside, as if to convince herself that they were still intact.

"Careful," he warned as she picked out a glass nugget. "You'll cut your finger."

She held the jagged piece up to the light, as though she could view the spectrum of her past through it, as though everything she had ever seen or felt, were captured in that tiny prism. But it contained no answers.

Alan read the distress on her face. "Chris," he said gently, "things that are broken . . . you can't always glue them back together. Sometimes you've got to start fresh." She knew that he was talking about himself. About her. Maybe even about them together. But she felt too numb to respond.

She closed the camera case and stared at her Leica on the bedstand. "Cameras are so fragile," she said. "So delicate. One strong jolt is all it takes, one violent act, and they...." She picked up the Leica. "Did you know that inside, under that strong-looking shell, this camera's made almost entirely of glass?"

"Like people?" he asked.

She stood up from the bed and paced back and forth across the room. Her impotence overwhelmed her. The walls were closing in, and the picture window was shivering in the wind, threatening to shatter.

Her mind was spinning out of control, and to steady herself, she stared at the clock again: 11:56. Was it possible? Only *two* minutes had passed? She couldn't stay here for three hours more. *In three hours* the jungle would crawl up to her window. *In three hours* the shrunken heads would gnaw their way out of the cupboard like rats. *In three hours* the dangling idols would loom so large they would blot out the sun, eclipse the sky into darkness, and then...? She stopped herself. This wasn't a room, she thought. It was a cage.

She snatched up her camera and ran out.

43

CHRIS STOPPED RUNNING WHEN SHE REACHED THE
patio, her hair flying in a jungle wind. The breeze bore with
it the stench of the garbage pits, as unsavory as the thoughts
she was trying to escape. But anything was better than staying
locked indoors, where the air was thick with fear. She listened
for a hint of the plane's arrival but heard only the roar of waves.
Overhead, black clouds hovered like a locust swarm.

She loaded her Leica with one of her last rolls of film. Her
trigger finger itched on the shutter release, and her eyes took
on their hunter's squint. Perhaps she would soon be devoured,
but for the moment at least, her camera would do the devouring.

Confined to the 50 mm lens that had escaped destruction,
she had to roam to frame each shot properly, ranging from the
pool to the surf's edge and back to the patio again, crouching,
kneeling, stretching in the ballet of her craft. The traumas of
the past few days had done nothing to dull her gift for playing
off light and shade, for capturing the El Dorado's clash of
elegance and decay. She realized that the war against the jungle
was over. The burrowers, the crawlers, the creeping infestation
had won.

A long shot. Click. The pool, once transparent, was now
a pond of swirling algae. *She knelt. Click.* The high diving
board, its paint blistered from wind and sun, was transformed
into a gibbet. *A low angle. Click.* The flagstones buckled as
roots wedged them apart with unrelenting force.

There, she thought, that's better. The narcotic still works.
Lulled by the shutter's tempo, she could take refuge in more
mundane anxieties than matters of life or death. Because if she
did make it back to New York, Graner wouldn't give a damn
about her brush with danger. He would want *coverage*.

Click. The tendrils that engulfed the patio furniture seemed
to be dragging it inexorably toward the jungle. *Click-click.* The
beach that had once been raked every morning was now strewn
with stingrays, suffocating in the air. *Click.* It felt good to flex
muscles that panic had tightened for so long. Fifteen minutes
and three rolls of Kodachrome later, she perched on the bal-

ustrade and panned the beach in search of fresh perspectives. How many days had it been since her tête-à-tête with Dr. Tobias in this corner of the patio? The wrought-iron table where the professor had daintily sipped tea was engulfed in twisted lianas.

Click. Chris wondered what would be left of *her* in twenty-four hours. The camera, perhaps, and its pictures. Would they be her last will and testament, the only clues to her demise?

Click. The narcotic was wearing off. As she framed her next shot, her hands trembled. Was that shadow among the vines an intruder? *Click*. Was that silhouette on the thirteenth floor the enemy? *Click*. She leaned on the mahogany of the outdoor bar to support her unsteady camera arm. A black widow skittered past, and she caught it crawling across a bottle of champagne. *Click*. The roll was finished. She rewound it and slotted in a fresh one.

Her photographer's trance drew her irresistibly toward the jungle. She had to stand with her back against the green wall to frame the entire hotel in her viewfinder. *Click*. She composed the shot first vertically, then horizontally, bracketing her exposures. *Click-click*. Through the lens, the building no longer stood out boldly against the sky. It was starting to fade, like a painful memory. *Click*. She could almost believe that the El Dorado had only existed for them, and that when the last of the guests perished, it, too, would dissolve, like a jungle mirage. *Click*. She was drenched in sweat, and slipped her finger onto the shutter release for a final salvo.

She stopped, riveted by a distant drone. She lowered the camera and glanced skyward. But it wasn't a DC-3's engines. It was a much less welcome sound: the buzzing of maggots. When she spun around to face the jungle, she almost dropped her camera.

A specter was emerging from the web of vines. A tangle of lianas strangled its arms and legs, and maggots crawled across the skeletal face, adorning the khaki shirt and trousers like sequins.

Backing away in horror, she tripped, holding the camera above her head to protect it from the impact as she fell. Sprawled on the ground, she had no time to scramble away. As the specter lifted the machete above its head, she raised an arm to block the blow.

He didn't lunge at her. He did something even more unsettling. He offered her his hand.

She took it cautiously, and the warmth of the fingers told her the intruder was very much alive. As he pulled her to her feet, she realized that maggots had crawled from his hand to hers.

The stranger slid the blade back into its moldy sheath. In spite of the overcast, he shielded his eyes, as if they had been weakened by prolonged exposure to the jungle twilight. He opened his mouth and his tongue clucked, preparing for speech. But the words were reluctant to come out, as if he had not spoken in days. "I guess I don't make a pretty picture," he rasped. "But then, you wouldn't look pretty neither, if you'd been . . . where *I've* been."

Perched on his head like a parasite, his toupee betrayed his identity. Beneath the crust of dirt, she recognized a familiar face. "Curzon . . . ?"

On closer scrutiny she realized that despite the filth, his skin was flushed, his posture confident. Under the gray stubble he seemed younger, somehow, more robust than before. To her astonishment, she realized that his sojourn in the jungle had, in some perverse way, agreed with him.

"Where . . . where *were* you?" she asked.

"East of the sun and west of the moon." He chuckled. "I've lunched with cannibals and kings. I've visited the Pope and the King of the Hebrews. Where I've been, what I've seen, you could take some mighty fine pictures, that's for damn sure!"

She noticed his backpack. "Did you go . . . far?"

"I couldn't rightly tell you that." He chuckled. "What matters is, I'll never have to go back there again. Never!"

"But . . . what were you *doing* in there?"

"What've you all been doing *here?*" His sarcasm made her suspect that he knew exactly what had been happening. But before she could question him, he strode off toward the hotel.

Even with his backpack, his spry gait kept him several paces ahead of her. She took a desperate stab at stopping him. "Let me buy you a drink."

He laughed. "No, thanks. All I need is some salt."

"Salt?"

He lifted his arm. It was covered with leeches from the elbow down. "Got to sprinkle a little salt on these mothers. Only way to get them off, don't you know." He stepped into the lobby. When she opened the door to follow him, he had vanished.

44

BERGER KNELT ON THE ICY FLOOR OF THE MEAT
locker beside Irv Florsheim's corpse. On the shelf above lay
the headless bodies of Lopez and Dawn. The walk-in freezer's
supply of meat, poultry, and suckling pig had been cleaned out
by the staff, leaving the cadavers as the last occupants. As he
spread a winding sheet over what was left of Irv, Berger's
breath hung on the air like smoke. He found it a reassuring
sight. He wasn't one of them . . . yet.

He was loath to lift the corpse. The prospect of its chilly
embrace repelled him. Still, Stokes's plane would be arriving
at three, and he felt compelled to complete this task before all
the others. If he had failed as a host, if he had allowed his hotel
to become an arena for murder, he would at least heed the
rights of the departed and assure them a decent burial on their
home soil. The bodies had to be at the airfield when the plane
arrived. He didn't want anything—*anything*—to delay the
flight's departure.

Trying not to remember that it had once been alive, he lifted
Irv's corpse in his arms and dragged it out of the meat locker.
When he stepped into the kitchen, he realized that the body
stank of rot. Somehow, even in the freezer, microscopic scavengers had infested it. He covered his nose with a handkerchief.
Why did a living thing become leaden after death? Even without
its head, the body was almost too heavy for him to lift, and
he grunted as he shouldered it down the kitchen steps to the
patio.

The noon glare beat down like a piledriver. He loaded his
burden as gently as possible into a wheelbarrow and struggled
to push it across the flagstone terrace. Sweltering in his suit,
he skirted the algae-green pool and headed down the dirt road
to the airstrip. When he passed the useless minivan, he cursed
his staff, the deserters who had reduced him to this grim task.
Most of all, he cursed himself.

The rutted road fought Berger's every step. The path was
powder dry, dust rising in a plume behind the wheelbarrow,

burying his footsteps one by one. The pallbearer focused his eyes on the road, avoiding the piercing gaze of the forest, a legion of corpses mocking him. He was running a gauntlet. At any moment sinister shadows might leap out and drag Irv away. The jungle flourished on death, and he had no intention of giving it one more cadaver to swell its ranks.

The wheelbarrow's rusty axle resisted shrilly, making each step an effort, but he steered the load resolutely forward, throwing all his weight behind it. The heads of the victims—Irv, Lopez, Dawn, and doubtless Dr. Tobias, too—had gone over to join the enemy, transformed into *tsantsa* with their own evil powers: lips sewn shut to utter curses; eyes closed to see with second sight. But if their souls had been lost, then at least he would see to it that their bodies escaped corruption. He would ship Irv's and Dawn's remains to the States as penance for the tragedy. Flies swarmed over the corpse, drawn to the severed neck, and he pushed with mounting difficulty, as if the weight of the insects somehow made the burden twice as oppressive.

By the time he reached the airstrip his hands were blistered and his shoulders ached. He surveyed the harsh red dirt: desolate, so barren that even the jungle's vegetation couldn't take root here. The air was still, as stifling as his own isolation. Summoning the last of his strength, he pushed the wheelbarrow toward the steel cart that would be used to transport luggage to the plane.

He looked up and realized he wasn't alone. A squadron of vultures had been circling overhead. Now they perched on a tree stump, mesmerized by the corpse. The scavengers rustled their feathers, clucking hungrily. He growled to keep them at bay. They ignored the threat and scuttled onto the ground, starting to scrabble closer. He grabbed a handful of rocks and hurled them at the birds, shouting curses, venting his hatred for the jungle.

Under his barrage of epithets the vultures flapped skyward, and as if fanned by their wings, a wind whipped dust into the air. At first, he was relieved by the breeze, but soon the flurry stung his eyes. With a moan, the dust swirled around him, thickening from a haze into a blizzard.

As he fumbled to tie his handkerchief over his nose and mouth, he lost hold of the wheelbarrow, and the wind toppled it over. Irv's headless corpse rolled out, slipping from its canvas winding sheet. Berger leaned over to pick it up, but stopped himself. The body quivered strangely in the cyclone, its dead fingers drumming on the ground, its legs twitching. For one terrifying moment, he feared it was stirring back to life. Then the movement subsided, as the corpse succumbed to a heavy layer of dust.

Bracing himself against the howling wind, Berger leaned over to lift up Irv's body. He held it close to him. But the dust devil tore the corpse from his arms, splintering the wheelbarrow. He lost sight of everything through the billowing cloud as trees, earth, and sky melted into one red inferno. The pillar spun taller than the El Dorado, threatening to sweep him away in its vortex. He tried to cry out, but dust clogged his nostrils, caught in his throat, and he gasped for breath.

As the maelstrom engulfed him, he glimpsed a spellbinding vision: *Irv's headless body was standing up.* It balanced on one foot, its arms extended, Christlike, as it wheeled in a St. Vitus's dance, seemingly transfixed in a moment of ecstasy.

Howling through the air, chanting a shrill Kaddish, the dust masked the approach of the hunter, drowned out the hiss of the blade as it slashed downward with the suddenness of a guillotine. Berger's throat was so dry from wind and dust and fear he hardly felt the incision. Swept off his shoulders, his head bowed down in humility, toppling to kiss the blood-red earth, to yield to the verdict of the Whirlwind.

45

THE SKY WAS A COFFIN LID, HINGING SHUT. CHRIS and Alan tore a tangle of creepers from two patio chairs and sat down, searching the clouds in the fading light. Her ears probed the skirring of jungle birds for the drone of propellers, and she remembered her words to Alan, what seemed years ago: "It's better to be down here wishing you were up there than up there wishing you were down here."

Not anymore, she thought. Not anymore. She turned to him. He was scanning the clouds with his binoculars, searching for the twinkle of wingtip lights. "See anything?"

When he lowered the binoculars, she could read despair on his face. As if hoping her ability to conjure up the sight would surpass his own, he handed them to her.

She shook her head. "It's too dark." It was an admission of defeat. But then, the plane was already four hours late. That was worse than Panaguan time. Much worse. Because if they didn't get out by nightfall. . . . She felt a chilling certainty that tonight the jungle would swallow them up in one gluttonous gulp. Tonight there would be no poolside buffet, no strolling mariachis, no carved ice swans. There would be another spectacle, much more awesome. And unthinkable.

She avoided Alan's gaze with the sinking feeling that darkness was close at hand. Whatever happened, they would delay telling the other guests for as long as possible. The others had chosen to remain in their rooms until the plane's arrival. She couldn't blame them. Now that nowhere was safe, each of them had to cling to their own illusions of security.

Neither Chris nor Alan spoke, as if the DC-3 were an endangered species which a single word might scare away. He gestured toward the gathering night and took a puff on his cigar. "How much more time do we have?"

She knew his words had a double meaning: how much more light; how much longer could they survive. "Maybe half an hour of daylight left," she said, and tried to keep from sounding like the voice of doom. But after that precious half hour was over, they both knew it would be impossible for the plane to touch down. Already dusk was tinting the wall of green into reds and browns, like a dollar bill crumpling into flames.

"There's got to be some way he can land after dark," Alan said.

"No way." But the very finality of her statement made Chris look for a loophole. Suddenly she recalled their arrival. "We could extend the time if. . . ." She was already out of her chair.

"If . . . what?"

"The smudgepots," she said. "They were on the airfield when we landed. They've got to still be there."

He nodded. "Let's get Berger to help."

She glanced up at the darkening sky. "To hell with Berger." She strode off down the dirt road toward the landing strip with Alan close behind. With every step, she cursed the hotel manager. In spite of his meticulous attention to detail, he had overlooked the key to their survival.

The jungle rose up on both sides of the road like a sea that had parted reluctantly and that, she feared, would come rushing together to engulf them. On the threshold of darkness, the noises grew strident: macaws shrieking; howler monkeys crying out as they passed. She didn't want to be here when the pitch rose still higher, to its shrill peak, in the rapidly approaching hour of the hunt. She scanned the ground ahead of her, alert for snakes, and noticed footprints in the dust. Perhaps she had judged Berger too hastily. Perhaps he had gone to light the smudgepots after all.

They rounded a bend in the road and found themselves on the red earth of the landing field. A guttural squawking startled them. Two vultures were squabbling over a heap of carrion, tearing at it with their hooked beaks. A few steps closer, and there was no longer any doubt: the scavengers were feeding on human flesh.

Alan lit a palm frond with his cigarette lighter and advanced toward the vultures holding them at bay with the makeshift torch. As she neared the corpses, Chris was grateful that dusk concealed so much. But it could not hide their identities. Even without their heads, the bodies were all too recognizable: Irv, in the blazer he had worn at the séance, and Berger, in his conservative gray suit, the gold watch still ticking on his lifeless wrist. Reeling from the sight, she wanted to run back to the hotel, to barricade herself into a room like the others.

"Over here!" Alan shouted from the fuel pump. He had discovered the smudgepots in an empty oil drum. "Quickly!"

She knew Alan was right not to linger over the dead. They would have only a few minutes to position the smudgepots. But before she could help Alan, she had another, higher priority. It took all her strength to wrestle first Irv's, then Berger's body over to the baggage cart, under the vultures' hungry gaze. She slammed the steel doors to the luggage compartment, sealing the bodies inside. The scavengers rustled their feathers and retreated into the dark.

There was no more time to mourn the departed. She was determined not to join them. She hurried over to help Alan fill the smudgepots at the fuel pump. As she aligned the cans along the runway, he ignited them with his lighter, first one row, then the other, flickering pinpoints in the twilight. A hollow ritual, she thought as the last one was set aflame, like lighting candles for the dead.

Lightning flashed on the horizon. The smudgepots sizzled as a light rain fell.

"Hell!" Chris growled, but Alan didn't reply. He had disappeared. Her eyes searched for him in the darkness on the far side of the runway. She gave a start. She could see his body. *But not his head.*

"Alan!" she shouted, her voice shrill with fear.

"What's wrong?"

Her senses were playing malicious tricks on her. While his white shirt stood out boldly, his tanned face had blended into the jungle's dark backdrop. "I . . . I guess I'm going bananas," she said.

He walked over and put his arm around her. "Join the club." They fell silent to the rumble of thunder. They had done all they could, and the awareness left Chris paralyzed. Should she wait here or return to the hotel? She stared at the airstrip. Suddenly it felt like a bullring. A hushed crowd was waiting for the bolted door to fly open. She knew that the beast that would charge in would be no bull from the plains of Córdoba, but a minotaur from the jungle's labyrinth, its hooves pawing the earth with taurine sinew and human cunning.

She listened.

Impossible. Her ears must be deceiving her.

Wait. A fragile drone rose above the thunder.

Her senses were lying to her, worse than they had ever lied before. This was the prelude to madness, she was certain of it. But suddenly it seemed that Alan was the one who had gone berserk. He jumped into the air, yelling hoarsely, flailing his arms. He stabbed a finger up at the sky. "Look!"

Three lights were blinking against the storm clouds, three meteors descending. He was laughing now, and she was laughing, too, pointing up at the sky to convince herself. "I can't believe it!" she cried. *"I can't believe it!"*

With a mighty roar the DC-3 tilted first its left wing, then its right, before straightening out to make a perfect three-point landing. The plane taxied toward them over the rutted airfield. She felt tears welling up in her eyes. It must be the dust, she thought. No, she was sobbing in a surge of relief. Let the gale from the propellers blast her; let it cover her with dirt. Anything, to confirm that this was *real*. She mopped an arm across her face, smearing it with grit. Enough tears, she thought. Cut it out. You're blubbering like a . . . goddamn . . . woman.

The engines revved for a minute before power was cut, the propellers glinting as they spun to a stop. There was no sign of life from within the plane. In the ghostly glow of the smudge-pots, it was almost possible to believe that it had flown here by magic and landed itself, summoned by the urgency of their need to escape.

The hatch swung open, and Harley Stokes climbed out, chewing matter-of-factly on a toothpick, clad in his cracked-leather flight jacket, jeans, and cowboy boots. She never would have thought she'd see anything heroic in that lethargic figure, but she did now. He had braved a storm to rescue them. He deserved a medal. She noticed that in addition to the Colt automatic in his belt, he clutched an Uzi submachine gun. Once Chris would have branded him paranoid for carrying such heavy armament. Now she blessed him for it.

"God, are we glad to see you!"

Stokes scratched his belly. "The food that bad?" He squinted into the dark. "Where the fuck's Fernando?"

Chris didn't answer.

"Well?" His voice grated with impatience. "He's got to gas this mother up."

Alan shook his head. "Fernando's gone."

Stokes bit his toothpick in two and spit it out.

"It's been horrible," Chris said.

"Yeah?" Stokes yawned and zipped up his jacket against the drizzle.

"Some of the guests have been murdered," Alan said. "And Lopez. The radio's been smashed. We couldn't call for help."

Stokes cocked his head, listening intently. "Who did it?" he asked. But she didn't reply, refusing to mention the *tsantsa* that dangled in her mind like question marks.

"What's Berger doing about all this?"

All she said was: "The staff panicked and left."

"You shittin' me?" Stokes' mind was slow to turn over, like the engines of his DC-3. "Then who lit *them?*" He pointed to the smudgepots.

"We did," Alan said.

Stokes frowned. "Guess I'll have to gas her up myself." He strolled over to the pump.

She ducked under the wing to follow him. "You're missing the point. We've got to get out of here. *Fast.*"

He turned a crank and snatched the nozzle off its hook. "I can sympathize with that, ma'am, but you'll have to hold your water." After popping open the fuel lid, he rammed the nozzle in with a clank. "It'll take a good hour to get this baby ready for the flip side back. When I'm set, I'll give a shout."

"*An hour?* We're ready *now*," Alan said.

Stokes ran a thumb along the edge of a propeller blade. "Sixty big ones."

Chris and Alan looked at each other helplessly. They couldn't risk pushing him too far. He was a big enough prima donna to climb back in, slam the hatch, and fly away. "Okay...okay.... An hour," Chris said. "But give us a gun until then."

"What the fuck for?"

She exploded. *"People are getting killed back there!"*

Stokes shrugged. "House rule. Never give a gun to a broad."

She set her jaw and strode over to the baggage cart. She had avoided resorting to this, because she didn't want to face it herself. But he left her no choice. She opened the steel door, revealing the corpses. Stokes let out a soft whistle, the most extreme expression of emotion she had ever seen him show. "Holy shee-it!" He looked at Chris, at Alan, and back at the corpses. "What happened...?" He ran his thumb across his throat and swallowed hard. "What happened to their *heads?*"

When they didn't reply, he turned and climbed back into the cockpit. She followed Stokes up the ladder. As she pulled herself in beside him, the snub-nose of a Colt Cobra stared her in the face.

With a wince that told her he was acting against his better judgment, Stokes handed it over. "Don't pull the trigger 'less you want to do some damage. You got six hollow-point slugs in there."

"I'll be careful," she said, and squeezed the pistol grip. It was the best reassurance she'd had in days.

Alan pointed toward the road, shrouded in darkness. "Could you lend us...?" Before he could finish, Stokes threw him a flashlight.

"I get them both back before takeoff," he said, "or nobody boards."

After whipping another flashlight out of his hip pocket, Stokes raised the cowling of the starboard engine and peered inside. His face fell, as if he'd discovered another corpse. "I've got problems," he said. "If you don't leave me be, we've *all* got problems." He pulled out a screwdriver and pointed it at them. "Now get this. I don't want nobody back here bugging me for an hour. Understand?" He disappeared again under the metal flap.

As she joined Alan on the road to the hotel, the drizzle turned to a driving rain. Chris tried to convince herself that they could last one more hour, but even such a modest hope seemed farfetched. A cold wind knifed against the back of her neck, and she cocked the hammer of the pistol. As they walked, every shadow, every sound taunted her. Wherever it was, she thought, just let it show itself. She was ready to kill.

46

FIGURES LOOMED OUT OF THE DARK, AND CHRIS
slipped her finger onto the trigger.

Alan stopped her. It was the guests, rushing toward them
in the rain. They had promised to wait for Chris to announce
the plane's arrival, but the promise had been forgotten. Caught
in Alan's flashlight beam, their eyes gleamed with panic.

Scott took the lead. Clad in his caftan, his long hair streaming behind him, he looked like a crazed prophet of doom. Inez
and Rima ran at his side, and their fear gave them a wild,
demented beauty. Jesús trotted behind them, trying to keep up
on his stubby legs. In sharp contrast with the others, Curzon
seemed serene in his freshly pressed white suit. Holding an
umbrella as if he were out for an evening stroll, he took up the
rear.

Chris's head count came up one short. "Where's Margot?"

"Who the fuck knows?" Scott growled. "We checked her
room, but she wasn't there. And if you think we're going to
wait around till she shows up, forget it!"

Chris glared at him: a selfish child. He continued toward
the plane, but she stepped in front of him, blocking his path.

"Get out of my way," he snapped. "We're getting on that
plane. *Now*."

"Stokes wants us to wait at the hotel. He wants time to work
on the engine . . . *alone*."

"I'm waiting *inside* that plane. We all are." Scott pushed
past.

"No, we're not." She leveled the pistol at his chest. "We're
going back to the patio, till we get the signal from Stokes."

"The lady's right." Curzon's teeth gleamed in the darkness.
She was surprised at her unlikely ally. "I know Harley Stokes,"
he continued. "You do like he says, or he gets bent out of
shape. We wouldn't want him so mad he ups and leaves without
us, now would we?"

Scott hesitated, then turned without a word and started back
toward the hotel.

When they reached the patio, the group wearily put down

their luggage. None of them dared to enter the hotel's shadowy corridors, and they huddled under a canvas umbrella at one of the poolside tables. Jesús scrounged up a few candles from the outdoor bar. The flames flickered in the wind, and the guests leaned close to them, as if seeking warmth as well as light.

Scott stared nervously into the shadows. "How long did you say it's going to take?"

"An hour," Alan said.

"An *hour?*"

"We'll be okay." Chris lifted the pistol.

Curzon yanked his luger from its shoulder holster and pointed to the butt of a shotgun sticking out of his backpack. "It worked fine for skeet shooting," he said. "It could come in nice and handy tonight."

Their panic was subsiding. Even Scott seemed reassured by their weaponry.

"*¡Aquí!*" A smile spread across Jesús's face as he slid his cardboard suitcase up onto the table, and flipped open the lid, revealing a dozen bottles filched from the bar. He came up with a burgundy, and tilted the bottle toward them like a sommelier, so they could appreciate the vintage and year. "*¿Vino?*"

Nobody responded, but he uncorked the bottle anyway and, after taking a hearty swig, passed it to Chris. She took a sip. The wine soothed her. She passed it to the others, each of whom followed suit with grim formality. This was more than just a way to pass the agonizing minutes, she thought. It was a kind of sacrament.

When the bottle came back to her again, she felt compelled to speak. She thought of those who had died, of Tobias... Lopez and Dawn... Irv... Berger. Days or weeks from now, at funerals thousands of miles apart, they would all be laid to rest with noble sentiments. But only this handful of survivors could understand the victims' ordeal. Right now, on this tainted ground, there had to be some observance of the tragedy. Yet when she tried to recite the names of the deceased, it was too painful to say them aloud. Choking back her grief, she passed the bottle to Curzon.

He refused it, and reached into his pocket to remove a pouch of white powder. Sprinkling some on the table, he snorted it through a rolled-up one-dollar bill. "Any takers?" he offered.

"For sure!" As Curzon heaped a mound of the powder on the table in front of Scott, the singer's eyes bulged. Chris understood his amazement. In Los Angeles, a mountain of cocaine that size would bring $10,000.

Scott inhaled the powder through his left nostril, then hesitated before sniffing more with his right. "Like...you sure you can spare it?"

"Be my guest." Curzon's teeth flashed. "There's plenty more where that came from."

Chris hoped that Scott's snorting would shut him up, but it only made his mind scramble faster. "So, like, you said Harley Stokes is working on the *engine?*" he asked.

She nodded. They all shared a worried look.

"Why? I mean...there's nothing *wrong* with it, is there?"

"He didn't say." There was no point in mentioning the way Stokes had grimaced as he had set to work.

Together they endured fifteen minutes of excruciating silence. Then Scott voiced the question on all their minds. "Can a DC-3 *fly* on just one engine?"

As if in reply, an aircraft motor sputtered in the distance, struggling to turn over. When, at last, the engine caught and smoothed to an even pitch, they breathed a sigh of relief.

This time when the bottle was handed around, smiles went with it. "To Harley Stokes," Alan said. Chris sipped the wine again, comforted by the drone in the distance.

But when she heard the *second* engine starting, her smile faded. Both props were racing now, running up to maximum rpm, and suddenly the sound grew louder. *Louder*. It was coming. *It was upon them*.

With a terrific roar, the plane swooped by, wings glinting sharp as machete blades. The DC-3 hurtled straight for the hotel, but at the last moment it swerved toward the ocean, nosing upward in the stiff sea breeze.

The guests ran out into the rain, shouting for the plane to stop, but the engines drowned out their voices. Chris watched as the landing gear folded under the wings. A door was closing, she thought. Their escape hatch had slammed shut.

The DC-3 circled once, taunting them, before it roared out over the jungle, banking to gain altitude.

And then it was gone.

The guests lowered their eyes from the sky and looked at each other. Raindrops rolled down their faces like tears.

"You made us wait, you fucking bitch!" Scott went for Chris, but Alan wrestled him to the ground.

"You make us stay...." Inez and Rima lashed out. "You make us *die!*"

Chris glared at them. "If you want to know why the plane left," she said simply, "ask Curzon."

They looked around them. "Where *is* he?" Scott asked.

"Señor Curzon!" Rima shouted, her voice echoing in the shadows.

"Cut the bullshit," Scott snapped at Chris. "What are you trying to say?"

She pointed to the empty space where Curzon's backpack had been. "Harley Stokes came to get *him*," she said simply. "He had no intention of picking us up at all."

"Christ! Why couldn't he take us, too?" Scott whimpered.

Chris remembered Curzon's jungle trek and the obscene mound of cocaine. "I have a feeling he has his own destination."

"Son of a bitch!" Scott buried his face in his hands. "I don't believe it!"

"Believe it," Alan said.

They retreated under the umbrella. The rain had doused the candles and Alan relit them. Borne by the wind, distant sounds took on an icy clarity. Chris could hear night birds cackling, laughing like hyenas. She looked up at the roof of the restaurant pavilion. Vultures were gathering, their huge wings flapping down out of the storm, dozens, scores, so many flocking there that they squabbled for perches. She glimpsed strange breeds with fleshy heads and yellow beaks. They looked as if they had flown from far away, summoned by a sixth sense to arrive tonight.

She longed to aim her pistol at those voyeurs and start shooting. But without Curzon's shotgun or Luger to defend them, the Colt was too precious to waste on an emotional outburst.

Alan reached for the gun, and reluctantly she let him take it. He weighed the pistol in his hand, then flipped open the ammunition chamber and peered inside, spinning the cylinder. The haunted look on his face made her wish she hadn't given him the weapon. She tried to snatch it back, but he was too quick for her.

Alan cocked the hammer and pointed the pistol at his temple.

"What are you doing?" she shouted, struggling to wrench the gun away.

He squeezed the trigger. Once. Twice. Again and again. Six times, the hammer snapped into empty chambers.

The other guests stared at him, dumbfounded. Alan smiled bitterly, and handed the pistol back to Chris. "Merely a symbolic gesture," he said. "I wasn't committing suicide just now. *We already have.*"

As Alan's words sank in, the terror that had divided the little group suddenly knitted them together. Scott pointed toward the swimming pool. "Look!"

A vision had been spawned by their fear, a shadow gliding toward them through the rain: it wore a pearl-gray kimono, reflected luminescent in the pool. Like a messenger of the night, it mesmerized them.

"Margot?" Chris murmured.

She didn't reply. The spinster had been transformed into a wrinkled hag, but her eyes shone with a passionate intensity. *"I knew."* Her voice rang shrill. "From the beginning, I was *condemned* to know!" She gazed at them with the pride of the damned. *"We are lost!"*

Slowly Margot raised her hand into the candlelight. She clutched three *tsantsa* by the hair. "The night is *theirs,*" she said.

The shrunken heads of Dawn and Lopez stared Chris in the face. And Irv had joined his starlet at last.

Margot's eyes brimmed with tears, a grief for the departed and for themselves. She spoke with evangelical fervor, as if translating the words of the *tsantsa*. "Come, they say. *Come! You will join us.* Do not despair. Ours is a simpler world. Where there is no love, there can be no loneliness or pain. Tonight!" Margot cried out. *"Come join the tribe!"*

Chris realized that all the guests were eyeing Margot as if she were a witch, as if the *tsantsa* were victims of her magic. Then they read the anguish on the old woman's face and realized that she was, perhaps, the ultimate victim. "Tonight!" Margot cried out. *"Tonight!"*

She was right, Chris thought. If the Warak waited for their victims' last hope to vanish before they struck, they need wait no longer. Margot was holding the *tsantsa* directly over the candles now, and in the heat they started to sway as if imbued with a life of their own. Impossible, Chris thought. *Impossible.* She would accept anything but this: Death endowed with life. Death entrusted with a mission of evil. How soon until the *tsantsa* would outnumber them all?

47

THE DC-3 FOUNDERED IN A CHOPPY SEA OF CLOUDS, fighting a head wind that battered it mercilessly. Curzon sat alone in the darkened passenger compartment. With each lightning flash, the jumble of shapes surrounding him loomed brightly: antique furniture, crates of wine and whiskey, candlesticks glinting gold. The seats, the aisles, as well as the cargo bays, were crammed with the plunder of a lifetime, loaded on in the capital before Stokes met him at the El Dorado.

The plane jolted through a barrage of thunder, and Curzon winced as his possessions shifted violently to starboard. When they slammed into the next air pocket, he heard a lamp crash to the floor. Cursing, he stood up and headed for the cockpit. It had taken him twenty years to collect this booty. He wasn't about to let Harley Stokes wreck it in a single flight.

"This isn't a goddamn beer wagon!" Curzon bellowed. "Why don't you fly her with some *class?*"

The pilot ignored him, the instruments bathing his face in a sickly green glow.

Grumbling, Curzon slumped into the copilot's seat and watched the stick in front of him bob in tandem with the one Stokes gripped between his legs. The DC-3's windshield wipers thunked back and forth furiously. Useless, Curzon thought. Beyond the cockpit window, it was pitch-black. "How far've we gone?" Even shouting, he could barely make himself heard above the storm.

Stokes checked the airspeed indicator. "We crossed the border out of Panaguas ten minutes ago."

"Hot damn!" Curzon sank back into his seat with an air of triumph. To hell with the storm. He was in fat city. "I'm retired," he said. *"I'm officially retired!"* He picked up a canteen from the cockpit floor, crumbled two Alka-Seltzers into it, and sipped the brew. "Panaguas! If God ever gives the planet Earth an enema, that would be the bodily orifice where He'd ram it in."

"Panaguas's been damn good to you," the pilot grumbled with a trace of jealousy. "Whatever you got, you owe to her."

"Yeah, she's been good to me, the old whore," Curzon conceded. "I screwed her royal." When he lifted the canteen to his mouth, they jounced through an air pocket, and the liquid sloshed onto Stokes's pants.

"You sombitch!" the pilot growled. "Bad enough I gotta save your ass in this shit weather!"

Curzon belted down the last of the fizz and licked his lips with a reptilian tongue. "You want out of the deal?"

Stokes was quick to shake his head.

Curzon snickered. "You'd blow the devil himself if the price was right. . . ."

Stokes eyed him suspiciously. "When you gonna pay me for the plane?"

"When we touch down nice and safe."

"What're you gonna use her for then? Hauling cargo?"

Curzon shrugged. He had purchased the DC-3 for this single flight. After that. . . . He studied the cockpit as if appraising a slum. "Like as not, I'll turn her into a diner or a bar or something." Stokes seemed appalled by the prospect, and Curzon twisted the knife. "I wanted the tackiest plane I could find. I got it." Stokes glared at him, but Curzon rambled on. "I could've hired a Learjet to fly me out of here. I could've hired a goddamn 747!"

"Sure," the pilot scoffed. "The radar would pick you up in nothing flat. And you'd never be able to land . . . where we've *gotta* land. Besides," he added, "I'd like to see one of them big birds hold together in this chop." The pilot stole a glance out the window to check that the wings were still glued on. Curzon was starting to retch.

"You gonna barf, do it here!" Stokes dropped a paper bag contemptuously into Curzon's lap. "You're more trouble than a planeful of *turistas*."

"Pay better, too." The pilot didn't disagree with that. Curzon winced from the taste of bile and yanked his seat belt tighter as the plane slammed through another air pocket. He heard a terrific crash from the passenger compartment. If that's my stereo, he thought, I'll kill him. "How you want to get paid?" He pulled a wad of cash out of his pocket, hoping the sight of the money would encourage a lighter hand on the stick.

Stokes shook his head and pointed toward the backpack wedged behind Curzon's seat. "I'll take a pound of that."

"Want my infrared scope, too? You can see in the dark with it, bright as day. Might help you fly in this soup."

"What for?" Stokes scoffed. "We're doing just fine."

His passenger wasn't so sure. "Just so you know where you're headed."

Stokes threw him a dog-eared map, and Curzon traced a pencil line with his finger: a zigzag from South to Central America, slicing across the Caribbean to Florida. The route was no joyride, he conceded, what with flying low to avoid radar detection at the borders and refueling stops on secret landing strips. But it was worth hedgehopping through Latin America to smuggle this booty into the States under the noses of customs officials.

He tapped the Florida coastline on the map with his finger and waxed nostalgic. "You know, it's been twenty years since I got deported. It's gonna feel good to come home. 'Give me your tired, your poor, your huddled masses. . . .'" He chuckled. "Well, I may be tired and huddled, but I sure as hell ain't poor." His eyes shot over to his backpack. Of all the plunder on the plane, it was the prize.

The next jolt slid the backpack across the floor and slammed it into the bulkhead. Stokes glanced over his shoulder. "Think maybe we should strap it down?"

Curzon shook his head. "Won't hurt the stuff to get shook up a bit."

"One thing . . . One thing I can't figure," Stokes said. "How come you went into the jungle to get it yourself? I mean, what about all the flunkies you've got to do your dirty work? You a glutton for punishment or what?"

"It was my swan song, don't you know," Curzon said. "Before I put myself out to pasture, I had to do one last job on my own hind legs. I had to prove I could still get it up." He fingered the scars from the leeches on his arm. "Well, there's no doubt about it now. I've still got brass balls."

A crescendo of thunder shook the plane. Then lightning flashes in rapid succession, as though a madman were fingering a light switch. A snowcapped peak loomed dead ahead. "Holy shit!" Curzon shouted as they hurtled toward the slope. Stokes slammed the stick to the left. They tilted giddily as the plane banked away from the crag. When the DC-3 righted itself, the next lightning flash revealed the mountain had vanished beneath a metallic crust of clouds. Curzon unhooked his seat belt and stood up.

"You may have been Mr. Big in Panaguas," Stokes barked, "but you're just another passenger here. Sit the fuck down!"

The plane jumped 100 feet in an updraft, and Curzon was seated in spite of himself. The passport slipped from his vest pocket, and he scooped it off the floor. Number B109879: *Arthur Felix Lombard*. He hadn't let one of the Panaguan hacks do the work. He'd sent away to the States for it, and for the fake birth certificate, driver's license, and Social Security card as well. They were beautiful forgeries, an art form of which he considered himself a connoisseur. He studied the "Place of Birth" on his passport: "Key West, Florida."

"Florida. . . ." Curzon whispered the word like the name of a mistress. The state was a popular refuge for deposed Latin American dictators. It would be an ideal spot for him to run his own shady government-in-exile. Plenty of time to play golf and hook a few big ones, while he kept tabs on his Panaguan operations: prostitution, cocaine, gambling, extortion. "You know what?" He nudged Stokes. "I'm thinking of settling down somewheres near Sarasota."

"Sarasota?"

Curzon's eyes had the same glint as when he had taken a snort of cocaine. "That's where the circus goes for the winter. Sarasota. The whole Ringling Brothers, Barnum and Bailey outfit. All the midgets and the freaks and the elephants . . . I hear it's quite a sight to see: those trapeze ladies gussied up in sequins. Froufrou girls riding Shetland ponies bare-assed. . . ." His voice trailed off as his mind swam in a rosy vision, both childish and obscene.

"Sarasota. . . . Won't be nothing like the El Dorado," he said, and took a few postcards of the hotel out of his pocket. "Nope. I don't think that hotel's going to make it. It's a crying shame. I should've stuck with building casinos and whore-houses. Yeah, the El Dorado was one lousy investment."

"Hey," Stokes stammered, "you shittin' me? You mean you . . . ?"

"Where'd you think the Panaguan government got the money to build the damn place?"

Stokes was dumbfounded. "The El Dorado's *your* fucking hotel?"

"I mean, I had to have some way to launder my profits, right? And the Panaguan government, well, their treasury's been broke for years. They put up what they could. You might say I took up the slack."

Curzon stopped. He could see that Stokes wasn't listening. The pilot was studying the gauges, as if debating whether to ask a question that might send the DC-3 into a tailspin. Fear crept into Stokes's voice. *"What the hell was going on back there?"*

"It's the jungle...." Curzon sighed. His posture sagged as if the thought cut him down to size. "Put a bunch of people together in the middle of it"—he shook his head—"and the damnedest things start to happen...." It was hardly a glib reply, more an admission of defeat. But then, he had given up trying to understand the jungle long ago.

Murder for money he could appreciate. There was a sound logic to it, the logic that governed his own life. But the slaughter at the El Dorado didn't make sense. It was the work of a power more malevolent than the underworld. He had spent enough time in the jungle to know that even human brutality paled beside it. He had seen enough to let the dark forces be.

As for the guests stranded at the hotel, he would waste no pity on them. In the jungle, there would always be predator and prey. In the jungle, the only crime was weakness. Those that were found guilty of it were bound to pay. He filed away the El Dorado among his life's more extravagant failures and tore up the postcards, letting the scraps flutter to the floor.

Already the plane was cruising out of the storm, into the balmy night. A bright path of stars beckoned through the clouds. The wings were dipped in moonlight, and they shimmered like the circus girls in his mind, who pirouetted in pink tights as they rode their dappled mares around the ring.

48

IT WAS CHRIS'S IDEA TO HOLD THE COUNCIL OF WAR in Berger's office. The brightly lit room with its walnut desk and file cabinets was thoroughly businesslike. In such a reasonable setting, she hoped that their extravagant fears would seem absurd and that they would be able to agree on a course of action. But when she stepped inside the room, she suspected she had made a mistake. Everywhere there were reminders of the terror they faced. Berger had been careful to replace the radio neatly on its table, but a few stray wires poked out of it, testifying to its destruction. And the doors of the mahogany cabinet in the corner yawned open to reveal the rack from which a dozen shotguns had been snatched.

As the guests filed into the room, she sized up each of them. Depressed since the plane's departure, Scott seemed malleable enough, though she knew he could explode again at any moment. As for Inez and Rima, they had already been so brutalized in their lives they were probably the best equipped to cope with a new ordeal. They sat down side by side, and soothed each other with caresses.

Margot retreated into a corner, a brooding presence, her hands fingering the *tsantsa*. Perhaps fearful of the shrunken heads, Jesús sat on the opposite side of the room, impassive and withdrawn.

And there was Alan. Somehow he had grown stronger from the trauma. But the threat tonight was so much more awesome than any he had faced before she wondered if he could handle it. Could *she?* Could she *shape* events, instead of merely reporting them?

She could feel their eyes watching her and was glad she had taken the pallor out of her cheeks with rouge, to convey a flush of self-confidence she hardly felt. Her mouth was dry; her hands were slick with sweat. She knew it wasn't just her words, but her tone of voice that would sway the others to calm or panic.

"Whatever it was that killed Berger and Irv and the others," she began, "it may already have left. We may already be out of danger." She was no actress. Could they hear the doubt that tinged her words? "But to be on the safe side—to be ready just in case—we need a plan to defend ourselves tonight."

"Defend . . . against *what?*" Scott asked.

"You're right. First we have to understand what 'it' is. . . ."

But before she could continue, Margot's voice rang out. "The dead! The vengeful spirit of the jungle is the killer. And *I* summoned it at the séance. . . ." Her voice died out in anguish. "*I* called it from the beyond!"

"No," Chris overruled her. "What we're dealing with is human," she said, as much to convince herself as the others. "This land once belonged to the Warak tribe. . . ."

"The Warak?" Scott asked.

"*Headhunters!*" Rima hissed.

"Lopez had them wiped out to build the El Dorado," Chris said.

Scott seized on her words. "Maybe it's *their* ghosts . . . !"

"In a way it is," Chris continued. "It seems that one of them survived. A warrior . . . a savage. The shrunken heads are his revenge. There's nothing supernatural about them."

"Don't make light of the *tsantsa!*" Margot warned. "Don't make light of the Avenging Angel!"

Chris feared that Margot was right, that the *tsantsa* possessed a power beyond reason. But to calm the others, she dismissed her words with a wave of her hand. "Our enemy is human . . . and primitive." She pointed to the empty cabinet. "He may have taken the firearms, but I doubt he knows how to use them."

"His machete," Scott murmured, his eyes wide. "I saw his machete cut through our door. He knows how to use *that!*"

Chris took another tack. "He's probably as scared as we are." A lie, but she hoped the thought of a gentle, noble savage would comfort them. "He may be sick . . . or wounded," she said. "He may even be insane." Her last words didn't come out the way she had wanted. From the look on their faces, the effect was anything but reassuring.

"There's no hiding place!" Margot's voice quivered with certainty.

"Wrong," Chris said. "So far he's only killed victims in small, dark rooms. A large, brightly lit space would discourage an attack."

"The lobby . . ." Alan said.

"We'll spend the night in the lobby, with all the lights on," she continued. "He'd never attempt a frontal assault against all of us."

Scott was already on his feet. "So let's move it!"

"First we've got to search the hotel," Chris said. "We've got to scrape up anything we could use as a weapon." She scanned the circle of faces. "Who'll help?" They averted their eyes. All but Alan.

"I'm game," he said.

"The radio," Scott added reluctantly. "I might be able to fix it. I used to be into electronics. CB's and stuff...." He pointed through the door into the lobby. "Then I'll join the others."

"Good," Chris said. "We'll meet in the lobby in half an hour. We should make it through the night without"—she hesitated in spite of herself—"without any problem."

"And what about tomorrow morning?" Margot asked. "What about *tomorrow night?*"

"No one's going to rescue us," Scott murmured. "Nobody even knows we're in danger!"

"Torres and his men are due back any time," Chris said, mustering what she hoped was a reassuring tone. "If they're not back tonight, they'll be here tomorrow for sure." They seemed unconvinced. "Look," she added, "if nobody shows up by tomorrow morning, we'll ... we'll just get the hell out of here. We'll set out along the coast. Follow the edge of the jungle. No matter what"—her voice was firm—"this is the last night we'll have to spend at the El Dorado ... Period."

"Right on!" Scott said. Inez and Rima nodded agreement.

Chris's plan sounded terribly logical. But her body wasn't so easily duped. It soaked her in sweat, wrenching her stomach with a gnawing uncertainty. She had better get moving while she still had the nerve.

Chris and Alan launched their search for weapons on the ground floor, hurrying down the corridor toward the cocktail lounge.

"That was quite a speech," Alan said. "It cooled everybody off."

"Did you buy it?"

"Sure...."

Chris stepped behind the bar and searched among the bottles.

She came out empty-handed. "I sure as hell didn't. The more I calmed them down . . . the more scared *I* got. I even. . . ." She hesitated. "It's crazy, but I even had this weird feeling. . . ."

"What?"

"Those shrunken heads . . . those *tsantsa* Margot was holding . . . it seemed like they were *listening* . . ."

She ducked back behind the bar to hide her embarrassment. She had revealed that she might be the first to crack.

She discovered a paring knife under a bar towel and tested the edge with her finger. She weighed it against the enormity of the danger, then stuffed it into her pocket. "It's coming," she said. *"It's coming tonight!"* It terrified her how much she sounded like Margot.

"Take it easy. . . ."

"I've seen it with jackals in Tanzania," she murmured. "They pursue their prey until it's ready to drop from exhaustion—until it has no hope of escape. . . ." She let out a sigh. "Then they tear it apart."

She was grateful for Alan's response. He didn't say her fears were groundless, but he didn't panic either. He put his hand on her shoulder to tell her that he understood and led her to the kitchen.

Rummaging through the pantry drawers, he found a screwdriver and an ice pick—puny discoveries, but worth keeping. Chris checked the cupboards. All but one. She couldn't bring herself to look where the *tsantsa* had hung. She turned away, as if fearing the doors might fly open to expose some new horror. *"Let's move."*

She was already halfway up the servants' steps. Alan caught up with her at the closet on the second-floor landing. It was locked, and he tripped the latch with the ice pick. She waited as he ducked inside the darkened cubicle. "Anything?" He pulled out a fire ax, and hefted it in his hand.

They chopped open the doors to the guest suites and ransacked them like thieves, pulling out drawers and leaving their contents strewn on the floor. They rushed through room after room, as if to linger would invite disaster.

But their search brought no new weapons. "Pack it in?" Alan asked. She nodded, eager to join the others.

They started back down the hall, Alan shouldering the ax, Chris clutching the knife, screwdriver, and ice pick. She looked at the meager weapons in her hands and thought of the brutal strokes that had harvested the *tsantsa*. She remembered Tobias's gutted room, the blood-soaked walls of the sauna. There was no way to combat a force like that, blow for blow.

They were about to round the corner to the staircase when they heard a *third* set of footsteps.

Alan placed a finger to his lips. Something was lurking around the corner ahead of them, its shadow falling across the carpet: a human form, it seemed, clutching a massive weapon. Chris's grip tightened on the ice pick. Alan swung back his ax.

A spear flashed through the air and stabbed into the wall, the steel shaft embedding in the paneling just inches from Chris's shoulder. She was amazed to see who staggered out from around the corner.

"What the hell are you doing?" Alan shouted.

Scott Hershey was holding a skin diver's speargun. Alan grabbed him angrily and slammed him against the wall.

"Don't! . . . Please!" Scott's knees buckled, and he collapsed on the floor. "I heard weird sounds. I wanted to *do something!* Don't . . . don't bite my head off!" When he realized what he had said, his mouth curved into a sickly smile. "That's what we're all afraid of, isn't it? I mean, *isn't it?*" He dissolved into tears.

"It's okay," Alan said, not very convincingly. "Everything's going to be okay."

Chris examined the speargun: a Magnum 450 model with 300 pounds of thrust. "Where'd you find this?"

"In Berger's office," Scott sniffled. "There was a chest behind the radio. Scuba supplies. . . ."

"Are there any more?"

He shook his head. "Hey, I'm real sorry."

"That's okay," she said gently. She was already prying the spear out of the wall. The barbed tip could pierce the hide of a shark. Perhaps they had found a weapon that could stop their enemy.

"The shaft's bent." Alan frowned. "It won't fire straight next time."

"It's the best we've got," she said.

Alan took the spear from her and skillfully notched it into its groove on the launcher. "I used to go skin diving in the Caribbean," he said, and cocked the trigger spring taut. "I've used these things quite a bit." She started to pull it away from him, but he wouldn't let go. "Trust me with this," he said. "Trust me."

She didn't trust anybody now. But she knew she had to accept Alan as her ally, or find herself totally alone. She let him keep the spear gun.

As they descended the staircase into the lobby, rain lashed the windows, and the wind moaned low. Beyond, lightning flared, and somehow it seemed to her that it was the jungle, not the sky, that was spewing forth those pillars of fire.

Huddled on couches, Rima, Inez, Margot, and Jesús seemed as bedraggled as the parrots in the lofty bamboo cage.

"Praise God!" Margot greeted Chris.

"Something . . . happen?" Inez asked.

"It almost did," Scott replied grimly.

Rima looked at the new arrivals with their makeshift weapons and crossed herself. "How you say? Our fate . . . in *your* hands."

That terrified Chris most of all.

49

A VENGEFUL RAIN DRUMMED ON THE WINDOWS OF
the lobby. Outdoors, as inside the El Dorado, the violence was
escalating, a cloudburst building into a hurricane. Chris knew
they had set forth on uncharted seas, where any minute they
might ram a hidden reef. Sink without a ripple.

She helped the others move the four leather sofas into a
tight square around the birdcage that dominated the center of
the room. When the furniture was in place, Alan slumped down
beside her. "Well," he said, "the wagons are in a circle. Now
what?"

She looked at the little group and at the caged birds. They
were all prisoners now. None of them could leave this strong-
hold until daybreak. She stared across the marble floor. "At
least it'll have to cross ten yards in a brightly lit room to get
us. By then"—she glanced at the speargun in Alan's hand—
"by then maybe we can get a shot off."

Chris was reluctant to distribute the weapons to the guests.
Their feelings were raw. She knew that once they were armed,
panic might turn any one of them into a murderer.

She handed Jesús the ice pick he had once used to make
daiquiris at the bar. After his near-lethal mistake, Scott didn't
complain when he got the screwdriver. Rima and Inez smashed
empty beer bottles into daggers of jagged glass, a skill learned,
no doubt, in the red-light district of Tierra del Mar. Chris kept
the ax for herself.

She had delayed giving Margot a weapon, for fear that the
spinster might hurt herself. When Chris finally offered her the
knife, Margot shook her head and opened her hand to reveal
the monkey's paw. *This* is my protection."

Maybe she was right, Chris thought. Would their weapons
do any more good than that scrap of fur? She eased Margot
down on a sofa. "Try to rest," Chris said.

The others followed suit, closing their eyes against the
lobby's glare. Inez and Rima flanked Scott on a sofa. He
rummaged in his shoulder bag, debating whether to take an
upper or a downer, and decided to swallow both. Jesús tried

to sleep sitting up, pressing his ankles and wrists together like a manacled hostage.

"You, too," Alan said to Chris. "I'll take first watch." But she had been vigilant for too long to remember how to relax. Trust him, she told herself. This may be your last chance to sleep.

1:15. Chris awoke with a start, as lightning exploded like napalm, searing the forest into stark relief. It looked as though the gale were hurling dismembered human limbs against the picture window. Rubbing the sleep from her eyes, she saw it was only palm fronds and broken branches.

She tried to ignore the ravings of the storm, to concentrate on the subtler sounds indoors. The electricity which crackled outside now charged the room, tingling her skin, raising the hairs on the back of her neck. Squinting through her camera's viewfinder, she scanned the brightly lit lobby, from the front desk to the curving staircase, then around to the elevators and the corridor that led to the bar, restaurant and patio. The polished surfaces, silent and cold, reminded her of a mausoleum.

2:37. The digital clock on the wall counted the minutes with sadistic tedium. "All things considered," Alan said, "I don't think this is going to give the Panaguan tourist industry much of a shot in the arm. I mean, it's been swell, but next time I think I'll try somewhere a little more laid back."

Chris was too preoccupied to hear him. "You know," she thought aloud, "if we took the insect coils from the patio and wired them across the doorways, we could give a powerful electric shock to any . . . late-night visitors."

A deafening crash cut her short. Margot opened her eyes and clutched the monkey's paw. "Thunder . . . ?"

Inez leaned up on an elbow and shot Rima a look. They gripped their bottle daggers tightly. Chris guessed that they had heard the same "thunder" during the rampage last night. When the next crash echoed down the corridor, they all sat bolt upright.

Scott winced, as if the sound inflicted pain. "Maybe . . . maybe a window just blew open."

"Maybe." Chris frowned. The sound was coming from either the dining room or the bar. Alan got up and started toward the corridor with the spear gun, but she stopped him. "We can't let it lure us into the dark. If it wants us . . . it'll have to get us *here*."

In the shadows behind the oak bar, something reared up, dancing in the strobe of the lightning. Spawned in the jungle, the savage was an innocent here. It wrenched open the door to the freezer, fascinated with the cold jewels of ice. The glassware on the shelves sparkled before its eyes, but it saw no beauty in the crystal. Fragile things were alien to its world of brute force.

A sweep of the blade sent Baccarat tumblers to the floor in a shower of tinkling glass, the machete flailing so quickly that the steel itself seemed transparent. For a moment the savage hesitated in front of its reflection in the mirror, marveling at its twin, until, mistrustful of the apparition, it shattered the image.

The sorcery of the bottles had attracted it here. Hiding on the roof and peering through the stained-glass skylight, it had watched the guests draw strength from the potions. It had concluded that this must be the shrine to their gods. It turned toward the altar. The guests' magic was now its own.

As it gulped from the bottles, the elixirs seared its throat. Endowed it with an unholy strength. In its might, it towered above the condor, the jaguar, the anaconda. And minute by minute, inflamed by the alcohol, the intruder's homicidal urges grew. The shrine had to be destroyed. The machete mutilated the oak bar, splinters flying helter-skelter. Bellowing, the savage dashed the bottles to the floor, absinthe mingling with burgundy in blood-red pools. And nothing dulled the blade. The cutting edge was sharper than before.

3:06. Chris listened to the din and struggled to conceive what force could cause such destruction. She refused to believe it could be a human being. The temptation to go look, to capture the intruder on film was almost irresistible. But she didn't dare. The cries she heard from the bar were like the sounds of no other living thing, a bellow both human and bestial.

Margot clamped her hands over her ears.

"Someone's wasting an awful lot of good booze," Scott whispered, his voice cracking. Rima and Inez embraced, their bodies stiff with fear.

Another salvo of bursting glass, bottles dashed against tile with such force that Chris could feel the vibration through the floor. Followed by the haunting cries.

Jesús took off his crucifix as he listened, hypnotized, to the bedlam. Long before Christianity, his people had named gods for such forces. She could see his lips moving. He was praying to them now. He put down his ice pick, as if it would be foolish to resist.

Alan balanced the spear gun in his hands. She guessed he was calculating how the bent shaft would affect the trajectory. There was only one spear to fire. He would get no second chance.

"It's strange," he said as the crashing echoed down the hallway, "I'm scared stiff. But if it doesn't come tonight . . . I'll be disappointed." Their eyes met. "I'm ready for it. I feel like I've been waiting for it for a long time."

When all the bottles were smashed, the machete glittered with flecks of glass like a magic wand. Now that their shrine had been destroyed, now that their gods had abandoned them, the time had come for the guests to yield to the sorcery of the blade. The time had come for the savage to garner fresh *tsantsa*—the only wealth the Warak knew—treasures of flesh and blood, sanctified by death. It walked across a floor strewn with broken glass, yet felt no pain, as it set forth on the hunt. It had drunk deeply. But now the savage had a thirst no alcohol could satisfy.

3:28. The mayhem in the bar stopped, and as if the intruder had dissolved into the night, the storm lashed out with a drunken snarl of thunder.

Suddenly, with the blinding brilliance of a white phosphorus grenade, lightning burst right on top of them. The hotel chandeliers glimmered, as if a murderer were being electrocuted in a distant room. Then the lights dimmed to a sickly yellow. The turbine, Chris thought. God in heaven. The lightning bolt must have scored a direct hit.

"Pray," Margot whispered. "It's the only answer now," and Chris could see that Scott, Inez, Rima, and Jesús *were* praying, each to his separate god.

But the time for supplication was past. As if to show their contempt for such prayers, all the lights winked out, plunging them into a darkness deeper than night.

Without the comforting glow of the digital wall clock, it was as if time itself had stopped. The whoosh from the air-conditioning ducts died, and insidiously, a jungle wind filtered through the ventilation system. Humidity thickened the air, drenching them in sweat. Suddenly blind, Chris felt her other senses heightened. The stench of the droppings from the bird-cage filled the room, and she could detect the sickening sweetness of spilled liquor, wafting down the corridor from the bar.

On the horizon, the lightning flashes faded as the storm swept out to sea. The artillery barrage had smashed their defenses, Chris thought. Now it was time for the bayonets.

50

4:03. CHRIS READ THE TIME OFF THE GLOWING DIAL of her watch. The rain had calmed to a soothing whisper. Moonlight filtered through the clouds, reflecting off the foliage outside the window, tinting the darkened lobby a glacial green. This cool aftermath chilled her, this turning point when the predators that had taken refuge from the fury of wind and rain came out of hiding to renew the hunt.

On sentinel duty, Chris watched over the others sprawled on the couches, cradling the spear gun in her arms. It had been hours since the air conditioning had died, and the humidity cast a drowsy spell, tempting her to believe that drunk and exhausted, the intruder too had dozed off; that its violence, like the storm, was spent. The others looked as if they had already succumbed to the sweet illusion. Bathed in sweat, each breathed with a private rhythm, the tempo, perhaps, of his dreams.

Chris squirmed. Though she avoided sleep, she could not so easily escape her nightmares. For the emerald aura of the jungle was far more disquieting than darkness. Staring out the window, she imagined that they were descending underwater in a bathyscaphe, descending inexorably toward moss-green reefs. They had already passed the familiar landmarks: plankton, seaweed, the shimmering schools of fish in the shallows. They had left them behind hours ago. Now, as they approached the ocean floor, she waited with her finger on the trigger. Any minute she expected to glimpse the predator that had been watching their descent, lying in wait until this moment, when they entered the most profound chasm of night.

4:24. Inez and Rima embraced in their sleep, as if both were swimming through a single dream. Sensual pleasure was their antidote for fear, and they stroked each other's breasts in a slow-motion caress. Their lips touched; their fingers groped in the clefts between their legs. The intimacy seemed to calm them, to keep panic at bay.

Scott awoke and eyed the two women, jealous of their embrace. They had abandoned him just when he needed them most. A dozen pills of as many colors were a poor substitute for the comfort of their flesh, and his mouth was so dry from fear he had trouble swallowing them. The capsules grated on his empty stomach as he lay back on the couch. And when the ingredients seeped into his brain, he found that they too had betrayed him. The jumble of chemicals distorted his perception, transforming the jungle outside the window into a realm of carnivorous plants, where greedy leaves engulfed their victims as surely as a Venus-flytrap devoured an ant. His eyes shifted focus to the caged birds, in search of a more comforting sight. But the birds were transformed into harpies with razor-sharp beaks. He closed his eyes in self-defense, but in the darkness he could feel the legs of spiders prickling his skin, like nettles.

Scott groped for his guitar, but his fingers trembled too violently to pluck the strings. He struggled to conjure up lyrics to drown out the fear, but his mind was blank. He snapped open his pillbox and swallowed another handful blind.

Alertness was what he feared most—he would do anything to block the awareness of doom. Whatever gruesome surgery they would be subjected to tonight, he prayed the scalpel would wait until the anesthetic had time to take effect.

4:33. Curled up on her sofa in a fetal ball, Margot rocked fitfully, swaddled in threadbare memories. As her body hurtled into old age, her mind snuggled back into long-lost childhood. *"I've a dear little dolly and her eyes are bright blue.... She can open and close them and she smiles at me, too...."* She felt the starched collar of a sailor suit against her neck, the one she had worn at the age of eight on summer afternoons when her nanny sang her a lullaby. *"In the morning I wake up and go out to play....But I like best to rock her at the close of the day...."* She pieced together a mosaic of the few happy days from a troubled childhood: parasols and merry-go-rounds, bouquets of balloons, and a sun that cast no shadows. She smelled the tang of taffy apples and the showers of spring.

The china doll she cradled in her arms had blond curls and innocent blue eyes. She kissed its cupid's-bow lips. To love something, to hold it close—she found comfort in that. *Until.* Until the lullaby ground to a halt, like a tune on a rusty music box. She opened her eyes. And shuddered. Instead of the smooth china skin of her beloved doll, she was fondling a shrunken head, its features twisted in hate. She held the *tsantsa* in one hand, the monkey's paw in the other, and vowed never to allow the shriveled relics to touch. For she felt certain that the moment she placed them together, a new being would fuse and grow, a cunning monster coagulating from dismembered limbs, piece by piece.

4:46. Alan leaned back on the sofa, and begged for the mercy of sleep. But the dream that seized him was far from merciful. His subconscious had a malicious intent of its own. He relived a night, long ago, when he had been a student in Istanbul, during the feast of Ramadan. All the hotels had been booked for the holiday, and it was well past midnight when he finally found himself a flophouse. The manager had one bed left, but Alan would have to share it with another male guest. Even so, it beat sleeping in the gutter, and after taking the key, he had walked up the rickety stairs to the room. His bedpartner had already fallen asleep, and Alan slipped under the sheets beside him.

At dawn, Alan had awakened to the muezzin crying out from the Blue Mosque in the distance. Turning to his sleeping companion, *he had found a corpse....*

Alan opened his eyes in horror and stared at the others. In the green glow, they all looked like corpses now. He feared that they had died in their sleep, leaving him alone to face the onslaught.

When Chris saw Alan was awake, she handed the spear gun back to him. As he took the weapon, his fear was replaced by determination. Either he would kill it, or he would die, but this would be one act in his life which was not left incomplete. He understood now how hunters yearned to end a long wait with bloodletting. They were right, he thought. There were certain conflicts—the most basic ones—which could only be resolved by murder.

4:56. It was Alan's turn to stand watch. Chris knew she should try to sleep, but with only one hour before dawn, she intended to stay awake for the duration.

Like a Chinese water torture, rain dripped from the roof, ticking off the seconds into a puddle outside the window. She knew the last hour would be the slowest to pass, a steep uphill climb. But for the first time that night, she allowed herself the luxury of hope. Perhaps the stalker was sated on blood. Perhaps it had taken mercy on them. God knows, they had suffered enough. Even if they survived, they would be haunted for life.

Perhaps the Warak that stalked them knew that years of mental anguish were a more exquisite revenge than death: every night for the rest of their lives they would sleep with the *tsantsa* dangling in their minds; every dream would end with the caress of the cutting edge.

She could feel her arms going numb. She shook them to reassure herself that her limbs were still intact, that they hadn't been sheared off in a surprise attack.

She rubbed her eyes, and to keep the room in focus through the haze of her exhaustion, she forced herself to study minute details: the water leaking from a seam in the roof, like seepage from a wound; the glow filtering through the window, tinging the Carrara marble a sickly green. She found herself drawn to the birds huddled in their bamboo cage an arm's length away. The cylindrical enclosure reached all the way to a skylight in the ceiling, but the birds had clustered near the bottom, as if craving human companionship. In the past, Chris had kept her distance from the cage, but now she identified with the creatures trapped inside.

Though it was still dark, the birds were beginning to stir, ruffling their feathers with restless beaks, clucking with thick black tongues. Perhaps dawn was coming sooner than she had thought. She leaned over to study them more closely. As she grasped the bamboo bars, she was surprised to feel the cage quivering under her fingertips. Was a wind flowing through the room, causing the vibration? No. The air was still. But the bamboo latticework was *shaking* now, as if from the first tremor of an earthquake.

For an electrifying moment, her eyes met the cobalt pupils of a parrot, and an awareness shot between them—the simplest message that could pass between two living creatures: mortal terror.

Then—frenzy.

With suicidal force, the birds threw themselves against the bars, wings flapping desperately, cries harsh and shrill. *Something reached through the bars and seized her by the throat. It was inside the cage. It had entered through the skylight, then climbed into the bamboo enclosure, descending the latticework rung by rung.*

The fingers that clutched her neck from behind were human, but the nails that bloodied her flesh were as sharp as claws. She couldn't see her stalker, but she could *smell* him—daubs of ocher mingled with sweat and caked blood. *And she could hear the blade whistling through the air.*

"Help me!" She tried to scream, but her captor was choking her, and the words came out a hoarse whisper. *"Help me!"* Raising its arm from inside the cage, the savage snatched her effortlessly off the floor.

As helpless as a marionette, Chris reached out to the others. Her cry had torn them from sleep, and paralyzed, they gaped at the apparition. It was as if their nightmares had hardened into this specter of vengeance, silhouetted in the green glow.

"Help me!"

She saw Alan step backward, aiming the spear gun.

"Shoot!" she whimpered. The hand was clutching her by the hair, and from the corner of her eye, *she could see the blade.*

"Shoot!"

His finger tensed on the trigger, but he held his fire for fear of hitting her.

Chris could feel the muscles of the savage stiffen to level the severing blow, and with a desperate twist of her head, she sank her teeth into the massive arm that held her. Her canines drew blood. Its grip loosened just enough for her to tear free, in a movement so violent, that she left the intruder clutching a fistful of her hair.

She fell to the floor, as the hot wind of the machete whipped past, narrowly missing her head and slicing through the bamboo bars. The birds poured out of the gaping hole, flapping up to the ceiling, where they hovered in a raucous chorus.

The other guests had fled, and as she lay on the floor, dazed, Chris thought she had been abandoned to die. But a hand gripped her shoulder. Alan pulled her behind him as, with a vicious blow of the steel blade, the stalker burst out of the cage.

Alan flicked off the safety catch of the spear gun. The target loomed before them in the green aura from the window, and suddenly, Chris's fear was matched by a sense of wonder. The powerfully muscled body had to be more than seven feet tall. How had this giant descended so stealthily to seize her? Beneath a shaggy mane of hair, the enormous figure was masked in darkness, but to photograph even that murky vision, she would have sacrificed anything. Anything, but her life. There was no time to aim her camera, for an enormous fist loomed out of the shadows wielding a four-foot long machete. In one leap, the savage was upon them.

Alan took aim with the barbed tip of the spear and squeezed the trigger.

A jolt of compressed air sent the projectile flashing, but the target moved with a speed that belied its enormous size, and the spear missed its mark. Deflected by the bamboo cage, it stabbed into a crested macaw, pinning it by a wing to the wall.

As the savage lunged after them, Chris dashed away, down the hall. She glanced over her shoulder and was appalled to see that Alan stood his ground and was taking a swing at his attacker with the butt of the spear gun. In the selfishness of terror, she kept right on running. There was nothing she could do to help Alan now. There might be nothing she could do to help herself. She wondered if she would ever see him again. Then such pangs of regret were forgotten in her race for the next step, the next yard, that she could put between herself and the savage.

51

THE GUESTS SCATTERED IN PANIC, EACH CON-
vinced the intruder was after him alone, the Angel of Death
bent on swift and certain retribution. Of all of them, Scott
seemed the worst equipped to survive. But despite his overdose
of barbiturates, a jolt of adrenaline sobered him into action.
He stumbled up the staircase to the second floor, racing past
the demolished rooms. All the doors had been ripped off their
hinges, depriving him of a hiding place. When he reached the
end of the corridor, there was nowhere left to run.

Then Scott noticed the elevator. He couldn't pry the sliding
doors open with his fingers, but when he took the screwdriver
Chris had given him and slipped it into the crack between the
steel slabs, they yielded. The opening was barely six inches
wide. In his desperation, he managed to squeeze inside before
the doors slammed shut behind him. In total darkness, he
groped for the buttons on the wall. If he could ride the elevator
up and down, from one floor to the next, he would be safe.
His fingers pushed the buttons frantically, but nothing happened. Finally, it hit his sedated brain that the electricity was
dead. He wasn't going anywhere.

He pressed his ear against the cold metal, listening for his
pursuer in the hallway. Nothing. It must be hunting the others.
For the moment he was safe. But how long could he hold out
here? The air in the cubicle was stifling. Sit perfectly still,
told himself. You'll last only as long as the oxygen. He slumped
into a corner and buried his head in his hands.

The total darkness, the surge of terror plunged him back
into the past. The last time he had run so frantic a race was
in the sixties, to escape a mob of his fans. Scott stroked his
beard, savoring the silken texture of pleasant memories from
the days when he was *big*. He had worn disguises, hired bodyguards, and still, the tenny-boppers had pursued him, smashing
through police barricades. That screaming horde would have
settled for a lock of his hair, or ten minutes in his bed. He
wished to God he were playing for such meager stakes tonight.

He let out a sigh and ran his hand along the steel doors to

reassure himself. But even locked in the elevator, he feared he
was being watched. He struck a match. The flame danced off
gilt-framed photos proclaiming the joys of the hotel's Sunday
buffet. But the centerpiece in the picture—the head of a suckling pig with an apple in its mouth—made him blow the match
out. Better darkness than this grotesque reminder of decapitation. He pressed his hand against his chest. The thump-thump
of pumping blood was proof that he was still alive. And he
heard *something else,* ringing in his mind: a fragile melody.

The high, sustained notes were transparent as a dragonfly's
wing, exquisitely sweet and gentle, and as he listened with his
inner ear, a smile played across his lips. This was no hard-rock
explosion, but a harmony as comforting as a lullaby. It forced
him to face the truth: all his music had been bubble-gum pop.
Commercial trash. But this was different. If he could capture these haunting strains, it would catapult him back to star-
dom. He strummed an imaginary guitar to the tempo:
C . . . A . . . B7. If only he had a pencil and paper to write down
the fleeting chords. . . . Then all spasms of ambition subsided,
and he succumbed to the melody, serene beyond imagining.
He drummed his fingers against the wall to the beat. His eyes
filled with tears. This was *his* song.

But as he continued to tap his fingers, he heard more tapping, *other* tapping, like a reply from a hidden recess in his
mind. It must be a moth trapped in the lighting fixture overhead,
he thought, an insect fluttering against the ceiling. But wait.
The rustling had turned into a persistent thumping no insect
could make. He struck a match and looked up.

On the ceiling, the emergency hatch was creaking open. He
blew the match out, hoping that it was all a hallucination of
his drugged mind. But no. The elevator shook. *Something was
walking on its roof.* Had the savage climbed down the cable?
Had it been up there in the elevator shaft all along—waiting
for him?

An oily stench flooded the cubicle as the hatch in the ceiling
yawned wide. Scott scrambled to his feet and clawed at the
hairline fissure between the steel doors. They were sealed shut.
A tomb.

He remembered the screwdriver and rammed the shank between the doors, slamming his body against the handle. It
snapped off at the hilt. Trembling, he turned to face the intruder
as it slid inside. The fragile melody in his mind was all he had
left to cling to now, but it was no use. The gentle chords

thinned to a shrill scream, a razor's edge of sound.

The blade slashed so swiftly that it did not seem as if Scott's head had been severed at all. Rather, it appeared to levitate from his body. And suspended in midair, his head seemed holier in death. With his golden beard, his halo of blond hair, he was St. John the Baptist in Epiphany. His eyes rolled heavenward until only the whites showed, and his mouth opened to sing one final chorus. One last amen.

52

TORN FROM INEZ'S ARMS, RIMA DASHED DOWN THE corridor out of the lobby. After bursting through the door to the patio, she stumbled out into an obstacle course of canvas furniture scattered helter-skelter, like an SOS in an alien alphabet. She debated whether to run along the beach or hide in the jungle, but decided that the pool would offer more immediate protection.

Her body cleaved the water at an angle that hardly raised a splash, and she swam beneath the surface to the shallow end. There she crouched up to her neck in the pool, a black head disembodied in the shadows, her heart pounding. It was a relief to be free of the hotel's imprisoning walls. She inhaled air sweetened by night-blooming jasmine, and slid out of her shift, the water pleasingly cool against her flesh. The chase had both terrified and excited her, leaving her nipples erect, her thighs and buttocks taut.

Moonlight filtered through a cleft in the clouds, turning the gently falling rain to quicksilver. As the water licked her body, she could almost convince herself she was out for a predawn swim, awaiting a lover. The shrieks of night birds, the screams of howler monkeys, even the threat of the assailant who might appear through the hotel door at any moment didn't scare her. She knew the jungle. She knew many jungles—from this tangled forest to the capital's shantytown. She had learned to survive in all of them, certain that even the fiercest predators would rather possess her than devour her.

She pulled her wet hair back from her face and thrust out her breasts seductively. All her life, jealous men had come to her bent on revenge, and always she had been able to sway them. She possessed the magical power to turn rage into lust, then quench it with her flesh. She even dared believe she could seduce her enemy tonight, entice it into surrender.

Lounging against the pool's edge, she succumbed to the water's caress, and stared at the lobby entrance, where the shadows were too deep for the moonlight to penetrate. Her mouth was parched, and she opened her lips to allow the rain to moisten her tongue. The pool's swim-up bar was a few yards away, and she eased toward it, through water where dead insects floated. Her fear had dissipated. Naked in the night air, she felt free, like a fish in the deep blue sea, too strong to fear the hook, the net, the harpoon.

A sudden wind sent a shiver through her. The breeze rippled the water, concealing the shadow that glided toward her beneath the surface, as silent as the clouds. The incision was made with a blade so sharp, it felt like a fleeting kiss. But when the warm crosscurrent in the water pulsed over her breasts, a tincture swirling in the moonlight, she realized she was swimming in her own blood.

"No!" She flailed her arms wildly, reaching out for the pool's rim, but her panic only made her heart pump faster, the dark current flow more swiftly. Her legs refused to obey her command to kick. She drifted, helpless, at her attacker's mercy. But instead of devouring her like piranha in feeding frenzy, it allowed her a final arabesque, as she felt her entrails trammeling her, dragging her down. She had set out to seduce, but the night had seduced her.

Although her body floated face down, the blade rescued her lovely face from the indignity of drowning. One blow, and the blood oozed from her severed neck, the coagulating liquid a jellyfish hovering near the surface. Headless, her body had a new center of gravity, and it hunched over, floating across the water to the deep end, a tangle of limp arms and legs, like a spider torn from its web.

53

AS ALAN PUSHED OPEN THE KITCHEN DOOR AND stepped onto the patio, he felt blood trickling down his leg. But compared to what might have happened, the gash in his thigh seemed a blessing. For the Warak had spared him from the final lethal chop and had turned to chase after the others. Perhaps, Alan brooded, he had only been spared for an even more grotesque end.

As he skirted the patio, he thought he could see someone floating in the pool. But there was no time for a closer look. Already he could hear the kitchen door creaking open. He was forced to escape to the beach, and painfully he dragged his injured leg down the steps to the sand. Glancing over his shoulder to see if he was being followed, he realized that he was leaving a trail of blood.

It had been a mistake to flee to the beach. He was exposed here, an easy target against the moonlit sea. He scanned the shore for cover, and a hiding place caught his eye: a rowboat at the water's edge. He ran for it and crouched down inside.

The planking stank of seaweed. He waved away a swarm of flies drawn to his wound. He could feel the surf slamming against the bow, and a grinding beneath him as the riptide grated the hull across the sand, pulling the rowboat toward the waves. He was gripped by indecision: should he stay in the boat and risk being swept out to sea, or leap out and run across the sand, exposing himself to attack? Suddenly the decision was made for him. On the patio he could see the flash of a blade, hear a frantic thrashing in the pool, a woman's scream. Her voice. . . . It sounded like Chris.

He buried his face in his hands. In a lifetime of failures, this was his most tragic. More than any challenge he had ever faced, he had wanted to save her life. And he *might* have, if only. . . . His tears tasted saltier than the ocean spray. His attempt to defend her had been as futile as that steel spear flashing into the night. It made him doubt, more than ever, whether he could save himself. And it made him wonder whether he was *worth* saving.

In spite of his harsh verdict, he refused to yield to suicide, even now. He had come too far for that, grown too much in these days of terror. He vowed that his act of defiance would be to survive.

He climbed out and shoved the stern into the waves. A gunshot forced him to dive back into the rowboat, groaning from the impact of his wounded leg against the planking.

Another salvo. As the boat drifted away from shore, the hull shuddered from a hail of buckshot. The stolen shotguns, Alan thought. Chris had insisted that the Warak wouldn't know how to use modern weapons. *This* savage knew.

Another blast, and another, peppering the hull. He feared the next salvo would pierce the rotting planking, and he slid into the water, clinging to the far side of the boat. His leg wound stung from the salt, but he bobbed among the waves until he could see the buckshot falling short, splashing harmlessly in the water. He had drifted out of range.

With a sigh of relief, he turned toward the open sea. The moonlit waves were a benign presence. Until he noticed an ominous detail. Twenty feet away, a dorsal fin knifed through the water. Trailing in the current, the blood from his leg wound must have sent out an irresistible invitation. He heaved himself out of the water and over the slippery side, collapsing into the boat with a grunt of pain. The dorsal fin skudded by on the port bow, just seconds behind him. For a moment the prowler disappeared among the waves. Then it appeared again—on the starboard side. It was circling. Once. Twice. By the third time, as if by some incantation of the deep, its circling had spawned two more dorsal fins. The leader had summoned members of its pack, all of them aroused by the scent of blood.

As he lay back against the rotten planking and stared up at the stars, Alan wondered whether this boat was to be his coffin. The sharks were still circling. Why hadn't they given up by now? He was out of the water, protected by the hull. Why didn't they move on to other prey?

Something gushed down his arm. For a moment, he thought it was a fresh wound, that perhaps the buckshot had found their mark after all. He *hoped* it was blood. He didn't dare consider the alternative. It was too dark to identify the liquid that drenched his shoulder, so he moistened a finger in it and stuck it in his mouth. The briny taste confirmed his worst fears. Now he knew why the sharks lingered. Perhaps he even knew why the savage had driven him out to sea. The liquid was seawater. The boat was leaking.

The black fins poked up through the waves like the hats of witches, a coven surrounding him.

54

CHRIS DASHED PAST THE GUEST SUITES AND, WHEN she reached the end of the hall, leaned against the elevator to catch her breath. Should she hide in one of the shattered rooms? She noticed blood trickling between the elevator doors. The sight drove her up the servants' stairs.

It was all she could do to keep her balance as she climbed floor after dizzying floor, spiraling into the smothering darkness. Rushing headlong, she tried to avoid asking herself *which* guest's corpse was entombed inside the elevator. But as her feet clattered upstairs, each step resounded with a different name: Scott . . . Inez . . . Rima . . . Margot . . . Jesús . . . *Alan?*

The staircase dead-ended. She teetered on the landing and listened for footsteps. The silence reassured her and she wrenched open the door. After the darkness of the stairwell, the moonlight that suffused the vast expanse seemed as bright as day. So bright, in fact, that she could read the 13 on the wall beside the elevator.

Memories of her ordeal here at the hands of Torres swam like piranha in her mind. She scanned the floor, hoping that the mercenaries had left some weapon behind, a bayonet or hand grenade she could use to defend herself. She found only shards of broken glass.

She walked over to the window ledge. The glass panes had not yet been installed, and she inhaled the salty ocean breeze. High above the jungle, she was spared the growls of predators, the shrieks of their victims. From her godlike vantage point, she could sense the tranquility of death. Was it worth the price to cross over to the Other Side, to become a shrunken trophy, serene and wise?

Chris's wrist ached from the weight of the Leica but she wouldn't put the camera down. She couldn't risk losing it, too. She squinted through the viewfinder and adjusted the lens until the dusty floor jumped into focus. The lens was still sharp. She tried to convince herself that her brain was just as acute. But she could feel her faculties starting to blur.

Spinning the lens barrel nervously between thumb and forefinger, she glimpsed something scrabbling along the floor. But when she caught sight of the intruder, her tension eased. It was only a parrot, a refugee from the cage in the lobby. Clucking, the bird scratched the ground in a vain search for food. It seemed as lost as she was, a pathetic companion but, in her loneliness, a welcome one.

Chris sat on the window ledge, and the parrot flapped up and perched beside her. Her thighs ached, and she massaged them with her fingers, but the muscles were stiff and sore. She wiped her forehead on her sleeve and realized that her face was gray with plaster dust. A death mask, she brooded, and racked her brain for some way out. But no matter how she fed in the equation, no matter how she phrased it, the computer in her mind always spewed out the same answer: Death. It was the only solution now. The only reasonable end to a most unreasonable chain of events.

To deny her computer's cold analysis, she searched the horizon for a hint of sunrise. But sea and sky met in a black weld. She suspected that dawn would never come. Night would linger until it numbered her among its victims.

She glanced over to the ledge beside her. The parrot was gone. It had silently abandoned her. As she climbed down from the ledge, her foot stepped on something soft. The bird had been cut in half.

Holding her breath, Chris scanned the thirteenth floor: no trace of the murderer. With queasy certainty, she turned to the one place where she had *not* looked. *The ledge*. Incredible, she thought. Impossible. No human being could scale a sheer marble wall. But then, hadn't Dr. Tobias said the Warak were more than human?

There. Climbing over the ledge. He pulled himself over the side with ease, and despite his weight, he landed on the floor without a sound. Had the savage known she was there all along? Had he clung like a gargoyle to the facade until she drifted into a false sense of security?

She screamed—but who would hear? She ran—but her knees locked in terror. If he had stalked her all this way—climbed sheer walls to trap her—a few steps couldn't save her now. As if sensing her paralysis, the man-creature made no attempt to lunge for her body. For he had already seized hold of her mind.

Chris was mesmerized by his silhouette in the moonlight. He opened his mouth to reveal teeth that had been filed to sharp points. Was that a *smile* on his lips? Yes. The smile of the executioner.

The Kakaram took a step toward her and swung back the blade. Above high cheekbones, his eyes gleamed with a hatred as eternal as the all-knowing *tsantsa*. Chris was spellbound, staring into the face of Death—an ageless face gifted with the vigor of youth, the wisdom of old age. Did he recognize her? Did he know she had already escaped him once? He stared at her like a carcass to be dismembered, studying the way her neck joined the base of her skull, as if gauging the angle of his blow.

Her lips trembled. She opened her mouth to beg for mercy. But before she could shape a sound, his snarl silenced her.

She staggered over a floor littered with broken glass, and he followed barefoot, seemingly immune to pain. Her shoulder bumped into a pylon, knocking her off-balance, and as she fell backward, she accidentally triggered the shutter of her Leica.

Click. The 330-volt flash flared. The burst of light exploded off the machete blade, blinding him. The savage clutched at his eyes and bellowed in rage.

Chris scrambled to her feet. In four steps she was across the room. Sobbing, gasping for breath, she staggered down the stairs. In her dizzying descent, she clutched her throat to convince herself that her jugular was still intact, her head still attached to her shoulders.

As she clattered down the stairs, she had no idea where her feet were leading her. For in the remotest corner of the hotel, he had found her. Where was there left to hide?

55

LIKE A SOMNAMBULIST, MARGOT GLIDED THROUGH
the kitchen, the dining room, the devastated bar. She had
watched the others flee to the outer reaches of the hotel. And
she had seen the hunter pursue them, drawn by the spoor of
panic. Now that both predator and prey were gone, she held
dominion over the shadowy building. A stately figure in a
flowing gown, she felt like the high priestess in a temple hallowed by death. She stepped out onto the patio, and even the
sight of the headless corpse floating in the pool didn't repel
her. She felt immune to the contagion, convinced no one would
dare to interrupt her sacred purpose.

When, at last, she discovered a drawerful of candles at the
outdoor bar, her quest was over. She returned to the lobby in
triumph. There, with a mystical design only she could understand, she positioned the white tapers inside the vast, empty
birdcage and lit them one by one, to fashion a glowing tiara.
Bathed in the radiance of the candles, her gray hair shimmered
blond, her wrinkled hands transformed into those of a young
girl. She was a virgin, bent on seducing almighty forces. Margot lit one last taper and reached inside the bamboo latticework
to press it into the wax drippings. Then she stood back to
admire her handiwork: reflected in the polished floors, the
marble walls, the score of candles in the cage were transformed
into thousands of twinkling stars. Her own sacred constellation.

Her voice rang out, clear and strong. "Let these candles
bring life to those on the brink of death and stay the hand of
the Reaper. May this bright forest combat the dark jungle which
threatens to devour us!"

Perched in the darkened chandeliers, fugitive parrots, toucans, amd macaws had gathered to watch her. They were her
congregation, and she spoke on their behalf, as well as her
own. "Spirit of the jungle, essence of the deep forest, we have
shut you out of our hearts. You, the all-powerful ruler. Now
we open our arms to welcome you into our souls!"

She backed away from the glowing birdcage and pushed the
lobby doors wide, as if opening the Ark of the Covenant. In

the sudden breeze, the flames flickered like endangered creatures.

The hallowed moment had come. Reaching among the folds of her gown, she removed the shrunken heads and hung them tenderly at the core of the shimmering altar, knotting the hair around the bamboo bars. The candlelight seemed to imbue the embalmed flesh with life. "My children, my fair ones, my tender loves," she intoned, "I burn these tapers for your departed souls!" In the updraft from the candles, the *tsantsa* started to quiver. Their faces turned toward her, and she was certain they were responding to her invocation. She studied them lovingly and tried to remember Irv, Dawn, and Lopez as they had been in life. "To your wandering spirits, who left us so suddenly, we offer our prayers: that in the world beyond, your bodies will be made whole again, complete and perfect beings."

The time had come for her plea. "You who have crossed over to the Other Side know how desperately the living cling to life. How irreversible is the darkness." She extended her hands to them beseechingly and tried to bore behind their closed eyelids. "Speak now, in defense of the living. Plead on our behalf. Cry out for mercy. An end to blood!"

The *tsantsa* were gods now. Her fate, the fate of them all, was in *their* control. And they were listening to her, she was certain of it. They would not ignore her plea.

"From the unknown, *spare us!* From the evil power, *deliver us!* From the *savage, save us!*"

In reply, a breeze stirred, blowing through the open doors, spattering her gown with hot wax like unholy semen. She spoke with the voice of a high priestess. "Spirits of Good or Evil, I beg your forgiveness! I have led my friends into the Valley of the Shadow of Death. *Now I must lead them out!*"

This would be her life's work. The forbidden books, the hours of training, the loneliness—yes, even *that* hadn't been in vain. The candle flames danced in her eyes. "Take *me!*" she cried out. "But . . . spare *them!*"

She stopped to listen. The *tsantsa* had heard her supplication. Already their answer was borne on the jungle wind. "Nooo . . ." it moaned, *"Noooo . . . !"*

The wind rose up, swelling from a purr to a howl, flaring the candles, which licked at the bamboo cage, scorching it. *Igniting it.*

The garter snake of flame thickened to anaconda width as

it slithered up the bars. The wood was tinder-dry, and it took seconds for tendrils of fire to shoot up to the ceiling. The birds fled the blaze on singed wings, reeling away in the drunken flight path of bats.

Though the flames terrified her, though the smoke suffocated her, Margot couldn't bear to part with the *tsantsa*. She tried to snatch them out, to rescue them from cremation, but the heat scorched her fingers. She had lost the *tsantsa* forever, lost them to the Other Side. What have I done? she thought, and eyed the shrunken heads with a twinge of suspicion. What have *they* done?

56

NESTLED WITHIN THE PYRE WHERE THE BLAZE WAS spawned, the *tsantsa* nodded hysterically, a satanic vision in the heat. Their warped faces seemed to revel in the hotel's immolation. Hadn't they already been scourged by scalding water, subjected to a trial beyond any the living could endure? Yes, they had reason for revenge.

The jungle, *their* jungle, had invaded the hotel at last. Vines of flame crisscrossed the walls of the lobby, fiery orchids blossoming two stories high to the ceiling. The *tsantsa* watched with seeming satisfaction as the precise angles of the architecture warped in the heat; the plaster moldings melted like wax, and the mahogany doors were charred to kindling. The inferno uprooted the parquet floors of the hallways with earthquake rumblings, and wavering like a mirage, the lobby's picture window shattered. Smoke billowed up the staircase, a messenger to the upper stories of the destruction to come.

The disembodied heads of the *tsantsa* had acquired limbs at last, for the tentacles of flame did their bidding. With awesome strength they pried the marble slabs from their concrete underpinnings, sending them crashing to the floor. Then, with a scream of shearing metal, the elevator cables snapped, and the steel cubicles hurtled to the lobby. Their doors slid open on impact, and Scott Hershey's body, what was left of it, was cremated in the blaze.

At the vortex of the fire storm, the *tsantsa* spun by their hair in a dance of ungodly rejoicing. Even now their flesh resisted the withering heat, but the thread from the bark of the kumai palm that sewed their mouths shut was charred to a crisp. Their jaws opened, with a hiss of escaping breath, and sputum foamed from their toothless mouths. Gurgling, the pink gums curled into smiles of joy.

57

IN HER HEADLONG DESCENT DOWN THE SERVICE
stairs, Chris reached the fifth-floor landing. At first she mistook
the glow under the steel door for the first hint of dawn. But
when the acrid smell reached her nostrils, she drew a more
ominous conclusion.

She yanked open the door to the corridor, and a funereal
shroud of soot billowed out to meet her. Coughing, she
slammed the door. The hotel itself had become the enemy.

The smoke floating up the stairwell was thickening. Her
eyes were tearing badly. She fought her way down two more
flights. On the third floor she opened the door a crack, enough
to see flames licking greedily from the rooms. She ripped off
the tail of her shirt and held it over her nose and mouth as she
groped her way down another flight, step by step, with her
eyes closed. In one, two minutes at the most, she knew her
oxygen would run out.

The second floor. The shirttail was useless against the smoke
now. She was suffocating on the edge of the holocaust, and
the once-distant crackle of flames had grown into the roar of
a blast furnace. In the blistering heat, the fire door to the
second-floor corridor wilted on its hinges, the metal reduced
to putty. Hunched over against the heat, she could feel her
flesh simmering. The smoke scorched her throat and began to
impregnate her lungs.

She tottered against the stairwell wall. A steel knob burned
her fingers. She was leaning against the handle to *another* door,
opposite the one to the corridor. In desperation, she twisted it.
Locked. She threw her weight against it, beat it with her fists,
and still, it held. Finally, with trembling hands, she unsnapped
the steel bar that attached her camera to its flash and stabbed
at the latch with it, trying to jimmy the lock.

The door clicked open. She staggered through. Wiping the
ashes from her eyes, she found herself on the roof of the
restaurant pavilion adjoining the hotel. She coughed up soot,
and as gulps of fresh air replaced the smoke, her mind began
to clear. She had almost been killed on this very spot, her first

night at the El Dorado. Now the roof promised safety. She stared at the hotel towering above her, flames billowing out of a hundred windows like an apocalyptic vision.

Suddenly the roof started to tremble beneath her feet. The fire was rampaging through the dining room below. She could hear the restaurant's stained-glass ceiling crash to the ground and realized that in minutes, perhaps seconds, the rest of the roof would cave in, plunging her to her death.

She remembered the ladder on the far wall and edged toward it. But when at last she neared her goal, she burst into tears. The heat tremors that shook the restaurant had popped the ladder's bolts, hurling it to the ground twenty feet below.

She was stranded.

Had all her narrow escapes from danger spared her for *this* . . . ? Teetering on the edge of the roof, Chris squinted through her tears down at the patio. It glistened in the rain, as alluring as the life she could already feel slipping from her grasp. She imagined what a fall from this height would do to her—the impact of her body against the flagstones. Her eyes darted to the pool. Could she dive into it from here? It was a difficult target. Both the patio and the pool shimmered, reflecting the flames, and the boundary between them was blurred.

The rafters sagged with a groan, the roof shuddering beneath her feet. She poised to jump, but the shaking walls threw her off-balance. Before she could gauge the distance to the pool, she plunged off the roof.

For a moment her body hovered in midair. Then she tumbled end over end, in a clumsy free-fall. Narrowly missing the flagstones, she struck the water on her side, and the impact knocked the breath out of her. She blacked out and plummeted fifteen feet to the bottom of the pool. The shock of cold water against her scorched flesh sent a shiver through her, wrenching her back to consciousness. She shot back up to the surface, and her mouth burst open, gasping for breath. Her body was smeared with smoke, her eyelashes and hair singed. But she choked out a shrill laugh.

She was alive.

With a mighty rumble, the roof of the restaurant pavilion caved in. The earth trembled from the impact, debris littering the patio, ashes blanketing the pool. Chris lay on her back in the water, hypnotized by the spectacle overhead: the fiery tentacles had finally reached the top floor of the El Dorado and whipped in the wind. Had the savage perished? No, she felt certain that he had survived, that this blaze was one more facet of his revenge.

A clammy hand slid against her thigh, and Chris shuddered. The headless corpse floating beside her was bloated with water, but she knew that it was Rima. As if fearing it would snatch her, she scrambled out of the pool.

The night sky hung low, like a pall of smoke. The beach was black with ashes. It seemed as though the fire had spread to the ocean, for the waves glowed red, reflecting the inferno, giant flames licking at the shore.

Trapped between the roaring fire and the roaring surf, Chris fell to her knees and buried her face in her hands. Her teeth chattered from exposure to the searing heat, the shock of the cold plunge into the pool. She longed to run down the beach, but her weary body refused to move. It was all she could do to drag herself across the sand to a heap of beach umbrellas. They provided a nest, and she huddled there, shivering in the night air.

Even now, she clutched her Leica, hopelessly drenched from the dive. It had saved her life once tonight. It would not save her again. The sight of the ruined camera hurt more than any other harm she had suffered. It had been the last part of herself to remain intact. Now it, too, was mangled.

She tried to prop herself up, and face the hotel. But her eyes drooped shut. As she sank down among the canvas umbrellas, drifting into fitful sleep, her mouth tasted of ashes. She could feel the waves slamming into the beach, attacking it blow after blow.

58

THE RISING SUN CREPT UP STEALTHILY ON THE beach, a scavenger ready to pick the carcass clean. Though only one wall stood amid the rubble, the El Dorado possessed a permanence it had lacked before. With all twentieth-century frills reduced to ashes, the charred slabs that remained seemed timeless, a temple from a civilization that had vanished thousands of years ago.

Chris awoke in a spasm of coughing, nauseated from the soot impregnating her lungs, her throat as raw as if she had sobbed for hours. Peering out from her hiding place among the beach umbrellas, she was riveted by the devastation: the building lingered in its death agony, rumbling as beams collapsed and reinforced concrete gave way. Fires smoldered in isolated rooms, guests that refused to be evicted, even now. Dully, she aimed her broken camera at the ruins. She could only glimpse a blur through the shattered eyepiece.

As if spawned by the flames of the night before, a hot wind blew. She licked her blistered lips, troubled by the cackling overhead. Crows circled above the debris, with probing eyes and sharp black beaks, more cunning and voracious than vultures.

She turned toward the beach. A man's body lay near an overturned rowboat. It must have been brought in by the tide, she thought. Already the undertow was starting to pull it out to sea again. On the chance that it might still be alive, she decided to risk leaving her hiding place and ran to the water's edge.

She waded in up to her waist and fought a tug-of-war with the surf, to haul the body onto the beach. Her efforts were futile. Sharks had mangled the body beyond recognition. *Almost*. She knew the tattered shirt: white Oxford-cloth, too tweedy for this tropical climate. The silk monogram on the sleeve: "A. R."

After all she had suffered, Chris had thought herself immune to grief. But though she had no more tears left, she broke into sobs. A wave of helpless rage engulfed her, as fierce as the surf that crashed on the beach. Alan had cared for her, perhaps even loved her. During her violent stay here, he had provided what little tenderness she had known. All the other victims had been strangers. But Alan had been so much like her, that in his death, she felt the inevitability of her own.

She lifted the body in her arms, and let the waves sweep it out to sea. It was the kindest act she could perform for him. And the last. She watched the corpse float away, past the murky green of the shallows, out to where the ocean cleared to a turquoise blue. For a moment she longed to join him out there, beyond the reef.

To be the last one, she brooded. To be the last one to go. That was the worst punishment of all.

A shot rang out—a twelve-gauge hunting piece, she judged, from the throaty echo. But scanning the beach, she could see no one. *Another blast,* this time so close that it showered her with ocean spray. She ran up the beach and crouched among the canvas umbrellas.

The next salvo splintered them, leaving her vulnerable. A low stone wall bordering the patio seemed to provide surer protection. She dived behind it and huddled a few yards from the jungle's edge.

A giant shadow was moving across the beach. He wasn't going to waste another cartridge. He was coming to kill her with the blade. Already she could hear his footfalls approaching, heavy in the sand. *He knew her hiding place.*

She wavered, helpless. The shadow neared.

"Chris!" The whisper came from the jungle, a dozen feet behind her. *"Chris!"* An urgent voice barely audible above the surf. Impossible, Chris thought. Wasn't *she* the last survivor? *"Hurry!"*

The stalker was almost within striking distance. She turned impulsively and ran in the direction of the voice, sprinting the vulnerable steps across the sand into the sheltering foliage.

She waded into the jungle, and strained to adjust her eyes to the emerald twilight, to find the one who had spoken to her. She gave a start. A warm hand patted her shoulder. But . . . what was there about it?

The hand had only four fingers.

Suddenly it all came clear to her, in a moment of blinding revelation.

59

THOUGH THE SEERSUCKER SUIT WAS STAINED WITH mud, otherwise the ordeal of the past few days seemed to have changed its wearer little. "Are you all right, my dear?" she asked. Chris could make out a familiar face, pocked with insect bites. It was a sensible face, a wise face. And, understanding it as Chris did now, knowing the secrets that it concealed, she found it a most fascinating face indeed.

"But . . . I thought you were dead," Chris stammered. She tried to sound surprised, and nothing more—She didn't dare reveal to Dr. Eleanor Tobias that she *knew*.

"Better hurry." The old woman stared through her spectacles at Chris with maternal concern. She pointed in the direction of the beach. "There's a *maniac* loose out there." Tobias pulled aside a curtain of vines and ushered Chris deeper into the jungle. "That night in the hotel room," Tobias continued, "Lopez's men tried to kill me. . . ." She held up her arm to reveal a makeshift bandage. "They botched it. Well, I hotfooted it out of there and hid in the forest, like you did just now. Only, the farther I went, the more lost I got."

Incredible, Chris thought. She sounds so goddamn convincing. Every bit as convincing as she had sounded on the patio what seemed years ago. No wonder, she thought, *no wonder I was totally taken in*.

"I couldn't find my way back to the hotel for the longest time," Tobias went on. "Until last night. The fire . . . It lit up the sky three ways to Christmas." She was so good at this, Chris marveled. So *damned* good. . . .

The anthropologist paused to poke a rotting log with a stick. "Lucky for me, I knew about jungle survival. While I was lost, I lived off roots and insects. As a matter of fact, in this part of the world, some of the grubs are quite a delicacy once you develop a taste for them." She selected a pulpy larva and popped it into her mouth.

The never-ending green surrounded them now, the air heavy and stagnant. Impelled by her compulsion to know, Chris let the old woman lead the way. Chris had to allow the tale to unwind to its own insidious conclusion. And who but Dr. Eleanor Tobias could reveal the subterranean motives that had driven events so far?

Chris took a perverse pleasure in goading her guide to continue her deception. She wanted to draw her out in her lies until the slender thread, pulled taut, finally snapped. "Who . . . *what* did all this?"

Dr. Tobias helped her through a cleft between cypress boughs. "Before we can go into that, let's wait until we're safe."

Safe? Chris thought. Knowing—what she knew—each step she took at Dr. Tobias's side led her into greater danger. But it was worth this steamy trek, with the mosquitoes biting at her arms and legs, the birds shrieking in the treetops, to know the whole truth. It might almost be worth death itself.

Tobias stopped and studied Chris carefully, as if detecting the awareness in her eyes. "Don't worry," she said. "I'll take good care of you."

The trail was blocked by two thick vines. Tobias unsheathed a machete, and hacked through them in a shower of splintered wood.

"There." She patted Chris's shoulder reassuringly. "That wasn't such a bad hike, now was it?"

Through the foliage, Chris could make out the tumbled-down walls of the temple, the weathered slabs chiseled with skulls. Chris sniffed an odor: the smell of cooking meat. Tobias entered the ruins as though she were coming home and walked toward a pillar of smoke rising from a campfire concealed among the stones. She beckoned for Chris to join her.

"I've got a surprise for you," she said.

Chris glimpsed a familiar face nodding at her through the foliage. "Margot!"

From a distance, through the veil of leaves, the spinster's face seemed calmer than it ever had before. Chris wanted to run over and hug her. Was her sinister theory about Tobias merely a paranoid delusion?

Then Chris rounded a moss-covered slab. With a stab of horror, she realized why Margot's eyes had lost their haunted intensity. Her head had been severed from her body, her hair knotted to a sapling, and as the branch nodded in the breeze, it dipped her face into a caldron of boiling water.

Tobias knelt over the steaming pot to study her handiwork. With loving care, she untied Margot's hair and let the head drop into the scalding water. "I know," she said, in her most reasonable voice, noticing Chris's revulsion. "I know how it must look to you. A barbaric ritual. That's the way it seemed to *me* when I first came here, lo these many years. But I learned better. I can see the splendor of it now."

Chris's mind was spinning. Tobias's gentle tone clashed with the gruesome reality before her eyes. Chris leaned on a massive stone slab but feared even that might not support her weight as she tottered, faint from the stench of blood. To *see* this with her own eyes.... To *know* that her worst suspicions were true....

Her lips tried to shape words. She struggled to control her voice, to sound rational, to fight the nausea welling up within her. "I think I understand," she said. "You did this ... you did *all this,* because the tribe was massacred."

"You don't understand at all," Tobias interrupted with profound sadness. "My revenge came out of love, not hate. You see, in my work in Samoa, in West Africa, I had always been able to maintain my objectivity—to live with a tribe, yet somehow to keep them at arm's length. But the Warak were too seductive for that. In their strength, their serenity, their courage I found a better life than any I had known. By the time I had studied them for a year I chose to stay. But I didn't know whether they would accept me. Until ... *the day.* The greatest moment of my life."

"What ... moment?"

"The day the Warak asked me into the longhouse. For the ritual of Sastram."

"Sastram ...?"

"They asked me to become one of them. *To join the tribe.* First, I had to give...." Proudly Tobias raised her four-fingered hand. Chris was riveted by the scar. "But there was a joy that made up for the pain. For that night, in the longhouse, I gave *myself.*" She smiled wistfully at the memory. "The ritual of penetration. The seed of the Warak was planted within me."

Chris's voice was hushed. "That night ... one of them ...?"

Tobias shook her head. "No, not one of them. *All* of them. In the darkness ... in a sweet moment of love, each of them gave his gift to me. It was a night of pleasure," she said. "A night of pleasure like no other." Tobias let out a sigh, her eyes clouded in recollection. "For nine months I could feel life grow inside me. Sprouting . . . blossoming . . . like the jungle. I was old to bear children. I was over forty. But their seed was potent. It *grew*. Warak midwives brought the child into the world. *My daughter!*"

"Your . . . daughter . . ." Chris repeated the words in amazement.

"Latai. . . ." Tobias spoke reverently. "The name meant spring lightning, for the stormy night she was born. She was a loving child. I nursed her at my breast, and the Warak accepted her as their own. They taught her the ways of the jungle. The magic herbs. The paths of the hunt. And I taught her to read. Imagine. A child reading poetry *here!*" There was a melancholy in her voice, a yearning. "Latai was my gift to the Warak, and the tribe's gift to *me*."

Her words took on a hard edge. "The day Lopez's men came, I was returning from the forest with one of the Kakaram. . . . We *saw* what they did to her." There were tears in the old woman's eyes. "So you see?" Her voice dwindled to a whisper. "To know all . . . is to forgive all."

Chris *did* pity Tobias. No, she decided, the old woman wasn't insane. She realized the horror of her crimes. But for Tobias, the murder of her daughter had been a much more monstrous atrocity.

"I'm glad you're the one who survived," the old woman said. "I'm glad you're the one I could tell. I knew you'd understand." The woman sniffled, tears sliding down her cheeks. "You *do* understand, don't you? *Don't you?*"

"Yes," Chris said. "I understand." But even as she spoke, her compassion soured to disgust. For matter-of-factly Tobias was lifting Margot's head out of the boiling water. The skull had slid away from the flesh, and the face was shriveling before her eyes. Tobias reached down to pick up a bone needle and bark thread and bent to work, starting to stitch the flesh of the lips closed.

Chris turned away, assaulted by a wave of nausea, and scrambled over the tumbled slabs to escape the horror while she still had the strength. But when she reached the edge of the clearing, a figure blocked her path. It was *him*.

The Kakaram had approached silently through the jungle. Had Chris really been so deluded as to think that Tobias would let her *live*?

The savage seemed even more fearsome in daylight than he

had in the night shadows. Daubed with foul-smelling ocher paint, his muscular body was naked, except for his penis sheath and the breechclout where his machete hung. His chest was scarred with tattoos: skulls, the same death's-heads that adorned the ruins. Echoes of the hatred that burned in his eyes.

"Please . . . help me!" Chris begged Tobias. But the presence of the Kakaram seemed to imbue the old woman with a sexual frenzy. Feverishly she unbuttoned her suit jacket and pulled it off. Her naked torso was disfigured with ritual scars—more skulls, the death's-heads from the stones.

"Please!" Chris begged her.

Tobias's reply was to bare her teeth. They had been filed into sharp points. When she spoke now, it wasn't in English, but in a harsh guttural tongue. Obeying her, the Kakaram stepped toward Chris, opening his mouth in a hideous grin. But he stopped, riveted by the battered camera in her hand. Was it possible? Chris wondered. Did she see fear in his eyes?

Tobias saw it, too, and wrenched the Leica away from Chris. "The mercenaries that destroyed the village snapped pictures of the dead," the old woman said. "The Kakaram believes they cast a spell on his people. That a camera can steal his soul. That fear—it saved you on the roof the first night. And it saved you last night too." Tobias hurled the Leica against a granite slab, shattering it to bits. "It can't save you now."

"You've *had* your revenge," Chris pleaded. 'You don't need to kill me, too. . . ." But Tobias was deaf to her. A primitive lobe of her brain had seized control. She grunted to the savage, and he nodded.

Chris took three panicked steps backward, but he snatched her. Threw her down. His body pinned her to the ground. She could smell his breath, the stench of putrefying meat, and she struggled to wrench herself loose, but the Kakaram's mighty arm encircled her breast like the limb of a tree. She couldn't fight free. She thrust out a hand to Tobias in supplication.

The old woman was *smiling.*

Chris heard the squeal of metal as he unsheathed the machete. Her right arm was trapped under her body. She groped desperately along the ground with her left. All she could feel was the thick mesh of vines. Then her fingers stumbled across a shape: a jagged piece of glass, a shard from her camera's lens. She snatched it up and with a vicious swipe of her arm stabbed it into his eye. The Kakaram bellowed, and rose to his knees, blood gushing down his cheek. As his hands flew to his face, he lost his grip on the machete, and she wrenched it away from him.

In her trembling hands the weapon was almost too heavy to lift. The blade had taken so many lives she thought, by now it must have a murderous will of its own. But that made it no easier for her. She had never killed anyone. She couldn't bring herself to thrust the machete into his naked torso. And as she hesitated for a crucial moment, he lunged down at her in blind rage.

She raised the blade in a reflex of panic. He impaled himself on it.

Chris fought free of his grasp and scrambled to her feet. Even with the machete buried in his stomach, the savage leaned up on one knee and roared defiance. Then he collapsed on his side, blood gurgling from his mouth. Tobias rushed to him and touched his shoulder with surprising tenderness. In that single act, it was as if his life force possessed her, all the strength of the Warak infused into the old woman's body. She reached for her machete. "Murderer!" she shrieked.

Chris scrambled back along the trail toward the hotel, snagged by vines, tripped by rotting logs. She could hear Tobias crashing down the path after her, just yards behind.

"I'll cut your heart out!" Tobias snarled, dashing through the undergrowth with the grace of a much younger woman. *"I'll cut you in half!"*

The howler monkeys in the treetops echoed her cry. The jungle, Chris thought, as she tore down the trail, the entire jungle was out to kill her now.

At last, sobbing for breath, she could see a shimmering through the foliage: the gleam of the beach. But Tobias was closing fast. Chris could hear her heavy breathing, the machete whistling through the air.

How could it be? The old woman seemed to gain strength from the chase, while Chris's pace flagged from exhaustion.

Clawing her way through the last yards of jungle, Chris burst into the sunlight. The glare blinded her, but with her eyes shut, she kept right on running, staggering across the sand. She ran toward the roar of the waves. She would plunge into the surf and swim out as far as she could go, swim until she sank into the sea.

Her flight was cut short. Even with her eyes closed, she could sense the wall of shadows blocking her path. Squinting into the sun, she glimpsed them in silhouette: the warriors bore machetes—all of them. She collapsed in the sand at their feet, certain they were brethren of the savage. *All of them, Warak.*

They surrounded her in a tight circle of shade. She felt a blade poised against her throat.

60

ONE WAVED AWAY A FLY. ANOTHER SPIT ON THE ground. Their leader stepped closer. The weeks in the jungle had reduced him to skin and bone, and his khakis hung loose on his spare frame. His sunken eyes smoldered fiercely, his once-fleeting look of anger hardened into harsh lines around his mouth. Despite his transformation, Chris was certain she knew him. But like a victim of amnesia, she felt that his face, like every face in her life before last night, had been erased from her mind.

He barked an order, and the man who held the machete to her throat backed away. That voice—arrogant, aloof—brought it all back to her. Through the layer of mud and stubble, she recognized Manuel Vargas. From his cold gaze, it was as if they had never met. As if she had never risked her life for him. Without a word, he turned away to confer with his lieutenants.

Watching the heavily armed revolutionaries as they picked through the charred rubble, she realized why they reminded her of the savage. They, too, reeked of vengeance.

One of them leaned over to offer her a canteen. Chris drank greedily, until she looked up at the guerrilla's face and choked on the water in astonishment. The blonde had traded her cocktail dress for coarse khakis, an AK-47 slung over her shoulder.

"Inez?"

She nodded, seemingly amused by Chris's surprise. "Didn't you ever guess?"

Chris realized that she *had*. The crucial moment when Inez had discovered her in Lopez's suite, the look that had passed between them. . . . But that ordeal seemed ancient, insignificant now. Reeling from exhaustion, she closed her eyes and lay back on the sand.

"Vargas trapped Torres and his men . . ." Inez began, "ambushed them—" But she cut herself short. There was no point in continuing. Chris had passed out.

It was only a few minutes later when she regained consciousness. With her eyes closed, she could still hear the men picking through the rubble. And she could hear a voice. A *woman's* voice. Even before her drowsy mind could identify the voice by name, its timbre gave her a chill, like the echo of a nightmare: *"Thank God you're here. . . .It's been horrible, just horrible!"*

Chris kept her eyes closed and hoped the voice would retreat back into her dreams.

"What happened to the hotel?" she heard Vargas ask.

The voice answered: "It was the storm. Lightning started the fire. The guests were trapped inside. . . ."

No, Chris realized, she wasn't dreaming. She could no longer delude herself. *She opened her eyes.*

The top of the seersucker suit was, once more, primly buttoned, hiding the ritual scars. And when Dr. Eleanor Tobias spoke, Chris noticed how cleverly the old woman concealed her sharpened teeth. "I did what I could to save the guests, but"—Tobias shook her head sadly—"I'm afraid there wasn't much I could do."

Chris couldn't let Tobias seduce them, too. She climbed back onto her shaky legs and pointed an accusing finger. *"That woman!"* She had meant to shout, but it came out a whisper. Tobias's crimes seemed too monstrous to put into words. Chris's legs gave out, and she collapsed onto the sand.

"Why, you've *saved* her!" Tobias beamed. "Thank God!"

A shadow sliced across Chris where she lay. The old woman leaned over and patted her shoulder with motherly concern. "Just take it easy. You're safe now." She exchanged a knowing look with Vargas. "After all she's been through, I'm afraid she's not herself."

Chris spun to the attack. "She planned *everything!* The shrinking . . . the murders. . . . There are *skulls* on her chest, and. . . ." She choked on sobs. She knew she wasn't making sense. Vargas turned away to join the others. No one believed her. They thought she had come unhinged.

All, that is, but Tobias. "Just rest, my dear," she clucked gently, smoothing Chris's hair with her scarred hand. "Everything's going to be all right. After what you've been through, why, it's enough to make *anyone* lose their head."

"¡Hola, *hombre!*" one of the guerrillas shouted, herding a survivor out of the ruins. He limped toward Chris, his face smeared with ashes, his clothes in tatters.

She gasped as though she had seen a ghost. He reached out

to her. She lost sight of him through her tears.

"You're . . . alive," she murmured in disbelief.

Alan nodded weakly, trembling like an old man. Tears streaked his grimy face. Before she was aware of what she had done, she rushed into his arms. He wasn't a mirage. He was flesh-and-blood. He held her so tightly that it hurt. And only now, as she hugged him, as she felt his hand on her cheek, did she realize that she, too, was alive. That she had survived.

"God, it's good to see you," he said. "It's been forever."

"Yeah." She tried to smile. "It must be at least five hours." His bruised arm brushed against hers. After so much pain, it felt like a caress.

Even now she wasn't satisfied; she had become suspicious of miracles. "But . . . I saw a corpse on the beach, wearing your shirt. . . ."

He nodded grimly. "I promised Jesús I'd give him the shirt off my back if he ever learned how to make the perfect Bloody Mary. Well, he learned." In a weary monotone, Alan unraveled the tangled thread of events. "I drifted out to sea in a rowboat. . . . Sharks surrounded me. Then Jesús staggered down to the beach, into the water. . . . He must have been wounded because the sharks went right for him. I started to row toward shore. . . . Then the riptide picked me up . . . slammed me down on the far side of the beach."

But even as he spoke, Chris realized it was premature to celebrate their deliverance. They were still in danger, nine fingers waiting to snatch them, the blade sharpened, ready to descend. She turned to point out Tobias to him—to warn him of the beast waiting to pounce.

She blinked in disbelief. The old woman had vanished.

"Alan. . . ."

"What?"

She stopped herself. Even if she could explain the bizarre chain of events in her shellshocked state, what good would it do? When he heard her story, he'd think she was insane. Besides, all that mattered now was that Tobias had avoided a final confrontation and returned to the jungle.

An electronic hum interrupted her thoughts. The guerrillas had deployed the tripod antenna of their powerful shortwave radio. Vargas was speaking into the microphone, but his Spanish was too fast for Chris to understand.

"He's calling the capital," Alan explained. "He's telling the government we're here." He listened to the reply crackling over the receiver and broke into a smile. "They'll be here in a couple of hours."

Even after the good news, Chris felt little relief. At first it baffled her why Vargas would surrender them to his enemies, but she realized he would rather turn them over to the government than waste his own meager supplies on them. She had been in jeopardy for too long. It was difficult to accept that they were saved—that she was going home.

She lay down beside Alan in the shadow of a fallen marble slab. Her mind struggled through the wasteland of the past twenty-four hours, like a scavenger picking through dry bones. But as she breathed the ocean air, it cleansed the smell of the scalding pot from her nostrils. With each heartbeat, she could feel her muscles relax.

Now that she was safe, the thought of Dr. Eleanor Tobias no longer evoked such terror. After all, the old woman was a figure as pitiable as she was monstrous. By now Tobias had no doubt returned to the shrine, to give the savage his proper burial. The last of the Kakaram. It would be punishment enough for the old woman to linger, marooned in the jungle, surrounded by the ghosts of the Warak tribe and the memories of her daughter. As she closed her eyes, Chris conceded that there was a poetic justice to Tobias's fate—a murderer locked in a leafy prison, surrounded by reminders of her crimes.... Until the old woman, too, finally succumbed to the insatiable night.

61

THE GOVERNMENT HAD PROMISED TO COME IN TWO hours, but just as Chris suspected, it was almost dusk by the time the helicopter actually swooped in, its rotors whipping up the sand as it landed on the far end of the beach. Faced with the wreckage of a 200-room hotel, the soldiers didn't know where to begin. They settled for an accounting of the dead. Chris watched a stretcher detail pick through the rubble, covering each corpse they found with a tarpaulin. The work was tedious, the humidity draining. But the men worked quickly. They wanted to complete their task before sunset, to avoid having to spend the night.

Chris could see that one soldier was snapping pictures, to record the devastation. The thought of photography repelled her now. She wanted to experience her last minutes here with a deeper part of herself. At least the past few days had taught her that much: that she could face the world without hiding behind a camera.

Restless, she turned to Alan, who lay in the shade beside her. Medics had bandaged his leg, and he was sleeping off a shot of morphine. Her own wounds were hidden, and they were still raw. But she had refused painkillers. She *wanted* to feel the pain, to purge herself of it. Otherwise, she would leave here with it locked inside her forever.

The bodies of the victims had been lined up beside the helicopter, to be transported to the capital. She felt a twinge of guilt—the guilt of a survivor. Terror had somehow linked all the guests with a bond closer than friendship. This would be her last chance to pay her final respects to the dead. Perhaps it was the only way she could do penance for not being one of them. She started up the beach toward the helicopter.

At first it took a monumental effort to put one foot in front of the other. But step by step, she felt her strength returning. The surf was gentle, the waves a soothing whisper. With the soldiers and the gutted hotel behind her, the vista of palms, sand, and sea sparkled like a picture postcard. Stretch, she told herself, reach out, or sink helplessly into the past, where *tsantsa* tick off the hours like pendulums in the mind. She ran a bare foot through the sand. It was a luxury for her mind to wander, to think beyond the next moment's survival, focusing on the starfish at her feet, the gulls skimming the horizon.

The chopper crouched ahead of her on the beach, a giant praying mantis, the bodies lined up in its shadow like morsels for its next feeding. There wasn't a soldier in sight. All of them were back at the hotel ruins, 100 yards away. And when she neared the bodies, she understood why. They had begun to rot.

She tried to see, in those swathed shapes, the human beings with whom she had shared the past few days. But the bodies had somehow been transformed. Without their heads, in their winding sheets, the strange forms seemed hardly human. She was tempted to peek under the canvas to reassure herself that they were, after all, only the bodies of men and women.

Wait. One of the shrouded forms still had its head. She thought back to the carnage, and ticked off the victims in her mind. Hadn't *all* the bodies been decapitated? She stared at the swathed corpse more closely, searching for a clue to its identify. Her scrutiny only left her more perplexed. The canvas was *twitching*. It was just the wind, she told herself, a freshet ruffling the shroud. But when she glanced at the delicate ferns on the edge of the jungle, not a leaf was stirring. It was as if the fronds were cast in iron. Uneasily she turned back to the corpse. It was starting to *sit up*.

"Aaaaah!"

Before Chris knew what hit her, a body lunged out from behind the canvas. A hand with four fingers locked itself around her throat, threw her to the ground, pinning her to her back. Chris looked up into the eyes of her attacker. The old woman's face was twisted in hate. Tobias was stripped to the waist, her naked torso livid with ritual scars. She straddled Chris's body— *and raised the machete with both hands*.

Chris rolled aside a second before the blade sliced into the sand. She scrambled to her feet to shout for help, but she realized it was no use. All the others were on the far side of the beach, out of earshot.

Tobias wrestled her down to the ground again. But now, as she was locked in a murderous embrace, it was Chris's turn to feel her body charged with rage. She wasn't just fighting to save herself. She had to avenge the others.

She lashed out, biting and scratching, her frenzy rivaling

Tobias's own. In her fury, Chris pinned the old woman down and wrapped her hands around her wrinkled neck. But Tobias clawed at her eyes and with a surge of strength, forced Chris down on her back. Chris choked as the old woman's scarred palm throttled the breath out of her.

Again Tobias lifted the machete. Chris hurled a fistful of sand into her face and scrambled to her feet. But her back was pressed against the helicopter's fuselage. She was trapped.

Tobias looked her victim up and down, her eyes wild with triumph. She smiled and bared two rows of sharpened teeth. Then she swung the machete back slowly, *slowly.* . . .

All that stood between them now was the six-foot-long rear rotor blade of the helicopter. Chris could feel the edge of the blade sharp against her thumb as she grabbed it with both hands. She gave it a violent shove.

The rotor sliced through the air, and spinning around once, it caught Tobias in the neck.

With a snap of breaking cartilage, the blade sheared through flesh and bone. It seemed that the severed head rolling along the sand was alive: Tobias's eyes bulged wide, staring up at *herself* in amazement. For her headless body was still standing, blood gushing from its severed aorta. Then the machete slipped from her fingers. Dr. Eleanor Tobias toppled among the white-shrouded cadavers, joining her victims, the headless fraternity of the dead.

Numb, Chris teetered against the fuselage to keep from fainting. She could see Alan rushing toward her, along with the troops, who had finally noticed her struggle. She wondered whether some new wisdom might spring from her intimacy with violent death. But if there was any such wisdom to be had, it was hidden from her now.

For though she had slain a demon, other specters still dangled in her mind: shriveled beings that would not, she feared, die as quickly as the old woman that lay at her feet.

Epilogue

A CLOUD OF FLIES SWARMED TO A BUZZ-SAW PITCH, ripping into the jungle silence. The light that filtered down from the treetops tinged the tumbled walls of the shrine with the aura of a shark-infested reef. The scalding pot was empty, and spiders swarmed over it. Roots had soaked up the dried pools of human blood, and drinking deeply, the jungle flourished even thicker than before, the green tentacles of peperomia vines writhing, grasping, growing.

As a hot breath of wind rustled the leaves, shadows played tricks on the eye. The death's-heads carved on the granite slabs seemed to stir to life. Their combined wisdom encompassed many secrets, many mysteries, one intelligence greater than the sum of its parts. And they were laughing now, laughing by the thousands at a final sinister joke, their voices as raucous as the howler monkeys in the treetops.

For the savage lived. A trail of red droplets stained the earth, leading deep into the jungle. And with each step, the wound was healing. Armed with his machete and his appetite for murder, he prowled to a place where no trails led. And a *tsantsa* bobbed from his breechclout, as if the tiny brain were hatching new plots, new schemes of destruction. Already the lips whispered to him, inciting him to bloodshed. Soon he would nestle the *tsantsa* in a dark hiding place where the next victim least expected it, planting his ominous gift in a closet, a cupboard. Under a pillow. In the hollows of the mind.

She is 12 years old, bright, pretty in an odd way.
Adopted as an infant, no one knows who her real parents are.
The kids at school don't seem to like her very much.
Her mother finds her harder and harder to love.
Then the strange and violent things begin to happen.

Come meet . . .

ARIEL

Turn the page for a preview of Lawrence Block's chilling new novel, coming in January from Berkley.

1

WAS there a noise that woke her? Roberta was never sure. The old house was full of night sounds. Floorboards creaked. Curtains rustled. Windowpanes, loose in their frames, rattled at the least touch of a breeze. She had been a light sleeper all her life. Caleb had just recently taken to sleeping through the night, and she had not yet entirely adjusted to his new schedule. The slightest sound could rouse her.

Or had she dreamed a sound? There might have been music, that thin reedy music Ariel made on her flute. Roberta sat up in bed, curiously troubled, straining to hear something in the silence.

Then she saw the woman.

A dark shape hovered in the far corner of the room near the window. A woman, wrapped in a shawl, her face averted.

Roberta pressed one hand to her breast. Her heart was fluttering, her mouth dry. She thought *David,* and her other hand reached out to her side, patting at empty air.

In the other house they had shared a bed, and she had always been able to reach out and touch him in the night. Now they slept in twin beds separated by the width of a night table. She had selected the bedroom furniture and donated the old double bed to Goodwill Industries. And she had been the one who picked this house. And now David slept, his breathing audible now in the room's stillness, while this woman lurked in the corner of their bedroom.

There was a lamp on the night table. Roberta's hand left off patting the air between the two beds and groped tentatively for the lamp. Her fingers found the switch, then hesitated. She was afraid to turn the light on even as she was afraid to remain in the dark.

She closed her eyes, opened them. The woman was still there.

Then a windowpane shook in its mullions and suddenly the woman was gone. It was as if she were a creature of smoke, and as if the wind that rattled the pane had slipped into the room and dispersed her. Roberta stared, blinked her eyes.

There was no woman in the room.

But she had seen—

An illusion, of course. Some trick of lighting, some shadow cast by moonlight through the old handmade windowpanes. But how extraordinarily real it had appeared to her! And what menace the shape had seemed to hold!

Unafraid now, she switched on the bedside lamp, then flicked it off again. There had been nothing and no one in the bedroom. Some forgotten dream must have awakened her, an unpleasant dream that left her anxious and suggestible. And so she'd seen a shape where there was no shape, and her imagination had cloaked that shape in a woman's shawl and touched her with a sense of evil.

Roberta lay down, closed her eyes. After a few moments she opened them again and stared at the corner of the room where she had seen the woman.

Nothing.

She closed her eyes again and tried to summon sleep. But it wouldn't come. Her mind was racing, and every stray thought that came to her seemed to increase her anxiety and focus it upon the baby. She had seen a woman who wasn't there, and now she was worried about her son.

It was ridiculous, and she knew it was ridiculous, but she also knew that she would not be able to sleep until she had checked Caleb. And wasn't it even more ridiculous to lie awake until daybreak? She sighed, then slipped out of bed and padded barefoot across the bedroom floor. David had wanted to carpet the whole upstairs, even as the other house had been carpeted wall to wall. She'd explained as patiently as possible that you didn't buy a house almost two hundred years old and cover its random-width pine floor with Acrilan broadloom. Now, though, she could almost sympathize with his position. The floorboards were cold underfoot and she found herself setting her feet down on them with exaggerated care to lessen their creaking.

Halfway down the hall, she hesitated at the open door to Caleb's room, then entered and approached his crib. There was enough light so that she could easily see his face. He was sleeping soundly. She stood there for a long moment, listening to the night sounds and gazing down on her son.

Before returning to her own room, Roberta walked the length of the hallway and stood outside Ariel's door with her hand on the knob. Then, without turning the knob, she went back to her bedroom.

Of course there was no dark shape in the corner. She shook her head, amused at her own fear, reassured now by the sight of her sleeping infant son.

Funny what tricks the mind played...

David stirred in his sleep and she looked down at him. The smell of alcoholic perspiration touched her nostrils. It was a sour smell and she wrinkled her nose at it.

Odd, she thought. He was never drunk, not as far as she could tell, but after dinner he would sit reading in his ground-floor study and during those hours he always had a glass in his hand. It didn't seem to change him—as far as she could tell it didn't do anything to or for him—but while he slept his body eliminated some of the alcohol through the pores, and in the morning his sheets were often damp with it. But he never staggered and he never slurred his words, and if he had hang-overs in the morning he never mentioned them.

She got into bed, settled her head on the pillow, let her thoughts drift where they wanted. Now the night sounds comforted her—the wind in the branches of the live oak outside her window, the loose windowpanes, the occasional creak of a floorboard, the inexplicable sounds that come from within the walls of an old house, as if the house itself were breathing.

Once she thought she heard the piping of Ariel's flute. But perhaps she was already asleep by then, already dreaming.

She was up later than usual the next night. She often went to bed right after the eleven o'clock news, occasionally hanging on for the first half hour of the *Tonight* show. But something kept her in front of the television set. She watched Johnny Carson through to the end. Even then she was faintly reluctant to go upstairs, and she dawdled on the ground floor, rinsing out a couple of cups and glasses she'd have ordinarily left for morning. She checked the pilot lights of the large old six-burner gas range. There were three pilots, one for each pair of burners, and they were forever going out in the damp brick-floored kitchen. One was out now, and she took a moment to light it.

She checked both outside doors, making sure they were locked and bolted, and she found herself testing the window locks and became impatient with herself. She felt like an old maid checking under the bed for burglars. What on earth was she afraid of?

She checked the children. Ariel was asleep, or pretending to be asleep. She lay on her back, her arms at her sides under the covers, her breathing deep and regular. Caleb, too, was asleep, and while Roberta stood beside his crib he stretched and made a sweet gurgling sound. Air currents in the room shook the mobile suspended over his crib, an arrangement of gaily-colored wooden fish equipped with tiny bells that sounded when the air moved them. Caleb made his gurgling sound again, as if in response to the light tinkling of the bells, and Roberta felt a rush of love in her breast. She lowered the side of the crib, bent over and kissed Caleb's forehead.

How sweet he smelled. Babies had the most delicious scent . . .

In her room, David was already sound asleep. Maybe that was what the drinking did for him, maybe it enabled him to get to sleep and sleep soundly. Maybe she should have had something herself. But that was silly—she was tired, she would sleep with no trouble, she had never needed help getting to sleep.

And indeed it wasn't that long before she slept. Nor was it too long after sleep came that she was suddenly wide awake, fearfully awake, with her heart hammering against her ribs and a pulse working in her temple.

Her eyes were open and the woman, wrapped in her shawl, was standing by the bedroom window.

"Who are you? What do you want?"

There was a gust of wind. She heard it in the live oak, rustling the leaves, tossing the branches of Spanish moss. It rattled the window glass and seemed to blow the woman about, as if she were a bundle of old rags. But she was a woman, it was very clear that she was a woman, the same woman who had been there the night before. Her form was quite distinct in the dim corner. She stood facing the window, her hip and shoulder toward Roberta, her face invisible.

Roberta reached for the bedside lamp. Her fingers rested on the switch. She thought *David,* but did not speak his name aloud.

The woman turned toward her. She had a quick impression of a pale face. And the woman was holding something in her arms. Roberta squinted, trying to focus on the woman's face, trying to see what she was holding, and even as she narrowed her gaze the woman began to fade away, to merge with the shadows.

She switched on the light. The woman was gone.

She couldn't seem to catch her breath. She was drained, exhausted, and for several minutes all she could do was remain where she was, breathing raggedly, willing her heartbeat to return to normal. David slept on. She checked the time on the alarm clock, something she hadn't thought to do the night before. It was a quarter to four.

She told herself to go to sleep. She turned off the light and tried to lie still but it was impossible. She had to get up, had to check the baby.

She hurried down the hall. Caleb was sleeping like a lamb. The sight of him was evidently all she needed. She sighed with relief and tiptoed out of his room, returning to her own room without bothering to check Ariel.

In her own bed, she had a sudden impulse to go downstairs again, to check the doors and windows, to make sure none of the pilot lights had gone out. But she resisted the urge and sleep came to her with surprising swiftness.

When she awoke a light rain was falling. She changed Caleb and fed him, then went downstairs. David had made his own toast and coffee and was sitting behind the morning paper. Ariel had helped herself to orange juice and a bowl of sugared cereal. Roberta joined them at the table with a cup of black coffee and a cigarette.

No one spoke during breakfast. Twice Roberta was on the point of mentioning what she'd seen in the room the past night, but both times she repressed the impulse. The sentences she tested in her mind proved inadequate. *"I had the strangest dream last night."* But had it been a dream, last night and the night before? If so, it was unlike any dream she'd ever experienced before. *"I thought there was someone in the room last night."* But it was more than that, more than a trick of lighting and shadow. She'd sensed a menacing presence, had seen the woman turn to her before disappearing. *"There was someone in our bedroom last night."* But was there? Or was her own mind conjuring up images?

David was the first to leave. They chatted briefly, perfunctorily. Then he carried his briefcase to the car while she poured a second cup of coffee and lit a third cigarette and picked up the newspaper he'd abandoned. As usual, it told her precious little about what was new in the world and rather more than she needed to know about Charleston. She scanned an article about plans for the next Spoleto festival, skimmed a report on activity in the state legislature at Columbia, and read wire service pieces on arms-limitation talks and congressional maneuvering without really taking them in. She turned with some relief to Ann Landers and immersed herself in other people's problems. A secretary found her boss's wife domineering, a man felt guilty about putting his old mother in a home, and an adolescent girl felt unloved, unwanted, and singularly unpopular. Ann told her to make a list of all the positive things in her life.

"Time for school, isn't it?"

Ariel nodded, rose from the table, carried her dishes to the sink. How pale the child was, Roberta thought. Pale skin, pale blue eyes. Expressionless eyes—looking into them gave her a feeling that verged on vertigo, as though one could fall through the child's eyes into a bottomless abyss.

"Have a good day, Ariel."

"Thank you. I will."

"You'll be home afterward?"

"Where would I go?"

Where indeed? The child didn't seem to have any friends. She spent all her time alone, reading or doing homework or playing her horrible flute. Had she been as isolated when they lived in the suburban split-level? It seemed to Roberta that Ariel had been less thoroughly alone, that she'd had a playmate or two, but it was hard for her to be certain. That had been before Caleb's birth and so many things had been different.

But she was always a solitary child, Roberta thought. She seemed most content that way, as if she required solitude as other children required companionship.

The door closed. Roberta hesitated a moment, then went to the front room and drew the drapes a few inches apart. She stood at the window long enough to watch Ariel walk to the end of the block and turn the corner, disappearing from view. Then she opened the drapes all the way.

Back in the kitchen, she rinsed the dishes and thought about Ann Landers' column. Perhaps she ought to make a list of all the positive things in her life. Well, there was the man she'd married, the daughter they'd adopted, and the son she had recently borne. And there was this house, historic and well-preserved, on one of the best blocks in the Old Charleston section south of Tradd.

An impressive list. So what if the marriage had turned loveless? So what if there was something strange, almost frightening, about Ariel? So what if the house made sounds in the night, and the pilot lights wouldn't stay lit, and the damp was so pronounced you could grow mushrooms on the kitchen's worn brick floor? So what if sleep was interrupted by nightmares, or visions, or whatever had possessed her two nights running?

Caleb fussed in his crib, demanding her attention. "I'm coming, sweetie," she called out, crushing her cigarette in the ashtray, hurrying up the stairs, grateful for the distraction from her own thoughts.

Around one-thirty she was seated on a green-slatted park bench at the Battery, gazing out at the ocean. Off to her left, several old men were fishing, their poles extending over the iron railing.

"They don't be catching nuffin but a cold," a voice said. Roberta turned to see an old black woman ease herself down onto the far end of the bench. She had frizzy white hair and very dark blue-black skin. She was tiny, small-boned and gaunt, and her skin clung to her bones like leather that had been soaked and left to dry in the sun.

"A million fish in the ocean but they don't be catching none of ems," the woman said. "You got a fine baby. A manchild, innit?"

"Yes."

"What do his name be?"

"Caleb."

The woman nodded, halved the distance between them, got up on her feet and peered down at Caleb. She nodded again, smacked her lips once and sat down. "You live round here," she said.

"Yes."

"One of them old houses?"

"Yes. Just a few blocks from here."

"Do there be haunts in it?"

"Pardon me?"

"Do there be haunts or ghosts?"

Roberta stared at her. "Last night," she said. "And the night before."

"You saw sumpin?"

"An old woman. She was standing by the window. And then she ... disappeared."

The woman nodded. "A haunt," she said, satisfied. "Must be she lived and died there."

"I thought she was a real woman. And then I thought I was seeing things, and—"

"Haunts is like that. She lived there and died there. Happens sometimes a body dies and don't know it. Could be she were murdered. Killed of a sudden." She rubbed her old hands together and shivered with delight. "All them old houses has their haunts," she said. "That's what you saw."

"I was afraid."

"Only natural. Anybody be fraid. Nuffin to be fraid of, though. Haunts don't *do* nuffin. They just *be*."

"I never saw her before. And then I saw her two nights in a row."

"Maybe it be the season. Fall comin on."

"Maybe."

"Maybe it be she died this time of the year. Haunts will do that. One house I lived, long long ago, you could hear a dog. He would howl the night away. And there were no dog in that house. He were nuffin but a haunt, and you never did see him. You only did hear him."

"I think I really saw her."

"Course you did."

"I thought maybe it was a dream, or a lighting trick. But I really saw something."

"What you saw were a haunt."

"Maybe you're right."

"Haunt won't never hurt nobody," the woman said. Then her face grew animated and she was pointing. "Look at that! I said they wouldn't catch nuffin and look at that! That be a flounder." The man who'd caught him, an elderly white man in bib overalls, gripped the fish in his right hand while deliberately disengorging the hook with his left. This done, he held the fish aloft for a moment, then dropped it into a galvanized pail. "Them flatfish be good eatin," the old woman said. "Flounder be sweet clear to the bone."

Just a ghost, Roberta thought. A mere haunt. Nothing to be afraid of. An asset, really, on the house's balance sheet, like the original glass panes in the mullioned windows and the brick floor in the kitchen. An authentic touch of pre-Revolutionary Charleston.

She wondered idly who the woman might be. Perhaps she'd been around at the time of the Revolution, when Francis Marion, the old Swamp Fox himself, had harried the British with his own brand of guerrilla warfare. Perhaps she'd occupied the house in the early days of the Republic, perhaps she'd known John C. Calhoun when he was the clarion voice of South Carolina. Or was the Civil War her time? Roberta hadn't felt anything of the southern belle in her aspect. She'd seemed more like an immigrant woman in one of those sketches of nineteenth-century slum dwellers in New York, a new arrival freshly transported from Ellis Island to the Lower East Side. Huddled in upon herself, wrapped in a shawl, carrying something—

She didn't mention the woman, not at dinner or afterward. Ariel spent the evening doing homework in her room, interrupting her work now and then to pipe tuneless music that pervaded the old house. David talked with her a bit over coffee, telling her about something that had happened at the office. She kept up her end of the conversation without paying much attention to what he was saying, and in due course he withdrew to his den to smoke his pipes and drink his brandy.

But she did talk to Caleb as she readied him for bed. "We're not scared of haunts, are we?" she cooed, powdering his soft little bottom, fixing a clean diaper in place. "We're not scared of anything, Caleb." And she kissed him again and again, and Caleb gurgled and laughed.

David went to sleep early, taking himself off to bed without saying goodnight, and she was grateful to hear his heavy step upon the stairs. She had spent a solitary evening, but now she could enjoy the special solitude that came when one was the only person awake in the household. She sat in the front room with coffee and cigarettes, her coffee flavored just the tiniest bit with some of David's brandy.

Would she see the ghost again?

She hoped not. It helped, curiously enough, to think of it as a ghost, although she was by no means certain she believed in such phenomena in the first place. Believing that the house was haunted, however, seemed to be rather less threatening than believing either that the woman was a real living creature or that she, Roberta, was going quietly mad. Perhaps that was how people had come to believe in the supernatural, she thought; perhaps they were relieved to latch onto an alternative to something even less acceptable.

If there was a ghost, did that mean she had to see it every damned night?

Perhaps not. Perhaps she could sleep through the nightly appearance of the ghost, even as Caleb had learned to sleep through his two A.M. feeding. The fact that she had only just taken to seeing the ghost did not mean the ghost had never walked before. Perhaps the ghost had appeared every night for years but she'd slept through the performance until the night before last, even as David had continued to sleep on through it.

And perhaps familiarity would eventually breed some form of contempt, so that if a night sound woke her she could sit up, blink at the apparition, say *"Oh, it's only the ghost again,"* and drift calmly back to sleep.

Had Ariel seen the ghost?

The child had certainly said nothing, but would she? She was so secretive she might have witnessed the apparition nightly for weeks without seeing fit to mention it.

If Ariel encountered the ghost, she thought, it would be the ghost that ran screaming.

She giggled at the thought, then flushed with guilt. Something was happening, some change in the way she related to Ariel, and she didn't know what it was or what to do about it. She penned a quick mental letter.

Dear Ann Landers, / Twelve years ago my husband and I adopted a baby girl, and now I've just had a baby of my own, a son, and I don't know what to do about my daughter. She's not what I had in mind. Do you suppose there's a way I could give her back? Just sign me / Having Second Thoughts.

Her own thoughts disturbed her. She frowned, crushed out her cigarette in the ashtray, and tried to force herself to substitute thoughts from an earlier time. Images of the three of them immediately after the adoption, she and David going on long walks with Ariel, then a montage of mental family pictures over the years. Ariel growing, learning to walk and talk, developing over months and years into a person.

A person Roberta knew less with every passing day.

She gave her head an impatient shake. This would all pass, she told herself. She had a new baby now, and any negative thoughts and feelings she had toward Ariel were almost certainly part of the process of nurturing that new baby. Older children were traditionally assumed to resent infants, and it struck her that their jealousy was well-founded.

In time, when her great love for Caleb became less obsessive, when she took his presence a little more for granted, her feelings for Ariel would be what they had once been.

Or had they started to change *before* Caleb was born? Even before he'd been conceived? She *was* a strange child, curious and remote. There was no gainsaying that. Even David admitted as much, although he seemed to take delight in the very strangeness that Roberta found unsettling.

And just when had she begun to find it unsettling? Before Caleb's birth? Before his conception? Well, she'd been so unsettled herself during that stretch of time that it was hard to separate causes and effects. Twice-weekly visits to Gintzler for maintenance doses of therapy and Valium. The whole business with Jeff was going on then, impossible to handle but more stimulating than the therapy and more addictive than the Valium. She could see now that she'd been skating closer to the edge than she'd ever realized. Now that she'd come back from the edge, now that she was settled again with a baby and a house and a stable daily routine, she could begin to appreciate just how unstable her life had been for a while there.

She put her cup down. Shouldn't drink coffee late at night, she thought. It made her mind race. She'd come a long way from ghosts and haunts and things that went bump in the night.

She lit another cigarette. If she just stayed up late enough, perhaps she'd sleep through the ghost's command performance.

She was dreaming. In the dream the old black woman from the park bench at the Battery was sitting on her haunches beside an enormous wicker basket filled with fresh fish. She was taking up one after another, gripping each fish in turn in one bony hand while with the other she wielded a nasty little knife, slitting the fish up the belly and expertly gutting it. While she did this she spoke of the supernatural, of ghosts and haunts and the walking dead, of voodoo curses and the power of a mojo tooth. The wicker basket gradually emptied and the pile of gutted fish at the woman's feet grew steadily.

Then she was holding not a fish but a human infant. "The manchild, he be good eatin," she said, and smacked her lips. Roberta noted for the first time that she had no teeth. Her mouth was black and bottomless.

Roberta tried to move. She was frozen, incapable of motion. She could neither act nor cry out. The old woman cackled, and the knife flashed, and Roberta sat up in bed and wrenched herself out of the dream.

It was a dream, she thought, fastening onto the thought and repeating it to herself.

Then, in the corner of the room beside the window, she saw the woman. As on the previous night, the figure was facing the window, with hip and shoulder toward Roberta. Tonight, however, her form was more completely defined, as if her presence became more concrete with each appearance.

She's a ghost, Roberta tried to tell herself. *Ghosts are harmless. You had a bad dream and now you're seeing the ghost, but dreams can't hurt you and ghosts are harmless.*

It didn't help. The dream had shaken her badly and the sight of the woman was considerably more frightening than it had been on the two previous nights, her thoughts notwithstanding. An air of evil was present in the room. The woman bore it like a perfume and it was palpable in the thick night air.

"What do you want?"

Had she spoken the words aloud? Was she talking to this apparition?

Slowly, like a statue on a revolving platform, the woman turned to face her. Roberta saw the heart-shaped face, the bloodless lips, the pale eyes burning in the pale face.

The eyes held Roberta's own eyes. Something unspoken and unspeakable passed between the woman at the window and the woman on the bed. Then, against her will, she dropped her eyes to see what the woman was holding in her arms.

A baby.

A male infant, his body swaddled in a part of the woman's shawl, only his face visible. His face was as pallid as the woman's own and his wide eyes burned with the same pale fire.

Slowly and magically, like trick photography in a television commercial, the baby's face lost flesh and turned to a gleaming skull. And the woman, too, was a bare polished skeleton wrapped in a shawl. And she drew away, the skeletal infant in her arms, floating through the closed window and out into the night.

Roberta cried out. She opened her mouth and screamed.

There was a gap, a blank space. Then she was being held, a hand patting awkwardly at the back of her head. She breathed in the smell of alcohol sweat and knew then that David was holding her, trying to comfort her.

"A dream," he was saying. "You had a bad dream. That's all."

She wanted to correct him but she couldn't, not right away, because her heart was racing and she couldn't catch her breath, and if he didn't continue to hold her very tight she felt she might shake herself apart.

Then, when she could speak, she tried to explain. She told about what she'd seen for three nights running.

"A dream," he said.

"Night after night?"

"A recurring dream. I've had one off and on for years, I'm someplace dangerously high and trying to get down from it, endless fire escapes and catwalks, and I'm frightened and I can never get back to ground level. Variations on a theme. You know about dreams, all those months with Gintzler, stretched out on his couch."

"This wasn't a dream."

"All right."

"I had a dream first, a crazy dream about a black woman cleaning fish." She hurried on, not wanting to recall the dream's ending. "Then I was awake and I saw her again. She was standing right there."

"She's not there now."

"Of course not."

"You think you saw a ghost?"

"I don't know what I saw. I don't know anything about ghosts. It was some sort of . . . some sort of spiritual presence."

"A being of another world."

"It had that feeling to it, yes."

"Why was it so frightening?"

"She was holding—I can't say it."

"What do you mean?"

"I can't make myself say it. I'm afraid."

He looked at her.

"Hell," she said. "She was holding a baby."

"So?"

"The baby died. She turned to show me the baby and I watched while the baby turned into a skeleton. Then the woman was a skeleton too, and they went out the window and disappeared."

"Jesus."

"I'm telling you what I *saw*, David."

"Now tell me why it's frightening."

"Are you crazy?"

He shook his head. "Why's it frightening to *you*? What are you scared *of*, Roberta?"

"You know."

"Tell me."

"Why do I have to say it?" She turned her eyes away. "The baby," she said.

"You're afraid of the kid she was holding?"

"You know what I mean."

"I think you should say it."

She closed her eyes, lowered her head. "Caleb," she whispered.

"What about him?"

"I'm afraid."

"Afraid of what?"

"God *damn* you!" She made a fist, struck out at his chest. "I'm afraid my baby's dead, you son of a bitch!"

He said nothing. Her hands dropped and her shoulders sagged and she wept soundlessly, the tears streaking her cheeks. After a time the crying stopped and she wiped her tears away with the back of her hand.

"Roberta?"

"What?"

"Do you really believe—"

"I don't know what I believe. I never believed in ghosts until I saw one. Or whatever the hell I saw."

"Why don't you go check Caleb."

"Now?"

"Why not?"

"I don't—I'm afraid."

"I'll go with you."

"I'm afraid. Isn't that ridiculous? I don't know what's the matter with me."

"You had a bad dream and then you either saw something

or thought you did, and maybe it amounts to the same thing. Would you like me to check him?"

"Would you?"

She sat up in bed and waited for what seemed like a very long time. He returned with a comforting smile on his face. "He's fine," he said.

"You're sure he's all right?"

"He's sleeping like a baby. Do you want to see for yourself?"

"No." She took a deep breath and let it out very slowly. "Thank you," she said. "I'm crazy tonight, I really am."

"You had a rough time there."

"Thanks for going. And thanks for making me work it out."

"You're all right now?"

"I think so." She looked at him, drawing from him a sense of strength he hadn't given her in years. His body was growing softer with the years. A sedentary life had changed his body shape, and the droop in his shoulders mirrored the quiet desperation of so many nights spent in his study with his pipes and his brandy. He was bare to the waist, his chest hair matted with perspiration, and as she looked at him now she felt an unfamiliar surge of desire.

"Well," he said. "We'd both better get to sleep."

"Could you—"

"What?"

"Could you come into my bed for a little while?"

He slipped out of his pajama bottoms and joined her under the covers. She really only wanted to be held, but when he began making love to her she was surprised by his passion and at least as surprised by her own. Afterward she held onto him but he deliberately extricated himself from her embrace and returned to his own bed.

She felt herself drifting off to sleep. She was on the edge of it when he spoke.

"When you screamed," he said. "Do you remember what you said?"

"I just . . . screamed. And then you were holding me."

"You don't remember what you said."

"No. What did I say?"

She didn't think at first that he was going to answer. Then he said, "I don't know. I was asleep. Maybe you just cried out. I thought you might remember."

"Maybe I called your name."

There was a pause. "Sure," he said at length. "That must have been it."

She heard his alarm clock when it rang. But she stayed in bed until he had showered and dressed and gone down for his breakfast. Then, reluctantly, she dragged herself out of bed. There was an emptiness within her, a hollow void, and she didn't know what it meant.

She went to Caleb's room. He was lying on his back in his crib. His eyes were wide open, rolled back in his head, and his face had a blue tinge to it. She made herself extend a hand to touch him. His skin was cool beneath her fingers.

Then she must have turned from him, because the next thing she knew she was in the doorway of his room, her back to the crib. Ariel was just emerging from the bathroom. Roberta stood still, feeling her breasts rise and fall with her breathing, as the child approached.

Ariel said, "Is something wrong? Is something the matter with Caleb?"

Roberta couldn't answer.

"That's what it is, isn't it? What's the matter with Caleb? Is he dead? Is Caleb dead?"

Roberta threw her head back and howled like a dog.

More Bestsellers from Berkley
The books you've been hearing about and want to read